BARD IV
Ravens' Gathering

SPEAKING VOLUMES, LLC
NAPLES, FLORIDA
2020

Bard IV: Ravens' Gathering

ISBN 978-1-64540-293-0

Gudrun yelled as black-nailed hands seized her.

Felimid rounded the tree, drawing Kincaid as he went; Kincaid, the sword of Ogma, the first steel weapon ever forged in Erin and forever the best, made from a fallen star brought from beneath a lake.

Gudrun struggled on the ground with something grotesque. The bard glimpsed a hairy, goat-tailed rump, misshapen legs, a curved manlike back, shaggy hair, and horns. Red-eyed goat's face, distempered, lustful glare, hairy chest—all this he saw swiftly as he leaped over Gudrun, his sword aimed at the god's stomach.

It inhaled and blew at him.

The blast stopped him short with its slamming force. He stumbled over Gudrun. Kincaid lightly slashed at the seed-god's ribs before the black-nailed hands ripped Felimid's shield from his arm. Gudrun's own sword, Kissing Viper, which had lain beside her, was now held in her hand....

"For lovers of magic, history, and/or swashbuckling adventure, *BARD* is an exciting novel about an earthy and genuinely likeable Irish hero."

—*Science Fiction Review*

BARD IV: Ravens' Gathering

Books by Keith Taylor

BARD *series*
Bard I: Bard
Bard II: The Return of Felimid Mac Fal!
Bard III: The Wild Sea
Bard IV: Ravens' Gathering
Bard V: Felimid's Homecoming

DANANS *series*
The Sorcerers' Sacred Isle
The Cauldron of Plenty
Search for the Starblade

For more information
visit: www.SpeakingVolumes.us

BARD IV
Ravens' Gathering

Keith Taylor

Prologue

The warriors moved at him from different sides. He caught one stroke on his shield, snarling at the jar. In the same heartbeat he struck backhanded with the flat of his axe at his second adversary, a seasoned fighter with mouse-colored braids. The damaged shield was batted aside with an ease that argued formidable strength, and Mouse-braids received a brisk whack on the rib cage with the flat of the weighty axe. From the corner of one eye the big man glimpsed him tumble down.

"Now you!" he growled at the other, a yellow-haired Saxon.

The man stepped back, throwing out both arms. "I yield, lord! You're not in the sweetest of moods. How is the arm?"

"It will serve," the big man said. He glanced at Mouse-braids, who strained to breathe on the ground. "Nay, but you're right. I think I struck harder than I meant. Are you sound, Accahere?"

"I've . . . had worse, lord," Mouse-braids croaked. "Yet it won't . . . astonish me . . . if you have sprung a rib or two."

"Is that all?" Sliding the shield from his left arm and transferring it to his right hand, the big man allowed his axe to dangle from his wrist by its looped strap. He flexed his shield-arm thoughtfully. It ached a good deal.

In itself, that did not trouble him. He reckoned himself fortunate that the limb was still attached to his shoulder. Still, the ache reminded him of things he was obliged to do.

"Enough for today," he said.

Presently he lay on a pallet of skins, bare to the waist, while his wife Haithabu massaged him. He looked even bigger with his fighting-gear discarded, thick-boned, thick-muscled, a shag of rust-red hair curling on his chest. Half a dozen children

1

romped in the room, some his, some the get of his brother-in-law, who sat nearby.

"So soon?" the latter asked.

"Yes, Edric. It must be soon. That island cannot be taken if it is well-provisioned. Now's the end of winter; they will have eaten everything and be unfit to stand even a short siege. Now's the time."

"And your arm?"

"It serves," the big man answered tersely. He had wearied of that question. The previous summer he'd been wounded in a fight against pirates. He'd also been taken alive and held for ransom, although that was not nearly the worst of it, and he did not savor being reminded. Yet that accursed question came now from his brother-in-law and chieftain, and must be answered more fully.

"It healed well," he added. "I exercised it all through the winter." So he had, not minding the pain, exercising the wounded limb with care and judgment, yet never slacking off. "It's sound again now. I fought four men today; Uhtred, then Cudebert, then Neith and Accehere together. It's sound. It aches like the cold of Niflheim, and will never again be as strong as it was before," he conceded, "or I'd have shoved Neith through the wall, but I am fit for business."

Edric shifted his enormous bulk in his chair. He was far bigger than his brother-in-law, so ponderous that he couldn't move swiftly enough to fight, yet a fair and shrewd chieftain to his people, the Elbe Saxons. He earned enough of their respect by being an excellent seaman. His brother-in-law did the fighting so redoubtably that he was nicknamed Edric's Axe.

"We have allies who know those waters," Edric said. "They sent their answer last autumn. Ricsige surely, Cerdic and Cynric perhaps. *She* has made friends of the Dane-kings, but we're between them and her."

"They won't interfere." The other smiled mirthlessly through his red beard. "And she's been estranged from her kin for years. That's her weakness; she has made too many foes, too few friends. She's careless that way."

"She captured you once."

"And outwitted me finely," the big man agreed without rancor. "Not again, brother."

"See to it," Haithabu said, ceasing to knead the scarred, great-muscled arm she held. "Slay her, Vithils."

"It's what I intend. I'm fit again. I have the allies waiting. I need only ships and men."

"They are yours," Edric said. "You can leave provisioned and equipped with the first fair weather."

In Kent that night King Ricsige dreamed. He saw a ship on sparkling blue water, a huge long ship with a serpent's head uplifted on the prow, the kind of ship that no men anywhere knew how to build. He recognized it at once. It had belonged to his father Oisc, but its sail no longer displayed the White Horse of the Kentish rulers. Now it was crimson, with a raven spreading its wings on that background of blood. A woman stood laughing in the bows, laughing at him, at the gods, at the world.

The raven moved on her sail.

It turned its head, thrust its beak forward and flapped its wings. Launching itself over the prow, above the woman, it covered both with black shadow. The crimson sail was left blank.

With a vast flap and whir, the bird flew by. The king saw it divide into a flock of smaller birds as it mounted into the sky. Like a wind-driven cloud, the flock approached an island, a natural fortress atop red granite cliffs. A surf-roar of battle came up to greet the ravens, and figures tiny as dolls struggled on the green plateau above the sea. The ravens flew down.

Gashed, bloody dead men lay scattered for furlongs. Even as the birds descended, so did the sun, swifter than ever it did in the waking world, and the noise died. The battle was over. Weary with their hard-won victory, fighting men stood about. The king recognized some of his own henchmen among them. He knew others, too; noted Saxon warriors from the Elbe, and some from Westri, the new kingdom at the sunset end of the Saxon shore.

The birds fed.

King Ricsige awoke. The dream remained vividly in his mind, and although he had succeeded to his kingdom less than a year before, he knew that a king's dreams were often meaningful for his folk. His own had often proved significant even before he was a king. He called for lights and ale.

In the morning he held a council with his spokesman Anlaf and some of his *gesiths*.* It was no formal affair; the invaders

*Personal companions of a king or chieftain.

of Britain were a rough lot, and if a king could carry his chief men with him, he might have things his own way. Ricsige was aware that his dream could not be other than pleasing.

The *gesiths* were delighted indeed, but they questioned freely.

"That hellcat Gudrun has served the Father of Victories all her life," said Chamo the Frank, once a pirate, now a farmer wed to one of Ricsige's many daughters. "Why should he deny her his favor now?"

"Maybe she has displeased him," Ricsige said. Brown-haired, only middling tall, with a full beard and mild eyes, he knew too well that he hadn't the physical presence of his great sire. "The raven flew away from her ship's sail; Odin's own bird, and it deserted her. The omen could not be plainer."

"The island of red granite cliffs is her lair—Sarnia," Ealdred offered. "All men know that."

"Her men lay dead with ravens eating them, and we were standing. Allies stood with us, too; certain Elbe Saxons among 'em."

"Vithils the Axe," Chamo breathed. The former pirate did not quite finger his neck to be sure it had not been suddenly collared with hemp, but almost. "His brother sent you word last summer, lord."

"True. Blackhair did some marauding in their parts, and Edric means to come south the settle the account—or maybe he will stay at home and send Vithils. They want our help. I'm inclined to give it," Ricsige said in kingly fashion, "For we've a duty of vengeance against Gudrun Blackhair ourselves."

Ha! Anlaf thought. *I served your father for long. He was a greater man then you, and he got nothing but his death when he met Gudrun Blackhair in combat. Surely you will welcome Vithils, for I doubt you would care to move against Gudrun without him.*

Nor would Anlaf have advised his new king to move against the Sarnian pirates alone. That would scarcely have been good service, and the graybeard gave such service, even if he saw his masters too clearly for their pleasure.

"I think, lord, we should ask your, ah, brother and nephew to the feast," Anlaf suggested. "They, too, have a right. It would offend them to be left out."

None smiled, though all knew whom he meant—and that

4

Cerdic and Cynric of Westri were no more Ricsige's kin than the Huns of the Euxine Sea. That story had been agreed upon between Oisc and Cerdic to suit them both. Many now believed it.

"Cerdic, yes," Ricsige said, albeit a bit sourly. "And Cynric." It appeared that he was going to be surrounded by stronger, bolder men than he. Not that that would be wholly bad, he reminded himself, when he must deal with Gudrun Blackhair. "Take Wave-Snake, Chamo, and bear them that word."

"In the first clear weather, lord."

Far away, north of the Danish kingdom, north of Skaggerak, north of Sogne Fjord, seventeen men clustered about a bonfire. They gnawed meat that had barely been introduced to the flames. Two, having disagreed about something, growled and roared like beasts as they wrestled.

Except for variations of height and build, the seventeen could scarcely be told apart. Their stolen deerskins were stiff with dirt, blood, and grease, their furs almost as bad, and their beards made their deerskins appear fastidiously clean.

"I pledge the south!" one of them bawled. "South, where ale is! South, where ships are! South, where good fighting is!"

"We'll go there soon," another grunted.

They had spent much of the winter trapping for furs, the rest killing and robbing Lappish hunters for *their* fur catches. They had obtained many bundles of reindeer skins in the same way, and they knew of some nearby settlers whom they could murder for their ponies to transport the loot. Although the settlers lived in a defended, well-manned camp, the seventeen felt little concern. They had all been berserks since their beards first grew. Ever a terrible thing, this was worst of all when it ran in a family.

The biggest hairy, stinking hulk impaled another chunk of elk meat and held it in the flames. They changed before his eyes to a lurid blue and no longer crackled. Their loudest noise was a faint, dry hissing. The berserk fell backward with a bray of astonishment. His meat dropped into the coals but did not char.

The seventeen gaped. Their bonfire burned three times its former height, all of an icy, sibilant blue. Black shadows danced with wan light among the surrounding boulders and over the crusted snow. A figure wearing the blue flames like a cloak stood on the coals.

He rose vaster than the hugest of them. Gray hair fell to his shoulders, a gray beard to his chest. One socket contained only darkness, the other an eye with an implacable gaze. He held a spear, staff-fashion, with runes cut on the shaft and a ball of the blue northern fire hissing around the head. His mail glittered like ice. He wore distance behind him, around him, above him—a distance of mist and darkness in which dreadful shapes moved.

"Greetings, Ottar, Hall, Bjarni," he said, naming the brothers who were the spine of the clan. "Greetings, Thrain and Leidolf," he added, naming their cousins. "Greetings to all your sons. I have work for you."

The berserks did not question. They recognized their lord, their only lord, the source of their peculiar battle-madness. He was, besides, the source of all other things that lift a man beyond himself and make him feel more than human—poetry, drunkenness, magic, the trances and visions of seers—but always and foremost he was the lord of war, and as such he was served by the berserks, the death-lovers, the mad fighters.

"Vithils, Edric's Axe, takes ship from Elbe-mouth soon," the spear-wielder said. His voice resounded, deep and slow. "He goes south to Kent. Thereafter, he fights against Gudrun Blackhair. I will that you seek him. If he has left Edricsburg on the Elbe, then follow him to Kent. Serve him against Gudrun Blackhair until her death or yours."

"It will be so, lord," Ottar answered in awe.

The shape with its vaguely seen attendants vanished. The fire blazed orange and yellow again, hurling up sparks, crackling loudly under the late winter sky. The biggest of the seventeen killers picked up his elk meat and bit it thoughtfully, not minding the charred stench.

"Vithils," muttered one of Leidolf's sons. "He doesn't love berserks."

"He's no fool," Ottar said. "If he's fighting Gudrun Blackhair, he won't turn us away.'

"*Hahrr!*" Thrain bellowed at the sky, showing all his foul teeth. "Victory-Father has spoken! South, south, south! Cross water, cross land! Gudrun Blackhair dies!"

"What of the skins?" the youngest berserk asked.

"Useless!" Thrain shouted, stamping his feet. "Baggage to slow us!"

Others were howling now, making hideous faces and swinging their weapons. Bjarni stamped like Thrain, chewing the

6

leather-bound rim of his shield and foaming as he gnawed. The youngest berserk seized a bundle of reindeer skins and hurled it into the fire.

"There goes my share!" he howled. "For Odin, Victory-Father!"

His kinsmen roared their approval and copied him. They grabbed hides and furs, the gain of a winter's hard work, and gave them to the flames. Smoke darkened the air. The stink of burning hide and hair spread for miles. The berserks tossed all their spare fuel on the blaze, too, lest their sacrifices smother it out before it was complete. They danced around the fire, howling like wolves, roaring like bears. In three hours nothing was left.

The berserks marched southwards with only their weapons. They no longer needed ponies, so the settlers they had planned to rob kept their ponies and their lives and never knew of their escape.

In Britain, forty leagues west of Kent, King Cerdic and his son talked over ale in the former's hall. Chamo the Frank was present, having delivered his master's message, and now he occupied himself with Cerdic's rich brew while father and son discussed the matter.

Cerdic had built and furnished his hall in a splendor even he could not afford, despite his success at plundering. It didn't trouble him in the least whether he could afford it; Cerdic seldom fretted.

"So, little Ricsige wants our aid." He chuckled. "My brother. I wonder how long he will rule Kent?"

"For a long time, it may be," his son said. "He has some good men to support him. I'll back him against the bitch Blackhair, and gladly, no matter what I think of him!"

Chamo carefully did not hear.

"Ah, Blackhair," Cerdic sighed. "She has made game of greater men than you, cub. Had she not stolen away my daughter-in-law and slain my, hmm, father, I might ha' sought to wed her. From her reputation, she's one of the few women worth my time since your mother died."

If he spoke truthfully, he had given his time to many women who were not worthwhile. His hall thronged with them. There were Britons, Frisians, Gauls, Burgunds, Spaniards, Thurings, even three Slavic sisters, a Greek, and a Persian, bought, captured, or received as gifts, and all of striking beauty.

"You'd have had to take her and tame her first."

"Just so." Cerdic grinned. "It would have been sport to bring her to bed." He lifted hs powerful shoulders and let them drop. "It won't do now. There's a blood debt to be paid, and the matter of your good name. I wonder, should we both go? With the Warlord and his host our neighbors, it seems foolish.

"The Warlord is back in the west?" Chamo asked sharply.

"Gods! He's been at Camlodd all winter. Is it deaf you've grown in Kent? I mislike it, too. Artorius is the one man who can make me anxious. If he takes it into his head to visit me here with his mare-pronging horsemen, I might not be able to kill enough of them. I'd have to retreat to Wight for a while, and that would hurt my reputation until I gathered a strong force to counterattack."

"Then you remain and guard the kingdom while I take the ships against Blackhair!" Cynric said.

He wanted the glory. Cerdic and Chamo both saw that, which was not an especial sign of their perspicacity; it was obvious. Natural, too, in a youth of twenty, so much the younger image of his father, tawny-haired, bearded, strong and vital, with gray-green eyes set wide apart. He didn't altogether like being so conspicuously Cerdic's son, even though it was a physical endowment most men envied.

"It's a great force," Cerdic said. "Lead it other than well, and the ghosts of your men will haunt you—supposing you live. You may be too eager to reach Gudrun Blackhair's heart."

"Her head is what I want!"

"Then stand in the line!"

"It's my right," Cynric insisted. "She carried off my wife." *Chosen for me by you*, rang the unsaid words. "I still think she knows where Vivayn is, whether or no she was responsible this time."

"Maybe," Cerdic agreed. He wet his throat and considered before he spoke. "She's borne you no children, or conceived since that first time when she miscarried. The gods could be speaking to you. Wed another and get sons. Any man should have them, but a king must."

"Forget her? Vivayn?"

"Why not? Her sorcery was useful, but I never trusted her."

"I did."

The bigger fool you, Cerdic thought, but didn't say. The British snowflake he had married to his son so that his conquest might be the more bearable to British slaves had frostbitten her mark on the atheling. This was no time to mock him with it. The matter at hand was aid to Kent against Blackhair.

Cynric wanted to go; someone had to go; there were reasons why Cerdic should stay. The cub had been leading pirate expeditions since the summer of his seventeenth year, and leading them well, all in all. He would have old Ulfcetel and a leavening of other trusty men.

"You want the work, then?"

"I do, sire."

Cerdic felt strangely deflated. He didn't ponder why. If he had, he might have recognized Cynric's youth as the cause. Being who he was, he simply acted. He engaged in fierce weapon-practice with four of his best men that afternoon, not as Vithils had done in Edricsburg—deliberately to test the limits of his body after recovering from a wound—but to prove to himself that he was still the mightiest man in Westri. He followed it with a mammoth drinking bout that night, and then took two lively concubines to his bed. They left it rather sore. However, they were avenged upon Cerdic by Cerdic himself, who moved in a leaden, half-crippled fashion all the next day, wishing that his head belonged to someone else.

Cynric, by contrast, had drunk lightly and bedded with one woman, and he was younger, which helped. He moved about whistling to select his ships and warriors.

I

Vivayn has cut her red-bronze hair
  Aye shoulder short and more;
She has brent* the fathom tresses
  Lest magic strike her sore,
And fled across the Narrow Sea
  To Lesser Britain's shore.

In Broceliande Forest
  She listened to the wind
And rested from her travels
  Till they should new begin.
                    —British Ballad

Felimid mac Fal went through the forest with a light, easy gait, singing as he passed, aware of the stirring life around him through nose and skin and the soles of his feet as much as through his eyes and ears. Winter had almost passed; spring had almost come. The world as yet remained tumultuously undecided from day to day which season reigned.

Beech, oak, and an occasional ash formed the heights of the forest. Over in Britain the oaks would be scarcely budding. Here in Armorica the buds had burst in a yellow-brown froth of newness, while the hazel leaves nearer the ground were already wide open. Odors of anemones and pale violets were subtle in the air. The first returning bird flock swept through the gusty sky.

Magic scented the air, too, heady and wild. Here in Broceliande a man might meet anything, though to Felimid the

*Burnt.

ancientry and power of ever-renewed life was worth the danger.
In places like this he remembered his heritage from the Tuatha
de Danann, the strange, skillful children of earth-mother Danu;
remembered it with his blood, flesh, and marrow.

He wore unremarkable clothes, though he might have gone
richly clad. His shirt had been neatly patched, his doeskin kilt
had seen a deal of wear, and the green linen wrapping his
calves was held in place by plain leather thongs. Only the
yellow, fawn, and thrush-brown cloak fastened with a bone
pin at the breast was new, and few would risk the curse of
killing a bard (or even a common harper) for that. The instrument riding on his back was a better safe-conduct in this land
than a hundred fighting men behind him.

He entered a birch grove. The gracile silvery trunks rose like
pillars, and the delicate twigs veiled the sky. Within it a spring
gurgled.

The woman who waited in Felimid's path might almost have
been a birch spirit. She was sufficiently slender, and had white
enough skin. However, no birch spirit ever had human hands,
or hair the color of red bronze, and even if Felimid had not
known that, he had met this woman twice before.

"Welcome, Felimid," she said. Her voice made him think
of cool light wine.

"Good day, Lady Vivayn." He'd a pleasant voice himself,
essentially tenor but with an earthy strength deep in the timbre
of it. He could pitch it baritone when he wished, and make it
carry in a way that seemed magical. Perhaps it was; bardic
training included magic. "I'm happy that you escaped from
Lansulcan. We'd have taken you off, you know . . . we happened to be there, but . . ."

"You would never have reached us through the drowned
forest, even in that ship of Gudrun's. No, Felimid, I know
you'd have aided us had it been effectible, but I think we all
did well just to survive. I'm told the sea still roars like an angry
dragon off that shore."

"You heard no lie, though it is less than the full truth. By
Cairbre's fingers! A man fit to hold opinion said the wreckage
of the forest would be washed from sight within a decade, and
one season has nearly done it! The sea will rage against that
place for nine generations, and nine and nine." He asked,
"What became of Sulghein?"

Sulghein was the mad priest who had brought about the

catastrophe. Vivayn said briefly, "*He* did not survive."

"Ahh. Well, I'll not be feigning great sorrow, Vivayn; not for that one. Are you settled here, or was it just an expedient for the winter?'

"I'm undecided. Eldrida likes it. Come to our hut and eat, Felimid. Maybe we will talk about that."

The enigmatic "maybe" did not escape him. As he walked through the grove beside her, the leather budget hanging from his belt clinked stonily.

Vivayn was different. The woman he had met in King Cerdic's dun a year previous had worn her face like a faintly amused mask, hiding her actions and herself within layers of illusion. Now she spoke directly, walked freely in her long-belted tunic, and wore a gray wolfskin cloak instead of the hair that had been long enough to serve her as a cloak itself. Among other things, that had been a sign that she could have several tiring-women look after it and did not need to consider the practicalities of action. When she had decided to abscond from her status as a royal wife, that ankle-long mantle of red hair was the first thing she had had to discard. Felimid, who knew her a little by now, was ready to wager she had found it a relief.

Her dwelling proved to be somewhat more than a hut. Eight paces long, five wide, with solid posts and beams, roofed with rainproof birchbark, it merited the name of a house to the bard's mind. However, he'd been a placeless rover for some years. Probably Vivayn had inappropriately high standards yet.

"Oh, Felimid! Or is it Bragi now?" Vivayn's companion Eldrida appeared, to hug and buss him enthusiastically. Yellow braids a-swirl, she turned laughing to Vivayn. "I will swear you didn't greet him like that."

Vivayn smiled herself. "True. And were I you, I would hope that Gudrun Blackhair never learns that you did. She would behead you."

"She would not, you know," Felimid said amiably, stepping through the doorway. "For one thing, she has been Eldrida's lover, too, as we're all three aware, so why dissemble? For another, if Gudrun were so unreasonable, I should prevent her."

He drew two stone bottles from his budget and set them on the table.

"From Gudrun's cellar," he explained. "I should be saying Decius's, for he's the one who stocks it, attends it, and best appreciates it. He promised me this is good."

"Wine!" Vivayn said with pleasure. "You're a true friend. I'm sure Gudrun's reivers rob nothing but the best."

She produced a pair of beechwood cups and one pewter beaker, then filled them all brimming. Before long they were eating bannocks, roast duck, and herb sallet. The meal had been partly ready when Felimid arrived; Vivayn had expected him, of course, or she could not have waited in his path. She knew how to commune with air elementals, just as he did. Any wind blowing in her direction might have carried news of him.

"And now," the sorceress said at last, drinking a little more wine, "what brings you here, Felimid, so far from Sarnia?"

"*Ormungandr* brought me to Aleth," he replied, naming Gudrun Blackhair's enchanted ship. "My legs carried me the rest of the way, and as to why . . . there is trouble a-move for us, Gudrun and I and all her pirates. The gift of seeing the future I have not, but Gudrun has made mighty foes, and I can see a furlong ahead of me. Cynric will come against us in the spring, and maybe his father will bear him company—and the King of Kent will be in it surely, for his father's sake and his own good name. Now it is advice we are needing, Vivayn, and none knows Cerdic and Cynric better than you, nor is any woman like you for cleverness, or more skilled in magic."

Such was Vivayn's nature that those words pleased her far more than hearing her beauty extolled, extraordinary though that beauty was. Still, she did not forget that Felimid traded in words. For troubled moments she sat silent, while the bard watched her undemandingly and Eldrida's glance moved between the two faces, the one oval, snow-fair, and symmetrical, the other fair-skinned and comely also, but with an engaging disproportion of snub nose and long jaw about it.

"You ask a difficult thing," Vivayn said at last. "I lived as Cynric's wife for years. Oh, I would not go back! His father slew mine, then had us marry for his purposes. I wasn't even faithful to him, as you of all men have reason to know, Felimid, and I looked to the day when the charade of our marriage would end. I never thought of us as truly wed. Yet I would not betray him to what might be death."

"He's my brother," Eldrida interjected.

"Ah, now. He's your half brother, and one of dozens the fecund Cerdic has sired—one of the rare few born in marriage, true, but still you can hardly be knowing him."

"Not these past few years," Eldrida admitted. "I used to

know him well, though, and love him. I want him to live.''

"Honor to you for that," the bard said sincerely. "I like him well enough my own self. Still it's in my mind that he can be a monster from the black depths when his pride is hurt. Whether or no, it's Gudrun who has my loyalty. If he or she must die, I'll do what I can to ensure it is he. I will so. Gudrun carried you both away for ransom once, to be sure, but I would say she has been fairer to you than Cerdic or Cynric.''

Neither woman disputed that.

"If Cerdic were slain tomorrow, I would not grieve," the sorceress said. Her words hummed in the air after they were uttered, though her tone had seemed dispassionate while she spoke. "Yet it is Cynric who is likely to come looking for us, not his father. He'd take me back, and you, I think, Eldrida, he'd very likely murder for aiding me to flee. Felimid is right; wounded pride would make him savage.''

"He plans to come looking for Gudrun first," Felimid said, "and it's in my mind that after that he will never seek anyone again. Why should we await him, though? Gudrun is for striking first.''

"Yes, she would be." Eldrida grinned. "She never was one for waiting upon others' pleasure. How is your back holding out?''

Felimid swatted her delectably rounded behind. "Finely. Now remember your manners.''

Eldrida stuck her tongue in her cheek.

"If the byplay's done," Vivayn said patiently, "I have a thought, maker of fame. Cynric will come with allies. Why should you not seek yours first?''

"What, among the Franks or the Armorican corsairs? Or maybe the Saxons of Gaul?''

"In Britain itself! The island of the mighty was not wrongly named. You know Count Artorius and what he has done. He was settled at the fortress of Camlodd with his war band, what last I heard, and that is within easy striking distance of Westri. Go to him, Felimid. Offer to strike from the sea while he strikes by land with his riders!''

"That would be a fine thing for Britain, and might bring Gudrun more fame and plunder, but I cannot see how it will benefit us in Sarnia this spring. It might shatter the kingdom of Westri and make an end of Cerdic. By the time all this is arranged, though, if ever it is, his son will be in Kent. Soon after that he will be at Sarnia.''

"Yes," Vivayn agreed. "Now if Cerdic be slain, the son will have to return at once to inherit his kingdom—and save it, for that matter. If he can. The Kentishmen must then fare against you without him. Never let your enemies unite. Ours united at Badon, and if it had not been for Count Artorius, they would have opened the lock to our island then.''

Felimid considered that advice over a slow inspiring swallow of wine. "I like the last part, Vivayn; it's fine. But I do not see how dividing our own forces to strike at Westri—for that'd entail costly fighting, and my Blackhair is too recklessly given to such now!—would achieve it. Better to just intercept Cynric on his way to Kent, it appears to me. Confess now and be candid. You didn't advise that because it is his sire you'd rather see bloodily dead.''

"Of course," Vivayn said, lifting one dark-dyed brow. "I said as much. Little use to talk of it more, I think, Felimid. If Cynric comes within sword's reach of you or Gudrun, you won't submit tamely! That I know.''

"No use at all to talk of it more," Eldrida agreed, with a certain grimness which was not like her. The big brother, the kinsman and royal heir she had all but worshipped as a girl and towards whom she had learned irreverence later, still had her love; none the less, it was a while since they had been children, and she knew that if they met again, he might strangle her.

"If I have my way," the bard declared, "she will dissolve her band and make for Erin with me. Her enemies will be left with nothing to fight.''

Eldrida hooted. "*Gudrun*? Oh, dreamer! She will never do that, Felimid—never!'

"She's promised me that she will," he answered.

"Has she?" The yellow-haired girl was astonished. "Well . . . as may be . . . . I'll take oath she gave you no promise to turn her back on a fight first.''

The bard made a wry mouth and drank more wine. He hadn't any answer to that. Instead he said, very nearly at random, "Where are Cerdic and Nys?" These were Eldrida's children.

"The village is taking care of them. They will be none the worse, except for being spoiled rotten. And where is Kincaid?''

Eldrida pertly asked in return. Kincaid was Felimid's sword, an ancient treasure which had once belonged to the god-champion Ogma.

"I left him aboard *Ormungandr* for the time. Wearing a sword invites trouble. You show that you are prepared to fight, and some fool demands that you do. A harp makes a better safe-conduct, but there is a curse on Kincaid, so, and I never could leave him with any I trusted enough, before."

"You trust Gudrun Blackhair that much?" Vivayn said.

"I do." He softened the declaration with a joke. "There's none to ransom me."

It wasn't as funny as he'd intended it to be. The mocking jest did not distract Vivayn. She listened to the first two words, the words that mattered.

"Gudrun's health, then," she said. "Perhaps you should take her to Erin as soon as the fight has been won, Felimid—and pinioned, if need be. Is there not a song you made for her?"

"More than one. Her saga's in the making yet, but I have a half-score ballads. Lady, it's a relief to make songs for Gudrun! Part of the reason I left Erin was to escape fangling praises for any chief who manages to gain a hold on three or four tuatha.* I heard bald or gray men described as golden-haired heroes until I'm nauseated with it. Not a king in the land but has a crystal-clear gaze; there isn't a cataract or squint from the Giant's Causeway to Kerry, to hear it told."

"And is it so much better outside Erin?"

"Hmm, no. In—rising five years?—I have encountered just two I would say were truly worthy of a bard's praise. Two. Their names will endure, and the bards of all generations will thank them for living; Count Artorius of Britain, and Gudrun Blackhair. Did we hate them and try to bury their reputations in muck, they would grow green and flowering out of the dunghill. Oh, they'll be changed and all. Their stories will be altered with each telling, each rendering in some yet-unknown tongue, until their own ghosts cannot recognize themselves. But forgotten they will not be."

"Is that why you stay?"

"I stay on Sarnia for Gudrun's sake, lady. Surely I do not take over-much delight in the pirate life. After spending an entire winter with them I can say that their company does bore

---

*Tribal kingdoms; the basic political unit of Erin.

in great portions. I make one or two exceptions, but for the most part I'd be feeding them at the back door of my own house, if there. One of Gudrun's own captains tried to run her through the back in the confusion of a battle.''

"Are you astonished by that?" Vivayn inquired. "If so, you are something wide-eyed for a man who has rambled at large for five years. I see well how you might grow bored with putting such deeds into song. I have heard enough of them the past four years myself . . . how Bilbert Bloodynose killed eight hundred men in a five-acre feasting hall with nothing but a beef bone, and lacking armor. Ovid and Sappho are more to my liking—but to the sea wolves a book, any book, is a repository of magic." She sipped the wine. "Hmm, your friend Decius is a good judge. Will you play us a song that is to your own taste, Felimid?"

"In a while, yes. It'll be my delight." Felimid touched the worn leather of his harp bag. "It seems in another world now that I made a song for that old shepherd Murd, and as for the horse songs and love songs I gave the Count of Britain's men before Badon, all gods witness me, it feels like another life . . . and Erin itself . . . ''

"You should go back there," Vivayn said crisply. "You agreed to exile yourself for three years—to avert a feud, wasn't it? It has been five now. You are fortunate; what you left behind is likely to be there yet, since there are no sea wolves in Erin. Cease dreaming and do!''

''Oh, lady,'' Felimid laughed, "we don't need sea wolves in Erin so long as we have each other!''

Vivayn shrugged gracefully. "Then do not go back if you dislike it. Remain on Sarnia with your wild pirate. In your place I would appreciate having the choice."

"If I wait awhile, I may have both. Now that's worth waiting for. You are quiet, Eldrida."

"I'm listening," the yellow-haired girl explained. "Also, I'm weary. Hunting and gathering fuel . . . pardon me." She yawned, and tipped the wine bottle. It yielded a bare last drop or two, but the other was still virgin. The bard opened it. "A good thing winters in this land are mild." She added, "And that the people are frightened of ghosts.''

"Ghosts, is it?" Felimid scented a story.

"One only." Vivayn's pale gray eyes were luminously clear in the firelight. "One lost, restless spirit I was able to lay, and so become persona grata with the village here. It helped at first. Eldrida has done more. I am still learning to work for myself and look after the children. You do nine parts of it, comrade. Nine parts of everything.''

"Yes," Eldrida said affectionately. "You've lazed and ridden on my back all winter. Show Felimid your hands.''

Felimid had noticed them. Vivayn did nothing ridiculous like suddenly snatching them out of sight. She merely occupied them in a smooth, natural fashion with bottle and cup, in a way that made courteously clear that they were not on display.

"This place pleases me," she went on, having moistened her white throat. "It is filled with enchantment and can teach me much. Yet that is scarcely as profit to us if we go hungry, fall ill, or work ourselves mindless. Now the winter is past, I think we may go to the city. I can find something to do there. A name as an astrologer-seeress should not be hard for me to acquire, and I can stay on the Church's right side if I step carefully. Do you think I could succeed, Felimid?''

"Sure, the difficult thing is to imagine you failing," he said gallantly. "Of what it takes to stay on the Church's right side you know more than I. Whatever, gold has a way of smoothing most paths. You carried some with you from Britain, no doubt, but maybe you lost it among the Children of Lir. The wine was my thought; Gudrun sent this.''

He produced a purse which chinked fatly. Within lay gold, in the form of studs, rings, one massive jeweled cloak pin, and some coins.

" 'Call it your honor price,' is what she said," Felimid added, " 'and consider us equal.' ''

"Accepted," Vivayn said past a certain tightness in her throat. This would indeed smooth her path if used wisely, and Gudrun had not had to do it. Still, she had abducted Vivayn for ransom once. The young sorceress had her full share of pride. "It's my due, therefore I will take it. And I thank Gudrun Blackhair, because nothing but her own honor compels her to pay. Now, that song . . . ?''

"You shall have it.''

He sang of a birch wood and three women who lived there; the yellow-haired daybright girl whose flesh made ripe peaches seem unpromising, the sorceress whose loins were ravishing fire though her mind and heart were twin precise snowflakes, and the woman of the white hand it was madness to offend, the last being the birch spirit with her dangerous touch. He sang of an enclosure of birches, a parlor of bright green trees, a place for two in spite of the cuckold's wrath, and Vivayn smiled. He advised forgetfulness of the harsh, imprisoning winter. Vivayn drew closer to him, while on the far side of the hut Eldrida curled up and breathed more slowly. Before long she was asleep.

Felimid laid his harp away. Vivayn held a cup with the last of the wine toward him. They shared it in the dim glow of the hearth, their fingers touching around the cup, and smiled in each other's eyes by the dim hearth glow. Vivayn's smile for one was the least bit ironical.

"Stiff and brittle as ice, indeed," she murmured.

"I know I never said that. My memory is better."

The soft luxury of her mouth told him his remembrances were indeed accurate, and the textures of her long white youthful neck confirmed it, but wishing to be certain, he let his mouth wander to her breasts, with their nipples like small, juice-crammed berries. Unlike Eldrida's, they had never suckled children. By then her own hands were roving, and his were upon her waist.

They kissed, mouth to mouth, relearning blindly the shape of lips once known, the capabilities of searching tongue, the underlip's soft texture without equal. Mouths wandered from shoulder to hand, waist to belly to breast. They moved from stool to floor to a standing position, stages in a journey which ended in a rising series of gasps, with an urgent tightening of hands on Vivayn's waist and Felimid's shoulders. Then they sank almost bonelessly down, to touch and murmur until desire became imperative again. They slept only in naps of an hour or so that night.

It was Eldrida, whose slumber had been continuous, who prepared breakfast. The porridge had cooked on the hearth all night to a creamy texture. She sang as she dished it out, a cheerfully bawdy song.

"Enough lickerish humor." Vivayn yawned. "Will you fetch the salt, my dear? I would, but I can't stand."

"Salt, is it? And royal salt, I see. You love like a princess still, Vivayn."

He had meant to say "live," but his tongue pursued its own path. Eldrida smiled.

"At present, a little. This hard-wearing world is apt to tarnish its princesses, I have noticed. I think it is past time I learned to be something else. Visit me at summer's end, Felimid. By then I may know what.''

"Meanwhile," Eldrida said, "are you guesting another night with us?''

Felimid made a polite show of considering. "No, best I return to Aleth quickly. I know Gudrun's rogues. If I keep them waiting long, they are likely to shatter the town just because they are bored, and so far they have kept it friendly disposed.''

He finished his breakfast, eating at his unhurried leisure, and kissed both women farewell. Vivayn watched him disappear through the purple-twigged birches, shaking her head a little, half bemused, half frowning.

Eldrida put a hand on her arm. "Come, what is it?''

"I am not sure I know," Vivayn admitted. "We spent the entire night enjoying each other, he and I, and . . . I have the oddest feeling that I've been done a, a courtesy!'' She flushed carnation.

"Maybe you were. He's Gudrun Blackhair's man now. You knew it. He was nobody's when first he met us, but all has changed since. He loves her, and she him. Even a night of carefree sport isn't the same when another woman is holding his heart.''

"I suppose it must be so." Vivayn grew somewhat bitchy. "I can think of no other reason why they should want to have anything to do with each other. Between me and God, it's extraordinary!'' She looked at her friend. "And is that why you did not join us?''

"My bloodtime's with me.''

"And if it were not?''

"You are asking some spiked questions today. I've two children! I don't wish to bear a third for a while. That's something you should have considered your own self.''

"I'm barren," Vivayn said. "Come, you know that.''

"I don't! I don't at all! I know you conceived once to Cynric, lost the child early, and haven't conceived since to him or any other man. I know as well that you're a sorceress, and far more than other folk a sorceress's wishes and fears and hopes rule her body. You were captive in a forced marriage, and now you're free. You may learn that you're more fertile than you think.''

Vivayn looked very startled. "You think so? That would be inconvenient just now."

"By Frigg!" Eldrida said. "About everything except magic you have a deal to learn, Vivayn! Look. You were fifteen, and a virgin, when Cerdic married you to his son. You used glamor to give you my seeming when you took lovers, because what I did was never a killing matter. Fine. Now, though, you must do your own loving in your own guise and bear the reputation it gives you. That, or be pure as a Christian nun is said to be."

Vivayn burst out laughing. "Then it seems I must be virtuous for a time! Are we quarreling, Eldrida?"

"No, we're not quarreling. Unless you quarrel with me for speaking my mind. Listen, I will go to the village and fetch the kids. While I am gone you might sift the wind for tidings, and each day from now on. We have to live. A name for being farsighted does much."

II

Lir the Sea and earth-mother Danu have loved since they came to be,.
Never gently, and never tamely, they couple unendingly. The wave
*   to the shore, the soil to the ocean, the cliffs rising out of the main,*
To be hollowed in caves and undermined till they topple grinding
*   again.*
The land and the sea change places through generations of flesh,
While Children of Earth and Children of Lir encounter, battle and
*   mesh.*

The Children of Earth are slower; they sometimes know peace and
*   ease,*
But their cousins of surging tumult are restless, harder to please.
They go with the tides of passion, they move with the pulsing green,
They belong to currents and eddies that lift or deny unseen.
They were never fathered for patience, or to plough the ground for
*   their bread;*
They live by instinct and magic. They desire no graves for their dead.
> —Felimid mac Fal,
> *Earth, Sea, and Stars*

Felimid, too, had been discovering that. Nearly as adroit as
Vivayn in air magic—the magic of words and sight governed
by the reasoning mind—he understood the speech of winds as
well as she. The boisterous, veering gusts of March shouted
to him as they dealt their buffets, and he shouted back, high-
spirited as they.

Crossing the water from Aleth, he waxed less cheerful. The
enchanted ship *Ormungandr* was still a ship, although very
likely the only one that could have ridden those waters at that
time of year with any degree of safety. It bucked and slammed

its way toward Sarnia in a horrid chop, and the bard, as usual, was seasick.

Gudrun Blackhair had thoughtfully not come along. She knew Felimid's weakness by now, and appreciated that it did a man's pride no good to be groaning, retching, and greenish before his lover, especially if she was immune to that sort of discomfort. She had entrusted the great serpent-ship to her lieutenant.

"There," he said, nodding at the red granite cliffs which rose to the north. "There, Bragi—firm ground."

Felimid, who went by the name Bragi among the Sarnian pirates, stared longingly at the nigh-impregnable isle. Although pale, he was standing and walking about.

"Wonderful seeing it makes, too. May I perish if I'm ever inveigled onto green water in March again." The ship lurched then, and seemed to drop sickeningly. "There! The waves themselves heard."

Gudrun's lieutenant smiled slightly. "They may have. After some things I've lately seen, I can believe it. Better you do not say that carelessly; the powers hear our words, not our intentions. Have your wind spirits told you more news?"

"Decius, I've been too sick most of the time since we left the Rance to give ear, much less inquire. I could well have missed any winds that blew from Britain. It's in my mind that we've had 'em chiefly from the southwest. There's rich gossip about the Prince of Domnonia and a mandrake; his people were ready to depose him for impotence, and having no mind to accept that, he—"

The ship bucked on a wave. Felimid staggered. Decius caught his arm, and perhaps kept him from knocking himself silly on a thwart. The bard was not so sure on his feet just then as usually.

"You had best tell me later," Decius said. "I have to bring *Ormungandr* to harbor unscathed, or the lady will have my head. She'd be sorry afterward, but that would console neither of us."

That Gudrun had great hopes of her enchanted ship was true. Felimid doubted that she would demand the life of Decius even if he shattered *Ormungandr* on a reef, though; that was dry exaggeration. Decius knew his own value.

Nonethelesss it said something about Gudrun Blackhair that Vivayn and Decius should both speak in terms of her removing heads when displeased, and within a few days of each other.

BARD IV

The long serpent-ship moved like a live thing swimming, into a sheltered bay on the island's eastern side. Two pirates clewed up the gray-green sail, and others manned twenty of the oars. Soon *Ormungandr* had been dragged ashore through cold waves on a shelving beach.

"How long before the other ships are brought out?" Felimid asked.

Decius scratched a salty eyebrow. "I'd give it a double fortnight, were it up to me, but the lady never has been one for waiting. It may not be left to us anyhow. I know I'd not fare on the sea in this month in any ship but *Ormungandr*, of my free choice."

"In this month," Felimid said fervently, "I'd sooner not go to sea in any ship, including *Ormungandr*! Past man's prediction is March's wild weather, winter contesting his empire with spring. . . . . Let those others come to us."

"Yes. Your sentiments I know." The Spaniard hitched his sword around so that the hilt should not drive into his side as he mounted the steep cliff path. His dark, experienced face, in which one destroyed eye had been replaced by a smoldering red-and-brown jewel, turned toward the cliff tops and then toward Felimid again. "You need to walk on hard earth and to stop complaining so much. Come. That poetry—yours?"

Felimid shifted his own sword, the legendary silver-hilted weapon Kincaid, and went lightly up the path behind Decius. The land went up and down under his feet, though not so badly as it had when he first took to the whale's bath the summer before.

"Mine, yes," he said, answering the Spaniard's query. "I have bowed before the glory chant, I have played in the night, I have slept in the dawn." He paused in his speech while he negotiated an especially steep and tricky bit of path. "I made it last year while I was following a man who had stolen Kincaid from me. The poor fool."

"I won't ask what became of him. I think I can guess."

"And I think your guess would be right. Mind, I did not kill the fellow. Not even a little bit. I never had to. There's an infallible curse on this blade, for any who withhold it from the descendants of Ogma. I have never known it take more than a nine-night to work."

"I appreciate your leaving it with me, by God!"

The tough back and compact shoulders ahead of the bard

24

shook a little with amusement. Clearly Decius did not believe. He probably did not believe more than a tenth of all Felimid told him. That was all right. Felimid did not have to convince him, and would never have tried to represent himself as infallibly truthful. He answered lightly.

"I'd have been mighty inconsiderate toward you to be getting myself killed in the Forest of Broceliande, yes. It is why I took care not to."

"You're a true friend."

As they mounted the winding path through crags and pipes of stone, it grew steeper. Nonetheless Felimid felt better with each step. The motion of the solid earth lessened. They reached the top no more than a quarter mile from the narrow isthmus separating the island's two parts, a path barely wide enough for three people to cross abreast. In places it wasn't even that wide. Behind them, on the greater part of the isle, cattle grazed.

Crossing the isthmus always reminded the bard of walking across a hatchet's edge. Cliffs fell steeply on either side to the booming sea. There was no other approach to the lesser part of Sarnia but one cliff path, a good deal steeper than the one he and Decius had just used. Beyond it lay Gudrun Blackhair's rambling hall and the isle's rich silver and amethyst mines.

Entering the hall was not an unmixed pleasure for Felimid. He had spent most of five months in the place, confined by winter. Both he and his darling had grown restless and jaded toward the end, despite their joy in each other. Spring was not approaching a day too quickly.

The place stank ripely, as all places did after a winter's occupancy. Coming in out of the clean, cold wind, Felimid noticed it, but once his vision adapted to the smoky dimness, he saw other things which banished the reek from his mind.

The Children of Lir had come back.

There they sat, the passionate, suspect allies of last Samhain, the sea people who had contrived to destroy the Gate to the otherworld where their fellows lived, rather than see it forced by questing children of earth. They had lost one world to Felimid's kind.

There was Turo the shapeshifter, cocky and playful, wearing the skin of a man-sized otter over his shoulders, brown against the whiteness of his human body. Near him sat Idh, beardless though old, counselor and spokesman for the third of their race present, their ruler, green-haired Niamh. She had inherited royal power when her brother died, and among the Childrèn of Lir that was no empty show, no matter of titles and political support, but a magical thing.

In her own way Gudrun Blackhair ruled by magic, too. She rose with a sudden glad laugh as the sea-stained men entered. "Bragi!" She vaulted the table to embrace him before all. Tall as he, very strong and splendidly made, she was beautiful in a big-featured, clear-cut way which showed to best advantage in fine battle gear or the man's garments she habitually wore.

"Welcome, Decius," she said to her henchman. "Join my council; you see our friends from the Veiled Isle are with us."

Niamh's changeable eyes clouded with grief. She said quietly, "Oblige me, Gudrun. If you would show courtesy, don't speak of the Veiled Isle. It is gone."

It was, indeed. Gone, overwhelmed, swept away by the wild sea, on the same night the otherworldly Gate had been destroyed. The mad priest Sulghein had actually pronounced the curse, yet the Children of Lir had allowed him to do so, led him, all but summoned him to serve their purpose.

"Well enough," Gudrun said carelessly, seating herself again. Although often generous, she would never be compassionate or subtle of feeling. "Bragi, Decius—you know these folk. Yes? Now they are seeking a new Gate to return to their own world, and since I am seeking such a Gate myself, we might join forces. That is why they are here."

It was unbelievable. Decius clamped shut his jaw lest he say so outright, and did some swift thinking. Felimid filled the gap with some swift talking.

"Wait, now. Maybe you drive on too fast, Gudrun. I don't understand at all why the Children of Lir would ally with *us* to that purpose! I'm puzzled. Lady Niamh, my lord Idh . . . your strongest purpose was to hide that Gate from the like of ourselves, maintain its very existence secret, and failing that, to prevent our kind using it at any cost. So you did, most ably. That you now wish to find another way home makes sense to me. Why you'd be ready to share such knowledge with us is less easy to ken. Will you instruct me?"

"I'd like to know that, too, lady," Decius said. He was looking at Gudrun when he said "lady."

"Gates grow rare," Idh said. "They vanish or are destroyed, and we know of no other which leads to Mag-Mell. If we seek one separately, we are likely to be drawn together in finding it, and that could lead to battle. Is it not better that we should each know what the other is doing from the first?''

''And begin to cut each other's throats directly we find this damned Gate? If we do.''

Idh met the Spaniard's scorn with honest anger. ''There speaks a sea thief! Yes, truth, we do not want you in Mag-Mell; we want to find our own way there. But there are many sorts of Gate, and we do not know what sort we will find. Some lead to different worlds at different times. Others stand open only at sunset or sunrise, or on certain nights of the year. Some are on land, some on the sea. A few lie beneath it. To find and use a suitable one may tax all our talents. Sure it is that we will have to attempt more than one Gate if we do this thing at all. Our world Mag-Mell is not for you; this I say plainly again. But lady, you may find another that pleases you to enter, and holds enough marvel and freedom and newness for you.''

''May,'' Gudrun said slowly, tasting the word, bridling her enthusiasm although her gray eyes shone. ''What do you say to that, Decius?''

''I have two questions, lady; one to ask of you and another of the lord Idh. Suppose you like this Mag-Mell best of any otherworlds we may see?'' (He thought the notion ridiculous, Felimid could tell, even with the Children of Lir seated beside him.) ''Will you still enter it? And what would your folk do then, Idh?''

Idh glanced at Gudrun. With a gesture she invited him to speak first.

''They would destroy our clan as traitorous,'' he said definitely, ''And they would destroy you. An entire world of our kind would be against you.''

Gudrun liked such direct talk. She said, ''Then I will not go. When the time comes to seal such an agreement, I will swear to that on my sword if you like. But I cannot go seeking any Gates yet. I have enemies who owe me a blood debt. They will come for me soon, but I know how to greet them.''

''Why wait?'' Decius asked. ''Lady, if you're determined to commit the madness of sailing through a Gate, the earth will not know you again in any case. Disband the men, all save a chosen crew for *Ormungandr*. Give the rest the other ships, divide the wealth among them, and leave Sarnia to those who want it. Let Cerdic, Cynric, and Ricsige find nothing here when they come.''

BARD IV

"Now tell me why I will not do that."

"Because you're Gudrun Blackhair, with three hundred good men and a fortress isle, and you won't scamper," the Spaniard said, grinning dourly. "Because the chieftains of our neighbor isles are friendly, and you won't leave them to Jutish raiders. They would scour and burn in their disappointment, and kill all they found on Agnia and Lesia."

"I am glad you still know me," Gudrun said, returning the smile with none of the grimness. "You have it right! They will come, and I will break them—whatever the sea leaves—and any who survive will not be back, unless it is to beg peace of me." She laughed aloud then, in her pride and cheerful ruthlessness. "The business will be settled this spring. Then I will help you find your Gate."

"You?" Niamh was startled into speaking directly, rather than through Idh, as was her custom. Her visionary eyes widened. She seemed to gaze beyond the confines of the hall, to some future day when ships met clashing on a windy, opaque sea.

"You? It is our help which is being offered to Sarnia! We know all that happens on the water for fifty leagues around, our ships sail invisible other than to magic-sighted eyes, we can seduce what you earth folk call ships to their destruction—"

"Except that these ships, I dare say, will sail with all the right blessings, and blood sacrifices, and charms, to ward them 'gainst such danger," Felimid said objectively. "I don't suppose they will take wergild, either. Forgive my ill manners in cutting off your speech, my lady, but you did seem to be believing that earth folk are wholly helpless before the subtleties of Lir. That is not quite so."

Niamh knew it. The children of earth, in their slow, stubborn way—with tame grain, iron, and wrought stone—had made the land their own, and were ploughing the sea with a thousand keels, until the Children of Lir could no longer hold it. She gave the bard a violently poisonous look.

"Nor are they immune to us," she said. "The sea is *ours*, and if they come here, we will make them know it."

"And Sarnia is *mine*," Gudrun said. "When they come here, I will make them know that. What advice did Vivayn give, Bragi? Anent Cerdic and Cynric?"

"To seek allies in Britain, and Count Artorius particularly, black jewel. You and he between you could destroy the kingdom of Westri if it came to that. It seems excessive to me, mind.''

''Destroy a kingdom!'' Gudrun repeated. ''By the Battle Crow, and some call me a hard woman! That carving of snow will trouble the earth in time. Yet if Cynric should fall, it is sure we will have to deal with his father. Allies would be no bad thing to have then. Is it true? Vivayn counseled destroying the kingdom, slaying father and son? I was not born to work her vengeances for her.''

''She pretends to be dispassionate, hates the father, has both softness and hardness for Cynric. She would use her sorcery to save him, I think. All by the way. A visit to Westri itself, before they are prepared to sail, might indeed repay us.''

''Yes,'' Gudrun said thoughtfully, considering those words, liking the possibilities they contained. ''Yes, by the gods. A visit to the Count of Britain might not go amiss, either; he's a man, and you have his friendship, Bragi. Was that true and no idle brag?''

''You wound me,'' he declaimed. ''The name is *Brag*? *I*? Not *I-brag*! The count will receive me. It's a considerable favor I did him last Beltaine, and I fought with his auxiliaries once. I've friends among his companions, too; Caradoc, Gareth, and maybe Palamides still, though I had to trick him when last we met. Are you wanting me to go to him?''

''Yes,'' Gudrun said. ''My lover, I do. Indeed, *we* will go, in *Ormungandr*—and if you will send one or two of your ships with us, Niamh, we will make some trouble in Westri while we are about it.''

''I am sure one or two of my husbands-of-ships would enjoy that.''

''If you went to Count Artorius in person, girl, he'd be apt to hang you,'' Felimid said dryly, ''and he's one of the few with the strength to manage it. Don't be forgetting that you have pillaged your share in his beloved Britain. Leave Artorius to me.''

''I plan to, my herald Ratatösk. I will do the sea work. You choose an escort and some gifts for the count.''

Decius grinned at him. '' 'May I perish if I fare on green water in March again.' I'll take oath I heard someone say that of late.''

''I did, did I not? But that was before I was reminded how stale this hall smells and how long I have been here. It's movement I want, Decius, and it's even worth seasickness to

me . . . most of all with a peaceful visit to some old friends
capping the journey.''

"Enjoy it," Decius advised him. "The fighting will start
soon enough.''

Those realistic words sounded in Felimid's head many times
as he sloshed in the bathhouse, rinsing salt from his skin, and
again on the other side of a heavy curtain as he sweated pleasur-
ably in a hot fog. Gudrun rubbed his shoulders and back with
a strong, sensuous touch.

"Now this is life," he said, with blissfully shut eyes. "Gudrun, we could have more of it and less of the blood-spilling,
if you wish.''

She dug her fingertips stimulatingly into the muscles of his
long back. "You are about to talk to me of Erin again. I know
the signs by now.''

"It's a fine place among all the places on the ridge of the
world, and you have been there. You could have honor; fighting
women do, there, and the time you raided, you raided Leinster,
not in the west. There is—''

"Bragi! There is a language I do not speak, and I do not
learn languages with your ease. There are ways I do not know.
Granted, I might like them when I did know them, for they
sound like good ones, and you have told me all about the warm
summers, mild winters, the beauty and fruitfulness. It is what
you have not told me that gives me doubt.''

"*Not?*"

"*Not.* I have heard what a fair land it is, its trees, cattle,
and matchless horses. I have heard your stories of old times,
of the Tuatha de Danann, of their wars with the Firbolgs and
Fomors, of their magic and skills and how they departed before
other invaders . . . and do you know something? Never have
you spoken of your own family, but in passing. When I have
asked, you have turned my question aside, not once but nine
times in a row.''

"Ah, surely not.''

"Surely so! Yes, Bragi, and yes, and yes! I do not like it.
I wonder what you are hiding. You have told me your line have
been poets and poetesses since bronze was the metal of war.
You have said that your father was Fal the Reiver, a pirate as
great as—as—as I am, by the gods! Or almost. You promised
once that you would tell me stories of him, a promise you have
not kept, although you had all winter. I do not even know if

you have brothers and sisters. You have never mentioned any.
Are you a man without family? Did you lie about your lineage
to me?''

"Come, you know better than that. Of course I'm of good
blood. Have I manners that show a loutish upbringing? Where
did I learn the harp and weapon-play and all the magic I know,
if I was bred a loon?''

"Then tell me. Between us only. You have even used a false
name all the time you have been with me. Bragi. 'Poetry.'
That does not seem like a man with nothing to hide. What is
your true name again?''

"Felimid mac Fal,'' he said slowly, tasting it.

"Felimid mac Fal. There! You have met my father and
brothers, you have seen his broad acres in the Limfjord, you
know my story and even my worst shame. I do not hide things.
I do not want you to hide things from me.''

"No, that is fair,'' he admitted. "Angus Og's half a hundred
swans, I have been in your bed nearly a year, and we have
saved each other's hides in tight places! I never thought, that
is all. I'll tell you. The name I use is nothing to do with my
own family, though. I took it because there are friends of mine
in Britain who might have suffered if it was known that I lived.
It should be all right now. A year is long enough for that
business to have blown over.''

"Then I will not ask about it. I do not want your life's
secrets, Bra—Felimid. I would know about your kindred, that
is all, and why you are mute on the subject.''

"So. I'll tell you, but for preference not here. In bed.''

"In bed?'' She came around by his hand and sank to one
knee, looking at him with her level, sea-gray gaze. "Are you
thinking to make love to me the night long and leave all my
questions unanswered?''

"Cairbre and Ogma!'' Felimid exclaimed. "Not when it
imports so much to you. Na, na.'' Puzzled, he cast his mind
back over his time with Gudrun. Had he shown that much
evasion and duplicity to her? She wasn't by nature suspicious,
he knew that. Yet he felt a strange, strong reluctance to talk,
even though he had nothing to hide. The story wasn't even
unusual. "I will tell you of my clan's affairs, and of my paren-
tage and my other relatives, until you are sick; and that will
leave time for lovemaking afterward, too. You shall hear.''

"No more do I ask.''

"Ahh. That is fine, Gudrun. Now I will rub you."

"Can you not begin telling me while you rub? I am eager to know."

"Oh, well," he said, standing and stretching while she lay down. "My tribe's called the Corco Baiscind, of the old Erainn blood that traces back to the Tuatha de Danann; the same blood as the Cruithni, whom you call Picts. We're like them, tall and fair-skinned, with brown or red hair for the most part, but we've blended with Milesian, Firbolg, even Fomor, I shouldn't wonder, and other tribes galore. My father's mother had more than a faint strain of the Children of Lir in her; Umai the Poetess."

"That strain has not come out in you, much."

"Na, that's true. My grandsire Fergus, now, who married her, he was a bard from a great line of bards and cared for little else in his younger days. He talked in cadence and slept with a harp, I believe. That same harp I carry. Golden Singer. He noticed Umai first for her poetry and only later as a woman. Then they bred a son, and he was the first of our line in generations past counting who did not *want* to be a bard."

"Oho! I can guess what your grandsire thought of that."

"You cannot, acushla." Felimid's voice had gone far away, remembering. "Family pride, family and tribe loyalty, the bardic calling . . . to Fergus those were everything until he met Umai, and for a long time after, I think. The bitter joke is that they were everything to my father, too. When Fergus sent him to a bardic college, he went, and he did well, if you discount pranks like lifting herds of cattle and driving them through the college in the misty dawn, while the *ollamhs** cursed and jumped and stepped in steaming cowpats to their hocks."

Gudrun chortled. Her sleekly muscled trunk quivered, "I'd have liked this father of yours, Felimid! What more did he do?"

"Much. He had an outlawed uncle, one of the Three Forfeited Hostages of Dar . . . a famous story, that, and not of the prettiest. Because of it, Uncle Misch had a blood debt to pay, and Fal aided him to pay it, which meant slaying a king. He had to flee—he was fifteen then—and took to the sea with a pirate named Nasach, a fisherman's son and a master of the trade."

*Bards of the seventh and highest rank.

"I never heard of him."

"Then maybe he was not as good as I have been told he was," Felimid said amiably. "Fal spent two years with him and became his lieutenant before the end, but he returned swiftly to Erin when word came of a battle in the making over the High Kingship. Fergus was there, on the side of Ailill Molt, who lost; and it was Fal got his father away from the battlefield alive. They were reconciled then, after Fergus had not spoken Fal's name in two years, but Fal never did become a bard or even train for it further. He followed the pirate trade in his own ship, the *Osprey*."

"At seventeen?"

"Well, no . . . I heard that he was two full years gathering a crew and making it what he wanted, and he must have made his common share of mistakes withal. He was nineteen when he obtained the *Osprey*. It's very little other than success he appears to have had after that, and each year he brought rich plunder home to the Shannon. By what I hear, he was his own man, and very much a man . . . along o' ruthless, self-willed, and insufferable. But I never knew him."

Gudrun had no difficulty in guessing that that was where the nettle stung. Why not?"

"Cradle your head on your arms again, as a favor, for I would not be seen blushing. My mother Caithlenn was another man's wife when Fal saw her, and a Christian. He saw her, and she saw him. They ran away together; her husband pursued and would maybe have killed them both, but that we will never know, because it fell out that my father slew him."

"This father of yours did not balk at much."

"Like a lover of mine. Now, Caithlenn my mother felt great horror and remorse. She left Fal and sheltered in a nunnery. Fal discovered where she had gone, but aside from warning the mother of the house to treat her well, and paying for her needs, he did nothing. He did not even let her know he had learned where she was. He waited, and while he waited he had trusty men watch over her night and day, and other spies with her dead husband's clan in case they learned of her whereabouts . . . as they did."

He paused. Gudrun asked quietly, "And what happened then? And where were you?"

"I was growing pink and blind in her womb, ignorant of all the fuss and murder. Fal's intrigues and great care had kept the dead man's clan ignorant until my mother's time was close, but he must have known they would learn someday. He couldn't send us to his family on the Shannon, for that would have provoked an open feud, and maybe Caithlenn would not have gone, any more than she would return to her own clan for shame . . . and they were determined to kill her to wipe out the disgrace. It made them more determined still when they learned that she carried me. Well, briefly, they made a compact with her slain husband's clan and came hotfoot to the nunnery.

"Fal was waiting. He put us both aboard the *Osprey* in the care of his ship's master, who took us to the Shannon while Fal held off the attackers and died doing it. His death satisfied both clans, and there was no feud.

"So, that is how I came to grow up with my father's kin in the absence of a father, and why my grandsire always hated my mother, and why she returned to a nunnery when the time came to send me to foster parents."

"Tyr's lost hand," Gudrun said. "What a story! Your mother sounds like a fool and a weakling to me. If you are going to sin, you should have the belly to stand by your sins and eat the fruit of them. Instead, I would say your father did the eating while she got off lightly."

"I see it another way. You are always hard on other women, Gudrun, but in the matter of this one your judgment is not wanted."

"I am tame. What was your foster mother like?"

"Much like a big warm she-bear. She licked, hugged and whacked her cubs into shape. Before she married she had been a famous fighting woman herself. She taught me weapon-skill, manners, and most of all what a great heart is. Her husband taught me to ride, to work—even though I'm by disposition lazy—and to get by rote the finest repertoire of bawdy songs from Shannon-mouth to the Leinster coast. Suibni's bardic college trained me to the third degree and polished my manners rather more. I have four foster sibs to whom I am closer than my one half sister, and a gaggle of my mother's kindred from whom I got little but hatred. Fergus and Umai live yet, so far as I know. He never could say very much to me, but when I left Erin he gave Golden Singer into my keeping and charged me to bring her back safely."

"That means much to you?"

"She's the greatest treasure of our clan; one of the treasures of Erin. What's more, she should rightly be in Fergus's hands until his death. He's chief bard.''

His hands had stopped in their work. Their heels rested on her upper back, the harp-hardened fingertips atop her shoulders. Gudrun stretched, her channeled white back, smooth waist, superb bottom and thighs displaying their conditioned strength as the muscles worked sleekly against each other in the glow of the hot stones.

"Thanks, my man. Do you wish you had not told me? For it means something to me to know.''

"Na, I'm not sorry I told you. I'll tell you more another time.''

His fingers moved down her spine, digging and loosening. As he finished by dancing his fingertips lightly over her ribs, she curled on her side, sat up and leaned against him.

III

For lifetime after lifetime
The legions kept the peace,
And men believed it eternal.
(All things mortal cease.)
Britain is now abandoned,
City, temple, and dome,
Yet if Rome has forgotten Britain,
Britain remembers Rome.
—Palamides the Thracian

"One of us ought to stay," Decius said. "Someone must look after this boiling of devils and enforce peace."

"I must have a trusty ship captain with me, too," Gudrun answered; but she did not deny the mixed, tinder-dry state of her own crews and allies. The sudden return of the Children of Lir had added water to the composition; however, they being what they were, their return might affect her men as the touch of water did the frightening Greek Fire of Constantinople, and set the sea ablaze.

"It shouldn't be me. Who does that leave?"

"I will take Pascent."

"I wouldn't trust him with the dregs of my wine!"

"All the better, then," Gudrun said cheerfully, swinging her legs as she sat on the table, like a young girl. Even a man who had witnessed her bloody deeds might in that moment have found it hard to believe in them. "I will be able to watch him. He will not be here to make mischief if he is that way inclined, or to fret you."

Because Felimid didn't trust the Gaulish captain either, he characteristically defended him.

"Come, Decius, you know nothing against him. Nor do I.

36

He's a fighter, and a crafty, seasoned sea captain. That's what we will be wanting, and since we can't have you—''

"Pah!" the Spaniard interrupted, his jeweled eye volcanic in his dark, hard-bitten face. "He's too hearty, and God knows he was thick with Hugibert before you slew the dungbag—for trying to murder the lady, I'll remind you."

"Remind me, then, if you must." The savagery of that bare-handed killing and of his own passions at the time gave Felimid no special pleasure to recall. "Yet I *saw* Hugibert drive his spear at your back, my bright fire. I know nothing of that sort, or of any sort against Pascent."

"I *know* nothing against him, either," Decius said, shrugging. "I just don't like him."

Gudrun laughed, and gripped his hard shoulder affectionately. "That is not much to the purpose! I need a trusty man here while I am away, and one who can keep order—your own saying, Decius."

"As for Pascent," the bard added, "when he knows our mission will annoy the British sea wolves, he will give his full power to it, or I mistake him."

Felimid was not mistaken. Pascent grinned through his russet moustache, jammed his repellent stocking cap on his head, and declared, "I'm ready."

"That is fine," Gudrun said. "I want some of the Children of Lir to come along, for I intend more than just setting Bragi and a retinue ashore in Britain. Let us visit them now."

The superstitions of a seaman thick within him, Pascent muttered, "I'd as soon not. The merfolk bring bad fortune. This is known, lady. Even when they mean well, they are not for mortals to mix with. Not that they often do."

"Better on our side than against us."

"And mortal they are," Felimid said. "They age and die like us, Pascent . . . all save a few who lengthen their lives by magic, which some earth folk also do."

Safe or unsafe, mortal or not, Gudrun wanted the Children of Lir beside her. They carried with them the living force of the sea she loved. The dull world borrowed brightness and mystery from them.

Even the little isle of Brechou, within spitting distance from Sarnia's cliffs, seemed changed by their presence. A greenish underwater tint had become a subtle dye in the air; a tree or clump of grass, seen at the edge of vision, appeared like swaying weed; a formation of brain coral, a leviathan statue. The sea caves below the island, where the sunlight never reached, had become places of unbridled glamor all in a few days.

That which was really there, like the light magical ships with their ivory fittings and bright sails of sea-spider silk, and the Children of Lir themselves, could not be seen at all by untrained eyes unless they were briefly given the power to see it. Niamh's doorkeepers gave that vision to Gudrun and Pascent as a courtesy. Felimid, through his bardic training, had gained it permanently years before.

They were welcomed by Idh, the young-faced, ancient-eyed spokesman, in a bone-colored tunic and sand-colored cloak. Lantern globes shone yellow, without heat, on fretted screens, couches, low tables, living tapestries, furs, and exquisite shells. From courtesy Felimid did not look too closely at these things. He did not really want to know how much was illusion. A deal of it doubtless was, for the Children of Lir had lost almost everything except their ships when the Veiled Isle was destroyed. (They had even lost a few of their ships.)

"All good be with you, Idh," Felimid said. "I do not see the lady Niamh. Is she near?"

"I cannot say. The lady Niamh comes and goes as she pleases. Since I am still her spokesman, you may say to me all that you would say to her, and I will answer as though with her voice."

"We are making a run to Britain to tickle our enemies the Jutes. It's questioning we'd be whether two of your husbands-of-ships would come with us, for Gudrun Blackhair would be honored to have them."

"So?" Idh looked amused. "You must ask them. Not I nor the lady Niamh herself would command them with you, and I would not forbid them, either. But I am sure at least two would go, for the sport of it."

"How are you managing to eat?" Pascent asked bluntly.

"The sea feeds us," Idh replied. "We're getting enough. Why do you ask?"

"Why, because you may be getting enough, but it doesn't look to me as though you are getting it very steadily, from one day to the next—and because that's likely to be a difficulty for us all, before May Eve." Pascent gnawed a curl of his moustache. "We go to Britain on short rations ourselves. Your captains will have to fetch their own, or else plunder some."

"Take it up with them."

Pascent scowled at that rather haughty advice. His sharp,

jutting chin came up, as with effort he strangled a choleric and profane reply. He did indeed fear the Children of Lir.

"Yes," he muttered. "And if I don't find them to be more forthcoming than you, I'll be as well pleased if they say no."

In the sunlight and raw sea wind again, they spoke with the husbands-of-ships they could find. Aidan, whom Felimid and Gudrun knew, was ready for the venture, a brisk and personable man not averse to making some trouble. He recommended Nacrantal, who snapped at the chance. This second husband-of-ships was taller than Aidan, with the able, predatory, single-functioned look of a shark about him. He was wholly willing to remind the Jutish pirates that they did not rule the oceans.

That settled, Gudrun chose the eighty men she could take aboard *Ormungandr* from the two hundred who wished to go. Decius's methodical aid and her lover's easy, pride-salving arbitration of disputes made it simpler.

"That Bragi," said Hemming the Saxon, "can soften any quarrel but those he starts himself."

Not even in *Ormungandr* would Gudrun cross the Narrow Sea to Britain by rowing or sailing due north. From Sarnia that would have meant passing through the lethal tide race of Ridune, and the British coast directly opposed had another tide which was swifter, if anything. The march weather made it worse.

Thus Gudrun's dark war serpent swam west to Lesia, the friendly neighboring isle with its Celtic chief. All Gudrun's neighbors preferred to be friendly with her, and she did not foul her own nest by raiding them. Also, she felt genuine liking for Lesia's chief.

"Bragi, you mind the dead monster that tried to shatter us here, last autumn?"

"I recall it better than I'd wish to, for the stink alone there is no way to forget. That would have been a bad day for us without the sea people's help."

"Yes. And these waters are cleaner now than they were then."

Ormungandr's double comb of oars carded the water, so that the island faded astern. Aidan's white ship with her figurehead of a swan raced to leeward and Nacrantal's to windward, its prow carved in the likeness of some bizarre fanged creature. Both were smaller and frailer than *Ormungandr*, though they rode the waves even more nimbly in their lightness. The crews of both included men and women. Some wore fish-scaled tunics, some kilts, some only their tattooed, salt-white skins.

"Sure, and it's well that the rowers cannot see them, or the stroke would be fouled past regaining in a moment," Felimid remarked.

Pascent frowned at the patches of water, stippled as though by cat's-paws of wind, which were the only signs of the accompanying ships then visible to him.

"Aye," he said, raising his voice in order to be heard. "The blessed powers are with us. We can't but do well."

He's sincere as a coper swearing his decrepit nag is seven years old, Felimid thought, smiling. *The blessed powers! Yet you are wise to treat them with respect, Captain. Ah, Cairbre and Ogma, my stomach . . .*

Pascent grinned at him. "Queasy, lad? This is mild weather for March, and it's far to Britain. Recall how we came past Kent in *Briny Kettle* with this very devil ship a bowshot astern? Saint Martin's fundament, how they hate for anybody to trade in Britain without their leave, the damned sea wolves! In a few generations they will be converted, and men like me can show them some righteous Christian swindling, aha!"

"Good luck to your successors, but the sea wolves may take to righteous Christian swindling themselves something well, if I'm to judge by their talents. They can haggle and levy tribute with the best. All they require," Felimid said, mildly detached, "is to learn that it is God's will that they should do so, and there will be no holding them."

A wind gust caused *Ormungandr* to buck. Felimid clenched his shaven jaw and once again became host to a rennetlike pallor. Pascent chuckled to see it, and swaggered aft calling orders. Felimid glanced Gudrun's way; her attention was elsewhere at the moment. He dashed for *Ormungandr*'s side.

Feeling better, he rinsed his mouth clean and walked forward. Although still pale and lacking his usual grace of movement, he no longer felt as though live fish inhabited his stomach. Gudrun stood by the shield-rail still, her crimson cloak flying.

The sea miles passed. Gray-green water hissed below, and *Ormungandr*'s gray-green sail strained above. A bay gelding stamped in an improvised stall abaft the mast. It had been the finest choice of horseflesh on Sarnia. The whiff of its fresh dung mingled with smells of brine, greased leather and weapons, sweat, oak, and pitch. Gulls wheeled above the mast, shrieking. Far higher above, the clouds were rippled like sea sand.

"The horse," Gudrun said as it neighed, "calls to my mind

your familiar, the black mare. She travels between worlds at will, Bragi! There is one who can tell me all I would know about the Otherworlds and the Gates.''

"Myfanwy? She could, true for you, but all else you do have wrong, my heart.'' He glanced humorously at Gudrun, aware of the adzed thwart under his thighs and the sour taste lingering at the back of his throat. "I'm scarcely a wizard, without certain limits, and Myfanwy is no familiar of mine or any thing subordinate; she's a goddess's daughter. I called her to me, once, in desperate need because she gave me that right in return for a service I'd done her. Now that debt has been paid. Gudrun, she's not a being I would summon on a whim to answer queries as to what lies beyond this portal or that.''

"I think you do not wish to. It's no matter for now. She may appear again of herself, and if she does not, there are other deer to skin first—Jutish deer, which have found a home in Britain.''

Gudrun wouldn't forget. Felimid knew that, and perhaps she was right when she said he did not wish to avail her of Myfanwy's knowledge. No. Not perhaps. Certainly. And yet he was right, too. The goddess's daughter was not one who could be called for convenience, to ask directions here or there. The seeds of another quarrel were in that, and in due season they would probably sprout.

Ormungandr drew closer to Britain. As always, the great ship moved with impossible smoothness and an utter lack of the normal popping, groaning, and squealing of timber. It had been made by the dour red dwarves of the north for King Oisc of Kent, and Gudrun had taken it as spoils of battle when she slew him in a sea fight.

Sailing northwest, *Ormungandr* came to a great bulge of land which would have been nigh impossible to miss. The fanged serpent head passed below beetling cliffs, with red soil and a huge, high granite moor behind them. Passing north along a frightened coast, it glared over a wide river estuary where shore larks picked among the wrack. Gudrun did not pause to explore it.

She turned east, working around the shore of a broad bay. This was the ancient land of the Celtic Dumnonia, who held it still. The invading sea wolves had not reached so far. Since the Count of Britain had now turned them back, it seemed unlikely that they would.

They landed when the lookout sighted a large dun on a

hilltop. Fifty of Gudrun's pirates went ashore with her and the bard. This formidable force alarmed the clan which possessed the dun; its head was glad when the bard came to parley, for he had expected an immediate attack.

"It's friendly we are," Felimid assured him. "Indeed, we'd be foolish to be other in a land of such valiant fighters."

With fifty seasoned killers behind him, well able to take the dun and slaughter the entire clan—and they not even Gudrun's whole strength—this was a little fulsome, but Felimid would never have become a bard at all if such exaggerations had troubled him.

"I'm a bard of the third rank," he went on, "and Gudrun Blackhair of Sarnia's herald, on my way to Camlodd to ask audience with the Count of Britain. I'm needing a score of horses for my party, if you will lend them. They will be returned when I return, and since we are strangers, the lady will give hostages."

He framed it gently, as a request, as though the clan were in a position to refuse. This allowed its chief to accede with pride intact, as it was intended to. The horses, or rather ponies, were forthcoming. Felimid saw them groomed and saddled, then inspected his escort of twenty, all Armorican Britons who at least knew one end of a horse from another and spoke the language. Taking Germanic sea wolves to the Count of Britain's base would have been poor diplomacy, and Felimid did not believe in giving offense—at any rate, not by accident.

He parted from Gudrun with a lusty kiss, and she went with her remaining three-score pirates, Aidan, and Nacrantal to induce some outrage among the Jutes of Westri. Felimid rested flat on his back on the solid, supportive earth for a few hours before he rode north through the land known as the Summer Country. He sang the lament for its last king, the hero Gereint, son of Erbin, as he rode.

> "Before Gereint, the enemy's punisher,
>   I saw white stallions with red shins,
>   and after the war cry a bitter grave.

> "Before Gereint, the enemy's depriver,
>   I saw stallions red-shinned from battle
>   and after the war cry a bitter pensiveness.

•   •   •

"Before Gereint, scourge of the enemy,
I saw stallions girdled in white,
and after the war cry a bitter covering.

"At Llongborth I saw vultures
and more than many a bier,
and men red before Gereint's onrush.

"At Llongborth I saw slaughter,
men in fear and blood on the head
before Gereint, his father's great son.

"At Llongborth I saw spurs
and men who would not flinch from spears
and the drinking of wine from shining glass.

"At Llongborth I saw armor,
and the blood flowing
and after the war cry a bitter burying."

Artorius, now the Count of Britain, had been in that fight, a youth of sixteen experiencing his first major battle. That would have been—what?—a quarter century past. Felimid's father had been alive then, his passionate love unmet, the bard unsired, and Fal about as old as he, Felimid, was now. Why should he think of that? The song, perhaps, the grim song of Gereint, and, of course, Gudrun's recent questions. He abandoned the lament not half sung, and began instead a bawdy celebration of the girls who inhabited a place in Ratuma called the Dolphin.

". . . she cushioned him neatly and circled her hips,
and lust had its way with that master of ships . . ."

The distance to Camlodd from the dun would have been thirty-five miles for a crow; on horseback, with river and forest to traverse, it was more like half a hundred. They made the journey in a leisured two days of cloudy, windy, but fairly dry weather, crossing a saddle ridge between two ranges of hills and low peat moors thereafter.

The Roman road, lined with mileposts like aging teeth, led them to a deserted town and across the Yeo—and Felimid, as always, felt the forlorn lack of his bardic powers while they clopped along it. The stolid, practical structures of Rome had a deadness about them. They held back magic as a dam holds back water. On leaving the road, Felimid felt a rush of delight, at once mental and sensual. Awareness of the living earth passed into his body through his horse's legs and back; he heard the voices of wind giants roaring between the clouds.

Before going on to Camlodd he made a careful toilet and changed into the clothes he'd carried in a saddlebag. His companions groomed their ponies and themselves. So prepared, they rode the last few miles.

> ". . . the sun in the morning shone over their bed,
>   the two lay entangled, the sheet was a shred . . ."

A patrol met them ten furlongs from Camlodd. Mounted on big horses, cuirassed in hard leather, armed with long swords and lances, they were unmistakably the Count of Britain's men. Few others in the island bestrode horses so large, and no others at all rode with stirrups. Felimid knew the leader.

"A good day I give you, Kehydi," he said, smiling. His smile could charm a brigand intent on murder. "That silver was delivered safe to the count's war chest, I'm told. Fine work."

The yellow-haired Demetian stared amazed, then rode forward laughing to wrestle Felimid from his horse. Lacking stirrups, the bard did not try to resist. He slid from the bay gelding's back to Kehydi's war horse, clamped his knees to its barrel and caught the warrior's arm in a lock that Kehydi, skilled wrestler, promptly broke. One of this feet left its stirrup; he seized his horse's reins and simultaneously gave Felimid a shrewd blow in the ribs with his elbow. The bard dropped lightly to the ground, to back away from the stamping, snorting war horse while Kehydi brought it within his control again.

"Enough, lout," the bard said, laughing. "I'm an envoy, you see, and I'd like to enter the count's presence acceptable to view."

"Acceptable, is it?" Kehydi looked him over. A grin split his yellow beard. Felimid's garments had been made by the same red dwarves who had refitted *Ormungandr* in the north, and covered him as though he had been delivered in them. His heavy linen shirt bore a pattern of brown and azure diamonds, his breeches were apple green, his buskins, tunic, belt, and wallet all made of the same wondrously supple leather, dyed a deeper moss green, and softer to touch than moss. He'd grown his hair longer since his vagabond days in Britain. It now gleamed in knots and coils. His people liked fine coiffures for men and women alike.

Kehydi's gaze traveled to the bay gelding, estimating the beast, its harness, the cloak folded neatly behind the saddle, and the twenty men ranged in a half circle behind that.

"An envoy," he said thoughtfully. "And whose, just? The emperor's?"

"I've not been quite that far! No, not the emperor. He heard of me and offered, but meantime I'd been approached by someone better." He smoothed his clothing without fuss. "Why don't you conduct us to Camlodd ere it rains?"

The hill rose ahead of them with its oak-wooded slopes, like a Roman tonsure about the cleared crown. Earthworks and ramparts enclosed a space of fully eighteen acres. The newest rampart had been faced with careful dry-stone work, for the art of mortared masonry was lost in Britain (as was much else), and a timber fighting platform added above it with the solidity of Stonehenge.

They entered through the southwest portal, a wooden lookout tower above two pairs of massive gates. If Count Artorius lacked masons, he plainly had the services of some fine heavy carpenters. Within the fortifications lay stables and barrack lines; the bard's limpid green gaze went roving, and he formed a swift estimate of the numbers of horses and men. No wonder such a large area was required! As he neared the hall which dominated the summit plateau, Felimid observed other things, such as the storehouses, armorers' and farriers' forges, the shrine to Mithras, the tiny church, and the exercise field. Most of all he observed the men.

"You are here for a long stay, are you not?" he asked of Kehydi.

"We've been based here the winter, o' course, and last autumn, and we'll be here this summer long, I fancy. We have no need to campaign in the north again, and we burned all Saxon nests out of the Thames Valley last year. It's my guess we will do little this year but keep a close watch on Westri, and award Cerdic a mauling if he gives us the least reason."

"A mauling only? That is more gentle than I'd think you

would wish to be with Jutes. The name of Artorius has never been higher, and surely he has the force to use. He could gather a thousand Cornishmen and Cymry behind the dragon banner after the seed time, and destroy Cerdic's kingdom entire.''

''We'd have another union of the sea wolves to contend with then. Kent, Westri, and the South Saxons would form it at the least, maybe the Angles and East Saxons as well. Myself, I'd return to Verulamium instead, and with that as a base, spend a couple of years destroying all the Angle thorps between there and the sea. Maybe we will, but as I say, we'll not be doing it this summer. D'you care to wager?''

''I think not. You know something that I don't.''

The bard soon discovered what it was. Had Kehydi not told him that Count Artorius was hunting—''with his guests''—he would have sought the man first among the horses, second among the dogs, and third only in the central hall, or perhaps in a barracks or the armory. After a battle he would have known with certainty where to find him—among his wounded men, unless Artorius himself were too badly wounded to move.

He returned late in the afternoon, by the northern gate. The broad-shouldered figure riding as though one creature with his huge, milk-white horse could not be mistaken, or his brindled wolfhound Cabal. The balding man on his right was surely royal, and on his left—Felimid lifted his eyebrows a little.

''Who's the lady?''

''Enid of Brycheiniog.''

She rode sidesaddle with jaunty poise, her dark head lifted. Although not fleshy, she had the fine bones to make the flesh she carried seem like a ripe abundance, and her skin was faintly tawny, like honey mingled with cream. She didn't compare with Gudrun, or Vivayn, or Eldrida for that matter, but she was a very pretty little thing indeed, and it was his nature to appreciate it. What else Enid might be he could not even guess. And apparently it was the Count of Britain who would be discovering. This was the thing Kehydi had known and the bard had not.

Surely, though, a princess of Brycheiniog would not keep Artorius from fighting for the entire summer?

He spoke with Felimid later in privacy. His quarters occupied the eastern third of the hall, with a tapestried screen between them and the feasting tables. They were plain quarters, a soldier's quarters, and at a glance the Count of Britain appeared a plain man.

He stood Felimid's height or a finger joint shorter, not tremendously tall. Broad of shoulder and chest, with wide flat hips and powerful thighs, he resembled the lithe bard only in having the slightly bowed legs of a horseman. His brown hair was stranded with gray. The square, steady, unremarkable face looked tired. A decent man and strong, one would have said, meeting him and not knowing who he was, but nothing uncommon.

He had created a force of armored horsemen such as had never been seen in Britain before, or elsewhere in the fragmented Western Empire. He had commanded great war hosts and shattered others. He was the one man who could lead the combined forces of the bickering British kinglets and chiefs, none of whom would endure to be made less than any other, because he was not royal himself. He had saved Britain, or so his people said in triumph. He was perhaps the one man who doubted it.

He also possessed the entire admiration of Felimid mac Fal, whose other name was not Bragi, but irreverence.

"Welcome, man," Artorius said, clasping his hand. "It's good to see you."

"Thank you, my lord Count. It's been some little while since Badon."

"So it has. You seem to have prospered." Artorius looked with some amusement at the garments which fitted as if woven and sewn on Felimid's limbs. "There was talk that you had died in a quarrel with the Atrebatian prince, Justin, and then one of my war parties brought the news that you were alive."

"Alive, meddling, and uncovering hidden things, as always," Felimid agreed blithely.

A steward entered through the partition then, bearing a flagon and two wine cups on a wooden platter. They were of polished silver as fine as the hilt of Felimid's sword Kincaid.

"Part of the treasure you found," Artorius said, touching his goblet.* "You outwitted Palamides over that, yet you left it for him—for us—instead of taking it yourself. Why? Have you no desires that a treasure like that could fulfill?"

"Oh, one or two. However, my lord Count, I had at that time a greater need to be traveling lightly and swift. As much silver as I could grasp in one fist sufficed me. Any man who tried to take that entire hoard should have a host to defend it!

*BARD, Part V.

47

One alone would have his throat cut within a nine-night. Besides, that treasure belonged to Britain.''

"It has worked for Britain," Artorius said simply, "and that's due to you." He grinned, and drank. "Palamides was disgruntled. Now, whose envoy are you?"

"Gudrun Blackhair's, my lord Count."

Artorius's face showed his astonishment, open and plain. Wrinkles entered around the small brand of an initiate of Mithras on his forehead.

"The woman pirate? I know she has raided in Britain, or someone of that name has. Still, I thought her three parts legend.''

"My lord Count, you have become three parts legend yourself, and in future years it will grow to nine parts! Receive my assurance. I know how these things go. Gudrun Blackhair is real as the noonday sun. She has three hundred men to follow her at present, and other, stranger allies. And she has me."

"You make me wonder what the Count of Britain can do for her, since all that is so! Nay, Felimid, to me she's one more sea wolf, and if I captured her, I would probably slay her. She must know this.''

"It may have occurred to her," Felimid said. The count's brows drew together a little. Felimid controlled himself. "Yet maybe, my lord Count, you'd rather be slaying Cerdic of Westri. Gudrun has made an enemy of him, or at any rate of his heir Cynric. It may lead to his dying at her hands this summer, for he plans to come seeking vengeance, the lovely, headstrong, misguided lad. If Gudrun does make an end of him, she will surely have to deal with his sire. That's another matter.''

"Yes. It would be."

"She wonders, does Blackhair, if you'd care to be the anvil to her hammer and shatter Westri between you. Vectis island is part of Cerdic's kingdom, the first part he conquered, and Gudrun could scour it free of sea wolves at her pleasure. The plunder would be worth it. The mainland part of Westri . . . you know better than I, my lord Count, how quickly your riders could reach it from Camlodd, and what you could achieve there.''

"I could destroy Westri," the count admitted. "It would be costly, for Cerdic is a mighty leader, yet it could be done by a sufficient force. I'll agree that your Gudrun could clear Vectis, though you may not be the best judge of that, Felimid. But what then?"

"Ha? Maybe I do not apprehend you."

"Maybe you do not. It's almost five years since Cerdic slew King Natanleod and conquered the kingdom. No British strength is left to rule it. Who could settle there and hold other adventurers at bay? There are more like Cerdic, Hengist, and Aelle; there will always be more.

"My brothers and I have driven the sea wolves from the north and out of the Thames Valley, so that those who remain dare not expand farther. But to retake the Saxon shore would cost Britain so much that we could not garrison the old forts, and there is no defensive fleet any longer. We have not had even one naval squadron for a century, man!"

"Surely, my lord Count. I never spoke of the entire Saxon shore, only of the newest, greenest sea wolves' kingdom — and Britain has plenty of bold seamen in the west. It doesn't lack restless princes with bands of fighting followers, either, that I have observed. Westri could be retaken and held, and carry a British name again, if it is thought worthwhile. That is not for Gudrun Blackhair or me to decide. I only bring the word that Gudrun has made Cerdic and Cynric her enemies — and I witness that even for such as they, she is not a safe enemy to have. You will hear soon enough that she has visited Vectis and Hamo. She is doing that very thing now. If it comes to more than a sudden raid and ship-burning, then the Count of Britain may wish to strike by land in concert with her. He should certainly be told if it is due to happen."

"Considerate," Artorius said, somewhat sarcastically. He poured more wine, and almost knocked over a goblet. Felimid remembered such little awkwardnesses in this man, from a few years before. They did not reduce him. They were endearingly human in one who had become three parts legend, and on a horse he was the least awkward being Felimid had ever seen.

"I'd feel safer for Britain if Cerdic were not," he conceded. "He's the greatest and ablest sea wolf left. Yet I'll require to know far more of your Gudrun's power and abilities before I consider her as an ally. She has a name for sudden recklessness. Also, if she can conquer Cerdic, she might prove worse than Cerdic."

"There is not the least wish upon her to conquer Britain, my lord Count. Or any part of it. Her dreams are elsewhere. Still, she did slay King Oisc, and she has his ship *Ormungandr* now. If you send a man of trusted judgment with me when I return to the coast, he will bear that out."

"Oisc! Light of the Sun! I'd heard that it was Gudrun Black-hair killed him. I didn't believe."

"I was there, my lord Count. She killed him with her own sword in her own hand. Because of it his kin and henchmen owe her a blood debt, and they will be coming to Sarnia to pay it erelong. That is for her to deal with, and it's in my mind that she will—but afterward . . ."

"Afterward we can talk of this further." Artorius took a long swallow of wine. "Tonight you are my guest, and you come at a good time for feasting. I have expected guests with me, too; Rhun of Brycheiniog and his daughter, the princess Enid. You will have seen them when we came in from the hunt."

Felimid agreed that he had. The matter of an association with Gudrun was evidently closed until there was more substance to it, but still, he would have expected Artorius to ask more questions.

He did ask a final one. "How old is Gudrun Blackhair, Felimid?"

"What? She has . . . two or three years more than I."

Artorius said something under his breath that sounded like, *"Mithras."*

Stepping into the hall, the bard was greeted by Gaheris and Gareth of Dun Eiddyn, two of King Lot's younger sons. He'd known them in the north, and in the war camp at Badon and met them again when he found the treasure of the abandoned villa in Kent. Gareth had accepted trouble then in order to let him go his way freely, as he desired. Felimid remembered. Their decent, guileless faces were a good sight.

"Felimid! What do you think of Camlodd? A change, isn't it, from those northern forts where the dung freezes solid inside the horses and you leave skin behind if you happen to touch the stone?"

"True for you. It's more like a king's hall."

That opened a door in his mind once he had said it. The long unused Roman forts along the Wall and elsewhere had been simply soldiers' bases for a soldier's purpose. Camlodd, too, was a fort, refurbished and rebuilt, yet it was in a fair way to becoming something else besides.

The same message could be read in Artorius's person at dinner. Clean-shaven in the Roman manner, he wore a tunic edged with the true Purple. Gold rings shone on his arms. A splendid bracteate, eagle within laurel wreath, glittered on his chest. Behind him, on the wall, a war banner was displayed, the red dragon of Britain on a golden field.

Enid sat beside him in springtime green and white, flowers in her rich dark hair. A certain awe of the Count of Britain was outweighed by her obvious pleasure in speaking to him, being his honored guest. The count appeared taken with her, too, despite a greater reserve. Her father Rhun could not have seemed more smugly gratified.

She sees the hero, the savior of Britain. She doesn't see the man I saw, tired after five-and-twenty years on the war trail, with his hair graying.

He wants to rest. He wants some honor and ease. He's no longer the young horse warrior with the sure, fixed intent of hurling the sea wolves back into the sea. He no longer even believes he can.

This is why heroes in the sagas die young.

"Unless I'm mistaken, your thoughts are older than your skin, Felimid."

It was Palamides the Thracian, who out of mistrust had wanted to confine the bard until the silver treasure they had discovered was safely with the Count of Britain.. The bard had eluded him. Now, although he looked the Thracian boldy in the face and smiled, he reddened a little while he did it, thus showing his impudence had limits.

"Greetings, Palamides. Are you maybe thinking you have a score to settle with me for last Beltaine?"

"No." The angular, pale-skinned face did not smile in return. "You were not under my orders. Those young barbarian fools who let you ride, they were—and they paid on the drill ground for disobeying, I may tell you. You left the treasure, though, and it is plain you told no others. That's the weighty thing."

"And have you heard why I am here now?"

The other occupants of the bench made space. Palamides fitted his tough-muscled body into it. "I've heard various tales. They have not ceased growing yet. Are you really the herald of a woman pirate who sails against the wind when she needs to, and sometimes turns into a crow?"

Mockery. The Thracian never had sympathized with Celtic fancies. Felimid, at any rate, heard it as mockery, and did not see why he should concur.

"You forget that you once met a man who turned into a

wolf. You did not believe that, either, until your raiding party was almost wiped out. Na, Gudrun does not turn into a crow, nor does she sail directly against the wind, although she has a ship which can do nigh anything short of that. Ride to the coast with me when I leave here. You will see how wild the truth can be.''

"Have I nothing to do here? I am second in command of a squadron, Felimid, not a bard who can travel where his next whim suggests. I would be gone for days, and I would have to take horses, men, and equipment. All this, if you'll pardon me, to edify myself by looking at a sea wolf's ship of which I have seen too many now, and a warrior woman with a moustache?''

"You're waspish, so," Felimid said mildly. "It's in my mind that you hold Beltaine against me after all. Wait, for I'd finish! Yes, I'm Gudrun Blackhair's envoy, herald, and spokesman, and here as such, but the count wishes that confirmed by a trusty man. I think he would have you go with me. Ask him.''

"Oh. Since it's that way, I shall." Palamides glanced toward his leader's table. With no mockery at all, he said, "He's a better man to wear the Purple than any of the barbarians or rebel generals who have.''

"His fame will last five hundred and five hundred and another five hundred years. Let's drink to it.''

"And the cause he fights for.''

Palamides was idealist and skeptic in the same skin, and never saw a discrepancy.

IV

The sea bride must carry us over the surge,
Our weapons to lend the wise chieftain:
Gladly you give her, as gladly we take her,
Or else we will redden your earth ruts.
　　　　　　—Felimid mac Fal,
　　　　　　The Lay of the Seventeen.

Far to the north a dozen and a half unkempt shapes came to a holding of broad acres near the sea. Wolves howled in the forest behind them. They slouched across unploughed fields, not troubling to announce their approach or to make any sign that they were peaceful. Dogs and armed men ran to meet them.

"Who are you?" demanded the foremost. "You show no courtesy, and if you're lawless as well, you have come to the wrong place. So many armed gangrels, all utter strangers, are not for men in their wits to welcome."

"Let me kill him!" growled one of Thrain's sons.

"Not yet," Ottar said. He grinned unpleasantly at the man from the farm, showing teeth as foul as his beard. "I'm Ottar the Berserk, little weakling, and these are my kinsmen. All berserks like me. We go where we like at any time, and we're on Odin's business now. That makes us worse. Just be mild and obliging toward us and maybe you will see another dawn. Are you the master?"

"Nay, my uncle Misk is that." The young man stood his ground, though he had begun to sweat. "I am Sigfus, Atkel's son, and there are thirty men in this household."

The berserks hooted laughter at that clumsy, defiant warning. Some of them stamped mockingly, slapped their own buttocks,

53

and made cruder signs of derision. One or two howled like wolves, and they were among the worst. Teg, the smallest and shrewdest of all that bizarre, frightening crew, simply grinned.

"Thirty? I'm frightened," he jeered. "We once cut our way through fifty king's troopers, and none of us died!"

"Now let's talk to Uncle Misk," Ottar said. "We're willing to be peaceful so long as things go our way."

"Peaceful," affirmed one of his nephews, in aspect as peaceful as a giant who had heard Heimdall's horn announce the last battle. "Yet if a dog comes at me, I'll bite off his head."

He glared at a black brute pulling at its leash.

"I think it would be the other way around," Sigfus said. "Our dogs are well spoken of hereabouts. Ask the robber band we buried last winter."

Yet he led them to the house. Several men with weapons stood in the yard, watchful and competent. They did not amount to the thirty Sigfus had claimed, so unless he had lied, the rest were not in view. The berserks cared little.

A bald, big-jawed man in a sheepskin coat confronted them, thumbs in his belt. "I am Misk the Roller. By coming armed and unannounced, you have done ill; you know custom, you know law as well as I. Is it guesting you wish? I can see that you are berserks, and it is asking a lot of a man that he should open his house to such a rough band."

"Guesting?" Ottar guffawed, and his noisome breath rolled about Misk in a cloud. "We are on the spear-wielder's business. We stop for nothing, we rest for nothing!"

"Never to bathe, anyhow," one of the bystanders muttered to his neighbor. Wearing a raw grin, the man replied with a cruder speculation, feeling glad he had given his axe a new handle. The air grew thick with a more then physical stink.

"Then let me not detain you," Misk said, answering Ottar's brag.

"I'll not. We must cross the sea, my kindred and I." Ottar's eyes narrowed then. "Who is that behind you?"

Misk did not turn his head. A man with a tangle of gray hair around a lined, beardless face had emerged from the hall. He said tonelessly, "It's I, lord."

Misk's expression showed distaste for a moment. He said brusquely, "Well, this man is asking who you are, and if you wish him to know, it's for you to tell him. All I have to say to that question is that you are my guest."

"My name is Aur," the stranger said. Ottar, looking him over for indications of his rank and conditions, came to the man's feet and recognized wizard shoes. "I am a priest in my own parts."

"Huh. Well. I said that we must all cross the sea. We can stay one night, no more. You have boat-houses down by the shore. What sort of ships are in them?"

"Is that what you want? Ha! You may get a ship, if you pay me what it is worth. Can you do that?"

"*Pay?*" Leidolf roared.

"Yes. Pay," Misk repeated. "You are not kin or oath-brothers or even neighbors of mine. Nor are you likely to come back this way. Should I give you a ship?"

"We're on Odin's business," Ottar said. He swelled and breathed hard. "It's bad luck to hinder us."

"Lord, I think you should oblige them," Aur said from behind his host. "I have some skill, and I can tell you a god is truly in this matter."

"Listen to that voice, Roller," a berserk growled. "We do not need it, but it says well for you."

"It says well for you! Misk the Roller doesn't hand over a ship for the mere loutish asking. Neither does any man of spirit. Aur, I would like it if you did not meddle. Now hear me, fellow. I will talk of selling you a ship. Can you buy or not?"

"If you will not give it," Ottar said, "we will take it."

"Clear them out," Misk ordered.

His order was rash. Ottar howled, and springing forward with eyes a-glare, he thrust two men staggering. Then he cut down the unarmed Misk while his thumbs were barely out of his belt. Turning, he hewed powerfully at a man to his right.

Teg raised a diabolical yell. He hurled his shield flatly skimming at the nearest farmsteader and broke his shins. The man went down. Teg put a long heavy knife into his neck and moved forward, a twisted, shrieking face atop a whirl of foul garments with a blade attached. Of them all he was quickest to take the berserker fit.

Ottar, terrible even when more or less normal, killed two men while his heart opened to the gift of Odin. He felt his muscles knot and convulse, his skin harden on his flesh. His vision turned red. Bawling, he flung his shield aside and chopped into bodies as though they were logs in a woodpile. Blows that fell on him he scarcely noticed.

The fit passed through his kinsmen like a swift contagion. Leidolf, crying that he was afire, cast away not only his shield but his axe, and ripped the clothes from his body, shredding the half-rotted buckskin like leaves. Foam in his beard, he seized a man by the neck and thigh. Raising him high, he dashed him with dreadful force to the earth of the yard so that bones crackled. His victim strove to rise. Leidolf stamped over him, snatching a weapon from the reddened ground as he passed, and the man strove no longer.

The yard was cleared now, though not as Misk would have had it cleared. Only berserks remained there. The other householders had retreated into the hall and barred the door, leaving a dozen fallen kinsmen and friends outside.

"Burn them!" Leidolf thundered. He raced to the cookhouse, where he raked among embers. His third son Jof stood near. Always the slowest among them to reach the berserk's way, he stamped and blew, working himself into the state.

"You feigning hangback!" Leidolf snarled, coming out ash-smeared and smoky with a double fistful of torches. He kicked Jof's backside. "Get on the roof and make the red cock crow."

Jof was boosted to the thatch amid gleefully bellowed advice. One firebrand after another was tossed to him. Below, his kinsmen ravened outside the doors, pounding on them with weapons. Jof pranced roaring for joy on the thatch, among the flames he had kindled, until the berserker fit truly claimed him. Then he jumped into the yard from a gable end without hurt.

In desperation the household men opened the doors and rushed forth among billowing smoke, led by the long-shanked Sigfus. He was the first of them to die. A remnant was driven back into the blazing hall after hacked, weltering bodies filled the yard. There they perished, trapped between fire and iron. The berserks did not even allow the women and children to come out. Only a couple of field thralls, who had legged it when the berserks first appeared, escaped alive.

Except for bruises and a few broken bones among them, the seventeen were unhurt. Careless of this as animals, they trod to the shore to examine Misk's seacraft. There were fishing boats, two trading knarrs, and a single mastless war boat large enough to carry thirty men.

"I should take one of the knarrs and sail," spoke a chill, colorless voice.

Hall, Ottar's brother, turned with his weapon raised. His

death-loving kinsmen gathered about the wizard Aur.

"You! How did you escape? Where were you?"

Blood-spattered and reeking of smoke, they pressed around him, growling. The passing of their fit left most of them weak, dazed, and sluggish-minded for a time, which perhaps was why none killed him outright.

"I am here now," Aur said, evading the question. "You are not the only ones to hear Odin's voice. I heard it, too, in the ash grove where I am priest. I came to this holding to wait for you, and I bring you a gift from the Father of Victories."

He displayed a leather sack, swollen drum-tight and secured at the neck with a curious knot.

"Take me with you, and I will open this when we are clear of land. It holds a fair wind to blow us across Skaggerak."

"*Us?*" Bjarni rumbled. "Take you with *us*? You bleached little owl, I'll feed you an anchor and just take your wizard sack!"

"Never will you puzzle out the knot, and if you slash the bag, you will get a squall to founder you," Aur replied in his bleached tone. "Also, the Norns have woven that only with me in your company will you ever see Kent."

"We take him," Ottar said flatly, ending discussion. "If he lies, we can kill him. You hear, wizard, Hel's get?"

"I hear you well."

The berserks did not question Aur further. Barely capable of thought in any case, they knew that Odin was lord of the winds, and Aur looked too much like his claim to be anything else. Perhaps he was even Odin himself, in disguise. It made no difference; Ottar was their chief, and he had accepted Aur as a passenger.

"The knarr, then. Load it, you manslayers."

The berserks returned to the farmstead to loot the storehouses. Ottar cast a spear over the scene of carnage, dedicating it to Odin. Afterward he ate hugely of freshly killed beasts, and in the morning his band departed over the trackless sea. Misk's neighbors had not yet gathered in strength to attack the berserks for their slaughter, and if they had, the berserks would have been convulsed with mirth.

They laughed and sang as they sailed.

V

Brilliant flames in Hamo's harbor
Scattered gold on the sea-wolves' path
When Gudrun came to trouble Cerdic
Careless of all his awakened wrath.
　　　　　　—Felimid mac Fal,
　　　　　　Gudrun's Saga

The cool night breathed the first heady, craving urgency of spring. The equinox had passed, and the season of wild, bursting new growth had unmistakably come. True child of that season, Gudrun felt a bright, diamond-hard eagerness to act, to strike. She stood mantled in her famous crimson cloak lest the glitter of her mail be seen from shore, and waited—the thing she did least gladly—with her blood rushing.

Some way astern, a henchman of Pascent's muttered, "Is that damned shapeshifter honest?"

The Gaul said shortly, "We are all in trouble if he's not. Now be quiet until you have something worthwhile to say."

He glared at the inoffensive half-moon because he must glare at something. Although it gave too much light for the comfort of a man lying hidden in an estuary ruled by Cerdic, it did mean that the difference between high and low tide was small at present. No matter what went wrong, they could not be caught at the top of this body of water with the tide ebbing swiftly. There were abundant other ways, though, to achieve cursory burial in the tide-flats with redshanks for mourners.

Bah, what the devil, Pascent thought. *We have allies with invisible ships, and our dice are loaded by the advantage of surprise. It's only that the otter-man should have returned by now.*

Turo the otter-man slid in his animal shape through the dark water of Hamo. Through his whiskers, through every hair-tip, he sensed and delighted in each swirling eddy as his feet thrust him sleekly onward.

Rising from the moon-dappled estuary, Turo frisked up one of *Ormungandr*'s oar-shafts, his fur dripping cold silver. He slid over the shield-rail, fluent and lively, more than eight feet from nose-tip to tail-tip, and rolled on the deck before Pascent. The Gaul was startled enough by his sudden appearance to partly lift the short-handled fighting pick he carried. Then, willing his hand down against his instinctive reaction to that which was not canny, he lowered it again.

The huge otter twisted and squirmed on the deck. Its pelt came off. A naked man with intricately tattooed limbs squatted on the floor timbers. With carefree naturalness he drew the otter skin over his shoulder.

"Ha! Welcome back!" Pascent said, cheerful now that something was happening. "What news, water-dog? No. Tell the lady, but first don some clothes. There's but one man she sees naked."

Turo laughed. "She'd be forever discontented with the man she has if she did behold me! Sa, sa. I will be decorous." He belted on a kilt of soft leather. "Is this less fearsome?"

The Children of Lir were never troubled by nakedness, living in the sea as much as they did, but earth-born barbarians like the Danes were stricter. Pascent, civilized in his somewhat sleazy fashion, deemed it ridiculous to be more perturbed by skin than slaughter.

"Fearsome?" he grinned. "I have more than that myself, but I take care where I show it. Do you know the last one who flaunted his manhood before the lady by taking a careless leak is searching for his plums yet? Now come along. I'll compare cock-prowess with you all month, after we teach these Jutes some manners."

Both had pitched their banter cautiously low. Gudrun greeted the otter-man in a like tone, knowing how sound carried across water at night.

"How went the scouting?"

"Blind are they in Hamo, lady—blind! They did not even

glimpse me. I saw enough to make up for their bleariness, though. They do have war-boats fitted, pitched, and ready to put forth, all excellent, and there are nine of them.''

"Nine!''

"Truly.''

"Four or five hundred men,'' Pascent said thoughtfully. "I give them this. They know what we are worth.''

Gudrun fisted his shoulder exuberantly, liking such talk. "How moored, Turo? How guarded?''

Turo held up fingers to illustrate his words. "They are roped to the east pier, lady, lashed wale to wale and touching, half a dozen guards in each. You can see the pier is torchlit from end to end, like all the ships.'' The flickering light could be seen for miles. Turo was mirthful as he pointed his arm shoreward. "They will be better lit soon.''

"They will.'' Gudrun braced the lower tip of her longbow by her feet, bent and strung it. Twenty fire arrows and a pot of embers stood handily arranged beside her.

"Now,'' she said, "let us make them know we are here!''

The ash oars dipped, shining like pewter in the moonlight. *Ormungandr* slid toward the town in that eldritch silence peculiar to the ship built by northern dwarves.

The two ships of the Children of Lir followed, silent as *Ormungandr* and even more agile to turn or back. They were invisible, besides, to common human eyes. Turo saw them, having as his natural birthright the vision that belonged to few among earthy mortals except bards, druids, magicians, and saints. Felimid would have seen them clearly had he been there, but he wasn't.

For greater trust and ease of mind among the strangely matched allies, Nacrantal had lifted the glamor from the sight of Gudrun and Pascent until dawn. Gudrun had accepted the eerie little rite with pagan unconcern; she had offered human sacrifices to Odin in her day, before she had angered the god. Pascent had clenched his teeth and promised a candle to the saints, but refrained from signing the Cross. It mattered more to him to be able to see the faerie ships whose captains he did not fully trust.

Ormungandr's baleful serpent-head rushed from the dark, water peeling away below it. The Jutes in Cerdic's ships stared. The extravagent yellow torchlight wavered raw on their faces.

"Jutes, Gudrun Blackhair is here!'' she yelled in the bow.

"From this night, Nastrand is your home!"

They were picked men. They sprang to arms at once. Three bounded up the steps of the timber pier—the stone docks of the Roman town had been destroyed by the invaders with immense labor, because the Jutes feared the Roman "magic" residing in them—and while two covered the third with their shields, he used an iron bar to sound a rattling, clanging alarm. It went on and on, jarring the teeth, arousing the town.

Gudrun fired four swift arrows at them by the torchlight, skewering someone's leg and driving a shaft clean through one shield. The iron racket continued nonetheless. Horns answered it from the king's hall.

Javelins flew at the serpent-ship. A few arrows hummed among them, although for the most part the Jutes were not bowmen. Then *Ormungandr* rammed the nearest Jutish war boat on the quarter, breaking in its timbers. The shock traveled through the entire line of closely lashed vessels. Men from Sarnia roared "Blackhair! and were answered with "Odin!" and "Westri!" On both sides they staggered at the impact.

Amidships in the raider four men kindled torches at a fire-pot and passed them to others. More axed open the heads of barrels, fired the pitch within, and—skin scorched, muscles cracking—heaved the barrels into the Jutish war boats. Red flame and black smoke rose, stinking.

"Ha ha ha!" Pascent bawled. "How's that for a love gift, you robbers? I wish we could have had it boiling for you!"

Gudrun's supply of pitch was small. Once the few barrels were gone, her men ignited bundles of oil-drenched wood and threw those instead. The Jutes who tried to swarm into *Ormungandr* were met with spear-points.

"Push off now!" Gudrun shouted. "Row down the line, my heroes, and save some fire for the rest!"

The Jutish commander heard that injunction. "Cut the ships apart and scatter!" he roared. Axes began to fall on cables at once. Still it was too late, and Cerdic's prized war-boats had been too closely linked that they might be defended as one. Crackling fagots spun into the other boats. Men swung short ash logs crowned with blazing pitch between them by rope collars, let them go, and watched the smashing, fiery impact with glee.

"Away now!" Gudrun ordered. "Port oars! Port oars! Port oars!" The rowers designated pulled strongly at each repetition.

BARD IV

"So. All oars now. Bend, my lads! Bend and pull!"

Ormungandr moved sleekly away from the wharves. Fire had taken a lustful grip on two of Cerdic's vessels, and was boldly fingering most of the others, while the Jutes battled like madmen to avert the threatened rape. As Pascent watched, grinning, a hundred warriors in two troops rushed to the wharves, their battle-harness creaking and ringing, shields banging.

"I wonder what those fine fellows believe they can do?" Turo mused. "Swim out and grapple us?"

As he gibed so, Nacrantal and Aidan took their own ships in, unseen by any Jute's crasser sight. At their ease they rowed along the burning line. White-skinned merfolk worked leather bellows, and streams of fine whale oil arched from fancifully worked nozzles to play over the hulls of Cerdic's war boats. Then the faerie ships flitted after *Ormungandr*. Their light hulls of a silver-gray wood which had never grown in any forest of earth glimmered in the moonlight.

Gudrun paid scant heed to their ethereal yet deadly beauty. Igniting her fire arrows and shooting them all, she bested her own record for accurate swiftness. The first still quivered in a strake when the last reached its oil-soaked target. The Jutish vessels burned inboard and out, beyond saving. Their guards had to scramble to the pier, singed, raging, shamed, and watch their lord's ships, loved as his own children, burn to the water-line.

"Scum of Westri, sea-thieves, heathen, how liked you our visit?" Pascent bawled. "Call yourselves pirates? Not one ship fully manned or free to move! Any man with aught but clotted suet in his head would ha' had this estuary patrolled! You hear, Cerdic, you drab's bastard by a ram afflicted with foot rot? You should be a Burdigala pimp!"

Gudrun liked Pascent and would have chuckled delightedly at his flow of language at most times. Now she knew a moment's sharp sadness as she looked back at the blaze she had ordered.

"Njord!" she exclaimed. "I hate to see ships die like that, even a foe's."

Have I turned foolish? Why, I have made other ships die, though never such a slaughter of sea brides as here. I have slain many men. Bragi, what are you doing to me?

Shaking herself out of the untimely mood, she gazed around her—and saw two beacons flame to life ahead, on opposite shores of the estuary.

"Look, Pascent! Whom would you guess they signal?"

The captain swore. "Can't say, lady. But maybe I jeered too soon and there is a patrol after all! We can still be trapped at the estuary head. Beyond it, even, if ships from Vectis be yare."

"Not in *Ormungandr*!" Gudrun said. "Not with *my* crew! Not with Aidan and Nacrantal beside us, either. Bragi will see us again. You are right, though; it may be close. We must earn our luck."

They went down the estuary with the gently ebbing tide. In the water ahead, white figures sported and dove. The Children of Lir felt out the way in that unfamiliar channel, rising unhurt to call instructions after intervals submerged which would have drowned any child of land-earth.

Turo remained on *Ormungandr*'s floor planks, in his human shape, looking ahead with faintly luminous eyes. He did not swim the moonlit waters with the others at their guiding work because as an otter he could not speak, and while as a man he swam as well as any Child of Lir, he saw better in the dark than any of Gudrun's pirates. Also, he could interpret his people's speech and signals to her far better.

"See yonder, lady?" Pascent said.

Two more beacons shone red at the estuary's mouth, and across the narrow strip of water which lay beyond, a third answered from the island of Vectis. Vectis had been Cerdic's first conquest, and now it was held for him by the heir who had such splendid reasons to love Gudrun Blackhair.

"I see it," Gudrun snapped. "I wonder if the cub has some ships ready to sail against Sarnia, too? We will not get near them if he has. He's too well forewarned. But maybe he will send them against us."

She sounded hopeful.

"Maybe, lady," Pascent said. "I would guess those nine ships at Hamo included his, all those he had busked and fitted to go. Belike any we do meet before we win clear will be in poorer condition. If I'm right, a happy farewell to them, poor fools, eh?"

He paused as Turo relayed a warning to turn from some snags. After giving the appropriate orders, he trod the length of the ship, inspecting the rowers, to curse and chivvy into full fighting gear all men he found unarmed, and to flatten a couple who argued. The merchant captain from the lethal stews of Massilia had always been tougher than most pirates, and possessed the perfect makings of one. Else he could not have risen to his current position under Gudrun.

Just after sunrise *Ormungandr* came into the strait between Vectis and the mainland. The wooded north shore of the island showed green and fresh in the dawn. Less lovely to Gudrun's eyes—because their condition was as poor as Pascent had suggested—were the four Jutish war boats that converged on *Ormungandr*. Two came from the west, one from the east, and one from across the strait. Moving swiftly under oars alone, they rushed to intercept and surround. Men swung grapnels.

"Blackhair, you whore of Niflheim!" someone cried. "You lose your stolen ship today, and your life besides! This is your end!"

Gudrun laughed savagely. "No, you son of a mare! It is yours!" To her steersman she said, through Pascent, "Turn west!"

The steersman threw his powerful back into working the rudder oar, while his mate began a chant for the rowers. *Ormungandr's* prow turned straight for the two Jutish craft which faced the rising sun. Each carried thirty oarsmen and ten or a dozen others, wild men in hard leather sarks, mostly bare-headed, their braided hair tossing as they bent back and forth, straining until the oars nearly broke.

Ormungandr drove like an arrow at the war boat nearer Vectis. Meeting it at a narrow angle, the black serpent of war splintered half a bank of oars and sent the looms whipping murderously forward, to break backs and noggins. The man who merely caught a cruel, bruising blow across his shoulders, which hurled him forward to bloody his nose and break his front teeth on timber, got off lightly. Then *Ormungandr's* copper-sheathed prow, cunningly braced within, struck the Jutish ship near its stern.

Nails shrieked and snapped. Planks burst. Those vessels, as few knew better than Gudrun and Pascent, saw hard service. Their useful lives were short. Their timbers constantly "worked." The long strakes, made of separate planks scarfed together, broke under the smashing impact. Cold brine poured in.

The Jutes kept their heads. Grapnels flew, biting into the wales and shield-rail of Gudrun's ship. The men behind them dragged their wallowing craft closer, until it rubbed grinding sides with their enemy. The second war boat came about, its skipper planning to bind to *Ormungandr* on the other side.

A sudden, inexplicable drag slowed it, because about twenty Children of Lir were clinging below the water. They began prying with bars and chopping with hatchets, to the consternation of their victims as their feet suddenly got wet.

"Row, you carls!" their leader cried. "Reach *Ormungandr*'s side and grapple! If we sink, we'll take her with us!"

They strained their backs to achieve it, while the leaks widened and their craft settled deeper. Javelins rained on them from *Ormungandr*'s port side, a volley of sixteen, swiftly repeated. The gift was returned, but *Ormungandr* held more men.

On the starboard side Gudrun's Sarnians fought redly to hold the Jutes back and rid the ship of the pestiferous grapnel irons. The sword Kissing Viper clashed and cut, its edge turning red. A Jute howled and fell back from the contested rail, clutching his face. Pascent's war pick, his favorite weapon in a sea fight, sank into Jutish flesh between the neck and shoulder. Bracing himself, he dragged the man forward like a hooked fish and hit him fatally with the boss of his shield before raising it again to serve its first purpose—warding Pascent.

The impact of a thrown spear jolted him backward. Its point had gone straight through his shield, and the shaft stuck out hamperingly before him. The thrower rose boldly, trod on the shaft to force Pascent's shield down, and hewed at his temple.

Pascent promptly crouched low. Missing his stroke, the man stumbled through his blow's unfulfilled force and his own very precarious footing on the shield-rail. Pascent swung his war pick, shattering the Jute's hip. He fell back into the war boat with a shriek.

"Blackhair!"

"Westri!"

"Cynric!"

"Die, ye mare's son!"

The war cries and curses rasped back and forth among the stabbing spear points. Beside Pascent a brawny, pot-bellied Frisian had at last pried loose a stubborn grapnel. He hurled it into the face of the Jute opposing him. A couple of heartbeats later someone's spiked bludgeon ripped open his arm.

Farther toward the bow Gudrun fought like a demon, conspicuous in her silvered mail and helmet, and easily known, too, by her red-covered shield. She liked to be known. Her own men fought with better heart when they could see her. If her enemies could find her more easily, too, why, they were welcome.

In her wildness she stepped to the gunwale to cut downward at the Jutes. An axe-man saw his chance. His blow would have bitten off half her foot had not one of Gudrun's pirates also seen his chance and rammed a spear point through the Jute's teeth, spoiling his aim for him. He fell, gurgling, while his axe remained stuck in the gunwale an inch from Gudrun's shoe.

"We're loose!" Pascent shouted. "Push clear, you dogs! Push!"

The vessels lurched and ground together. A strip of green water wide as a hand appeared before them, broadened, and was kissed by sunlight again as *Ormungandr* drew clear. The Jutish craft wallowed, slowly sinking, while their crews worked to stuff leaks, to bail, and make for the friendly land. It was near enough to reach by swimming, even if the other two war boats, too late to close with *Ormungandr*, had not been present to help.

Gudrun's men called out the farewells of their choice as the serpent ship raced west. The Children of Lir followed, in their ships which the Jutes could not see. Gudrun could not any longer see them herself, for that matter. The sight temporarily given her and Pascent had deserted them with the sunrise. They scarcely noticed the circumstance.

"By the Nails, lady!" Pascent whooped. "These Jutish wolves are eleven ships the poorer! Eleven! They cannot have many more decent, seaworthy ones among the whole boiling of them, mainland and isle. We've stranded them!"

"In their own dirty harbor!" Gudrun added with joy. "Bragi can make a ballad of this and a part of my saga besides. Raise sail, now, bucks! We will be waiting for my man when he returns to the coast. He and I have already been too long apart, and our news will please the Warlord of Britain, I take oath!"

They waited in the bay below the dun on the hilltop where Felimid had borrowed the horses. They waited for some days. *Ormungandr* traveled more swiftly than any horse on the ridge of the earth could, and Felimid dallied a while, enjoying the Count of Britain's hospitality. Except for daily weapon practice, Gudrun's crew had little to do but loaf and ripen for mischief. Seeing it with the eye of experience, Pascent ordered rowing practice each day as well. The master of the hilltop dun watched them at it and thanked God he had hostages, even if they did each eat enough for three and swagger as though they ruled the Summer Country.

Felimid appeared at last, riding out of the green spring distance with his twenty-strong escort and ten of the count's cavalrymen on their big Gothic horses. Palamides led the latter. They did not wear mail shirts, merely their hard leather corslets or loricae; Gudrun might have friendly intentions, but mail shirts were precious enough to tempt an angel, and Palamides had never heard Gudrun Blackhair called that.

"The horses are more to be valued still," he had admitted dryly to his leader, "but a pirate would find them of little use, and if she takes them aboard her ship, they will kick it to pieces."

However, even his sardonic eyes widened a little when he saw *Ormungandr*, and Gudrun's appearance truly astonished him. He had expected a woman with a body like a keg, unwashed and graceless, for he had wholly discounted the bard's enthusiastic descriptions. The tall, vital figure in man's attire came as a revelation to him.

"My sea eagle," Felimid greeted her, "I would say by the happy look of you that your raid went excellently, and Cerdic will be frothing yet. Now this warrior is Palamides, second to Gwalchmei in the Count of Britain's White Squadron. Palamides, you look upon Gudrun Blackhair of Sarnia."

They regarded each other and took each other's measure, the civilized, urbane child of the east and the wild north's wilder daughter. "My lady," Palamides said gravely, and bowed. "Your fame goes before you."

He did not say what he thought of the nature of that fame.

"Well . . . pleasantly said," Gudrun admitted. She did not trust diplomats. She often found Felimid himself too ready to agree and be peaceful, when she would have liked a rousing quarrel followed by a passionate reconciliation. "You serve a mighty man, who would hang or sword me if he captured me, so let us not pretend I am other than a pirate who has more than once raided this Britain of yours! But I am at odds with Cerdic and Cynric now." She smiled suddenly, with open delight. Pleasure in her daring feat shone from her. "I burned nine of their ships at Hamo's waterside, and crippled two more later! Your lord's spies will soon tell you the truth of that."

"Nine?" Palamides was startled. That was a fleet of considerable size. Cerdic had first come to Britain with only five, and he had been reckoned a notable young chieftain for it. Nine and two—why, that meant that the father and son could have few serviceable craft left between them! If the woman's boast was true, of course. As she said, he would soon know.

"Nine," he repeated, more coolly. "Lady, that's a most notable feat. Can you tell me why Cerdic had so many war boats made ready in one place? Kingdoms have been taken with slighter strength."

Gudrun agreed. "By Cerdic himself, for one. He meant to league with Kent against me. He may still come to Sarnia, or send his whelp, but I think he will be late to the banquet now."

"Doubtless." The saturnine Thracian, a little taken aback, raised a shield of understatement. "Kent by itself is a dire foe to have if you are not yourself a king. I wish you victory, lady."

Gudrun Blackhair smiled again. "Thanks. I expect to have it, friend, and I do not need to be a king."

The assurance of her, Palamides thought, partly amused and partly irritated. Then he looked again at the long black war serpent drawn upon the shelving beach below the dun.

"The Count of Britain," he said, "did not take your herald's message as seriously as perhaps he might. I did not take it seriously at all." He looked straight at the pirate leader. "I'll report to him that I believe second thoughts are wanted. When you win your victory, lady, we will hear of it in Camlodd—and afterward it will be Count Artorius who sends envoys to you."

"That makes good hearing, and they shall be welcome."

None but Felimid saw the Children of Lir or their ships riding offshore. To neglect those unpredictable, prideful folk, even the more easygoing of them, such as Aidan, was to ask for them to turn against you.

Once the parley with Palamides was ended and dusk covered the water, Felimid swam out to the faerie ships. The Children of Lir were blithe about bare skin, and Felimid, though less so, was not greatly bothered.

Nacrantal gave him a somewhat spiky welcome. "It's fine to be remembered at last. Are we not a part of your alliance, too? A bard should know better. I could give that man of the count's the vision to see us, for a short time. Surely that would 'suade him."

"Surely it would, husband-of-ships," Felimid said. "The sorry truth is—I know the man—it would have 'suaded him that the worth of us all as allies is no more than starlight and mist. For like reasons I warned the lady to say nothing of her dream of seeking the Otherworlds. He's Roman, that man, from the east. He doesn't comprehend the west, or the power of the old gods and their children. We showed him just enough, and just what he could accept.''

"Are you ashamed of us, then?" Nacrantal sneered. "Are you, a bard, abashed before *Rome*?" He spoke the word like a softly uttered curse. The shark's look of him was suddenly more pronounced, a matter of facial bones, planes and angles rather than anything overt in eyes or teeth. "Are you, Felimid of Erin?"

"Are not you?" Felimid countered. "I lose my powers where the things of Rome linger, and where the Cross which conquered Rome appears. Where are the Veiled Isles now?"

Nacrantal's teeth showed white as he half reached for a spear. Felimid stood relaxed but ready to move.

"In Manannan's name," the husband-of-ships said very softly, "you are lucky my own lady bound me to tread softly among you! But guard your tongue."

"I spoke cruelly, maybe," Felimid said, "but I will not believe you have never done the same—and did I say other than the truth, at all?"

"That is why I will not pardon it." Nacrantal brooded a moment. "Rome. Rome and the Church . . . Is there anything now to keep us here?"

VI

Berserks had come from the northern country,
Vithils the Axe sailed vengeance set;
Kings and chieftains swore agreement
To crush the foe none had conquered yet.

She replied with a chime of sword rings,
"Gladly I welcome high-stomached guests!
Come and be welcome in all your numbers,
To drink red ale and exchange sharp jests.

"Many others have come before you,
And found how Blackhair prepares a feast.
They ate and drank to such full repletion
Most haven't moved since the knives were greased."
—Felimid mac Fal,
Gudrun's Saga

Kent held the key to the trade of the North and Narrow seas. Firmly in the hands of the sea wolves, as it had been for sixty years, it grew rich from trade and tribute more than from simple piracy, which its lords practiced for sport while farmers worked the land and made sure their weapons were always handy.

Across the sea and far to the north, below the neck of Jutland, lay Edricsburg. The chief and sole town of the continental Saxons, it was hardly less rich than Kent. Most traders said it was a deal more honorable and better managed.

To Edricsburg came Ottar's clan of berserks, sea-stained now atop their other filthiness, wrangling and foul-tempered. They had mishandled their ship all the way down Jutland's west coast. Despite the magical wind Aur had brought them, tied in a sack, they should not have arrived at the bay of the Elbe.

The enormous town held about two thousand souls. Behind the oak jetties and docks lay many storehouses, boat-houses and barrack buildings for transient seamen. Few such had arrived in Edricsburg yet. The trading season was still to begin. Ottar's berserks would have drawn attention even had Edricsburg been swarming; as quiet as it was, craftsmen, fishermen, women and children all turned to look at the brutish strangers. Upon recognizing them for what they were, they quickly stopped staring.

The seventeen shambled up a sodden, mired street surfaced in the worst places by split logs over layers of stone rubble. The five massive hulks who were oldest led the way, but Teg, the youngest, stepped close behind them. Small by the standards of his clan, he walked confidently, darting quick glances about him from under dark brows. He had the most wit in that band when he was not frothing mad.

His elders knew it. "You talk, Teg," Ottar growled.

A charcoal burner the worse for drink blundered into them. Thrain backhanded him aside with scarcely a look. The charcoal burner rebounded from a storehouse wall and lay in the mud with a fractured jaw. One or two berserks trod over him; none heeded whether he recovered or drowned in the mire.

A troop of forty warriors was exercising with weapons in a yard. The berserks looked on them with contempt, sure that they could slaughter the lot if needful. They tramped onward to the chieftain's hall.

The doorkeeper set his teeth when he saw them coming. Edric's household troopers could subdue even these men, with their prowess and numbers. That, however, would be of small use to the first man they decided to kill. He reminded himself that questioning people like this was one of the tasks that made his post an honored one.

"Who approaches?" he asked.

"I'm Ottar Olsson, the berserk. These are my sons, brothers, and other kinsmen, and this my brother's son Teg. He will speak for us."

"I will proudly," Teg declared, with a strut. "We be all sons and grandsons of Ole Wide-Grip, who ate wolverines alive and was descended from a hero and a she-troll, and as our chief says, we are all Odin warriors. Few can resist us when we are in our ordinary strength, and none at all when the berserk fit is upon any of us. We were the first among those who set

Frodhi on the Danish throne, and the richest rewarded.''

The doorkeeper's eyes narrowed. He knew that to be true, and it was an ugly tale, if not unusual. Frodhi had slain his brother to become king.

"We killed eight men apiece at Bjorsat," Teg boasted. "We are worth gold to any chieftain with fighting to be done, and here we are to serve your master until one purpose is achieved, for no payment save our eating. And for why? Because Odin has so commanded us. If you smile, I will murder you.''

"Then you would neither take service with my master nor walk out of his town alive," the doorkeeper answered. He looked askance at the monstrous band before him. "He has no wars or feuds on his hands, and if he had, his own men would suffice. We have fought Angles, Frisians, and Franks here. We have cleared our shores of pirates and made this a safe place for outland trade. We did not need berserks to help us, either.''

"You will need berserks to help you against Gudrun Black-hair," Teg said.

The doorkeeper was startled. "You say that is a command from Odin? He has always favored Gudrun Blackhair. He has favored my masters even more, as is well known," he added.

At the implied doubt, Ottar frowned heavily. His patience was short, even for a berserk. He began to hunch his shoulders and growl.

Teg spoke before blood was spilled. "No longer! The black bitch has his favor no more! The Spear-Wielder told us so himself! Now, I've said more than enough to a doorkeeper. The rest is for Fat Edric's ears. Do we speak with him while you remain unhurt, or do we hack you limb from limb and see him anyhow? Do not stand havering, man. You can decide such a thing if you are worth all you squeeze out of your position.''

The doorkeeper drew a harsh breath and hefted his weapon. He expected to die. Instead, Teg tackled his legs and called on his clan to seize other parts of the man, which they did once their thinking lumbered abreast of his. The doorkeeper was pinioned, cuffed, mauled, lifted, kicked, hammered, beaten, and carried at last between the gang of brute men into the hall he had warded, to be dropped in a bleeding, senseless heap before Edric's high seat, where he had been hearing disputes.

"Your hall needs a better guardian, lord," Teg smirked.

"And one who uses his ears more shrewdly."

The merchant chieftain looked him and his kindred over slowly, frowning and self-assured. His massive body filled the famous seat which could accommodate two normal men side by side and support the weight of five. Edric could never fight, for although very strong, he was too ponderous to move suddenly. His round, heavy-mouthed face turned gradually red.

"You have found it easy to force a way into my hall," he said grimly. "By Frey and Forseti, you may find it harder to get out again." His voice boomed like North Sea surf. "Pick up that man again, scum! Set him on a bench and bear him gently as girls! You shall pay him wergild for his injuries and compensate me for this insult, and that is the least you shall do! I have not yet decided what the most is to be. Do not press me."

"Lord, we are berserks all," Teg told him. "We do not pay our debts in gold or gear, but in blood and meat—our own as freely as others. That is why we are here. We were told that you move against Gudrun Blackhair, and our god commands that we fight on your side."

"In the forefront, as ever," Thrain said.

"How do you know that I want you, loon? For that matter, how do you know we are fighting Gudrun Blackhair this summer? You have come far and only now arrived here."

The berserks' sea-stained clothes announced that much. Edric would not have had to ask, especially as such a rowdy band could not have gone unnoticed in Edricsburg for one hour. He always knew what was happening in his own town.

"Yes, lord. We're from beyond Skagerrak, and our arms are yours for this one purpose. All the pay we wish is to eat at your cost until Blackhair is destroyed. We know about it because our god told us. The Victory-Father himself gave us the command!"

Edric's round, heavy-jawed face changed. That was different. Odin, the war god, the spear god, the gallows god, gave or withheld victory in battle, and those who fell were his sacrifices. Berserks were his chosen warriors.

"Who is that man who hangs back and says nothing?" he demanded. "He has the look of a wizard. Come forward, fellow. What are you doing in such company?

"Lord," Aur said, his tangled locks moving as he bent his head. "I, too, serve Odin. I read omens in his grove and came

73

with these warriors to fill his purpose. As I am a priest, they tell the truth.''

Edric pressed his lips together. Teg seemed to believe what he said, like all his kindred, and they at least were too stupid to lie. The soft-voiced Aur was another matter, yet was not Odin the god of sorcery as well, master of the runes, knower of the road to Helheim? What other power could draw berserks and a wizard together?

He decided to be open and see what came of it. ''You have heard the truth. My sister's husband Vithils went south with four fighting ships but yesterday. He goes to Kent. They have a blood debt with Blackhair in that kingdom, too.''

''He has already gone?'' Teg asked.

''I said it. Were he still here,'' Edric said dryly, with a glance at his battered doorkeeper, ''be sure you would have met him by this. If you wish to join his company and fare against Blackhair, you must follow him to Kent and place yourselves under his command. Nor does he stomach raw behavior from those he leads, or have any great patience with berserks.''

In fact, Vithils had killed five. This was widely known. Edric did not mention it overtly, for he did not think it needful, as it wasn't. Teg and the older berserks, at least, were plainly thinking about it so far as they were able.

''If Odin's will is in this thing, lord, maybe it would be well to do more than just send these warriors on their way,'' a man of Edric's suggested.

''I'm considering it,'' the chieftain answered. ''Yet with due regard for your honor, strangers, I do not go to war on a bare statement that a thing is Odin's wish. The Victory-Father is a deep being. Now the spae-woman Skogul dwells in my town, and her powers as a seeress I know from long acquaintance. I'm minded to visit her and have her cast auguries. If she agrees with what you have told me, or if she does not, I'll decide what to do after I have heard her.''

''She had better agree,'' one of the younger berserks muttered to his brother at the rear of the band. ''I'll strangle her with her head in a sack if she gives us the lie.''

''I'll help you,'' the other replied.

Although Aur held his peace, his hatred of the mere thought of another practitioner of sorcery being consulted over himself could be felt like heat from a hearth by anyone who conversed with him. Edric did, and was amused.

Skogul lived alone in her widowhood. Her wide cheekbones and black eyes showed Finnish blood, which was reason enough for the folk of Edricsburg to gossip knowingly about the two husbands she had survived. Her ribbed reindeer-skin tent contained a rat's nest of wands, bones, herbs, curious pots, furs, ointments, and knotted cords.

Edric entered with some trouble, his ox-boned, ponderously fleshed body barely fitting through the tent's door flap. Clearing some litter so that he could sink to a pile of leather cushions, he explained his wishes to the seeress. Her bony face paled a little under her swarthiness and dirt.

"Lord," she said, "it is ill to meddle with the Spear-Wielder for one like me. He is a man's god, and ever goes his own way. My own powers of seeing are from Freya. To track *his* path, that of the One-Eyed, could lead me to danger. I must leave my body; he might prevent me from returning to it, and leave me to wing ghostly through the cold air."

She shuddered.

Without a word Edric placed a ramskin-leather purse on the floor between them. Its contents chinked fatly. He said, "I must know, Skogul. If the danger is too great, say no. If you wish something other than this, tell me. I think I would rather Odin had no purpose in this matter; it is never good to meddle with him too closely, I agree. Yet I want the truth, and if you bring me anything else, you will find me stern. Now tell me whether or not you will try."

Skogul stared at the ridgily rounded purse for a long time. At last she sighed. "I will try, lord."

After Edric left, she weighed the gold long in her hands before preparing for her rites of seer. The yellow coins and ring fragments gleamed richly, dropping between her stiff, arthritic fingers.

"Tears of Freya," she murmured. "It's fitting, goddess."

She opened her tent flap wide and laced it back. She donned a cloak of gray feathers, sat on a tall stool and closed her eyes. So she remained for some hours before she began to sing. Edricsburg heard the spell songs and for the most part resolutely ignored them. A few bold or chuckle-headed folk made derisive comments; even they, though, did not go near the spae-woman's tent. Its hide walls bulged too disconcertingly, as though unseen powers pressed from within. One child, on a dare, crept near the open flap and peeped within while her friends watched from a safe distance. After one look at Skogul, squatting with her mouth stretched wide in a taut face, the spellchant wailing from her, the child ran away.

Some said later that a white bird flew out of Skogul's mouth and flashed into the sky, returning to her after a day. In one version she spoke of hidden things to Edric after her trance had ended; in another, he sat with her and listened to the words she spoke while the trance of seer lasted. Some men said knowingly that the crafty berserk Teg had managed a word with Skogul before she gave her augury, promising her rich gifts from the plunder of Sarnia if her words favored him and death if they did not; but the men who said this were known boasters, loudmouths, and errand-runners, and hardly privy to such matters.

The entire town knew, however, that she wore her feather cloak and divined for the chieftain. He treated the berserks with honor after he had heard her counsel, ordered a ship made ready for their journey to Kent, and even announced that he would steer it himself. Surely Skogul's advice had been definite.

The sky darkened an hour after Edric gave that order, and a gale came shrieking over the North Sea. There would be no departure yet. Some said it was an omen that the berserks should not be given their asking and that Skogul had been wrong. Edric held to his decision.

"Vithils will have to seek shelter from this blow, wherever he is," Edric said, walking the shore on his short, massive legs and watching the black clouds boil. "We may even overtake him before he reaches Kent. If not, we will meet him there."

The beserks received the news with pleasure, and even grew something like well-behaved.

On the Narrow Sea, between Britain and Gaul, there was also foul weather. Not even *Ormungandr* could resist it. Despite all its crew could do, and its magical sailing qualities, the war serpent was driven eastward so powerfully that when Gudrun and Pascent brought it safely to the Gaulish side of the sea and found shelter in the Bay of the Seine, they reckoned themselves lucky.

Aidan and Nacrantal were nowhere in sight. Nor had they

appeared in the four days that passed before Gudrun was able to make for Sarnia.

"Ah, well, we will either see them there or we will not," Felimid said. "If we came through safely, it's in my mind that they will have survived."

"You say that as though they were better than we," Pascent said contentiously. "They can drown, too."

"Who argues otherwise? But I've sailed with them, and seen them at work upon the sea their father, and in it, and they impress me. I'll have a small wager that they are afloat yet, Pascent; maybe a large one if you feel a strong hunch that they are gone."

"No, I'll not take you."

Ormungandr flew on. In time they rounded the peninsula where the wrecker Urbicus, once a bishop, later a traitor, renegade, and sorcerer, had ruled as a lord and driven his bargains with sea demons. He might have prospered long before he went to his last accounting, had he not wrecked and plundered a ship of Gudrun's men. The accounting had come swiftly then, brought across sea and land on the edges of her weapons and her men's. Although he had eluded her once, she had trapped him the second time, helped by the Children of Lir.

Within view of Sarnia itself the bard saw what he had been looking for all the way down the shore of Gaul. An air elemental in the form of a tattered wraith came flying from the northeast. Such beings changed shape constantly. The appearance of this one told Felimid that it had come far, and through stormy skies.

"Welcome, traveler!" he shouted.
"You who wander the wild far air
Higher than strongest eagles dare
(For their wings would fail and falter there!)
Rest and exchange a word.
The bone and flesh of my body decree
That I cannot wander completely free,
But I have the eyes of a bard to see,
And ears for what you have heard."

"Now he speaks to nothing," Pascent growled, seeing Felimid's looks and gestures as he uttered more staves—and seemed to listen to a response. "I don't know about him. Lady, it doesn't like me to deal with things I can't see unless some uncanny fellow allows it, or that another can see but I can't. Is there anything there, or is Bragi astray in his wits?''

"I will vow there is something there," Gudrun said, "and you will have me to fight if you speak so of Bragi again. You may even have *him* to fight if he hears you. I should not have offered to do it for him . . . and I should not smile, Pascent. Tosti Fenrir's-get found it no smiling matter.''

"I'd heard that." Pascent did not say whether he believed it. "And yet there is something unchancy about a man who talks to the air, sees mermen and spirits . . . no offense, lady.''

"I do take offense!" Gudrun rounded on him, furious. "I take great offense, the more so since I have warned you once!" She gripped his tough weapon arm and glared into his face. "Now when Bragi has finished his collogue with whatever spirit is with him, I mean to hear you say to him what you have just said to me, that he talks to nothing and you doubt his understanding. No matter how fine a captain you are, Pascent, I will have you keep your mouth away from your betters.''

Betters! Pascent thought redly. *You haughty bitch!*

He remembered that the sea bottom was no farther away than the limits of her temper, and mastered his own.

"No ill speaking meant, lady. I'll . . . ask the bard's pardon.''

"That is not for me to say. It's between you and him. All I demand is that you tell him to his face what you told me. I will not have you talk behind his back to me, do you hear?''

"I do.''

"Then mind it.''

Rated like a schoolboy scribbling in his margins! The sea captain could scarcely believe it. Why, she was head over heels with the bard, as he was with her. The bloody slayer had turned into a yearning, milksop girl! It wasn't possible. Folk didn't behave like that unless they were crazy. Yes, maybe that was it, they were both crazy. . . .

Felimid was speaking to the air elemental still.

> "Give me advice of where you have been,
>   Councils heard and voyages seen,
>   The gray salt sea and the springtide green—
>   Scandal you needn't spare.
>   The stirring world is eager to move,
>   And many a foe has honor to prove—

The flower, the sun, and the sword's blood groove—
Which is waiting, and where?''

All Pascent heard by way of answer was a curious note in
the wind. When the bard lifted his hand in farewell, Pascent
thought he glimpsed something gray at the very edge of his
vision, but then it vanished astern, and it might have been his
fancy.

Felimid came toward them, treading with a slight misstep
past the improvised horse box where his erstwhile mount
stamped restlessly. Pascent, aware of Gudrun beside him,
worked hard to repress a sneer. *A year on saltwater and he
walks like a lubber yet!*

"I've news," Felimid said. His amiable, snub-nosed face
did not readily express grimness, but there were two vertical
lines in his brow which might have been cut there.

"Pascent has news, also," Gudrun replied, "and I am the
one who means to hear him tell it to you, my darling. Say on,
you backbiting dog."

Pascent gave her a poisoned stare. "I take that ill," he said,
his voice flat. "Bragi, I think that talking to the air is pure
proof of craziness, though for all I know you are no more crazy
than any other western bard. And I said so, and I say it now
to your face."

One brow lifted. Felimid looked at the trader captain with
the interested sympathy he would have given a three-legged
dog.

"So? That kind of talk is bad manners anywhere and a crime
where I come from. Besides, it's foolish. When you insult a
bard you invite a satire. It's foolish on another count, too.
You know fine that I do see and hear things most men do not,
and that such things are there to be seen. Why miscall me for
that? I fancy it irks and frightens you. Man, if you had been
initiated through one bardic degree you would have fled the
test as you have never fled any pirates!"

"Hogwash, Bragi. A magician of sorts you may be, but
you're dreamy-eyed. We cannot plan our fighting by your
visions."

"If your manners are gone from you," Felimid said, "and
if it is the way with you to refuse what you know like a horse
milling about in a burning stable, then I promise you a song
that will afflict you with phlegm, piles, and bellyache by the

next sunrise, and there will be nothing of a dream about it. Now be quiet and listen to me, for there is nothing of a dream either about the thing the wind has told me."

"What thing is that?" Gudrun asked.

"Why, briefly, an entire clan of berserks is traveling to Kent. The purpose of them is to serve our foes and fight on their side, and Edric the Fat is steering them to Kent in his own ship, and Vithils precedes 'em."

Gudrun Blackhair raised a hand to her face, and with her thumb against the angle of her jaw, tapped her clear cheekbone with her fingertips a few times, lightly and thoughtfully.

Pascent was more vocal. "Satan's arse! You mean the Saxon merchant chief and his brother-in-law? The one they call Edric's Axe? *That* Vithils?"

"That same one."

"I know 'em both. I've traded at Edricsburg in the past."

"Vithils the Axe," Gudrun said softly. "He comes for his quittance, does he? Yes, he was never the man to leave a debt unpaid for long, good or bad. How long until he reaches Kent?"

"That I can't say. The wind tells me he has sheltered among the Frisian isles from some very foul weather indeed, and as he has foes of his own in those parts, it may just be the last anyone sees of him. I'd not wager upon it, though."

"Nor I. Then it depends upon how long the weather delays him. By Ull's bow! If he reaches Kent and allies himself with Ricsige and Cerdic . . . ! Hardly a man between here and the Limfjord would not defer to him in a matter of this kind. He must not reach Kent!"

"No ship but *Ormungandr* could intercept him, if he's left the Elbe," Pascent said.

"Easy," Felimid advised. "We are scarcely a bowshot from Sarnia, and sure our own allies should be knowing what we know, and we should hold a council before acting. It's certain that if we race to intercept Vithils without greeting them, they will think us lost, and they all deserve better than the disunion they would suffer then."

"Aye," Pascent said into the silence. "That's sense. We'd have to provision and take a new, rested crew, besides."

"This crew is one of men, not a paddling of geese," Gudrun retorted, "and they will have all the rest they need while the council talks. We cannot be sure of intercepting Vithils no matter what we do. We can warn Sarnia and have the lads prepare. Home!''

"Aye, lady,'' Pascent answered.

Vithils! Mother of God, but this makes a difference!

Not only the famed pirate killer's prowess made the trader captain think hard second thoughts about his position. He'd friendly remembrances of Vithils and Edric. The one had helped him during a clash of Pascent's with some Angles, and the other had given him fair treatment on more than one trading venture. He'd no wish to be unfriends with them. All he had ever wanted from Gudrun Blackhair was a new merchant ship to replace the one he had lost, and some loot to finance his next trading venture. He did not intend to be hanged in her company.

Keeping his own counsel, he guided the ship to Sarnia through the dangerous waters Gudrun knew so well, until they entered the island's southern bay. Chanting as they threw their backs into the task, the pirates dragged *Ormungandr* up the gritty sand. Leaving a strong guard with the ship, Gudrun went at once to her hall above the cliffs.

That night she held a council there. At her own table sat Felimid, her lover, bard, herald, and messenger; Decius, her chief henchman; Waldin and Arnehad, the Frankish captains who both coveted the place left empty by Hugibert when Felimid had slain him for his sneaking attempt on Gudrun's life; Pascent, a former crony of Hugibert's; Niamh, the green-haired princess of the sea people, with her councilor Idh and the several captains of her ships, creatures of sea foam and bright water; and the Danish chieftains who had rowed south with Gudrun at the end of the previous summer. Pigsknuckle Hromund ripped a roast duck apart and devoured it as they talked. Njal the Sea-Gray drank in moderation and asked a shrewd question now and again.

Gudrun's own wildly mixed following, Franks, Goths, Saxons, Picts, and even a Basque shipmaster named Zucharre, shared the long feasting hall with many Children of Lir and five-score Danes. The walls very nearly bowed outward from the crowding. They boasted, laughed, quarreled, and drank extravagant healths, their spirits hearty.

"Quiet!'' thundered Decius, and repeated the word even louder. "We face trouble, as all of you know, for our enemies are banding together. Cerdic's brood cannot join the league in any huge strength; the lady, Nacrantal, and Aidan here have burned their means!''

The hall boomed like a drum. Stamping, shouting, banging on anything handy and ribald toasts to the achievement declared the men's pleasure. Not for moments could Decius continue.

''Aye, it's well,'' he said. ''But comrades, it seems we are rid of Cerdic to face Vithils. Is there a man here does not know what he is like?''

''I know!'' a bald Frisian answered, rising. He wiped greasy fingers on his cowhide tunic. ''I was one of Ingsel Widespear's men. We never thought any could reach us in our place among the lagoons and marshes. Vithils came with just forty warriors in shallow boats. I don't know to this day how he learned about our island and its approaches! We outnumbered 'em more than twofold, for all the good it did us. His Saxons just killed two or three apiece. When they left, everything was ablaze but the sodden ground, and I include the roof beams where my fellows were hanging! You could sniff roasting meat a mile. Four of us escaped alive. One died of's wounds later, one's mad, one's a cripple, and one's here telling you.''

Scornful hoots and thoughtful murmuring greeted the Frisian's account. Gudrun's hot raised voice called for attention.

''That was Ingsel Widespear, and I am Gudrun! That was a swampy Frisian island, and this is Sarnia! The local water that surrounds us has killed more ships than the dry rot, and it will be strange to Vithils. Some of his ships will crash and sink before he reaches us.''

''My people can wholly promise that,'' Idh confirmed, rising in his strange, beardless eld to speak for his princess, who lolled in her dragon-leather seat with its frame of monstrous bones, carried up the cliffs for this council. ''We will sink them if they dare approach, and none of them even dream the Children of Lir are in the matter. If they come, it is to their doom.''

''Yes,'' Gudrun said exultantly. ''We will break them together, and I will take it ill if you leave none for us, Idh of the Children of Lir! Our third strength is this isle. Who thinks it can be taken by direct attack? And will we let Vithils approach it by stealth? Are we such fools, and do we keep such poor watch?''

They shouted as one man that they were not.

Then Gray Njal the Dane spoke.

"Vithils is no fool, either. It's his way to study and know ere he moves. I'll swear he has had scouts and spies at work ever since you held him to ransom three seasons past, lady. Now suppose you were he, and wished to take this island in this season. How would *you* set about it?"

"I would get steersmen and sailors who knew these waters, the rocks, tides, harbors, and banks," Gudrun answered promptly. "I would come to Sarnia in force, and I would take the main bays on the northern part of the island. I would hold them, and not try to carry the cliff tops. Not at once. Then I would raid the southern landing places and destroy my enemy's ships."

"Aye, there it is!" a gaudily jeweled Briton cried. "We can bide atop the cliffs, but our ships are kept at the sea's edge, and it's not only Gudrun Blackhair can use fire against 'em! Also, we've but meager foodstocks left."

"More like none," Decius agreed, "as Vithils will bear in mind."

Hromund ripped steaming flesh from his duck and swallowed. "He'd not try to starve us down," he said past grease. "I grant it might not take him long, the way we're placed, but yet longer than even he could hold together a lot able to handle us. Kent, Westri, Edricsburg, it's not natural that they unite for long. They will quarrel, and a ship's company here and there will go home until the attack dribbles away."

"I believe you are correct, Pigeyes," Nacrantal said. "Your pardon. *Pigsknuckle.* Correct, save that you assume their foolish attack is going to get so far." He showed the edges of his teeth. "It will not."

"We're still at a disadvantage where food is concerned," the Dane grumbled.

"A little hunger would do you no harm."

"Enough!" Gudrun rose, tall and square-shouldered, her black hair tumbling about her face like dark water marking danger. "A single hundred of men can hold Sarnia against a thousand. The rest of us should disperse, ships and men, to wait in ambush at various likely places, and raid for food, too."

"My people can get all the food they require from the sea," Idh promised. "As for scouting, our friends the seals and dolphins will do that to your contentment."

"That's well! I thank you! Now I believe it when you say

Vithils and his ships will never reach Sarnia, yet . . . .'' She spoke now to the hall at large: "Why should he even reach Kent? I can meet him beyond the straits in *Ormungandr*, if bad weather delays him only a day or two more. Let none mistake this; if we meet Vithils on land or sea, it is his death or ours, and I want only those with me who are prepared for that, not fearing his name! See Decius if you are such a one.

"Lady Niamh," she said then, directly to the sea woman, "I wish two of your people's ships with their husbands and crews to help me. It comes hard to Gudrun Blackhair to say graciously that she wishes help, but if I lack it, I think Vithils may slide past me to league with Kent. He's crafty, that one. Will two of your captains go with me?"

"I think it very likely," Niamh answered, smiling.

"I will go," Nacrantal answered positively. "There is good sport in your company, Gudrun Blackhair."

"I will also go," offered Yrnruch Starknower, a third husband-of-ships famous for his navigation. He lifted the gold-rimmed spiral shell that was his drinking cup. "My brother Aidan has had his share!"

"I am glad of you both." Gudrun laughed. "Let others not be downcast, though. They will find plenty to do here! Food must be found, ambushes set, watches kept. . . . Best to stay aware of what Ricsige, Cynric, and Cerdic are doing, lest they surprise us."

"Surprise us they will not," Felimid declared, emphasizing the words with a ringing of his harpstrings. "The Children of Lir will know of their coming by sea, and I will know of their speech and their preparations by land, for the winds will tell me. I can summon fog to blind them on the perilous water, and rob them of heart with my satires; and I can fight with the sword's edge when the sword's edge must finally settle the matter. Oh, Vithils may be mighty and cunning, but it is great effort we would have to make not to triumph."

A drunken Frank muttered, "Loudly he boasts, but we'll see how the bench ornament fights when the iron is reddening."

"Ask Hugibert," laughed Griff, the west Briton beside him, "or just ask me, which ye'd find easier." Griff had been with Gudrun and Felimid on their northern voyage. "I haven't seen him backward yet."

The pirates would have caroused and boasted far into the morning, save that Gudrun did not allow it. She and her captains drove the bung back into the barrel, and posted a sober guard over the ships, with others manning signal beacons on the cliff tops. All carried horns and knew how to blow them. Then Gudrun and Felimid went to bed.

"Bragi, my joy," she said as his fingertips danced over her ribs and touched her spine from neck to waist in the way she liked, "I love it. I love it more than fame."

Felimid felt strangely sad. *More than fame.* His trade was the making of fame, and he knew how false it could be. Nor did he really believe Gudrun. She still wanted to leave her name behind, ringing loudly till the end of the world, more than anything else.

He slew that thought and swived her hotly, glorying in her, looking into her proud, passionate face as their bodies turned sweet with sweat, sliding and turning together. This coming battle would cap her fame on the ridge of the earth, for they would win. Vithils was not a god.

In the sea caves under Brechou the Children of Lir shared that opinion as they held a council of their own. A shimmering green-gold glamor hazed the air, giving the impression of far distances, and floating globes shed a yellow light such as once had illuminated Rothevna's hall on the largest of the Veiled Isles. Sea anemones half as tall as a man guarded the pools giving ingress, their deadly, exquisite tentacles waving in pink and purple ruffs, and golden seals lolled on the many-leveled cave floor.

Niamh smiled as she caressed the head of the largest. Two husbands-of-ships, Nacrantal and Yrnruch, drank wine on seats piled with furs. Idh was beside her, as usual.

"What is it to us if Vithils wins?" Nacrantal asked. His look of ruthless function, sharp as a knife blade, was stronger than its ordinary degree. "These pirates know too much. Let him wipe them out."

"Look further, my brother," Yrnruch advised.

"Yes, master of the barbed-spear feat," Niamh said. "Look and think further, then tell me yourself. Between Gudrun and Vithils I will choose Gudrun to thrive, though not because I love her. As for that bibble-babble on Sarnia, it did but prove what a fool she is! Having roved the sea for years, she knows nothing of it."

"More than most earth-bred," Yrnruch qualified mildly, "which says little enough."

"She wholly forgets the Cold Ones," Niamh said. "She fought their pimp the wrecker only last autumn, and was almost slain by two of them, and now . . . they might no longer lair by their hundreds in the black depths, for all she contains them in her bounding cry."

"They remain below unless some air-breathing wizard tempts them up." Nacrantal dismissed the possibility with a shrug. Then he grew very still as understanding came to him. "They will not trouble Blackhair—but are you by chance thinking, lady, that they might trouble Vithils?"

"I have hopes for you." Niamh smiled. It was not a pretty smile. "Urbicus had a bargain with them; Urbicus is dead. We did help slay him, and now he lies buried on Lesia with his severed head under his knee. Yet I took something from his ugly little body before it was dragged into *Ormungandr*."

She produced a squidlike image of gold from a casket on the table beside her couch, a small image on a chain, which she dangled pensively from her small fingers. It turned and gleamed.

"Urbicus used this to summon the Cold Ones to their feasts. What he could do, I could do far better—if it comes to that. The upper waters, bright in the sun, or the black depths where the ooze gathers and the corpses sink, it is all the same sea."

"Blackhair would not care for this," Nacrantal said, and he chuckled.

"Blackhair would burn like a comet with rage, and devastate these caverns," Niamh told him, with a nearer approach to the truth. Her hazel, slightly protuberant eyes gleamed with wicked laughter. "If she were to know." She closed her hand over the golden image. "She is not to know, or to hear one sighed word. I desire your vows to that, Nacrantal and Yrnruch."

"By our father Lir, I wear my tongue in a knot on the matter," Nacrantal said.

"May the sea rise and cover me, the earth swallow me, and the sky full of stars fall upon me and crush me out of life forever, if I talk of it but here," Yrnruch swore more grandiloquently.

The seal beside Niamh whimpered and blundered away.

VII

Worlds extend in their endless number,
Holding all that has ever been sought;
I will rove at my pleasure through them
when the battles I owe have all been fought.
—Felimid mac Fal,
Gudrun's Saga

Mist hung in cobweb masses over the Narrow Sea. *Ormun-gandr* moved through it on silent oars, the carved eyes of its figurehead seeming to glow as they gazed ahead.

"It sees," Gudrun murmured. "You doubted, Bragi, but it does see through the fog."

"I think so, too, and I was wrong. The dolphins will guide us, besides, so Yrnruch says, and I believe him. But we should only be needing them if this ship fails you."

"I trust it. Bragi, who are these merfolk, these Children of Lir? Who are they, truly? Do you know? I have heard you call them your cousins. What world do they come from?"

"I would I knew! I cannot say surely what world my own forebears, the Tuatha de Danann, came from! Tuatha de Danann, Children of Danu the earth-mother. Children of Lir, Children of the Sea. The races knew each other of old, some-times as friends, sometimes as enemies, but they called each other cousin even then. A bit of ancient courtesy, my darling."

"What befell?"

"The Danann were dispossessed from Erin by the first iron users. Their leaders fled beyond this world, and the Children of Lir to the sea's secret places or also to the Otherworlds. Some stayed and mingled with the invaders. There is no single answer to know."

87

"Whence came they in the first place, then?"

"No single answer to that, either. I can repeat any number of stories. From the sky, say some. From the north or the east, say others. From enchanted islands in the west, say still others. Maybe it was the east, after all. Our goddess Danu is called Don in Britain, and Palamides—the fellow you met, Gudrun—says that there are mighty rivers in the east called Danube and Don. That's a custom of my people; most of our rivers in Erin bear the names of goddesses, so. Boann, Sinann . . . many others. In Britain, too."

Gudrun's mind had been racing to its own conclusions.

"Tuatha de Danann," she repeated. "*Danann*. Danes?"

"Why . . . I'd not be knowing," Felimid said diplomatically. "It could be. Were they ever spread as far east as Sarmatia, they might have come into Jutland, too, before they reached Erin. It could be."

At first he had choked on the notion that his magical forebears and the ancestral Danes could be the same. Now he began to consider it. Gudrun might have hit a target there with her mind's arrows.

"What sort of folk were they?" she asked.

"The Danann? Tall, fair-skinned, red or brown of hair. They were great craftsmen, skilled in magic, and worshipped the earth-mother. They were farmers who could grow crops in the white sea sand, it is told. The tribes descended from them still reckon descent through the mother."

"Like the Picts?"

"The Cruithni are Danann-descended, too. Smaller, but they have the red hair and the customs and some of the knowledge. And they are of mixed ancestry, as we all are in these days. I have Milesian blood, and a trace of the sea people's through my father's mother, and Firbolg and Fomor, too, I shouldn't wonder—but the most of it is Danann."

"The earth-mother," Gudrun said, excited. "Freya, the necklace-wearer! That is what we call her. The feather-cloaked, whose chariot is drawn by cats. She belongs to the Vanir, and they are gods of the fruitful earth like your Danann, and the Aesir warred with them long ago. They won but did not wholly supplant them. The fighting ended with an exchange of hostages—and many Danes are red-haired! Mine is uncommon, a sign of favor from—" She stopped abruptly, and went on a moment later in a level, controlled voice. ". . . from the one whose name I had best speak no longer. Why, Bragi, we're of the same blood, you and I!''

Felimid wasn't sure of that. It appeared to him that Gudrun's reasoning bounded and sprang across some pretty wide gaps, but as the notion pleased her very much, he did not dispute it. And it pleased him, too.

"What about our friends yonder?'' he wondered, waving through the mist toward Nacrantal and Yrnruch's unseen ships.

"They must spring from Aegir and Ran," Gudrun guessed, naming the northern sea deities, the bountiful ale brewer and his fierce wife who netted ships to their destruction. "I hope for their sakes that these ones favor their sire. If they play Ran's tricks with me—"

She made a swift, sword-slashing gesture with her open hand.

"You do not trust them."

"I would have trusted Rothevna. That tiny, slippery sister of his, no. I suppose you do."

"I'll trust her until she proves false. More than that I can't say. I'll not pretend that I know her, or what she chiefly wants. I'd trust Aidan, though, and Turo, and maybe Yrnruch Starknower if I knew him better. Nacrantal . . .'' The bard grimaced and waggled his hand. "I have my doubts of Idh, as well."

"They all do what little greenhair says," Gudrun reminded him, with a note of viciousness. "It ever comes back to her. And I would not trust her as far as I could stay ahead of *Ormungandr* swimming—in my mail, with shield on back."

"She's a formidable ally."

"I like her where I can see her, and she may lead me to a Gate. A sea gate that *Ormungandr* can pass. The risk of treachery is a fair trade for that."

You like her where you can see her, Felimid thought, *but you do not like having her where I can see her, do you, my heart? Well, I do not like your craving to invade the Other-worlds, or this demon ship which can take you thither! Some time we will have to talk of that. . . .*

"Vithils first, acushla," he said.

"Never is he far from my mind, I promise you!"

The morning sun burned the mist from the sea. Until then *Ormungandr* had been dawdling, for the power of all its oars would have left the two light ships of the Children of Lir far behind. Under sail, though, Nacrantal and Yrnruch could keep pace with the great serpent ship. When a wind began blowing from the southwest, Gudrun raised a plain sea-colored sail and her allies their bright, intricately patterned ones. They covered as much sea in a day as the best Saxon war boats could swallow in three.

Beyond the Kentish strait, among concealing sandbanks on the Gaulish side, they waited with *Ormungandr*'s mast unstepped. The wind continued to blow from the same quarter, so Felimid could get no tidings of their prey from air elementals, since Vithils would be coming from the northeast.

"Maybe he has reached Thanet already," Decius suggested.

"It's in my mind that the weather he met will have stopped him," Yrnruch Starknower answered. "Still, you may be right. I will go and see."

He crossed the water to Thanet, a matter of thirty sea miles and five. Circling the island, and slipping unseen among the ships ready for launching on the beaches, he found none had crossed the sea recently. They were all new from their winter quarters. King Ricsige (or a canny henchman) had spaced them apart in ones and twos, and guarded them so well that only a glamor-cloaked son of faerie could have spied them out. Even Yrnruch's folk narrowly escaped from dogs who could hear and smell if not see them.

He retreated into the water, diving beneath the waves. He told his playful companions the dolphins what he had learned, and they sang the news in their complex picture sounds through the water. Nacrantal heard it where he lay in ambush with Gudrun Blackhair. He translated the message, his sharply angled features smiling.

"Vithils hasn't come there yet, it seems," he declared. "The King of Kent has eight ships ready to sail, though, which if they be fully manned would mean four and a half hundred warriors. They lie ashore ready for launching, and are guarded by at least a hundred."

"What chance of serving them as we did Cerdic's fleet?"

"None. They are not bunched together as his were, and we would have to go ashore to reach them. Ricsige must have heard that news."

Gudrun sighed briefly, but wasted few regrets. "We are in time to take Vithils, though! Maybe his ships were damaged by the storms, and he has had to repair them . . . or . . . . Bragi, where did he lie when your wraith saw him?"

"He was among the Frisian Isles, west o' the Elbe mouth," Felimid answered. "Then the storm broke and he had to shelter there."

"That was long days gone! Where can he be? I will not believe the Frisians could slay him or vermin like nicors overcome him."

"All men die, lady," Decius said, "and few die as they should. Still, I will not easily believe Vithils is dead, either. I'd wish to see his corpse, and even then I would approach it with care. I reckon he will appear."

Barely had he spoken when a dolphin raised her jaunty head from the water to chirrup and honk at them. Nacrantal listened closely from the rail of his glamor-cloaked ship.

"One sea is every sea," he said exultantly. "News, earth children! From the sea caves, by the stream, in the barking of seals and the motion of kelp, I have the news! This Vithils is wary. Lest he be expected and waited for, he crossed the open sea to Britain, lying out upon it for a full night. He hasn't made landfall yet, but when he does, he will be proceeding to Kent by the *British* coast."

"Njord!" Gudrun swore. "Njord of the Ships! The crafty wolverine! I'd have been waiting bootlessly here for days yet! My thanks, seaman. Where will he land? Do you know?"

"Not far from the mouth of the river called Humber, the word has it."

"Huh huh! He must pass by the Wash, and the Angle country, and the land of the East Saxons. They are bad shores all."

"Because he's Vithils," Decius said, "he will have mariners with him who know those coasts well, and foresighted agreements with Angle chiefs. I have no doubt he's been at this since Edric ransomed him. But we can still catch him before he comes near Kent."

"Yes, we can. We will. Hear me!" Gudrun cried to her crew, chiefly Danes she had recruited the previous summer, thirty of them skilled archers. "Vithils has reached Britain! We can trap him still, if we cross the sea and meet him east of the Wash. Liefer would I do that then meet him at Sarnia with half a thousand allies to back him! What say you?"

The pirates said a good deal. It included grumbles about racing elsewhere when they had only reached this fine ambush site, and much dissension and debate as to whether Vithils could be intercepted. Some did not really wish to intercept him. Many distrusted the source of the information. The debate lasted some hours.

Gudrun talked, and eloquently urged. Felimid persuaded, urged, and sang, making the course seem the height of reason, while Decius backed his leader in hard, practical terms. In the end the three carried the men with them.

The wind still blew from the southwest. They sailed north with it on their quarter, staying well out from the quicksands and deadly waters of the East Saxon coast. As always, *Ormungandr* slid through the sea as though water offered no resistance. Yet something was different. For a while Felimid could not name the difference, and then it struck him.

"The timbers are creaking," he said in surprise.

"I hear it, too," Gudrun said in ire. "Those maggoty dwarves have cheated me!"

"Have *what*? Cheated you?"

"Yes!"

The bard laughed at her. "Magnificent! All other ships afloat are a shrieking discord of creaks and groans all the time, and this one has ever been quiet as a shadow no matter what fearful demands of it you make, from sailing in autumn gales to ramming—and now that it moans a little, you complain! Oh, my sea eagle, you have your brass!"

"Little scuts," Gudrun fulminated. "Such wonderful makers they are said to be, huh. . . ."

She never accepted graciously that ships wore out, weapons rusted and broke, or that clothes needed mending—or for that matter that a virile, poetical lover could be seasick. She had gone to reckless lengths to obtain dwarf-made weapons and ships so that she at least would not have to suffer those inconveniences, and still they plagued her.

Felimid comprehended her better then—and felt a certain exasperation. This was child's pique. They were going to fight a feared and mighty man.

"In a magical Otherworld none o' this would happen, ha?" he said. "A faultless, unwaning wood, where the leaves are the color of gold."

"*Yes!*" she answered with desperate hunger. "If there is such a place, I will find it. There must be something better than this."

Better . . . than this world where empires fell and choices narrowed to submission or bloody slaughter, where sickness ran wild, where the Church ever widened its stifling embrace and taught that the earth was a cesspit ruled by demons, and woman a vileness, and slowly killed magic. Better . . . than the squalor attending even the wildest, freest of lives, and tarnished the halls of kings.

But that was only one side. Also, knowing something of the Otherworlds, Felimid did not think they were perfect. He'd been abducted into one at the age of nine. He'd ridden the black mare Myfanwy through a succession of them. He'd glimpsed the one so jealously guarded by the Children of Lir, which held wonders, maybe, but no more than this world he accepted as his own and loved. That other place had appeared to contain sea spiders and mud as well as enchantment. Although if Rome's legacy and the Cross worshippers were only missing from it, that might be enough of an improvement.

His fancy conjured seas of voluptuous water under thickly clouded heaven, amber suns and pearly moons, scented wood burning in nights of purple fog, dragons roaring in a swamp and Golden Singer sounding in his hands at a feast of the Children of Lir. Gudrun was there, in a spider-silk tunic of flaming crimson, and he, Felimid, wore a soft leather kilt and sandals in the enervating warmth. Wholly unknown oceans waited.

Cairbre and Ogma! Live without dreams and what do you have?

The wind veered at the instant of Felimid's mental query. *Ormungandr* lurched and slid bow down in a wave. The bard fell on his backside, banging his elbow at the same time, and for a while was too busy hissing oaths to consider the value of dreams.

They were plunging in choppy water off an unattractive coast where waves burst frothing on exposed shingle beaches. Wind howled desolately over the flat land beyond. By nightfall they had left this for a waste of lagoon and swamp containing the mouths of several rivers; scarcely an improvement, particularly as a sudden east wind threatened to push them into it, forcing them to battle past that foul lee shore until after midnight. Hands were skinned raw, muscles aching and tempers short before they could rest.

Nacrantal and Yrnruch shouted that they would rejoin the pirates later, and ran their ships in behind a large marshy island for shelter, lacking *Ormungandr*'s rowing power. None would molest them. Their vessels could not be seen.

Dawn saw *Ormungandr* waiting by a shingly island off the long bulge of the Anglian coast which ran eastward to the Wash. Iron-gray water, white and buff sand, gritty pebbles and shrieking gulls were most of the view, with low heath and an occasional sheep to be seen on the mainland.

"Let's take the boat and lift some fresh mutton," chestnut-haired Sigar suggested, "while we wait to carve the Saxon pork."

"Better bait some hooks instead," Decius advised. "That mutton yonder is probably riddled with fluke and foot rot."

Sigar led a raid anyhow. The meat soon crackled over driftwood fires, and wind carried the smell of roast mutton over the sea. Decius ate his share with pleasure, despite his pessimistic warning.

The next day was one of the finest any April month could be asked to provide, blue, bright, hard and clear as a diamond. Their allies rejoined them out of the east, their vivid sails announcing them far across the sea to Felimid's bardic sight; Yrnruch's flowing, interweaving spirals, russet, brown, and yellow: Nacrantal's sombre maroon with its ice-blue basket-weave border, a slashing armored pike in saffron and white on the body of the sail, slanting across the bunt, savagely jaunty.

"Good day!" Nacrantal cried. "No sign of Vithils yet?"

"None, husband-of-ships," Felimid called back. "Maybe the sea has swallowed him."

"That we can discover," Yrnruch said, as the dolphins sported around his ship. "If he comes this way at all, we will know."

Felimed interpreted this. Decius looked across from the fire by which he sat, rubbing grease into his leather war corslet. He'd taken out his jeweled eye, and that eyelid drooped skeptically over the void socket.

"Surely we will; that's no subtle prediction! I hope he hurries, that is all. If he doesn't, I will take a chill from all this wind."

Another day passed. Decius held weapon drill and kept the lookouts doubled. A quarrel or two erupted among the Danes. Gudrun and Felimid made love in the dunes. Although neither said so, both knew in their stomachs that it might be their last chance; there was a wholly possible outcome if they went to confront Vithils the Axe.

Yrnruch sat with them by their fire that night, the yellow

flames limning his fine-boned dreamer's face. He spoke of far corners of the earthly seas, of hot islands where the leaves of trees were like huge emerald feathers and the people amber-skinned, of one-eyed giants with monstrous flapping ears in which they wrapped themselves to sleep, of regions so distant that the stars one beheld in the sky were never the same as those seen in Britain at any season. Felimid matched his knowledge of the northern stars, at least, with the husband-of-ships; in his bardic training he had been required to master the true names of the turning stars and know their movements. Yrnruch proved his master, exposing his knowledge as patchy.

"I do not think you gave much attention to your teachers when it came to star lore," he remarked.

"I've forgotten a deal," Felimid admitted.

He understated. Some of his teachers had been doubtful about raising him to the third rank so soon; at his age it had been unheard of. His powers of storytelling, poetry, and music had been offset by ignorance or rank laziness in other areas, and his own grandsire, the chief bard, had been more doubtful than any other man. It occurred to Felimid that perhaps the old man had compromised his tough integrity for once, out of love for him, giving Felimid a misguided gift as he went into exile. Well, if so, he'd undertake the test anew when he went home, and earn the third rank of bard all over again, should that be called for. Rising higher after that would take years, he knew, but then he saw no need for hurry. He hated memorizing law tracts. . . .

It would be better to live with his family for a while. Five years was a long time. He would have to learn to know them, and they him.

"Hoy!" Yrnruch said. "Where are you, my friend?"

"Pardon," Felimid answered. "I was at home in Erin just them."

His clan's hearth had called, and his heart ached. He felt that if he allowed it, he could weep. He'd been free to return for two years, and why had he never gone?

A question for another time. He threw off his homesick mood and became lively. He talked of bread, of dancing and horses, of foolish quarrels over precedence, of craftsmen, warriors, farmers close to the powers of earth, of language and strong liquor—that marvelous blessing—of clothing, jewelry, and weapons.

Gudrun talked of ships, naturally, and weather and fighting. She leaned against Felimid and talked of love, without shyness. She had changed. At last they rolled into their cloaks fully clothed for a few hours' sleep. As it happened, they did not get it.

Yrnruch himself aroused them. Felimid felt the hand on his shoulder, stirred, smelled the faintly fishy scent from Yrnruch's sea-dripping flesh, and finally saw the graceful, bending form outlined against the stars as he opened gummy eyes. Gudrun sat up swiftly.

"What's toward, Yrnruch?" she demanded before the bard could speak.

"Vithils has been sighted. All his ships are whole, though his own is damaged and leaking. He should be here in the mid-morning, and if he passes us, he should reach Kent safely."

"He will never arrive," she said.

She had been sleeping in her sheepskin vest, with shoes on her feet. Now she reached for the leather sark placed handily beside her.

"Wake Decius, Bragi! Ah, he's awake and standing guard in *Ormungandr*, all the better." She was completely the fighting leader now, the lover, the merry woman, the healer of wounds, the darkly murderous slayer and the holder of otherwordly visions all subordinated to that one function. "I want the men in their war gear on the strand at once. I will inspect them myself, by Njord, and so will Decius. We put to sea with the morning tide." She stopped to think. "Yrnruch, I must have the faerie sight this day, and yon one-eyed Spaniard, too. He or I or Bragi might be lost, or any two of us."

"After the sun rises I'll endow you with the true sight," Yrnruch agreed. "You will have it until sunset then. Now must I get to my own ship."

He slid back into the sea.

The lover flashed out of Gudrun then. She held out her arms to the bard.

"If you should fall," she whispered against his neck, "I will not leave the place until I am dead or no foe lives! If I should fall, Bragi, I ask you this. Live! Save your own life if you can, and sing of me. Remember me yourself."

Felimid kissed her long. "I'll forget you when all the stars fall out of the sky."

Gudrun drew back from his embrace then. She laughed and

pressed a separating hand against his chest when he would have stayed her.

"No, son of Freya! One kiss before fighting is enough. Get into your war gear. In our bed I will follow your lead, as harper, poet, planner I will shout your mastery to the wide sky, but when a sea fight's imminent, my word has to rule."

"Be it so," he said regretfully. Pulling on the boots he had removed, he groped for the cuirass of heavy walrus-leather strengthened with whalebone, which was his own fighting harness, almost as strong as metal and far lighter.

Wearing her stiff leather sark, Gudrun reached for her famous silvered mail. Sorting it into the right position with a soft rustle of links, she slipped her hands through the short sleeves and bent forward from the waist to thrust her neck into the bunched garment. Then she squirmed and writhed her shoulders, straightening the while, until the mail shirt fell susurrating past her hips. She hissed softly at its icy touch on her neck and upper arms.

"Loki's malice! I always do forget to warm it at the fire beforehand. . . ."

Last of all she donned the harness of straps and buckles that held the shirt close to her body, preventing its heavy, fluent links from sliding in one direction when she moved, and upsetting her balance by their shifting weight. In minutes she was inspecting her eighty warriors before the ship. In two hours they were under way with the risen sun behind them.

VIII

Show me Vithils, the foe who seeks me!
Face to face let us meet and fight!
Tangled byways were never my ways,
But a net of fate is across my sight!
—Felimid mac Fal,
Gudrun's Saga

They were not enchanted, dwarf-built ships, the four that
came down past the Wash from the direction of the marshy
Humber. They had nothing to do with any hot quester like
Gudrun, impatient of all restraint and avid for new horizons.
Built under Edric's shrewd, loving direction, they were soundly
made and of good size, meant to defend his people's coasts.
The solidly stepped masts carried square sails stiffened with
rope at the edges. The strips of fabric had been dyed in alter-
nating colors, blue with white in three cases, green with rusty
black in the last. Northern men had not the dwarves' art of
weaving in one unbroken piece a complete sail.

They had not the magical skill to shape wood into an almost
organically living thing, either. The Saxon ships creaked and
squealed as the adzed strakes flexed over the frames of grown
oak. One wallowed a good deal, gaps in its planking stuffed
with wool which did not hold out all the beseiging brine. Storm
and tide had exacted their price.

"I'm not at fault, lord," Vithils's hireling pilot told him
stoutly. "Ye would cross the North Sea. Ye would take this
route to Kent. Look you, north o' here ye have the tide running
out in one direction, south in t' other. Ye're bound to meet a
foul tide now and then on the way. This, now, is taking us out

98

from land. I knew it would, aye.''

"Then if you knew it would, why did you not wait?" Vithils asked. His tone was reasonable, yet something in it suggested the pilot would do well to satisfy him with his answer.

"For because it's better to be lost on t'open sea for a few hours than run aground yonder among the Angles,'' the man said emphatically. A flat-nosed Frisian named Lambert, he had the confidence of one who knows his trade. "The Angle chiefs as took vows o' friendship with you are away to the east. These hereabouts . . .''

He spat to leeward to express his opinion.

"I know what they'd do if they could or dared.'' Vithils stood braced on his thickly muscled legs. "If they tried anything, they'd find us a bad bargain for that kind of trading. Not that I want to run aground to prove it. You have done well thus far.''

He glanced toward the stern. Like the others, this ship was closely packed. Thirty rowers and half that number of extra men assured that there would always be fresh hands for the oars, but with their battle gear and foodstocks, they loaded the vessel close to the utmost it could carry. A few friendship gifts of good worth and small weight excepted, this powerful force carried nothing not absolutely needed. Of course, that battle gear itself was worth any thief's while. Vithils's four ships held a score of well-made swords, a few scale byrnies, and—on Vithils himself—one mail shirt, work of a master human smith over a full laborious year. The very spearheads were of fine workmanship, narrow and grooved, the points reinforced to pierce even mail without breaking.

"Nothing but the best for you, Gudrun Blackhair,'' he growled.

His rough-hewn face impassive as an idol's, Vithils remembered the events of the previous summer. The news had come to him from trusty coast watchers that Gudrun Blackhair lurked near Elbe-mouth, and he had gone at once to bring her to account. He'd been circumspect enough, he had believed, given Blackhair's name for rashness. Yet she had outwitted, trapped, and held him to ransom—*him*, with his great name, Vithils the pirate's bane!

What truly scalded his soul, though, was the memory of the fighting men who had died in that dark creek mouth where Gudrun had captured him. Tribesmen. Saxons. His men. He owed it to them to avenge them. Until that was done, he would neither sleep well nor feel like a complete man.

Being Vithils, he did more than brood over the debt of blood; he prepared to pay it, and thoroughly. He sent out spies, wove alliances, learned all he could about Gudrun's base, her friends and enemies, and planned his own movements accordingly. Supposing that she would know of his intended journey to Kent, and await him in that cursed ship of hers, he had taken the perilous route across the open sea and around Anglian shores. He'd made other preparations, too, after planning them long and well with trusty, sagacious men. All that remained uncertain was Fate.

His half-brother Cudebehrt strutted forward, chiming with cheap jewelry. Men who judged by outward things had been known to laugh at those gauds, at Cudebehrt's bantam walk, at his short-sighted, blinking eyes, drooping moustaches, and squeaky voice. They discovered too late that laughing at Cudebehrt was an unsafe pastime.

He carried one of the best of the swords with Vithils's small fleet. Its name was War Shuttle, because it wove a red thread through the woof of every battle, and Cudebehrt used it like a master. His sight was scarcely so weak that he couldn't see what to do in hand-to-hand fighting.

"I see clearly enough to ten yards," he was accustomed to say, "and I never yet encountered a foe with arms that long."

Now he gazed shoreward, where for him there was only a gray-green blur. "I must say, brother," he piped, "that all I've seen of this land convinces me it's fit for Romans, Jutes, and Angles, in that order."

Vithils smiled through his rust-colored beard. "You haven't seen the best of it yet. Those ague-ridden marshes around Humber's mouth might as well be Nastrand, and that tide trap they call the Wash is a gateway to Fenland, though again there is said to be better land beyond. I've only been to Kent."

"The old king was a man. What of the new one?"

"I haven't met him. From what I've been told, he could never have founded the kingdom, but with strong supporters who don't wish Kent ripped apart, he should do well. He's had foresighted dreams from boyhood, and he says the omens are against Blackhair."

Cudebehrt made a wry mouth. "I say the same, but those yonder are the omens I mean."

He waved a jangling arm at the accompanying war vessels with their serpent figureheads.

"I wouldn't choose Ricsige to lead the host in a fight like this," Vithils admitted. "He's a man without any great name for deeds, and that matters. We will just have to see when we face him."

"Sail yonder, lord!" one of the fighting men near the bow called. He pointed.

Cudebehrt blinked, then gave up the attempt. He knew he could not discern it. Vithils gazed long, his blue eyes slitted in his rough-hewn, impassive face. The westbound sail drew nearer.

"Another ship, so far from shore?" Cudebehrt queried. "Maybe it was caught by the tide, like us."

"That's *Ormungandr*," Vithils said in the flattest of voices.

"*Ormungandr!*" The name went down the length of the ship like a spreading flame. Other things were uttered, some merry, some suggestive of fear.

"Gudrun Blackhair! She saves us trouble and comes to us!"

"How did she know—"

"She's a witch, see you!"

"Belay that!" Vithils ordered. "Yes, that is *Ormungandr*, but she seems alone, and we be four. I cannot say how Blackhair knew where to meet us, and it's no matter. We can finish her here as well as at Sarnia. Better."

He began calling instructions to the masters of his other ships.

"Arn, Euric, ready those grapnels! If Blackhair gives you any chance at all, I want you to bind fast to her so that she cannot move. Do that even if she rams you, and one of us will soon have her tied on the other side. We are two fighting men for each one of Blackhair's, and fighters of Edricsburg. We will cut them to dog meat!"

They roared back that they would.

"What if she's too cunning to allow that, Vithils?" asked Arn, youngest of the captains.

"That's what our bowmen are for," he answered. "String them now, all of you, and be ready to prickle her once she's in range."

Across the heaving gray water *Ormungandr* raced, in company with two faerie ships Vithils could not see. Gudrun scanned the water intently, noting how the Saxon ships had begun to maneuver.

"By the gods, they are clumsy," she laughed to Felimid. "They have suffered in crossing the open sea, I think. We can row circles around them!"

"In the wildest wedding dance since the Thunderer married the giant," Felimid agreed, excitement seething in him. In Gudrun's company he had fought a couple of sea battles, and he looked upon the Saxon ships with a more knowing eye than he had possessed a year before. "Shall I utter an invitation first? It's manners, my black darling."

"No! You are my spokesman, Bragi, and it is your right, but I want to have words with Vithils myself."

"Then I will be telling him so. It's my right, as you say, and I find I am jealous of all my rights where you are concerned. *Vithils, Edric's axe!*" he cried across the water. "*Greetings!*"

"I remember you, harper," Vithils answered. "I have little time to waste, and I would say a word to Blackhair before we fight."

"Time may waste you, instead—and fight? The lady can answer you there, and indeed she's as ready for a word as yourself."

An arrow or two hissed across the water from Vithils's ship. They fell far short of *Ormungandr*.

"You brought bowmen, I see," Gudrun said. "The notion was good, but they are not the equals of mine if that is the best they can do. I think you would be wise to turn back."

Vithils shouted with laughter, and he was not the easiest of men to move to displays of mirth. "When did you hear of four ships turning back for one?"

"When the one is *Ormungandr* and I command her, it happens. Your own ships are not in the best of trim, and I would be light of spirit if they were. If you swear an oath to return home and trouble me no more, Vithils, you may live."

This time Vithils did not so much as chuckle. The joke had been hilarious once. "Let fate determine that."

In one of the ships Vithils could not see, Nacrantal shrugged.

"Well, lady, he cannot complain with his last breath that he was not told," he said pleasantly. His eyes glittered in a way that belied his tone. "I'll go with a few friends and sink him from beneath."

Gudrun's anger flamed. "By every sea demon, you will not! This is between Vithils and me! Interfere and I will slay you myself!"

"If you don't use trickery, the odds are a little against you."

"Not so much. Two of those toy ships carry only as many men as *Ormungandr*. My bowmen will reduce that before we come to close quarters. You and Yrnruch may distract the other two, and open some seams if you like, but Vithils must be mine. I will not have you drown him like a rat. You hear me?"

"Indeed. Vithils is yours—or you are his—no Child of Lir hindering." To the purple-haired woman beside him, Nacrantal then said, "Earth folk are strange. I never have understood them."

"What is it?" the sea daughter asked, puzzled. "Does she wish the glory for herself?"

"Probably. Let her have it. Let her have the Saxon spears as well."

Although he spoke lightly, and even leaned negligently on his ship's rail to watch the outcome, Nacrantal's fingers were white against the wood. It was Yrnruch Starknower, the dreaming watcher of the skies, who took his ship against the Saxons, while his fiercer comrade remained aloof in offended pride.

With two steersmen plying the rudder paddle, and thirty rowers straining, *Ormungandr* danced over the gray-green waves. Felimid, his harp stowed securely away, sprang to help clew up the sail as it flapped and cracked a shade darker than the water beneath. No seamen, he had yet learned some skills during his year with Gudrun.

A knot came loose. Half the sail hung flapping while the other side was brailed loosely to the yard. Felimid gained the mast and went up it like the agile squirrel Ratatosk, which carries gossip and provocation through the branches of the World Tree. Gaining the yard, he threw a leg across it and took a one-handed grip on the heavy rope collar that held yard to mast.

Below him the sea heaved and *Ormungandr*'s flooring tilted. Suddenly the wind shifted. The great ship bucked, and Felimid almost fell. Spray stung his eyes. He reached for the flying cord, missed it twice, and stretched out along the yard on his belly to make his next attempt. An arrow hissed by him. He never noticed it, but Gudrun did.

Snarling, she bent her own bow, making the eighty-pound draw with practiced smoothness. Three dropping shafts in twice as many heartbeats sped toward Vithils's ship. All fell within it.

Even as Gudrun shot, she gave commands. Her Danish bowmen sent a whirring flight of arrows after Gudrun's three envoys. They thumped in timber, thudded in flesh.

Above, Felimid made another snatch at the whipping cord. His tough, graceful fingers grabbed it at last. Stuffing the end between his teeth, he gathered sail by the double armful like a drunken draper measuring cloth and clumped it against the yard. It fought him in the mischievous wind. He wondered furiously what had become of the vaunted lightness of dwarvish cloth.

Swiftly he passed the cord around the loosely gathered sail and secured it, letting his fingers remember the knots he had practiced for hours in the winter. Then he hitched himself farther along the yard and finished the job. Glancing around, he noticed for the first time that arrows were flying his way. None reached him, though. Gudrun and Decius were carefully keeping *Ormungandr* out of range of the short Saxon bows, yet within effective shooting distance for the Danish staves. The Saxons had taken some casualties.

Gudrun's men had not. Her plan was working thus far, and the superiority of her bowmen being proved, but the matter would have to be ended at close quarters. A fresh flight of arrows hummed over the water as he watched.

Yrnruch's ship skimmed like a gay-winged dragonfly toward the more distant Saxon vessels, while Nacrantal rode the waves and did nothing. Anger rose in Felimid's heart. Cairbre and Ogma! Who did that supercilious predator think he was? Let him call Gudrun to account later, if he felt insulted. Battle was imminent!

The bard squirmed back along the yard and descended the mast. His corslet and boots hampered him. He hadn't been aware of it in the urgency of climbing and doing; now they weighed an apparent ton. Luckily they were only thick leather and not metal.

"Well done!" Gudrun greeted him. "Ha, look at those Saxon river trout try to close with us! They will succeed when we are prepared to let them!"

Felimid picked up his sword and shield, set aside when he ran for the mast. Vithils's ship and Arn's were now coming straight for *Ormungandr*, side by side, meaning to catch the long sea dragon between them. A third Saxon ship moved to block *Ormungandr*'s retreat. It was like a game of *fidchell*, the bard thought, with the pieces reduced to four hounds attempting to surround the more mobile hart. Yet in *fidchell* there was rarely blood. In *fidchell* there were seldom two additional pieces with minds of their own allied with the "hart," and they invisible to one's opponent. Nor was *fidchell* played upon the waves of the unpredictable sea! He slid Kincaid restlessly in and out of his scabbard.

"To windward, quickly," Gudrun cried. "We will not be taken in this vice! And send them more arrows to show our regard!"

Ormungandr turned side-on to the waves and rolled dangerously. The bowmen aboard lurched, and invoked the Vanir in disreputable terms while trying to keep their bowstrings dry in the hissing spray. They sent one ragged volley at the Saxons, which mostly missed, and one more accurate volley as *Ormungandr*'s bow turned toward the open sea.

The water darkened and seemed to curdle. A shrieking black wind came striding across the sea from the east. Rain whipped in its ragged skirts. Waves rolled white-capped and violent before it. Decius barked urgent orders to the steersmen and rowers, who barely in time headed *Ormungandr* into the wind.

The squall vomited its main force over them. Bowstrings were drenched in seconds, with all else. Waves crested under the high serpent prow, tossing it higher. Skirling murk surrounded them; wind struck in gusty, staggering slaps, and *Ormungandr* bucked wildly. Reeling on the floor timbers, Felimid saw the air elemental who battered them as a rushing, formless giant. There was no time to reach his harp, much less play it. They were struck, spun, blinded, had their oars wrenched and twisted in their hands, and at last were driven helplessly westward. Vithils's force bobbled far behind.

Felimid saw no sign of Yrnruch or Nacrantal, either. Running, white-crested water merged into stormy darkness all around him. Staring upward, he saw shapes riding the wind, nightmare hags with gory talons, mouths stretched wide in shrieks of bloodlust. Their lean thighs gripped the flanks of demon horses.

"The *badb*!" Felimid cried, unheard by any.

He named the inciting war spirits of his own people, mad, inexorable, furious, dark, lacerating. Gudrun Blackhair saw them, too, as the bloody corpse-choosers of her northern tribes.

She knew whose agents they were. Staring into the ragged indigo clouds, she mouthed a name of two syllables which she had not spoken lately.

Ormungandr fled on, helpless for once among the wind-driven waves. They flowed a man's height and more, cold as the breakers of Nastrand, which is the shore of Hel. The sorcerous wind lashed and drove them, never letting them rest.

Felimid struggled to where Golden Singer lay stowed under the small foredeck, a mere triangular platform in the bows. Drawing her from her plain leather case, he swept his hand over the strings in a mad attempt to charm the wind-giant scourging them on. It was like throwing a handful of chaff at the fire consuming a town.

There was no commanding the elemental powers by a third-rank bard. They would either listen or would not.

"It *follows* us!" the steersman yelled. "This foul squall drives us!"

A few furlongs away the April sunlight shone clear, while the wind with its hideous riders hooted and yammered about the plunging ship. Dimness like an ugly twilight blew along with it. Thrand the steersman and his Cornish partner Reuel worked until their muscles cracked.

"It drives us into the fens!"

The feared region showed ahead of them. Pale water of lakes, rivers, and swamps, vast reedy stretches and a few islands merged into a uniform deathliness with distance. Yet the distance lessened. The wonderful swiftness of *Ormungandr*, the seeming freedom from water's drag or resistance, now worked against its mistress and rowers. It raced madly before the wind, and the fens drew closer.

Gudrun's men worked ship as a ship had seldom been worked before. Felimid worked with them, lithe, indolent Felimid, until the lines skinned his hands, his back ached in a white heat from bailing, and his arms turned to lead from tugging the refractory oars.

His efforts did no good. The labor of eighty other men was no more effective. The fens drew ever more near.

"Bragi!" Gudrun yelled through the black wind. "You have the sharpest eyes here. Is that a river-mouth?"

She threw out her arm, pointing, the while she gripped the shield-rail with her left hand to steady herself.

Felimid stared landward through the hard-hurled spray. Was it? There, by the little jut of high ground, receding back into the fens like a wide pathway?

"By the gods, I think it is!"

"You think! Ran's teeth in a hungry grin! Do you not *know*?"

"Make for it and take the chance!"

Miles away Nacrantal and Yrnruch conferred on the sea. The sorcerous wind which drove *Ormungandr* before it had all but passed them by, as it had the Saxons, who were now disappearing from sight eastward, rowing, bailing, and fighting the tide. The Children of Lir did not mind how far the tide might take them, so long as it did not take them aground.

"Are we honor bound to follow them into the fens?" Yrnruch wondered. "They may require us. That was a most inimical power that struck them, riding the wind."

"It was, and I'd sooner avoid it," Nacrantal said. "Maybe it will be content to leave them where they are, or maybe it will pursue them. Anyhow, they are earth's children, and the fens are earth for the most part."

"It's extremely wet earth."

"My thanks. I did not know. They will live there without us if they can live at all. Eighty strong fighters, with a leader of name and a bard who has the true seeing? They don't need our nursing, and *I* am not minded to nurse them."

"That's so," the purple-haired woman commented. She was a noted sea witch who kept her name and soul in the body of a salmon so that it would be safe from her enemies. "The water of the fens is dead. I'm for remaining away."

Yrnruch argued. He disliked the fens as much as any of his people, but reckoned that they were obliged to learn what had become of *Ormungandr*, at least. Only a few shared his opinion. Nearly all were of Nacrantal's view, and the purple-haired witch's. Yrnruch had not the personal force to prevail against them all.

"We cannot abandon them merely!" he said. "At the least we must wait and see whether they come out of that foul place. *I* am not returning to tell Niamh that I would not even do that. Are you?"

"Niamh is like the rest of us," Nacrantal said coldly. "She owes these folk nothing but the destruction of the Veiled Isles and her brother's death. I doubt that she'd care."

"Nonetheless, I do. Also, companion, you do not know Niamh's mind. I'll stay even if no one else does."

Then they agreed to wait, even Nacrantal. He was curious, he said, to see whether Gudrun would live up to her reputation. He would bide among the fighting tides of the Wash until he grew bored, at any rate.

The Saxons were gone, a fair long way to the east and gone, free to make their limping course to Kent after all. The Children of Lir let them go, having no great interest in them and possessing all the fickle wildness of the sea. Nacrantal might have pursued and destroyed them for sport; it would have pleased him better than waiting idle in such a deserted place. But he would not.

"Blackhair bade me keep my hands from Vithils, and said he must be hers," he recalled, smiling. "I'd like to see her live to regret that word."

IX

A temple of old stands somewhere hidden,
 Dreaming dreams that have soured with time,
And fields which once were a fertile glory
 Lie sodden under the marshes' slime.
                                   —Felimid mac Fal,
                                     Gudrun's Saga

The serpent ship moved upstream under ten slow oars. Other men stationed amidships poled and thrust when it was needful. Hauling the ship like a barge would have been better, save that the banks were too sodden soft, and no man there would have risked a tumble into a fenland stream. They looked about them as though expecting trolls or lake monsters to appear at their elbows.

More than the reputation of the place set them on edge. They had been assailed by something uncanny that day. The experience had left them raw-nerved, quick to bluster, and deep in their stomachs, frightened.

Felimid harped music now breezy, now lilting, to raise their spirits. Every so often a chord like a laugh of bright impudence would leap from his strings. An idea came to him during that slow progress, an idea for a song about an overweening chieftain who got his ship trapped in a tide marsh and boasted afterward of how he had robbed toads and plundered the eels; but that was a song for another time. It wouldn't suit the present company.

Gudrun turned her bare black head, gazing beyond the stream's banks. Reeds, rushes, and sedges stretched far, while in places a dozen kinds of willow grew mingled with shrubs.

"Who knows anything of this place?" she asked.

Felimid didn't, though he had wandered a few years in Britain. He never had a chance to say so. Rowan, the Saxon youth who thought Gudrun Blackhair as splendid as the sun, leaped to answer. He stammered a little, while his gaze ravened at her striking, large-featured face. The bard observed that she didn't appear to mind his adulation a bit.

"I—I do, lady. Some kinsmen of mine crossed the sea and entered Britain through the fens."

"They came through this?"

"Indeed, lady! Just as we're doing, and many others did. The rivers lead west and southwest from the Wash, so that in a ship or boat of small draught you can reach the good farming land beyond."

"We don't want to go that far, just to get back to sea once the tide serves us. Farmers, you say?"

This was the usual tale. Most of the so-called sea wolves who invaded Britain were farmers, crossing the water in any sort of ship they could purchase or build, wanting only land, stealing nothing more ambitious than sheep.

"Farmers. None settle in the fens, though. It's too much like the country across the sea they wanted to leave—marsh, mere and lagoon. You cannot cultivate it. Nothing *human* lives here but some British fishers and fowlers, and a Cross-worshipping monk or two, as I've heard."

"You need not trouble to tell me about the things which are not human," Gudrun said. "I can guess. Nicors, ghosts, and corposants, right?"

"All I know who have been here say it is no place to be."

Gudrun had a liking for this worshipping lad. It had begun when he was sorely wounded fighting for a place in *Ormungandr*, when she was about to make her first voyage in the serpent ship. He fought well.

"We will not flout that advice," she said. "This is a dreary place, and I have business elsewhere. Vithils was lucky today, and I want to be there to greet him if he comes to Sarnia. We cannot have him bragging that I was afraid of him."

She was shaken beneath her display of hard cheerfulness. Felimid knew it, and could do nothing to comfort her without exposing her terror before her men, for which she would not have forgiven him. Her terror's name was Odin, the god she had erst served so ardently. Father of Victories, god of war and the gallows, he was also the master of sorcery and lord of the winds. As surely as night followed day, he had sent the chill black wind that drove them hither. Cairbre and Ogma! His own strife-inciting valkyrs had ridden it, shrieking! Oh, yes, he was in this thing, in it and behind it, with all his cunning and implacable anger.

Felimid's fingers strayed to a halt on Golden Singer's strings. The harp had uttered a cry of furious protest, echoing his mood. He looked at Gudrun, who had heard it. She crossed the floor timbers and sat beside him.

"Cheerful country," she observed. "Do you know much about it, my man? Have you been here?"

"Never until now, surely." The dark-brown eyebrows climbed up his forehead a little as he scanned the flooded peat. "The Britons tell me that all this was once farmed. Some say the legions drained the marshes by the same magic that built their roads, and I've heard a bishop declare firmly that his god dried out the land for his favored people when they came from Troy—or was it Canaan?—but let it all go back to marsh when the people turned away from him."

"*You didn't have to speak of that!*" she hissed.

"Of . . . oh."

No, he had not had to speak of angry gods punishing recusants, not at all. He had spoken because it was in his mind, as it had to be in Gudrun's, she whom Odin had rejected . . . on the bard's account.

It had happened in the north. She and Felimid had quarreled bitterly and parted, over a hanging sacrifice she had made to the Father of Victories. Gudrun had followed her lover into the forest to find him again, and been warned by a stranger who called himself Grim to turn back, to forget the bard. She had refused.

"*From this decision you will get bitter woe,*" he had told her. "*Your vows are severed; call yourself no longer mine, nor invoke my name. Pass on, fool. Rush to your fate.*"

"Maybe we had better speak of it, after what we both saw this day," the bard suggested.

"Yes." Gudrun spoke low. "But later, Bragi. The men must see me brave, and you must aid me."

"Aye."

"There now," Decius announced with satisfaction. "That looks like a place which will not soak us to the knees if we walk on it."

The lowering, brassy sun shone on a five-acre island at the

junction of their river with a larger stream. A tangle of alders and osiers bearded the isle on one side, while funereal black poplars formed a sombre fringe on the other.

"We're unlikely to find aught better before sunset."

Gudrun assented, and *Ormungandr* was drawn up the margin, its keel crushing sedges which yielded a strong, rank smell and dark sap. Some pirates tramped about seeking fuel, while others remained with the ship lest a foe appear. Others yet began rigging shelter with osier withes. As Felimid stepped ashore, he felt a curious, ugly thrill pass from his soles to his belly and crotch. He did not care for it.

"Oh-ho-ho!" Sigar's roaring laugh came from among the poplars. "Come see this! The Romans have been here before us!"

Gudrun and Decius saw to establishing the camp and posting a watch, while Felimid went to explore. He walked through pale marsh violets and more of the peculiar sedges. In the last of the daylight he saw an occasional ear of grain, wild for generations, stunted in height yet swollen and ill-shaped at the head, unharvested remnants which must have been ripe the previous autumn.

Among the poplars stood a tiny stone temple, a rectangular box with its portico crumbling, the pillars specked with blackish fungus. A larger relative of it erupted in puffballs from the ground. Felimid trod on one. Its tough skin resisted the pressure briefly, then popped, giving the bard a morbid sensation of having stepped on an eyeball.

"Sigar!" he greeted the big chestnut-haired northman who had found the temple. Two wadmal-clad comrades with him were kindling torches. "It's a gloomy place you have discovered here."

The atmosphere of the place meant little to the northman. "There may be some loot!" he bellowed joyously, and rushed within, followed by his companions. Felimid listened with interest to the three men stamping about, kicking through a century's worth of silted dirt, and saw them come out shrugging and dissatified at last.

"No loot?" he inquired.

"None!" Sigar admitted. "Not even a sign of a hiding place! It's just some little Roman temple, to seed time and harvest gods by the friezes on the walls." He waved a long arm at the surrounding fens. "But who'd build such a temple *here*?"

"I'd never be knowing, Sigar. I did hear that this land once looked different, was drier and felt the plow. Maybe there were seed-time rites and harvest offerings in those days."

"Aye, maybe. I'll tell you this, Bragi! These Romans must have had rites to make Frey and Freya blush red. You should see the carvings on those walls and altar." Sigar whistled and made expressive motions. "Maytime at home is tame compared with it."

"Ah, that's a sorry thing." Felimid grinned and fisted Sigar in the ribs. "You ought to see Maytime at *my* home."

"Why didn't you enter?" asked one of the other pirates.

"It's forbidden to me," he answered glibly. "I lose my bardic powers when I deal with things of Rome."

This was more or less true. Something in his soul recoiled from those too-straight lines and ruthlessly ordered forms, the outward signs of a way of life that had thrust all flowing harmonies out of the way to further its own system. The magic he knew did wither in such places.

Yet the patterns of Rome had their kind of rightness. Here Felimid sensed something corrupted, warped, intrinsically wrong. Returning to the other side of the island, he experienced less of that sense of wrongness, yet he still felt it, permeating the soil and its growth. The soil smelled of something worse than clean decay. He saw malice in the outlines of the very willows.

Then Gudrun came to him. She had not removed her mail shirt or harness; they were unsafe here. But she seemed vulnerable for all that.

"Bragi?"

"You sound unsure. I've been Bragi since the day we met, and nothing is changed now." He took her hand. "A long hard day it has been, but we came through it."

"Do not cheer me. Vithils came through it, and he was not meant to. Odin's own wind drove me from his throat, let the man escape me! I might have ended this business off Anglia. The One-Eyed thwarted me, Bragi. The battle deaths I devoted to him, the times I reddened my sword in his name and hung or speared captives after the fighting, are not to be counted! I have never broken faith or been a coward. Now he turns against me because of you."

"Are you blaming me?" Felimid asked quietly. "Do you wish we had never met?"

"Do not be mild with me! Do not forbear! I hate it. I am Gudrun Blackhair, Bragi. I wanted you and went straight for what I wanted. You followed me into the north, shipping with danger to be near me, and still paused, considered, and weighed for long before you chanced your passion. Then you ran from me because I offered a sacrifice. You knew I served the One-Eyed, you knew! Yet when he demanded that I leave you to your fate, I would not. Do you think that was for a lawman's reasons? Because I owed you my life once or twice by then? Ha! I wanted you and would not give up my desire. You wanted me and gave up yours at the first excuse! Now you ask me if *I* wish we had not met! Do you? Are *you* shaking within at the thought of Odin's spear?"

"He's not my god, or the god my people swear by. I don't fear him. For the rest . . . I know my own mind now, Gudrun. It's you are the marrow of my heart and the mate of my soul, and I'll not be leaving you again under threat of Odin's spear or the nine-barbed, poisoned *gae bolg* itself. Red battle is not the amusement I love best of all, as you know, but I'll readily wade through it to win clear with you beside me. *The whole of the men of the world, from the rising to the setting of the sun, he would pacify with his three fair words. But by my word, it is no cowardly or no peaceful counsel that man will give his king today, but counsel of courage, and of strength, and of battle.*"

Then he took her in his arms and kissed her. She returned the kiss, though with no overwhelming passion, and sighed and rested her head on his shoulder with its covering of triple-ply walrus leather.

"Big words, Bragi. I'm glad that you will not leave me. Still, Odin is against us. That is no joke. He's crafty, far-seeing. He knows the roads to Helheim and what is being loomed by the Norns. You see things that others do not. Can you see into his schemes?"

Her face twisted. She turned away from him, gripped the alder tree behind her and sobbed. Once.

Felimid placed his hands on her mailed shoulders.

"What can Odin do to you? He cannot change your fate. He cannot change his own. Death in battle you must have long expected. You don't fear that."

"Who says I fear anything?" she snarled, wheeling upon him.

"Meseems you do. It's Odin himself, isn't it? Not death or maiming, or the loss of Sarnia. You saw Odin's corpse-choosers riding against you, and dreaded his enmity."

"Be quiet, you wordy bard!" she screamed. "Or . . . or . . ."

She seized her hilt, drew half a foot of Kissing Viper's blade. Felimid caught her wrist, then her other arm as she lifted it. They strained together.

The bard weighed a pound or two more and was strong beyond the power his lithe frame made manifest. However, Gudrun, too, was amazingly strong. The arms that had bent a steel siege bow fully equaled his, and all the force of his shoulders, wrists, and fingers was tried. His hand covered hers on the grips of Kissing Viper, and steel grated fractionally in the scabbard as they writhed and struggled. Gudrun panted. Felimid's mouth drew into the semblance of a lopsided smile, then an honest snarl.

He ceased to think. He only knew that he must push her sword back into its sheath, would do so if it meant breaking all his own fingers and her wrist, would do so if Vithils and all his Saxons came yelling ashore that instant, would do so whether he had the might or not, *would—do—so—*

Gudrun gave way suddenly. The sword rasped home. She fell against the alder. Felimid staggered the other way as the tension was released. From a raw throat he asked, "What is it, Gudrun? What is it, my heart?"

"I fear what Odin may do to me after I am dead!"

Felimid's blood ran cold. "What?"

"Yes! I know nothing—only the stories that are told, and that is the same as nothing! Odin welcomes dead heroes, they say, to fight in his host on the last day, and until then they revel and feast all night and fight great battles all day."

The bard almost made an unfortunate quip. He knew even better than she what such stories were worth. He made them up. Yet his love was frightened, so he shut his undependable lips and listened.

"They say that, Bragi, but then they say that Odin's valkyries are comely war maidens, each to her chosen hero. You saw those taloned hags! How if everything is like that? No hall roofed with glittering shields, no honor—just endless cold and the creaking of gallows? A grave mound to prison me and dead men's tongues to mock me? What then?"

BARD IV

Felimid loved life and beautiful things. Briefly, his skin crawled at the picture Gudrun painted. Never had he held pretty illusions concerning Odin, but now he saw all pleasant things beseiged, like a garden with purulent slugs crawling below it, all poetry and faith turned to moldering bones in the mound, while Odin laughed in his many disguises behind it all.

Laughter came to his rescue. Odin was not the only god, nor did he rule the many worlds. He wandered through them at will? Well, others, even mortals, could do as much.

"Gudrun, there's a saying. Every man must come at last to the sod where his grave shall be. Remember the Otherworlds. Seek you that eventual sod in a world where the One-Eyed has small power. I'll help you find it."

"Yes," she said. "Yes." Then she pushed herself slowly away from him. "But while I snuggle to you for comfort, my men may be falling into panic. Some are bleating just the way I have been. They should have their true leader to take them in hand. I suppose I thank you, Bragi—though I would liefer you had told me to find my backbone and be Gudrun Black-hair!"

She straightened fully. Her harness creaked.

Saddened, he said, "You are Gudrun Blackhair."

She departed, and Felimid remained in the gloaming, listening to the mosquitoes hum and the bitterns thunder. He missed the accustomed weight of Golden Singer from his back.

"She won't change for you, friend," said a grim voice. "Or you for her, I think."

He knew the voice of Decius even before he saw the dark, compact figure. The jeweled eye flashed red zigzags.

"How long were you listening?" the bard demanded in a smoking voice.

Decius strolled close with his thumbs in his belt. "For a while, and no harm was done. I see you are affronted—by the lady's behavior, I mean—and you need not be. If she hadn't remembered herself when she did, I would have said the same things to her. She doesn't like weakness, Bragi. She's a chieftain with men to lead. If ever you are one, you will see."

"My fine, earnest, well-intentioned seaborne cattle lifter," Felimid said, "I'll never be a chief unless it's chieftain of my own clan in Erin, the Corco Baiscind, and I'm not even the tanist to my knowledge."

"Then you don't know. Were she under the displeasure of

a dozen gods, it would be hers to ignore them and bring us all
safe out of this. What about you, my buck? How much of those
fine words did you mean? You don't want her to go to the
Otherworlds, nor do you mean to go with her. Make up your
mind to it; she won't settle in Erin as some petty king's foreign
mercenary. She'd want to be the king if she went there at all.''

"That we can decide at the time. I said I would help her
find her Gate to the Otherworld of her choice, not that I would
go through it with her.''

"Then once you are back at Sarnia and pillow-talking one
night, I'd make that wholly clear to her, and ask her what she
will do for you. You may love each other, but you and she
want different things, and neither of you will give them up.
You want to go home and live as a bard, true? Well, what the
lady wants we both do know.''

"A matter to decide once we are out of here, and have settled
with Vithils. Now, Decius, I have here some very bad wine,
so let's be sharing it while we decide when we will stand watch
tonight.''

They slew the flask between them. Decius declared it was
quite as foul as Felimid had said. The bard replied that he
shared it for that reason; no man should have to drink such
dreadful stuff alone. They savored its rawness and condemned
it utterly over the dregs, promising to one day raid the estate
that included such miserable vineyards and leave not a plant
standing, in the interests of true drinking men everywhere.

From the shadowy poplars a shape watched them. Eyes
gleamed redder than the agate Decius wore in his bereft socket.
Lean muscles moved in hunched hairy shoulders. Black-nailed
hands flexed. Mud-crusted hair cracked over bestial thighs as
the being shifted its legs.

It remained for a while, glaring at the pirates' smoking
campfires, listening to the sound of Felimid's harp. Then it
returned at a clumsy lope to the temple, unseen in the darkness,
and vanished between the fungus-mottled pillars.

X

Unhealthy shapes flock howling yonder
(Build up the fires and pour the ale!)
Tomorrow they will still be anguished —
Tomorrow we ride the laughing gale!
—Felimid mac Fal,
Song in the Fens

Sigar the northman and a hard-bitten Saxon named Hemming stood guard by the willows. As men keeping vigil in unlovely places will, they talked of other things.

"Those jellyfish-gutted Children of Lir deserted us," Sigar snarled. "I'll have their captains between the wands when I see them again. Where are they now? Fleeing back to Sarnia under the full spread of their pretty sails!"

"If you're right," Hemming said, "I'll dice you for which of the dolphin lovers to fight. Their women are fine, though, I will say that. Supple as seals and as lively, swiving on a beach."

"Ah, you've tried them?"

"One or two," Hemming said modestly. "Maybe I was lucky with the choices; still, they make most earth women seem passionless, I tell you, even if they do leave a smell like whale oil upon you! Their hips dance fast as a fish's tail netted. They haven't a grain of shame."

"By Freya, they sound like all a man could want! I'll have to try my luck with them."

"Have a care of that purple-haired sea witch who lacks a name. You'd never get her unless you fought Nacrantal — and if any man fights Nacrantal, it will be me!"

"He's yours. The other sea women, now —"

"I've told you. Aye, they were good," Hemming said reminiscently, "but I mind at least one earthy girl was even better. I knew her in Aleth last autumn. Eldrida, that was her name! Bastard of Cerdic's, and a lively darling. I'll go back to Lesser Britain and find her when this is over."

Sigar then began a tale of a swan-may he had captured in Skania, only to lose her when she retrieved her stolen plumage and departed in bird shape again. He lied as completely as Hemming had—anent everything except Eldrida, who would have clouted him in the teeth had she heard her name bandied—and neither man cared.

Sigar, though, did not have a chance to finish his story. A howling wail from out in the marshes interrupted him.

Both guards remained still, glaring into the darkness. A new ululation followed, then two more, coming simultaneously from a different direction. Sleeping men awoke reaching for weapons as more voices joined the racket

"*Fenrir!* What is that?"

"Ghosts?"

"Nicors, more likely! You should have been with us in Frisia, you'd know—"

"Nicors are mute, ye fool of a Goth! It's you who does not know. Whatever's out there is not made like a nicor!"

"Stop this yammering, all you men!" Gudrun blazed. She had been first out of the sleeping furs where she snuggled next to the bard, and now she clapped helmet to head. Her black hair escaped in a sleepy tangle. "It is only noise, thus far! Stand together and listen!"

She had them form a shield burg in case it should be more than noise, with the hollow side of the crescent against *Ormungandr*'s strakes. The racket went on, made by multitudes of creatures howling, shrieking, and wailing hopelessly.

"They do not sound of much account to me," she said.

"I see things," one man muttered.

"I see them, too," Gudrun told him. "Well, that is all to the good. I was more troubled when I could not see them. They still do not seem very terrible, do they?"

The pirate chuckled; a bit effortfully, but he chuckled. The pale, half-glimpsed shapes were thick as frogs along the riverbank. Their wailing never stopped. Felimid suddenly sensed that these creatures, whatever they were, clung to their misery. His stomach turned over.

With never a ripple or splash, something came out of the water, to crouch mouthing three spears' lengths away. Skinny tendons quivered. Its hollow chest heaved after breath that was only a memory. Sunken, brilliant eyes stared hungrily at Gudrun's company. It seemed to gloat.

Two spears went through its unlovely shape. Save the problematical satisfaction of hitting so narrow a target, the throwers gained nothing, for their spears had no effect. The thing crouched and moaned as before.

"No more weapon-striking but by my word," Gudrun commanded above the endless din.

"*Lemures.*" Decius said, his Hispano-Roman mind leaping to Roman beliefs to explain what tempted to madness. "The malign dead. They died of the fever that spawns in these marshes, by the look of them. God! They are foul!"

"But helpless to harm, if this is the most they can do," Felimid remarked. For him, disgust mingled with wonder. What could these creatures want? The living to share their miserable unlife? They had appeared so quickly and in such numbers that they must be powerfully drawn.

Danes made the sign of the Hammer against bale. The Christians invoked various saints. Decius belatedly did so, too, though with no better result. Well, he had not prayed since he was a child. He remembered a ritual from before the days of the Cross, involving bare feet, beans, and the midnight hour, for just such situations as this. He'd have been willing to use it, if they had possessed any beans and if the details had not slipped his mind. He felt a wild impulse to giggle, and hauled himself back from that sinister brink.

"Ghosts," he said disparagingly. "Just sorry, dead ghosts. We have made so many of those that we should not fear them."

More of the specters came ashore, to yammer, grieve, and mock. Although they seemed capable of little but noise, that noise as they raved on and on caused a peculiar shaking of the mind. Even Gudrun bit her tongue. If this continued until morning, her pirates might all rush into the river or spear each other in madness. She should do something. What, though? Weapons and invocations seemed useless.

The bard stepped out before the shield burg. His sword Kincaid lay at rest in the sheath, and his harp rode on his back in the familiar worn leather bag he would never replace with anything richer. He held his shield negligently to one side.

"What is it you desire?" he asked.

The ghosts ceased to yammer. The nearest ones stared at him avidly.

He repeated the plain query, in Latin and in two of the British dialects he knew. Silence spread among the loathly crowd, spread into the river, across it, and beyond. They listened. They hunched forward, shivering in their constant ague fit.

"What do you want?" Felimid asked again. "Is it to be freed from this state, and can that be done by us? For we will do what we may."

The nearest specter ululated like bubbling muck. The others took up the sound anew in mindless derision. They had heard, and perhaps even comprehended the sounds, but no true meaning reached them. Mean, corrupted spirits dead long ago of sickness, they flaunted their deformity and gibbered.

Felimid's mouth pulled into a shape of disgust. His intuition had been true. One being of the sort might have been pathetic. Hundreds . . . were an abomination of waste.

"Sa, comrades, it's a mannerless crowd we have here!" he shouted through the din. His voice, trained in bardic schools, was heard by them all. "Mannerless and dismal. I'm for building up the fires and telling as many good stories as we know, to show them how live men scorn their wriggling in muck. It's too long since these ghosts heard a bawdy song. What do you say?"

Laughter answered him from here and there within the shield burg. If it rasped and sounded forced, at least it was uttered. Northmen were not inclined to respect bodiless things that could only shriek and gesture. The frosty dark of their homeland in winter held real horrors.

"I agree with Bragi!" Gudrun declared. "It is beneath us to maintain a shield wall against sorry things like this. If they keep us from sleeping, we may as well be cheery while we wake. You, there! Yes! The gibberer showing all his ribs. Come warm your thin backside at my fire. Gudrun Blackhair is more hospitable than you."

The thing crouched, glared at her with huge fever-bright eyes and mouthed. She jeered at it again then turned her back. It followed her in lurching hops. As the sparks from her fire began to soar, it hunched like a frog in the flickering light, roasting before and chilling behind. Coughing in its throat, it glared at her through long beslimed hair.

"You invited it, Gudrun," Felimid said with a shrug. "A stronger magician than I could not force it to leave."

"Let it stay, then," she answered. "It can learn to be better company or be ignored. With Odin and Vithils ranging yonder,

BARD IV

I am not going to fret for the likes of this fenbound thing.''

She began telling the ghost riddles while she roasted meat. When she could not talk for chewing, she jested by tossing it bones, or fragments of the tough bread her teeth had ripped, as if it were her dog.

It babbled and chuckled wordlessly in reply. Hatred shone from its sickly bright eyes, and the noises it made were malignant, especially its laughter. It stared and stared at Gudrun Blackhair as though it loved, instead of hated, the sight of her. A gloating pleasure grinned through its chattering teeth.

Felimid loathed it.

Why is this thing so pleased? What does it know?

In his mind he saw a one-eyed god riding the wind. The specter hunkered beside them could know nothing of that; he couldn't! The Spear-Wielder was a god of the dead, yes, but of battle's dead, the warlike dead, and the sacrificial dead — not of sickly, impotent lemurs.

Yet the dead knew things the living did not. Odin, according to the tales, sometimes visited Hel, and the ghost at their fire belonged in her realm if anything did.

On impulse he drew Kincaid and sent the sword of Ogma hissing through the ghost's scrawny neck. It sat leering at him. He slotted the sword's point neatly between two prominent ribs, meeting no resistance and gaining no result. Venting a breath of frustration, he returned to Gudrun's side of the fire.

"That was no way to treat a guest, love! Anyhow, you knew it would be futile.''

"Not with this blade,'' Felimid said, sliding its blue-white glitter home. "He has killed vampires, werewolves, demons, and other beings no common metal will harm, so I thought it worth trying. And our guest offends me. Yes, cackle, you scut! If you cling to your state rather than risk the Caldron of Rebirth, the fault is your own.''

"What caldron is that you said?''

"The Mother's caldron. The Caldron of Rebirth. *A rim of pearls is around its edge; by the breath of nine maidens it is gently warmed. It will not cook the food of a coward or oathbreaker.* Maybe our friend here cannot enter it because of that — or loves to suffer, just.''

"Or is lost in this festering marsh which has taken over what used to be his land.'' Gudrun slapped a mosquito. "You are harsher than usual, Bragi. Our guest does offend you, does he

122

not? I concede that he's ugly. I have seen worse things, though."

The ghost squatted on puffy feet and yammered.

Toward dawn it rose and left the fireside, with a last hateful grin at Gudrun Blackhair. She hurled a smoking fuel chunk through it, with a curse that smoldered as hotly. She had grown very weary of it herself through the night, and wished her careless summons undone.

The dawn mist of the fens surrounded it. With a last malignant keening, its hundreds of fellows departed also, quaking in fever-ridden limbs. Their howling and coughing reached back muffled to those they had haunted.

Gudrun stretched her hands to the embers. "What a long hilarious night that was! Bragi, of all places I have seen, this is the one it will please me most to leave—except Jarl Ivarr's hall, maybe."

"And even to Jarl Ivarr's hall you returned," he said. "Once."

"Mmm, yes." Gudrun smiled at that memory. Jarl Ivarr was the man from whom she had suffered most, and for whose killing she had become an outlaw. "Not to this cesspit, though, I vow. We leave when the tide suits."

"To find Vithils again?"

"If he is about, I rely on him to find us. More likely he has gone on to Kent. We *might* catch him first. . . . Bragi, I need to make water. Will you guard me?"

Gudrun sought a clump of willows for her privy. Felimid leaned against a tree, hands resting lightly on his weapons, and wondered again about the *wrongness* of the entire island. The fen ghosts were scattered now, and daylight had come, yet still he was aware of something he could scarcely have named.

He recalled the discoveries of the day before; the temple to some agricultural godling the Romans had brought with them, the fungus, the distorted, wild-growing grain. He let his earthy senses of touch and smell reach out.

This earth did seem blighted. It smelled sick. It was, of course. Good farming land had reverted to sodden waste, and the powers of that farming land—

A sensation, a footfall, a pressure, touched him through the ground. The touch was strong. Another. Although his ears heard nothing, he was aware that some presence moved nearby, lifting and doggedly planting its feet.

BARD IV

It wasn't human. Felimid knew that, as he would have known cowhide from linen if he touched it in the dark. He restrained his urge to draw Kincaid and said quietly, "Gudrun, it's in my mind that—"

Willow withes crackled and ripped. Gudrun yelled as black-nailed hands seized her, tumbling her backward. Felimid rounded the tree, drawing Kincaid as he went; Kincaid, the sword of Ogma, the first steel weapon ever forged in Erin and forever the best, made from a fallen star brought from beneath a lake. The staghorn grips comforted his palm, and the shine of the slender blade comforted his eyes, in the teeth of the unknown. He threw aside a curtain of green withes, the half heartbeat's drag of them across his arm an intolerable delay.

Gudrun struggled on the ground with something grotesque. The bard glimpsed a hairy, goat-tailed rump, misshapen legs, a curved manlike back, shaggy hair, and ridged horns. He also whiffed a stink like an orgy on a midden.

Even as he had that initial glimpse, the sight changed. Gudrun writhed from under the being, her arms straining, to thrust it aside even as she rolled. Her white bottom flashed below a gathered-up kirtle; the beast-god vented a coughing grunt and lunged for her.

Felimid saw its front parts now, as he sprang to meet it. Red-eyed goat's face, distempered, lustful glare, hairy chest, wet member unsheathed and bulging navel high, clumsy, rocking stance on the damp ground—all this he saw swiftly as he leaped over Gudrun, his sword aimed at the god's stomach.

It inhaled and blew at him.

The gust struck Felimid in mid leap like a buffet of wind. But sky winds are clean. This had a warmth like rot about it, and a smell as of a grain basket opened upon contents gone musty.

The blast stopped him short with its slamming force. He stumbled over Gudrun. Kincaid lightly slashed the seed-god's ribs before the black-nailed hands ripped Felimid's shield from his arm. The wrench dislocated his shoulder. Still holding his shield, the god lifted Felimid and hurled him into the crackling osiers with one hand.

The bitter withes broke his fall, his walrus-leather cuirass protected him, and the action had been too sudden and furious for him to notice pain. But Kincaid had flown from his hand and vanished somewhere in the tangled osiers.

Through the damp leaves and through a daze, he saw the

god break his shield across a hairy thigh. It tossed the pieces away in opposite directions. Then it shambled toward Gudrun again.

She had dragged up her breeches, though she lacked time to fasten them. Her own sword, Kissing Viper, which had lain beside her while she relieved herself, she now held in her hand.

Confused by several impacts, filled with an urgent need to help his lover, Felimid had become aware that his right arm was helpless. Being left-handed, he could still fight if he had a weapon. Yes, but he'd lost his.

"Gudrun!" he croaked. "Hold him at bay. I have no sword and my shield arm is hurt."

He never knew if she properly heard. Breathing deeply, he summoned his voice and shouted.

"Come running with weapons, you men of *Ormungandr*! Your lady fights a troll! Aid, quickly, you slackers! Are your ears wool and your feet stone? *Ha-yaa! Sarnia!*"

He plunged into the willows and searched one-handed for Kincaid. In the dimness of early dawn it was a maddening task. Each drop of water looked like the gleam of steel, and each spray of green leaves might have the elusive hilt behind it. He probed with scabbard chaps, felt with his restricted right hand, and called as in a nightmare for the pirates.

"Gudrun! How do you fare?"

"I fend the thing off. I have drawn some of its blood. My blows do not go deep, though." Her voice rang clear. Suddenly she screamed, "Bragi! Help me!"

He left his frantic search for Kincaid at once. Sliding through the withes, he saw Gudrun struggling with the god once more, and swiftly losing in its inhuman clutch. Dark blood welled from its shoulder, to drip on the earth. One of its arms cinctured her waist while the other immobilized her weapon arm.

"Drop it, Gudrun!" Felimid cried.

She trusted him and did so. He snatched it from the ground, a blade just broader than his own and maybe a quarter pound heavier, with edges as sharp and a sea-gray glimmer running along its patterned blade. He struck with skill, teeth set against the pain he knew would jolt his other arm when the blow landed. Kissing Viper's edge cut into the seed-god's back, across the spine where the kidneys were in a man. Dense muscle resisted the stroke; a spine like iron all but clanged under the impact. A chip of meat flew up.

The godling swung about on malformed feet, still holding

Gudrun before him—it—so that Felimid could not strike again. Then Hemming the Saxon ran up behind it to sink an axe between its shoulder blades, and it staggered. Gudrun tore herself free.

It lurched toward her, reaching out with a lust the bard found dreadful and piteous. Seed-time rites in a place where seed-time and harvest were no longer known, a land decayed until both were meaningless. This sad god might have haunted his deserted temple for two hundred years for all they knew.

Gudrun was no sentimentalist, and she had known rape before. Standing her ground, she dealt the creature a savage kick where anything male and warm-blooded can be hurt. It roared.

Spears flew at the god from two sides. They pierced to the sockets, where they would have driven completely through mortal flesh of the same thickness. The being staggered, then fell down. As it attempted to rise, Felimid hewed away one mushy, diseased hoof, then put all his power and skill into a drawing cut that opened its hairy throat.

The pirates gathered about it to smash and beat. Caprine legs kicked spasmodically, then drew up in a slow, final reflex. The bearded face, part goat, part human, which had expressed a wild, demented power, in death was only grotesque. Yet it was all that remained of an earth divinity, and Felimid, too, had his descent from earth-mother Danu. He looked elsewhere when Gudrun cut away the goaty privates for a trophy.

He couldn't feel deeply horrified by her act. His shoulder burned like fire and his head seemed to float. His lover noticed then, after wiping her gory hands on the ground.

"Bragi! What is your hurt?"

"My shoulder's out of joint," he said between shut teeth. "It's nothing that cannot wait if you care to mutilate anything else."

"Bastard," Gudrun said with affection. "Brace yourself and be quiet. Yes, that is only out of joint. I will put it back for you."

She performed as she had said, swiftly and competently. Sprains and dislocations were among the injuries she handled most often. As Felimid's shoulder clicked back into place, he quivered, seeing visions, and the cold sweat poured from him. Then the bearded faces of Gudrun's rogues were real again, and a hot ache in his shoulder, and Gudrun's own face—square cut, wide of cheekbones and mouth, with full, forthright lips. When he noticed her still holding up her muddy breeches, he had to smile.

She had taken back Kissing Viper. He didn't remember that.

"My sword is in these willows somewhere," he said.

"You hear that? I have a gift for the man who finds it," Gudrun promised her band. "Do not stand there idle, my blood drinkers, for I have not changed my mind about leaving with the tide."

The pirates went through the willows virtually leaf by leaf. A Goth named Tiumals found Kincaid where the sword had fallen among rank sedges. Felimid thanked him and promised him a song; Gudrun gave him a gold thumb ring.

The sun had fully risen by then, and the fen mist had begun to disperse. The pirates dispersed also, going to the shore, few pausing to look at the dead godling. Those who did saw green shoots sprouting beside the hacked carcass. They grew throughout the trampled area of the fight, on every spot where splashes of potent blood had dropped.

Before the mist was entirely burned away by the sun, *Ormungandr* swept downstream toward the Wash, through a blue and silver day, through the endless reed beds. Lines of wild duck flew noisily over, and all the world seemed ocean.

With his bardic sight, Felimid saw the brilliant faerie sails in the Wash at once. The Children of Lir had waited to meet them, and came now with sails flying jauntily. It was well that Gudrun's crew, and Gudrun herself, could not see them unaided, so angered were they after their experiences in the fens, and so eager to have someone to blame.

The unpredictable sea folk had no apologies in them.

"Where are the Saxons?" Felimid asked.

"Well on their way to Kent by now, if they can reach it. I rather believe they will."

"You might have stopped them."

"We might have stopped them the day we encountered them. Your lady forbade it. Loudly. Then she mishandled her ship into the fens. Let her blame herself, not complain to us by your mouth. She scarcely *can* complain."

Gudrun seethed when Felimid repeated that to her.

"It went for nothing at all, then! Complain! Tell that shark from me that if I do complain, it will be to his face, if he has the courage to let me see it. Yes, there must be some explaining done . . . so, let us return to Sarnia. We had better prepare to greet some hard visitors."

XI

Oh, Gudrun's out again, mannies,
And Gudrun's word is law,
And Gudrun Blackhair's the bravest chief
That ever the green sea saw!
     —Felimid mac Fal,
     Ballad

Cudebehrt swung his sword War Shuttle. It sprang at Vithils's red head. The big man shifted his stance on the gurgling floor planks while Cudebehrt threatened his thigh, shoulder, hip, and other thigh in succession. Each time, Vithils turned or stopped the stroke with his deftly handled shield.

"Hah!" Vithils said. "I know this is practice, brother, but you can wield a swifter blade than that without peril of maiming me."

"Can I, now? How is this?"

Cudebehrt cut at his skull. Vithils raised shield with a circling motion. Sweeping it up and over to cover his head was the best way, though not the shortest. Lifting it straight past his face would have blocked his vision, giving Cudebehrt the chance to strike below his waist instead, while Vithils was self-blinded.

The red-bearded man had last made that mistake in his early training, as a lad with a changeable voice.

Although the right one, his action proved somewhat slow. Cudebehrt pulled the force of his blow in dismayed haste. He'd have opened his half brother's skull else.

Vithils resumed practice without comment. Cudebehrt and he both knew that the smaller man would never have come that

128

close to striking him down a year before. His shield arm was not what it had been, that was all, and a thing he had known already. He stopped only when he could barely lift the orbed round of linden wood for weariness.

Their practice had been straitly confined in the packed warship. For just that reason the two had exercised with weapons each day on the water. There was hard sea fighting to be done shortly, and practice under the same conditions was the most useful kind.

The green-and-black sail passed between long sandbanks. The other ships followed it closely. Ahead lay the isle of Thanet, rich trading depot and seat of the Kentish kings.

Flat, pebbled beaches lifted to dunes of buff sand crested with sea grass. Beyond rose the walls of a long stockade enclosing the royal dun. Felimid would have recognized it at once. He'd been a guest there in former days, and the view of it he had received going away had been the best one. Kentish hospitality had proved less than irreproachable for him. Of course, that had been in King Oisc's time. Ricsige ruled now.

The wakes trailing creamy behind the Saxon ships traveled straight as taut ropes to the margin. Few trading ships were there to crowd them for anchorage, the season having barely opened. Later, there would be many.

A band of king's men winking with gold rode down to the shore. Sand flew in spurts from under the hooves of their small British horses. Reining them in sharply with rope bridles, the riders sat clumsily by Celtic standards, their bright cloaks flying in the wind on one side, pressing against the wearer's bodies on the other in rippled folds. They gripped their steeds' barrels with breech-clad thighs cross-gartered with studded leather straps.

"Welcome, Vithils," their leader said, saluting. His followers echoed that cry, raising their spears. "The king will be joyful to know that you have arrived, you and your war men so proudly equipped. All Kent's fighting men are impatient to fare with you after Blackhair."

"And that will happen soon," Vithils answered courteously. "Meanwhile, we will share the banquet at Ricsige's table, and we will make warlike plans both drunk and sober, if we may greet in person his father's wise son."

"We will take you to the hall now, if you like."

Vithils left formal phrasing and shook his head. "You know

me better than that, Stur. I won't stand under a roof or sit at
my ease until I see my men settled in their quarters.''

Stur Worferth's son, who led the king's household troopers,
fingered his yellow-brown beard. He caught a louse and
absentmindedly cracked it as he answered.

"You won't find anything to displease you there. We can't
fit them all in the hall, yet we've provided for them. Come
and see. We've both slept worse ourselves.''

Outside the royal dun stood long barrack houses. Vithils
walked through them, finding them well built and appointed.
Clean sleeping straw rustled in heaps, the gray rounded cones
of clay ovens sat in threes like helmets, and cooking hearths
sheltered under leather awnings. Many of Ricsige's own fighting men, from all over Kent, camped in these barrack houses
already, but with some crowding there was space for the Saxons,
too. The royal dun itself would contain only about four hundred,
and Ricsige's feasting hall proved to be straining at the walls
when Vithils, Cudebehrt, and a score of fighters tramped sea-
stained into it.

They had kept their weapons about them. This was not a
sign of mistrust, but the reverse. It showed that they were
thought well-conducted men who did not have to be relieved
of their arms to prevent trouble. Ricsige greeted them warmly
in the dim hall with its great central pillar. It had carried the
name of a mirthless, niggardly house in his father's day.

"Welcome, my friend Vithils," the king said from among
his *gesiths*. "You're known as a mighty achiever of feuds, and
this will rank with the greatest. For you there is honor to avenge,
and lost henchmen, and a ransom paid for you, wealth of your
people to regain; for me a father's death, and the pride of all
ships now held unworthily in a robber's hands. *Ormungandr*
belongs to Kent. She must come back to Kent.''

Ricsige leaned forward in his seat as he spoke the latter
words, desperately eager. Vithils did not show that he thought
the speech untimely drivel, verging on rudeness. A slightly
longer speech of welcome before discussing their mutual purposes would have been fitting, and Ricsige had at least the
name of a courteous man. Perhaps he was so desirous of proving
himself a war leader as well as a dreamer that he had lapsed.

"Can we find *Ormungandr* in a harbor," Vithils said, "she
will come back to Kent indeed, lord. With a cargo of dead
pirates! And there you touch nearly on something I would say.

We met *Ormungandr* on our way to your hall. Yes. Gudrun Blackhair came to destroy us with a sudden onslaught!''

"What said you?" Ricsige leaned farther forward, in the midst of an outcry of intense comment. "Blackhair intercepted you? So! I can see that she did not destroy *you*, my guest. What became of *her*?"

"I cannot say. We were parted by Odin's own wind. The god favored us, in that she was driven into the Wash and may never come out again if the stories I hear of that place are a tithe true. We escaped the wind's whole force and made our way west to bring this word to you, for if she survives, she must pass this isle on her way to Sarnia—and here we have a great force gathered to sunder her as she tried to sunder us."

"You could have waited to waylay her," commented one of the *gesiths*, a rangy killer named Oswy with a jealous glint in his eye. Not among the greatest warriors, he yet liked to believe he was. "You did not have to scurry to us for help, if you are the men I've heard you are. Did she put a lasting fear into you when she captured you last summer?"

"Enough, Oswy!" Ricsige barked.

"I will answer that." Vithils looked unwinkingly at the pockmarked *gesith*. "You take a deal upon yourself for a man not even drunk, Oswy the Hasting. I'll concede that you might do better against a woman than I. You had more practice killing them, and children also, at the fortress of Anderida—didn't you? I have not heard of you killing any men of outstanding fame. Myself, as all know, I have slain more pirates than you have emptied horns of ale. However, let's see."

Vithils lowered his heavy buttocks to a bench and planted his elbow—his left elbow—upon the battered table. Even in the dimness, men saw the huge V-shaped scar impairing the muscle. Yet it remained an uncommonly strong arm.

"Care to match me?" he asked.

Long-armed, big-wristed, and big-handed, Oswy showed an arrogant grin. "You ask to be humbled. I'd spare you that."

"Kind," Vithils said. "Yet you'd be kinder to show me when I'm overreaching myself, that I may know better next time. Sit down, Oswy, here with me and pit your wrist against mine. Sit. Unless you are the one afraid of a humbling."

The foundations of Oswy's grin shifted a little. He hesitated for a moment, wondering if he could avoid the testing. A second look at the scar hacked into the meat of Vithils's upper arm gave him confidence. Spreading his hands in an indulgent gesture, he seated himself by the huge Saxon.

Their toughened palms smacked together. Oswy's grin became a rictus as he felt Vithils's grip. They strained back and forth for a long minute before the Axe slammed Oswy's hand to the table. Vithil's harsh face showed little strain; only Cudebehrt and one or two others guessed how his shield arm must be hurting. Oswy's pocked visage showed astonishment covering hatred.

"Blackhair bested me when my arm was sound," Vithils said, rising, "and I bested you after it was wounded sore. I look forward to the day that you meet her, boaster."

"So do I!" Oswy blustered, resisting an urge to nurse the hand that had felt Vithils's loving grip. "I reckon her henchmen have done all the things the stories credit to her, and that I'll demonstrate."

"Aye, as successfully as you humbled me. Gudrun Blackhair is mine if I can reach her, Oswy; be content with her henchmen. They did all her reputed deeds anyhow."

"That's no safe man to belittle," the king observed to his spokesman Anlaf.

"He's strong, lord."

"Come! You are over-safe, and there is no need of it with me. There are scores of strong men who do not impress me. This one knew that Oswy is a Hasting, and was at Anderida twenty years past. He knew it pat when they happened to cross wills. He has the story of each *gesith* here in that red head, and much else besides. Of this I'm sure."

Anlaf was also sure.

"Now let us draw some lots for who goes out to wait for Blackhair!" the king cried. "What do you say, Vithils? A few ships among the sandbanks off Thames-mouth, and others in a fair ambush site across the strait?"

"Good measures in themselves," Vithils agreed. "I'd add this. *Ormungandr* may never be taken back by you. She was your sire's, as all men know. Now the ship is a weapon in Blackhair's hands, and far too swift for gentle measures. The ship may have to be sunk or broken before we can take the pirate."

"Sunk? *Ormungandr*?" Ricsige turned red, then pale. "Never! She's the pride of Kent!"

"The pride of Kent has been mauled by Blackhair, like the

pride of the Elbe Saxons. Neither can be whole again while she runs free. Maybe she cannot be taken while *Ormungandr* rides the sea in one piece.''

"Is this Vithils speaking? She can be taken like any other pirate. No, my guest, I will not lend my word to that. Let Blackhair return to Sarnia if she must. Then we will go there in overwhelming force and get the ship that way. She cannot take it up her cursed cliffs for safe keeping!''

"Lord, we should take her when we can, in such ways as she can. Sending men against her with commands laid upon them to be careful of her ship is . . . is like shackling their weapon arms! It's almost to be guilty of their deaths! We may catch her here in the strait—I say *may*—if we hunt her hard and strike with all our might.''

Ricsige shook his head with the occasional great stubbornness of a weak man facing a stronger. "I will not sanction it! I tell you, Vithils, the gods have frowned on Gudrun Blackhair, and she will not prosper. I have seen this in dreams, and you say yourself that Odin's wind drove her into the Wash. We all know what a place of horrors that is! She may not come out. I may have to search for *Ormungandr* there, in the fens, and find her riding empty, unmanned. Or not at all! But she must be regained without damage if that can be done. You will not sink her.''

Controlling himself, Vithils said, "It's for your judgment, King.''

"Come, my friend." Ricsige may have thought his own smile friendly; it showed as triumphant. "If my way does not succeed, we can give some thought to yours. It's early yet.''

"Early, by the gods!" Cudebehrt hissed to his brother. "It is never too soon for warriors to die because their master is avid! Ricsige is a fool who wants to be his father and thinks his father's ship will fulfill that desire!''

"Quiet," Vithils said. His voice was pitched for Cudebehrt's ears alone, though some doubtless heard him in the packed hall. "If I dispute him more, he'll grow more stubborn. That will do no good. Maybe his own *gesiths* will talk him out of it later. Whether they do, or whether they do not, I won't wait on his permission. If I meet Blackhair on the sea with *Ormungandr* beneath her, I will forget in the heat of fighting that the dungbag ship is peace-holy, or supposed to be. It'll be very sad, but far beyond mending. Now let's drink.''

The servants poured great bubbling jacks of ale. Vithils and Cudebehrt imbibed with mature relish, and passed the word to the barrack houses with the trundled barrels. No men of theirs were to row in the ships that went to await Blackhair in the strait. No men of theirs would give blood to obey foolish prohibitions.

Gudrun did not appear for two days. Even her famous weather-luck could not always be perfect, nor could even *Ormungandr* sail against the wind. Thus another company, coming from another direction, arrived at Thanet first.

The ships were sighted as they rowed past the white cliffs that had fronted so many invaders; the seafaring brewers from Spain, the first Celts with their iron swords, the Romans, and lately the sea wolves. Three mounted shore watchers looked with experienced eyes and wondered, as a raw wind blew rolling waves onshore.

"That's a strong company, but can it be a high one?" asked a leather-capped man with a graying beard. He shifted his buttocks on the wooden saddle. "Those ships are old. I think they cannot have been much even when land-virginal."

"You're right," one of his companions said, a little cocksurely. "The sort of longboats farmers use for one crossing, if they make it! And bringing with 'em their ducks, pigs, and maybe a cow tied helpless on kelp. They are not commoners who row them now, though."

"Freshly tarred and carrying peace signs," the first man ruminated. "War shields along the gunwales. They row like warriors, and—that chant settles it." A loud war song carried over the sea. "Jutish! They will be the men from Westri, Eadwulf."

"It's likely," Eadwulf replied, sure of himself still. He chuckled. "Blackhair must have done a thorough fire-raising at Hamo, if Cerdic comes in ships that mean. Let's joke with them."

"Let's remain here and signal Thanet as we're supposed to do," growled his companion. "If you joke with Cerdic's pride, you have to be prepared for his jokes in return."

It was not Cerdic but his son who brought the three sorry ships to Thanet. Young and vainglorious, it hurt him to do so; but the hundred fifty warriors he led ashore, busked and equipped, filled him with enough pride to compensate. The forces of Edricsburg, Kent, and Westri thus gathered together

134

had one day to mingle before Gudrun appeared.

The fair wind she awaited came at last, blowing from the northeast down through the strait. She raised her crimson sail. The Children of Lir in their graceful faerie ships kept pace with her, and Decius stood ready to perform her orders at her left hand, while Felimid stood at her right with an arm about her waist. His enchanted harp nested in the crook of the other.

She went arrogantly through the strait with her crimson sail spread to the wind. Ships lurking behind sandbanks and below heedlands raced to catch her, their crew's efforts all spent for nothing. She had miles of open water to use, and possessed the most agile ship asea. Two unlucky vessels did crowd her a little; they began leaking badly when Nacrantal's folk sabotaged them unseen, and wallowed to safety with their crews bailing assiduously. Curses flew with the water from the bailing scoops.

"It is almost too easy," Gudrun said with real regret, as the sea broadened before them.

"Almost," Felimid agreed. "We might have been taken then, with a little bad luck. Your god-enemy could have seen to it, Gudrun. He interfered before. I wonder why he held back his hand just now?"

Gudrun looked at the free wide sea stretching far away. She smiled at her lover.

"Odin can do nothing to me that is not in my fate. He failed to have me destroyed in the fens. He failed to trap me here. The Norns weave." She threw out her arms and raised a joyful face to the windy sky. "They weave against you, old god! You and your thralls are going to lose!"

"That's the talk!" Decius said. Wind prowled through his black hair. "We missed Vithils by a gnat's wing; we'll have him at Sarnia."

Felimid's harp began to sing, a light song about a group of hunters who chased a lynx, only to meet with endless mishaps. Men joined in the refrains as *Ormungandr* sped on. The humor aboard was merry.

XII

Who will not when he may, may not when he would.
　　　　　　　　　　　　　—Waldin the Frank

Bitter smoke hung visibly over the land, and sent its odor out to sea. Felimid was sure the carved nostrils of *Ormungandr*, that great dark war dragon, widened and suffused to the stench, and that the ship turned of its own will toward the source.

"This is where Arnehad, Waldin, and Njal went raiding," he said. "Five gold coins says it is their work."

"I'm to wager with you?" Rowan asked. "You, who know the speech of the wind? That would be a fool's bet, and I don't have so many gold bits. Anyhow, I think the same. I'll just believe you."

"The company you keep has made you untrusting, and so young," Felimid sighed. "The wind has not spoken to me on this matter, and I've no more certain knowledge than you. I do not tempt my friends with fools' bets. Say ten?"

A lace-winged, white bird of air perched unseen on the bard's wrist as he spoke. It trilled laughter, yet Felimid had no reason to blush, and didn't. The sprite had flown to him from the shores of Kent. It knew no more of what might be happening upriver in Gaul than he did.

"They may be ours, or may not," Gudrun said. "We can await them at the river-mouth."

That course appealed to Felimid's indolence, and seemed practical besides. The river-mouth was their agreed meeting place. If the three chieftains were truly raiding upstream, they would have to return, and if the signs of plunder were due to some other band of pirates, the men of *Ormungandr* would gain nothing by seeking them out. The fire might not have been raised by sea robbers at all, if it came to that. Gaulish bandits or feuding landowners might be the culprits. Gaul under the rule of King Clovis's sons was anything but a quiet or orderly country.

They waited and kept watch. Felimid had learned by then that much of the pirate trade consisted in just waiting. One waited in ambush for ships which sometimes never came along; one waited throughout the winter for open seas, and grew dangerously bored; one waited for favorable weather; one waited for the right wind. The waiting was done in company Felimid would never have chosen, too, with some exceptions like Decius and young Rowan.

"What say you to some sword practice?" he asked.

Gudrun agreed at once. She took sword, shield, and helm to the water's edge, where Felimid joined her, his own shield a two-foot circle of linden wood instead of the small oval targe he normally liked best. For mass battle he wanted more of his body covered, and mass battle was coming.

"Let you fly inland, friend, and discover whose smoke that is and what they are doing," Felimid said to the lacy sprite. "I'll give you the story of Emer's only jealousy for that favor, and maybe the tale of Mac Datho's pig."

The insubstantial wings fluttered. Like a hawk from a falconer's wrist, the sprite rose from Felimid's hand, to circle above the trees before departing. Its absence removed no weight from his arm, for the airy being was weightless. Felimid drew his blade, smiling.

He saluted Gudrun. Her gray eyes lighted. She came to meet him, knees slightly bent, Kissing Viper angled back over her shoulder. Her red shield covered her from collarbone to waist.

Kincaid flickered in the bard's hand, a nimble blue-white tongue. The pair circled, moving with feet placed well apart for balance. The swords flashed, rang, and slithered together, whirled apart, sought a way past skillfully handled shields with a purpose that just stopped short of being earnest. It was rough, teasing play with excitement in the possibility of harm, and a needful trust in the opponent-partner.

Gudrun worked unpredictably around the edge of her red shield, sending Kissing Viper forth to strike from above, beside, and even beneath the rim. Felimid once had to leap like a dancer to avoid a cut of the latter sort.

"Have a care, Gudrun!" he said. "You will be spoiling your own fun!"

"Not I, lover. I did not come—within a palm—of your jewels. Nor would I! Ah-hah!"

Her gasp of triumph was uttered too soon. Felimid saw the feint and was ready for the real attack, turning it with shield and sword edge. They pulled the force of their cuts at the last instant, yet were fascinated by each other's skill and drawn to test it to the utmost. The pirates watched with appreciation, cheering their lady. They felt possessive of her against the stranger who had taken her fancy, and would have enjoyed seeing some of his blood spatter. Yet as the long minutes went by, only sweat ran. It stung their eyes. The pair moved their shields a fraction more slowly, and the feints and slashes themselves were a little less quick. They made slips.

Which of us is really the best? Gudrun wondered. *How hard would I force this contest to learn?*

She pressed a fiercer attack, and the bard responded, catching her blade with a twist of his shield. He took the initiative then, and made her back away a single step before she stood fast, her shield clashing against his. They strained on the river shore.

A veil of shadow seemed to fall between them. Was the bard not aware of it? His face expressed only gasping mirth as sweat ran from his eyelids, nose, and chin.

I could slay you.

The sacrifice might buy me Odin's favor again. All would be as before. . . .

No!

Gudrun sprang backward, lowering Kissing Viper's point.

"Enough, Bragi! We will have no strength for our real foes at this rate!"

Panting, he agreed. He generally agreed to her suggestions. She sometimes wished he would not. His ideas were a constant fountain, many of them feasible, all of them clever, but he left it to her to put them into action, to give the necessary orders. It was annoying sometimes. She did not want him to threaten her leadership, but . . . it was annoying sometimes.

She took off her helmet and undid her thick black hair with one hand, shaking it out, letting the air cool her head. In the singing darkness behind her eyes she saw a stark graybeard riding an eight-legged horse, followed by a troop of dead men.

Go embrace Hel, you wolf god! She is your sort of woman,

not I! You wanted me to slay Bragi. I beat you then!

Felimid, who had bruises and one red scratch, stepped gracefully close to her and kissed her between their two shields. It wasn't the most satisfying way to kiss, but all ways were good. For a moment he thought the cries from *Ormungandr* were comments of encouragement, then wondered if it might be alarm. He ended the kiss to look.

He hadn't noticed anything even momentarily amiss with Gudrun.

Something drifted from upstream. It moved idly, half submerged, with a live shape clinging to it—or maybe a dead one, for the shape never moved. It floated toward the margin where Felimid and Gudrun stood.

"A man," Felimid said, and then drew less obvious conclusions. "A peasant, from the tunic, and no knowing who hurt him or whether he's alive, but that appears to be a door holding him up. He'd the presence of mind to escape into the river from carnage, it seems."

"What of it?" Gudrun demanded explosively. She had just thought of killing this man, and now to have him obliviously turning his attention to some random stranger was enough to make her think of it again.

Felimid looked at her quizzically. "What of it? By Cairbre's fingers, he's coming to us as though expected. I'm not about to scorn a river god's gift before I even know what it is, and whether it's useful."

Drawing off his footgear, he waded into the stream and gripped the floating timber with its burden. Then, bracing himself, he dragged it to the water's edge. Exhausted and barely conscious, the river's gift muttered. He showed the marks of savage blows. Felimid felt him gently for broken bones and discovered none.

"Bragi, he's nothing to us," Gudrun said impatiently. "Cut his throat, for you need the practice."

"I dragged him ashore, Gudrun. He's mine, and I will not cut his throat. I'll confess I do not know just what, if anything, I can do with him, or what use he might be. When he recovers, I'll find out. It would be good to know who hurt him, strangers or our boys."

"He's an ignorant peasant who wouldn't know. He probably cannot tell a Dane from a Jute. Still, as you say, he's yours. Do as you wish with him, but get him out of my sight for now."

"What? Gudrun, that is how you speak to a dog you do not particularly care for. I'm your man! And were I not your man, still too good for that tone."

Gudrun Blackhair flushed scarlet. "Oh, Bragi! I did not mean to insult you. It itches me to wait here, that is all . . . and seeing this fellow reminds me of those on Sarnia. We should be there."

She would not admit to being haunted by Odin's curse.

Felimid frowned. "That's not reason enough."

"Pardon me, then. I've Loki's temper, as you know. I was wrong."

"Yes. Let us forget it." Still puzzled, the bard called Giguderich and Martin, two of the pirates, to carry the stranger into the ship. They handled him like a sack of grain and stowed him aboard with less care, so that he lay in a dripping huddle.

They waited the rest of the day. No vessels came down the river, nor did Felimid's white bird of air return with tidings—or without them, either. When the river's gift regained full consciousness, the bard was beside him.

A stubbled, heavily muscled man, he sat up suddenly. First he saw the bard, and then his glance raced *Ormungandr's* length, showing him the nature of the ship and its lawless crew, made obvious by the weapons, the scars, and the serpent head. He vented a wild laugh.

"More of you devils! More! Well, you are too late to rob my folk! You must take what your fellow thieving bastard dogs have left in other places! May you find flux, sacred fire, and the plague when you get there!"

He spewed water and coughed convulsively. Gudrun laughed merrily.

"You see what overmuch kindness earns you?"

"Exasperation! How well I do know. Hear me, fellow. I like your flow of speech, but it hasn't contained what I wish to know. Who are you, and what is your place?"

"I haven't one. Your friends burned it."

"So? How are you after knowing they were our friends? No matter." It did matter, but Felimid sensed that letting the man know might make him stubborn, whether or not it stood to reason. "What was your place, while you had one?"

He set his long-fingered, versatile hand on the pommel of his knife to stress that the question was serious.

"Ammian's estate," the man said grudgingly, as though the name was enough to identify it anywhere.

"Ammian's estate, and we missed looting it!" Felimid had never heard of it. "Maybe we can still take the plunder from those who have it. Were they many?"

"Three shiploads of raiders. They were Franks, or two lots of them were. I recall one leader, an ugly devil with half his nose missing, who killed whatever he saw."

Arnehad, Felimid thought. Then he spoke, changing the subject. "And your own self? Have you a name and a useful trade? What was it you did on Ammian's estate?"

It began to penetrate the stranger's dazed mind that this man was an unusual sort of pirate. He was not disposed to be friendly on that account.

"Who wants to know? Interested in the profit you can make by selling me?"

"I'm growing the least bit tired of discourtesy," Felimid complained. He took the stranger's ear between finger and thumb. "Continue surly, friend, and I may just begin cutting. Now, have you a trade or not? It may make the difference to you between getting a good master or a bad."

"They're all bad. Some are worse than others, that's the nutmeat of it. I was a baker . . . am a baker, and a brewer, of course."

"How good are you?"

"The best along nine leagues of this river."

"That will do. Pirates eat like honest folk, and the bread on Sarnia could be better. Get yourself dry and warm, and tell any who ask that Bragi protects you. In return you may speak with deference and answer when I call your name, which I haven't been hearing yet."

"It's Brac. Lord."

"Come to me on Sarnia and I'll put you to work."

The bird of air appeared before sundown, to confirm what Brac had unwittingly implied. The next day brought the ships themselves. Two galleys and a long Danish rowboat came down the river, expertly rowed and somewhat low in the water. The pirates chanted as they pulled on their oars. In each ship captives huddled, men, women, and children whose fate now was slavery, though belike it would be no worse for them than the lives they had known before.

The captains saluted Gudrun as they approached; Arnehad, the wild Frank from the northern *limes*, with the back of his head shaved to the scalp and a long, barbaric tress dangling from the top of his head, snuffling through the repulsive vent

141

in the side of his nose; Waldin, more civilized in veneer, his hair and moustache flowing long in the fashion of his tribe's nobility, his tunic and footgear showing Roman influence while his wolfskin cape and tattooed limbs betrayed how thin the veneer was: and Njal the Sea-Gray, a Dane like Gudrun from the lands around the Baltic, a big man whose hair had early turned the color of ashes. If anything he was more lethal than the others, and unlike them, he was not sworn to Gudrun Blackhair. Instead he had come south as her ally for a summer's raiding.

"How went the business?" Gudrun asked.

"It was not bad," Arnehad snuffled. "We ravaged one estate the Saxons hadn't touched. A sorry place and barely worth our while, lady, but it did have beasts and seed grain, and it burned well."

"The usual slaves, too," Njal added carelessly.

Arnehad trumpeted sideways, out of the grotesque hole in his nose. "Never mind that piddling stuff! How went *your* venture, lady? Did you meet Vithils? Never thought of that matter, did you, Waldin, you thickwit?"

Waldin looked murder, but kept his tongue behind his teeth. Gudrun clenched her own a little before she replied.

"We met him. Near the Wash we came together, he with four ships, and before we had passed beyond a few light greetings, we were parted by the wildest squall you might see in a year. *Ormungandr*—yes, even *Ormungandr*, my men!—was driven into the fens before it. I will tell you on Sarnia what happened there, and your eyes will freeze at the sights I conjure. But Vithils escaped me. He is safe in Kent now, plotting with that dreamer Ricsige. We must take him when he comes to us, that is all."

"All!" Waldin burst forth. "All! That is all! He was supposed to die before he reached his allies and formed their union. All we have to do now is battle the lot of them together, with Vithils's brain to benefit them. That's a large *all*, Blackhair."

"We can talk of that on Sarnia," Njal said. "We should be quitting this place before soldiers of Frankdom follow us here; the questions can come later."

Gudrun looked at him sharply but gave her agreement. Felimid thought it best to go swiftly himself. The crews of the four ships would have little chance to mingle at the river's mouth. They would do so freely when they came to Sarnia, though, and *Ormungandr*'s crew would talk of what they had seen and heard to their comrades. Cairbre and Ogma! How they would talk!

"And among all the exaggeration and bubble there will be two things emerging like rocks from the foam of the bright sea, my darling," he said to Gudrun as her serpent ship raced through the spring night. "That Odin brought the winds which tore you away from Vithils, and that ere it happened, the Children of Lir might have sunk and drowned him in gray fathoms . . . except that you ordered them not to do it."

"The first I could not help. The second I am proud of! That man is not a dog to be drowned, and I am not Urbicus, long may he rot! No, Bragi, do not expect me to rue that, ever."

"I'll not. I know better, believe me truly. But it's my neck and everyone else's you ran into a noose by your fierce honor, and I have my doubts that the men will understand. Na, that's evasion; what I am meaning is that they may understand too well. I foresee storm waters, Gudrun."

The storm waters burst. There was uproar and fury in the plunder-strewn hall on Sarnia when the story was told and its meaning appreciated. Not even Decius and Felimid approved what Gudrun had done, though they stood by her against the bawling horde.

Pascent's was the most forthright voice. Crushing his gaudy stocking cap in a heavy fist, he stated his opinions loudly enough to shake the rafters.

"Betrayal! You betrayed us to hang-nooses, all of us, nothing less! Vithils the Axe was helpless before you; Nacrantal there could have wrecked him *before* the demon wind you speak of started to blow. You wouldn't have it. You let Vithils go to join Ricsige, who's a weakling, and Cynric, who's a whelp. Once he lends them his backbone and experience, well, I can feel hemp on my neck, Blackhair! Without him, this vengeance fleet would be nothing to trouble us. Now it is a thing worth fearing. You betrayed us, you failed us. The chieftain who does that is not to be served."

"Njal and I do not even serve you," growled Pigsknuckle Hromund. "We came south for good plunder, not to fight Vithils the Axe and two kings in a quarrel that isn't even ours." He blew noisily from his nose on the rushes before he continued. "You bungled, Blackhair. I'm minded to take my ship and my men and try my luck farther south. We can pass this way again when all's over."

"So I do think," Gray Njal agreed. "Although it is not my

fight, I would partake of it because I am your guest, if you were managing it well. You are not.''

"I am with Pascent," Waldin said, standing in the trappings of his lost nobility. "You failed us all. When you spared Vithils the Axe, you were not sparing us. Many and many a one here will die for that gesture—if we are found! I, too, think I may take my ship and go. Who would go with me?''

The support that resounded was loud. Waldin folded his arms and stared challengingly at his lady.

Felimid, her spokesman, laughed aloud as at a splendid joke. Rising with all the confident grace he could summon, he smiled at the furious gang before him; the former noble of Frankdom, the gross Dane, the irascible, crafty one-time merchant with the Greco-Gaulish blood seething in his veins, and all the others.

"Is that right, now? You would all desert and flee from a name? Your lady has made one mistake and you will run from her?

"Waldin, how far will you run, do you think? You cannot return to Gaul, and Vithils will not forget you were a captain of the lady's, if he wins. I say if. I believe we will win, with you or without you—and we will not be forgetting that you scurried like a mouse, either! Sooner or later we will come for you, never suppose otherwise. Run, and you will face either Vithils or us with none to protect your back.''

"And who is *us*, you bench ornament?" Waldin sneered. "Most of the voices here sounded with me.''

"Not mine, you jumped-up barbarian," Decius said coldly. "Bragi is right; I will not forget you if you run. I did not hear Arnehad agree with you. Was I wrong, halfnose?''

Arnehad snuffled sourly. "Agree, Decius? So much as that, no. But the lady did ill. It's a thing she should answer. We're her eaters, and we did not deserve that. You should have rid us of Vithils when you had the chance. However you could.''

"You're still here, though," Felimid said. "The Children of Lir are not absent, either." He bowed to the magical company at the table's end. "You were given the greatest offense; have you nothing to say?''

Niamh spoke for the Children of Lir, in her own voice for once and not through her counselor.

"You slighted us greatly when you would not have Nacrantal destroy the Saxon ships, Gudrun Blackhair! Who led you to them? Who could have rid you of your foes' greatest leader in one opportune hour? You refused that favor, and more, you

forbade it. By my father Lir, I think with your own captains
that you did very ill! Henchmen of yours will die for your
glorious pride.''

Her anger surged like the waves, bursting in rushes of whelm-
ing foam. Gudrun stood fast before the tide and gave her answer.

''If Vithils comes here, it will be he who dies. I was there,
I faced him on the sea. Bragi did, Decius did. You did not.
Even your husband-of-ships did not, not truly. They were hidden invisible. As for my henchmen . . .'' She turned to the
hall at large and lifted her sheathed sword high over her head,
gripping the sheath at the midpoint. ''You are my henchmen,
my guests, and my allies, all here! When have I ever asked
anything of you that I would not do myself, and first? I went
to meet Vithils, and I will be first to meet him again, if it
comes to that! I will bid him fight me himself, just he and I,
sword against axe! I swear it. That is how I will amend my
fault. Who backs me now?''

They roared that they would. But only a third of them.

Pascent spoke for the doubters. ''What if he refuses, or his
friends do not abide by the result? This is not a hero tale from
your northern snows, lady.'' He twisted the final word into an
epithet. ''Now if the sea folk are still willing to aid us, I'd
have you ask their pardon first, and swear on your sword never
to reject any aid they offer again, whether it's to your taste or
not. We are pirates, not some golden warband. Your pirates.
Whether we stay yours depends on you, tonight.''

Waldin seconded him vehemently. Arnehad agreed more
slowly, being a slower man to think, but he agreed. Njal and
Hromund stayed apart, saying neither yes nor no, waiting to
see whether Gudrun would submit to conditions from her own
men.

She ate her pride. ''Nacrantal, Yrnruch! What amends do
you want from me? I swear my oath on this sword I meant no
slight to your honors when I warned you from Vithils the Axe.
It is fitting that he should be mine. He must be mine! I would
be sorry if you give me no further aid because you hold that
your honor is affronted. I value your help. You are my guests
on Brechou, and welcome to share what I have. But it is in
my mind that if you want Brechou, as a haven, you will have
to fight for it, will you or nill you.''

''That will be nothing new,'' Yrnruch said, with an edge
honed on his voice. ''For myself, I am tired of being disturbed
in any place I may happen to make my home, and by the like

of Saxon merchants. Your captains are right, though, Blackhair. If our help is valuable to you, you cannot scorn the manner of it.''

Nacrantal fanned the air mockingly. ''There is too sickly an odor of politeness here,'' he said. ''You are desperate, lady. So are we. We have spent the winter homeless, and Brechou is a refuge where we can rest and fatten for a while. I am ready to fight for it with weapons and sorcery, and any other resources I have. We need not love each other to fight as allies—but you, lady, are arrogant and a fool if you wrinkle your nose at our ways of fighting! Lir and Manannan mac Lir! You have sacrificed more men to Odin than are sitting in this hall! Can you wonder that we are angry when you pretend to be better than we?''

''All my slaughter has been done in the open, not from behind veils of glamor,'' Gudrun retorted, her pride resurging like the sea. ''I am not a wrecker.''

''But we are,'' Niamh said, poison-sweetly, ''and will be with a vengeance when Vithils and his friends come to Sarnia. Let me put it fairly to your men. Is that bad?''

They shouted their approval, stamped and swore and drank to it, Pascent and Waldin leading the chorus. Niamh looked at Gudrun. Her look said plainly, ''You will be deserted by at least half your men if you refuse those terms now.''

Gudrun knew it. She gripped hands with Niamh's husband-of-ships, and embraced Niamh herself before all, about as willingly as she would have embraced an octopus.

''Now, Waldin,'' Pascent said a bit later, grinning over a horn of ale, ''what did you make of all that?''

''The lady's a fiery dreamer,'' Waldin answered. ''I have always known that. Two in three of these dogs will turn like dogs if the fortunes of fighting go too much against them. I have always known that, too. I'm glad the sea folk are on our side . . . if they are.''

''Ah, come now! They are on nobody's side except their own. I think you are right about all the rest. Tell me, why did you join the lady in the first place?''

''I'm a younger son. I quarreled with my brothers, chose the wrong side in a little intrigue and murder, and offended a powerful woman, all at the same time. I have learned to sniff the wind a trifle more carefully since.''

''I'd hope so! Was the woman worth it?''

''No woman is worth it,'' Waldin said flatly. ''I wouldn't

inquire further if I were you."

"As you like." Pascent shrugged. "Do you think Blackhair can stand off the power that's coming against us?"

"You say Blackhair, not we. I know why you joined her, merchant. Your ship was sinking under you and she gave you the choice. Planning to run now? You heard Decius."

"Aye. I'm trembling with terror. Listen, man; I never intended to be a pirate for long. All I want is the treasure to come out of this with a profit, and a ship. I have earned that already. What of you? Are you ready to fight to the last beside your chieftain like some model of honor out of the sagas?"

Waldin smiled bleakly. "It is as you said. This is no hero tale from the lady's northern snows. The knife in the back rules this world, as I have cause to know. I don't trust those Children of Lir. They are fickle as mist. They do not know themselves what they will do next."

"Oh, I'm of your opinion there!" Pascent poured more ale into Waldin's cup, and let the man go on persuading himself. It didn't take him long.

His mistrust included Pascent with everybody else, however. He gripped the captain's brawny arm with bone-hurting force and shoved his face close to the raffish, big-featured one beside him.

"Do not take me for a fool, bully," he said softly. "I know you drank as affably with Hugibert as you're doing with me. Doubtless you spoke to him in this way, too, yet when things went wrong, it was he whom Bragi killed, not you, and I never heard you protest, although you and Hugibert had been such close drinking friends! Do not think to use me as you did him."

"You have it wrong," Pascent said innocently. He struck a sharp blow to the inside of Waldin's wrist and freed his arm. "If Hugibert did try to murder the lady by stealth, it was wholly his own idea, and like him to bungle it. I wouldn't have plotted with such an idiot. You and I can get along, Waldin—if you don't try too many of your Frankish noble's ways with me. I'm not one of the peasants you used to kick. I was born in Massilia, a free port and free city since Caesar's day."

"And one of the worst to be found anywhere," Waldin countered. "Be it so. For the present, we wait and see what happens."

"And if matters go too far wrong . . . we seize our chance," Pascent added.

Waldin nodded slowly.

In private with her lover, Gudrun raged against events, wildly miscalling her own pirates.

"The dogs, the swine, the gutless sea slugs! To talk of deserting me because I failed to make an end of Vithils! Few of them would have gone looking for him!"

"Easy, lover," the bard said mildly. "What else were you awaiting? It's not a tribe you have here, bound together by time and loyalty and blood. They are outlaws bound together by advantage, and they follow you because it profits them. Oh, they boast of you. They are proud to say they are Gudrun Blackhair's, and see folk cringe. But it's only a few, like Decius, Rowan, and I, will stand with you when the boot truly pinches. What you have made here on Sarnia was never meant to last."

"Fires of Surt, you are so bland! Does nothing anger you?"

"Many things. I cannot see this worth spoiling my digestion for, though, Gudrun. They do but want you to use every weapon you have to hand, against a foe who means to destroy us to the last man. I'll not fault them for that! I'll not even fault Vithils for wanting retribution, though I do not intend to let him have it. He's not wrong, he's only the foe we must fight. Remember this, besides. You were and are planning to leave them when it suits you. You mean to take *Ormungandr* into other worlds for a new venture, not so? You have talked of little else to me when we haven't been talking of Vithils and his friends coming south to visit. How long do you reckon most of these reivers will last without you? As soon as you are gone, they will fall apart in disunity and die at the law's hand one by one. Has that troubled you?"

"Later, Bragi! I will go my own way after I've met this threat to them all and broken it! Not before, as they would have done! By Njord of the ships, I have that right! You said it your own self. This is not a kingdom or a family I have here."

"Na, that it's not. You do have a family, though. I've guested with them and seen you make your peace. In your place I'd be thinking of going back to them. Not many who venture into the Otherworlds ever return."

Gudrun for once was slow in answering. "We . . . parted ways long since, Bragi. I know I have won the Dane-king's favor and could return to stay. It's not what I want. I have chosen my path, and I will follow it until I find something of my own that I want to keep."

"So? I thought you had."

"You? To be sure I do, lover, and I will! Do you fancy I would have another beside me, in *Ormungandr*'s bow or in bed?"

"And I'd joyfully be with you in either of those places. It's just that you have not asked me whether I want to be with you in the Otherworlds. I've spoken more than once of my own family in Erin, and of my longing to go there, and you have yet to listen."

"What? You are a man, Bragi! You do not need my leave to see your kin. But you promised to find a way to the Otherworlds with me! You gave your word!"

"I gave my word to find a Gate for you. That I'll do! I said there are more remaining in the west of the world than elsewhere, destroyed as they have been by time and Rome and the Church's ban. And that is true. Not once did I ever say I would go through that Gate with you once it is found! I've been to some of the Otherworlds, Gudrun, and found them not to my liking. You'll be chancing whether you can even eat or drink in the places you'll find. I told you that."

"You gave your word!"

"Then you did not understand what I said. Gudrun, I asked you to come to Erin with me and remain there!"

"You did, and I said no, straightly. I did not quibble as you are doing now! I know you, Bragi. Words are your trade, not truth and hard dealing, but this thing you promised me."

"Acushla, I know what I promised!"

"No sweet words now! Give me true ones. You might have returned to your kindred two years agone. What is so urgent now?"

"Oh, Gudrun, I bound myself to exile for three years and have been in wandering for five. Are you saying it makes no difference, because of that, if I never return to stay? It's what I am longing to do, once we've dealt with Vithils between us."

"You say? Then you can leave now! I do not need you to deal with Vithils, and I can find my way to a Gate of the Otherworlds without you, as well! You disparage my men because they are placeless and faithless, and then you do this to me . . . weasel-squirm out of your given word! You can go, Bragi! Take what you want of gold and raiment, go to Britain or Lesser Britain or whatever land will have you, such as your mangy Erin! Once you are there, you can dream and idle and listen to the blowing winds tell you what happened here on Sarnia! Make a song about it! Maybe one of your measly chiefs will give you a clout of meal to sing it! I see that is the real measure of how you love Gudrun Blackhair.''

''Take payment and go, leaving you to the storm? And that is the real measure of what you think of Felimid mac Fal?'' He used his true name in his heat. ''You do need teaching differently, my sea eagle.''

''Teaching? By you? Get out!''

He didn't; and if any servants heard gasps, blows, the crash of things thrown or overturned in the next hour, they knew better than to meddle or gossip too loudly. The pair were still in the same room at dawn.

In the sea caves under Brechou, at that same time, Niamh and Nacrantal spoke together.

''We do not require this island as desperately as that,'' the sea man opined. ''After tonight I say we do not require Gudrun Blackhair at all. Let's go, and leave her to her self-made fate.''

''We might, yet I would as lief stay. This is a fine place. Besides,'' the sea princess said pensively, ''I would rather see her win than Vithils and Ricsige. She shatters her kind's rule of the sea, with every merchantman she robs and every seacoast hamlet she burns. Those two increase it. Mortal fishermen and traders prosper under them, and their clumsy lumps of wood go out in greater numbers each year. The sea is ours.''

''Yet am I a man. She has not satisfied me for the affront she gave.''

''After the battle is over and she wins it, shark's tooth; only then. We have work to do. Take me to Coriallo, where the human wreckers once had their base and drove bargains with the Cold Ones. I must deal with them, too.''

Nacrantal showed the edges of his handsome teeth. Something in the glint of them, and the lines and angles of his lean face, justified the nickname Niamh had applied to him. He watched as she took the grotesque gold cuttlefish from its box, dangling it between her fingers in the yellow light, where it turned and turned at the end of its chain. Nacrantal's shark smile broadened.

''My ship has been kept ready to sail at a word since you first spoke of this to me.''

XIII

The cock will crow, the sun will rise,
And gore will drench the ships,
That we may prosper on the sea,
What time the oar blade dips.
                    —King Ricsige of Kent,
                        Invocation

Three sturdy brown ships moved across the sea under disciplined oar work, close as a well-made comb and as effective. Edric the Fat stood to the great steering oar of the leading vessel, solid as a tree butt, ponderous as a walrus with legs, breathing the salt air with pleasure. Yet beneath the joy of being at sea and doing a thing at which he was wonderfully skilled, he felt driven by a purpose that hurt. Lives and good treasure would be spent before this matter was concluded. Edric was usually a close man with both.

"Britain!"

The cry touched every man there. Britain, island of the mighty, province of Rome, temptation to every pirate, dream of every landless man, place of holiness and magic—even to barbarians it was an arousing name.

Ottar's berserks felt it, however dimly. Feeling it and despising it, they laughed like trolls coughing. Not for them was land or family, vowed as they were to the battle god, lord of wolves, ravens, and the noose.

"Britain!"

"Soft piece of mud not worth getting on a man's shoes!"

"I wouldn't slaughter its men for practice!"

"Haw haw haw!"

Edric blew through his cheeks like a restive horse. He'd

151

become wearisomely familiar with this kind of noise on their voyage from the Elbs. That each of these madmen was worth ten in a fight made them endurable, no more. He looked forward to having them meet Vithils.

Britain's shores, and the conquered Isle of Thanet at Kent's eastern tip, grew closer, more distinct. Sand and chalk sparkled in the sun. The drab royal hall raised its dark gables against the sky. Gulls shrieked, water slapped, and smells of stable, midden, and cook-house wafted from the low island.

A ship with the White Horse on its sail came out to greet them. Satisfied of the strangers' identity, the coast watcher led them to shore. A special gangway had to be run out for Edric, and even then it bent cracking under his immense weight as he plodded down to the beach of Thanet.

"Is that the lord of Edricsburg?" a scullion muttered, watching from a distance. "I'd be a full month rendering him for lard."

A spear butt struck him between the shoulders. He tumbled flat with a wail, his arm rising to ward further blows. A harsh word caused him to lower his arm again. The companion to whom he's spoken his joking insult began sidling away. He was ordered to stand fast, and did, with a face like curdled whey.

The warrior who had thus surprised them, a well-knit young towhead, set the point of his spear against a quaking belly. He laughed, enjoying himself.

"You'd render the lord of the Elbe for lard, would you? And be a month about it? Dog meat, you merit death for that word."

The scullion began to gibber and plead.

"Yes," the warrior went on. "You should die slow, cooked in a manure heap, but you may come to a better end than that. Get to your work, the both of you."

He gave a hard, careful glance at the pair to be sure of knowing them again.

"Run!" he shouted. "Have the cook set you the meanest, nastiest task he has!"

They ran. The scullion who had spoken so foolishly smirked with lowered head as he went. "Not even a lashing," he said triumphantly. "That Ohrtric is soft."

"Shut up, you fool!" his companion snarled. "Your mouth will dig your grave in the end."

"He's forgotten," the smirker said, but unease rested on his curved back. He had been unwise and knew it.

Ohrtric went down to the beach, spear on his shoulder, and watched mighty Vithils greet his brother-in-law. Legend with a rust-colored beard, huge of chest and limb, he smiled with evident love, smote Edric's heavy shoulder and asked roughly, "What brings you here? Think you I cannot manage the business, or that four ships' companies would not be enough? You cannot have left much to guard Edricsburg."

"It's in the good hands of three boys and a dog," Edric replied. "As for your business here, it's in the hands of a god or I miss my guess. Seventeen berserks have come with a message. Spaedom confirmed it. I'll talk of it with you in the hall, kinsman. You do not imagine I came so far to cluck over you like a mother?"

"You've done just that each time I have been wounded. And what's this of berserks? Yes, I see them coming, and I can smell them from here, too. What made you foul your ship with such?"

"In the hall."

"What, turn around as if I feared to meet them? That is Ottar leading them. I do not budge for him. He can give me civil greeting or walk around me."

"Brother, I say to you, Odin himself sent the clan to me. Slay one and you will have to slay them all."

"Who wants to slay them? I've slain enough berserks to know how it feels. All he has to do is behave as decently as a mad boar."

Ottar shambled up from Edric's vessel. Once he recognized the famed man standing in his path, he swelled with the need to live up to his berserk's reputation. He walked straight to Vithils and peered at him.

"I'm looking for the King of Kent," he said. "You are as good a signpost as any to point me to him."

"If I point you anywhere it will be to someone who can trim your beard and wash you. Then you might be allowed near the king. You might. My brother will see him first."

"Kings always see me when they want to mow their enemies, and they see my kindred. Afraid there will be no need of you, signpost Vithils?"

"I'm a signpost that shows you the way to the barracks only. You will like it. There is ale, plenty of hot food, straw for sleeping, and you are not expected to conduct yourself too well. If you get drunk and start cutting off heads, I will come and cut off yours.''

"The way you did at Mogloe?''

Mogloe was a former battle, at which Ottar and Vithils had fought on different sides. The redbeard grinned.

"I missed you there, in all the confusion. We're on the same side now, strange though that is. No doubt we'll be enemies again another day. If you want to wrestle or practice for it, I'm willing.''

Ottar swaggered around Vithils. He swaggered stiff-legged all the way around him. Vithils stood so relaxed that he yawned.

"You look like a signpost from all sides, Saxon. You stand as still as one, too.''

"One of my arms points the way to Hel. Go sharpen your weapons and your wit. If you haven't thought of something better than signpost to say to me when next we meet, don't say anything. My youngest son can lay his tongue to more than that.''

"I eat youngest sons at the Yule feasts,'' Ottar boasted, "and firstborns at any time.''

He shambled to the barracks, evidently content with those parting words, his clan stamping after him. Vithils went straight to the king's hall.

When he herd the tale of the berserks' coming to Edricsburg, Vithils grew thoughtful but did not look especially happy. King Ricsige's fresh, bearded face flushed with delight. Edric, accustomed to the knowledge, looked from one man to the other, weighing their responses.

"The Victory-Father is with us!'' Ricsige said. "I dreamed of it, and now I see it is true.''

"With us, yes,'' Vithils agreed. "You have just arrived, brother, or you would have heard how Blackhair waylaid me off Anglia.''

"*What?*''

Vithils shrugged and wet his gullet with Ricsige's ale. "The warriors are saying that all the stars were blown out of the sky and the sea bottom exposed. It wasn't like that, though uncanny enough. Odin rode the winds and drove Blackhair before him, into the fens. I felt his cold blasts and saw his valkyrs raging on the gale. We got away from the squalls and worked our way east. That was the last we saw of Blackhair for that time.''

"You do not know that she perished, then?''

"We know that she survived," Ricsige said with rue. "She has been seen at large since then."

"*Huhnhm*. That could be better."

"Yet Odin is against her."

"That doesn't show he is for us," Vithils said. "If Blackhair *were* dead, we could all go home. The Spear-Wielder and his wild hags would rather see mighty bloodshed. If he kept Blackhair from slaying me or me her, and then let her slip past your ambushes here, King, I am guessing that he wants us to come together with our full strength. Yet that does not mean he wants us to win."

"It's bad luck to mistrust the gods, Vithils!" Ricsige said sharply.

"It can be worse luck to feel too sure they are helping you." Vithils's look was dark and brooding. "When could Odin ever be wholly trusted? He has been known to deceive before. He has turned against his favorites before. We don't know. I'm saying that his purposes may not be ours, and that even those berserks and the wizard could be wrong."

"No offense," Edric rumbled from within his heavy chest. "My brother and I offer chiefly to the powers of the sea. We sacrifice to Odin on the greatest holy days and are as pleased when he ignores us. Stark is he."

"With him in the matter, I'm for making a great offering to the sea powers," Vithils said. "The greatest of all, to bring the ships luck."

"You mean—men?"

"Aye, so. Have you slaves or captives to spare, Ricsige?"

"Two or three, perhaps."

"A niggard insult for an occasion like this, with portents like this. One for each ship would be something like it."

"What? Nearly twenty?" Ricsige was aghast. "I—I—"

"A king shouldn't stammer," Vithils said.

"We do not offer that many men even at Yule!"

"This is not Yule! We go to the greatest battle any of us have fought yet, which the powers of the sea can do much to decide! I'd liefer it was only mortal strength against mortal strength and craft, but that's not so." Vithils absolutely glared at King Ricsige. The king shifted his gaze away. Vithils turned to his brother-in-law. "Edric, what do you say? I advise a man to each ship, and we may come to think it was none too much before this is over."

Edric nodded ponderously. His voice rolled slow and heavy as surf when he replied. "I say so, too."

Ricsige had withdrawn into himself, remembering dreams he had had of late, and by the haunted look in his eyes, they gave him small comfort. He shuddered.

"Will you sit there and shiver?" Edric growled. "Your father's blood is unavenged in the sea, his bones yonder in the grave. Behave like this and he will come walking back to madden you! What are twenty-odd thralls and captives to that?"

"Nothing," Ricsige said huskily. "We will make the offering. If I cannot spare so many here, slaves can be bought in London."

"Raid the Thames Valley farther upstream. Get Britons for nothing, and give your weapon men some work."

"It is too far," Ricsige said.

"You mean the Warlord cleared the Thames Valley of your people, and you do not want him riding back," Vithils said harshly. "Well, then, find what useless thralls you can, and the risk is yours if they offend the powers."

"And what would you do?" Ricsige demanded.

"You take tribute of merchants here, don't you?" Edric asked, knowing the answer. "The trading season has begun, and none but hardy men are shipping on the Narrow Sea thus early. Take the first ship that haps by, whether it has scanted your tribute or not. The cargo to your stores, and the crew to the powers."

Both Vithils and Edric saw the king's eyes kindle. He liked the scheme, or his face could not be read. Yet being Ricsige, he grew censoriously noble.

"And you are the men who boast of your fairness to merchants in your own place! What of Edricsburg's honor?"

"But this is Thanet," Vithils said with a carnivore's grin.

Ricsige flushed. He havered and evaded for a while; he called in his counselor and chief men and put the matter to them. He made the issue as complicated and thorny as he could, taking it into twenty irrelevant side paths, but in the end it was decided.

"Find some thralls who are of little use," he said to Chamo the Frank.

The exile saluted and passed on the order. One of the warriors who received it was Ohrtric, and he remembered the mouthy scullion at once. Whistling, he went in search of the fellow, and took his mate for good measure. One screamed and groveled, while the other tried to run, although he had nowhere to go. After fleeing into a cowshed, he seized a wooden shovel from a dungheep and fought with it, so fiercely that he cracked one skull and lamed another man before he was overwhelmed.

"We've one worthwhile offering, at least," Ohrtric laughed. "Ran's daughters will greet you finely on the sea bottom. You should be honored."

Then the thrall began to shake. He was dragged away, cursing his mate's loose tongue from a pit of dread and horror.

Ottar and his fellow berserks were given the task of capturing a ship. They accepted it with glee. In their bloodlust they killed all but eight of the crew, yet the number was made up with purchased slaves, a few Britons from the reed villages on the estuary of the sacred Thames, and one outlaw murderer.

"Eighteen," Ricsige said at last. "Twice nine. It is a good number."

With Aur the elf-locked wizard by his side, he watched the sacrifice performed. One by one the captives died. Some were chopped apart at the bows of the ships, their blood spilling over the cutwater. Some lay bound to logs while the ships were launched over them, crushing their bodies, leaving long red smears in the sand and long agonized screams hanging in the spring air.

One captured mariner walked to his death boldly. He spat on the vessel he was to honor and said loudly, "I hope this ship and all in her are sunk, lost, destroyed, and doomed, and it's to that end I dedicate my blood, long may you rot, King Ricsige!"

The priests gave him special treatment. Lashed to the stem while the ship was launched, he had his throat cut in the water. The blood trailed away in streaks, joining the many others that had dissipated in the sea that morning, from other reddened bows and keels.

"I wouldn't sail in that ship," Edric said to his brother-in-law.

"Nor I," Vithils agreed, finger-combing his red beard.

Ricsige heard them, although they had not spoken loudly. Raising his own voice, he said for all to hear:

"I'll take that challenge, for Odin favors our venture, and his power is stronger than any British curse, were it even a bishop's! I will sail to Sarnia in this ship and no other! Who goes with me?"

The berserks roared their eagerness for the honor. Aur would have declined it, but they vowed he should go with them, since he had taken it upon himself to join them and to come this far. They explained that his other choice was to be cut apart for an additional sacrifice, even if it spoiled the symmetry of the double nine.

"No, my friends, don't do that," Ricsige said. "Hang him for Odin if you must, since he's Odin's servant. It would be fitting."

Aur decided to go with the king and the beast warriors.

"What think you of that?" Edric asked softly.

"Just what you do, brother. Ricsige tries to show that he's braver than we, because we did not butter him. All he has done is show himself the more fool. Well, we have good leaders enough. If that curse comes home, he will be no great loss."

"Yet I'd be sorry to lose the berserks."

"Yes."

Vithils did not let his dislike of the creatures outweigh their value in breaking a battle line. He gazed at the blood smelling shore with its litter of mangled flesh, and his harsh-featured face settled into yet harsher lines. Many such sights had he witnessed before, and the coming battle would show him others. The berserks would make their complete share of the carnage, until one side was shattered.

Cynric, youngest of the leaders, had painted the prows of his own ships with human blood as readily as the others.

"I need the luck even more than you, considering the state of these keels," he laughed. But the laughter had thickened and died in his throat when the priests had used their heavy knives. Now he was more subdued than usual, and he ate sparingly that night.

The morrow saw him recovered and ready to set forth.

XIV

A grotesque figurehead shone back distorted from star-glit-tering water, utterly calm. Thin-bladed oars dipped and rose beneath Nacrantal's sail. The sea man stood with his cloak and hair unstirring, like the air.

Niamh stood beside him. She might have been leagues away. She did not ignore him; simply, she was somewhere else in her soul, a place those of the royal house of the Children of Lir sometimes went when their rank called them to do dreadful things. Thus had her brother Rothevna been, the night he gave himself as a sacrifice.

They entered a bay known to man as the harbor of Coriallo, old in the days of bronze. Rocks surrounded it on three sides, while the north was exposed to the sea. The foundations of a burnt mansion and the gutted shell of a tiny fort showed where Gudrun had done her work against Urbicus, the wrecker lord and former bishop.

Here he had made his pacts with those he called sea demons, known to Niamh as the Cold Ones. His had been a foul, simple

159

bargain; manflesh for goods and gold. This bay, so oddly quiet in the starlight, had resounded to the crash of waves and breaking ship's timbers, so that Urbicus might grow fat. Then he had made the deadly mistake of wrecking a Sarnian ship, drowning Gudrun's men.

Niamh had motives more complex for the bargain she would drive.

"If I have not come back when the ebb begins, I will not come at all," she said to Nacrantal. "Take word of me to Brechou in that case, and fight against Vithils. I know you would as soon fight against Gudrun—but I wish it the other way, and if this is my last command, I will have it obeyed."

"It will be," Nacrantal said, gravely for once.

Niamh glimmered white as she slid over the side, wearing only a small knife strapped to her calf and the cuttlefish pendant. Flowing through the water like a seal, she came to a place directly offshore from the burnt mansion.

Quietly she floated, gathering her psychic strength, her senses and passions flowing out into the sea. The great green body of Lir did not convey words or thoughts as did the air, but emotions, from the lightest to the most deep and powerful. It carried Niamh's emotions now. In time, colder, more alien passions flowed back to her. Yet it was not their alienness that caused her to twist slowly in the water, but the ways in which they were familiar.

Stroking downward a fathom or two, she began a weightless dance of summoning. As she turned gracefully, she took the knife in her hand and made a series of cuts in her flesh; arms, ribs, calves, and shoulders. Thin ribbons of blood trailed unseen into the dark water.

The tide began to come in.

The cuttlefish pendant Niamh wore dragged its chain into her skin, as though its weight had grown tenfold. She fancied that its tentacles writhed against her flesh. Her blood and her dance and her feelings called, called, called—and out of the deepest water in the Narrow Sea, a shape came. She sensed it long before it arrived, with no fear that it might be a shark. Not even a shark would have dared approach her as she performed this rite.

The being had authority among the sea demons, of whatever kind they recognized. Grotesque shining fish accompanied it, native to greater deeps than any in the Narrow Sea. Some looked like undulating ribbons with vast fins and jaws attached. Others were chunky wedges of muscle twitching natural rods and lures on their heads. Squid jetted beside them, glowing blue, pink, and purple. In their midst swam a scaled, finned, gilled shape with webbed feet and hands. Blue patches upon its manlike body also glowed. As it approached Niamh, its entourage surrounded her like living jewelry.

The creature circled her, its movements filled with meaning. They joined in a combination of dance, mime, and sign language. Yet most of what passed between them was emotion, a direct interplay of feeling both subtle and savage, through the ancient medium of the sea, with nothing hidden. The sea thing, too, had passions ranging from dark to bright.

It bore some enmity toward Gudrun Blackhair for the slaughter she had made among its kindred when they had attacked the shores of Sarnia. The sea demons seldom did such things, had done so then at the urging of the wrecker lord, and were not eager to do so a second time.

Asking it to take Gudrun's side and fight against her foes was asking much.

The mute parley lasted long. Niamh had to rise for a score of breaths in the course of it, and she could remain beneath the sea longer than a dolphin. Her blood ribboned about her the whole time.

At last the sea demon, twisting elastically, drew its own blood in a score of places with its fangs. The black gore mingled with Niamh's in the water. Then the demon clasped her with its webbed paws and placed its mouth to each of her wounds, a nightmare nuzzling illuminated by living jewels. The cuts closed one by one at the touch of the creature's tongue. In her turn she sucked each of its flowing bites. They tasted like vinegar.

Weary, chilled to her marrow, she floated on the sea. Through the water she heard the webbed kicking of the sea demon returning to its place. Slowly she stroked her way toward Nacrantal's ship, her remnant of strength inexorably leaving her.

Nacrantal was beside her then, one arm supporting her and the other oaring through the water. A woman of her kindred supported her on the other side.

"I can get aboard," Niamh said clearly, if faintly. "You will not have to handle me like a sack."

Nacrantal let her prove her words. She made them good.

161

Once in the ship she sat on the deck with her head low. The weariness filtered through all her veins like poison.

"Was it worth it?" Nacrantal asked angrily. "For that haughty earth woman who would be for killing you if she knew what you have done?"

"It was not for her. You know that well. Do not question me!"

"Pah! Will the Cold Ones even act?"

"The Saxons have . . . protected their keels with a blood sacrifice. Men, Nacrantal. The Cold Ones want a greater sacrifice from us before they will move. They do not care who is offered . . . and they will not give direct battle. That is not their way, anyhow."

"Then what will they do that was worth your kissing spawn of the ooze?"

"Nacrantal . . . do not go on and on."

Drawing a hard, sudden breath, Nacrantal shut up. He gave her his cloak and left her to her goosedown pallet, under the stars. As his ship put out for Brechou, he clamped his hands to the ship's rail, cursing Gudrun and Sarnia in a soft, intense voice, with great thoroughness.

XV

Eight hundred spears and fifty swords
   Were whetted and greased for me.
Compacted oaths and sworn accords
Of several mighty, furious lords
From isles and estuaries and fjords
Joined them as one and spilled their hoards
   Into the restless sea.
How fine they look in their warlike gauds,
   And how welcome they shall be!
                              —Felimid mac Fal,
                                   Gudrun's Saga

"No greater muster of ships than this has ever been seen in Britain!"

So declared King Ricsige of Kent, preening. His gold-worked tunic of blue and purple showed peacock bright in the morning sun. The only signs about his person of preparation for war were the sword at his side and his braided hair, swinging beside his unexceptional face. He held himself pridefully erect and threw out his voice to all his hearers.

These had the look of war in every way. From the hundreds of them the smells of leather, greased iron, and sweat permeated the air. Many wore mere cloth and went bareheaded, the limit of their arms a shield and spear. Others wore hard leather tunics, and bore axes or spears. Only the greatest men among them went busked in scale byrnies and helmets; only these, or warriors of a great chief's following, or men who had been lucky in battle or inheritance, carried swords.

All were hard-bitten fighters, however. The yeomen and farmers summoned by Ricsige's war arrow had all battled for the land they tilled; they would not have left it so close to sowing time if they had not already been burned and driven from it by the Count of Britain's armored riders, all the length of the Thames Valley. Most had crossed water at least once in their lives, to reach Britain, and were ready to cross it again for the loot of Sarnia.

"This woman Blackhair has offended men and the gods too long," Ricsige continued. "Has she a beard, that she struts with sword and helm? No! She murdered my sire, a king! She has given foul offense to my cousins of Westri, and done very ill by the lords Edric and Vithils. Now we are come together for the purpose of cleaning her smell from the sea! Odin himself has wearied of her, as the omens presage! We here are Gudrun Blackhair's fate!"

With a royal shout, Ricsige drew his sword and swept it aloft. His manner then was truly kingly, and more; it was as though this foresighted dreamer did indeed speak the mandate of Weird.

A vast roar answered him. Warriors rattled spears and boomed axe flats on their linden shields, so that birds flew shrieking and none heard them. Then they waded out to their ships, clambered into them, and stowed their gear between the thwarts. Each man hung his shield on the long rail just outside the gunwale, some covered with cowhide or leather, some painted with emblems.

Ricsige's own shield hung solitary near the bow of his warship. Green-surfaced, it displayed a running white stallion above the umbo and branded runes around the edge, within its iron rim. The seventeen berserks manned the forward oars, and they had no shields to display, for it was their habit to fight without any, protected by their invulnerable battle frenzy. Five and twenty picked warriors met amidships and aft. The wizard Aur stood with the wind combing his gray elf locks and chanted.

Seven other Kentish ships followed their king. Chamo the Frank commanded one, and loudmouthed but able Oswy the Hasting another, and captains as well or better known issued orders in the rest. Some vessels were new, a couple taking the sea for the first time, their raw yellow planks shrieking as they flexed together, while others were years old, nearing the end of their useful lives.

Behind them came the four Saxon ships which had carried Vithils's band from the Elbe, through storms, across the wide

North Sea, and down the dangerous coasts between Humber and Thanet. Broader and weightier than the lean Kentish warcraft, lately damaged, swiftly repaired and caulked, somewhat waterlogged, they lumbered through the water by comparison, though on the whole they boasted better sails and rigging. Red-bearded, redoubtable Vithils gave orders on one, with Cudebehrt his second, while leaders called Eglinth the Chapman, Gurth, and Stigand Seavain commanded the others.

Edric the Fat, who had followed his brother-in-law because of supernatural promptings, stood braced on his short pillars of legs, handling his own ship's steering oar like a master, with two more Saxon ships pacing him to leeward.

The three comparatively sorry vessels from Westri fell behind. Young Cynric drove his powerful sword fist into his palm again and again, a look of frustrated lightning about him. Before his eyes, men labored with scoops in the bailing well, throwing out water in clear weather lest the atheling's ship should founder. Glowing before his gray-green, tawny-flecked eyes was the remembered vision of flames in the night devouring a fleet as splendid as Ricsige's, which he, Cynric, might have commanded now. Oh, fierce and mighty gods, Odin, Tiw and the Thunderer, oh, how that knowledge scalded!

"Easy, youngster," Ulfcetel said beside him.

No other man could have addressed Cynric by that word except his father. The sailing master with his whitening hair was the oldest man in the ship, and the shrewdest, and one of the hardiest despite his years. He'd done more to teach Cynric seamanship than Cerdic had. Moreover, he loved the fiery, thin-skinned, great-hearted young man he had watched grow from an infant as he had never loved a woman.

"Easy?" Cynric repeated. "They distance us like hares, and we stumble like hedgehogs! By the time we reach Sarnia, they will have left us nothing to do!"

Ulfcetel grinned, showing his few remaining teeth. "Let you not believe it. They taunt us by rushing on. You would do the same in their place and think it a good joke, so do not rend your hair. They'll pause in good time, and be pleased to rest. We won't be that far behind them, and Sarnia won't be taken so soon. There will be enough for us to do, and space to increase your honor. Just let you be patient and grow a thicker hide."

Cynric gazed at the old man a moment. Then he laughed. "Aye, you're right! Will you look at them yonder, you heroes?

Let's see how far they draw ahead when the wind drops! We will be first to Sarnia yet, with a steady oar beat, or they will be too tired to do much but await our coming. Who wants to wager on it?''

A few men took the bet. They knew their atheling gambled for joy and paid cheerfully when he lost. In this instance they could not lose. They would have their share of the glory if he was right, and some of Cynric's loot if he was wrong.

"I'll take some of that myself," Ulfcetel declared. "I know of no way a man can come nearer to buying luck." Then he frowned. "I'd thought I was the oldest man here. Now, who is that one?''

Cynric looked casually at the man his sailing master had noticed. He saw a very tall stranger with his face in shadow, mantled and hatted, holding a great spear with a brilliant head and runes cut in the shaft. His long gray beard was plaited for war. Although he stood straight as his spear, Cynric and Ulfcetel both had the impression of a vast store of years acquired like treasure.

"I don't know," the atheling admitted. "He's none of ours. Maybe he was drunk and missed his proper ship, or boarded this in error. Go ask him.''

Ulfcetel approached the stranger, and felt a chill like that of a wind howling about high crags, sucking life out of the careless in an hour. His step faltered. He could not see the stranger's face clearly in the shadow of his wide-brimmed hat, yet his bearing was that of one accustomed to command absolutely in war. Ice-gray mail glittered between the folds of his cloak. This was no tosspot who had missed the right ship.

When Ulfcetel would have spoken to him, the stranger shot him a numbing stare from one cold eye. Ulfcetel's tongue seemed to freeze in his mouth. He stumbled back to his atheling with not a word uttered to the disconcerting unknown.

"What ails you, man?" Cynric asked. "You almost look fey!''

"Bad oysters last night," Ulfcetel mumbled. "That fellow is of a degree that cannot disgrace you, lord. I'll answer for it.''

"If you say so. I'd heave him over the side else. Where did he go?''

Ulfcetel stared at the place where the tall figure had been. Then he looked the length of the leaking ship. Nowhere did he see the distinctive wide-brimmed hat or glittering spear head.

The chill in his flesh seeped inward to his heart.

"I know not. But I beg, lord—if you see him, *let him be*."

Cynric stared in astonishment at the sailing master. Almost, he asked if his mentor had grown too old for battle. Perhaps it was his great regard for Ulfcetel, or perhaps he, too, had sensed something uncanny about the stranger, for after a pause he gave a pensive nod and did not question.

"As you wish."

While the eighteen ships sailed westward, some of Gudrun's pirates were out waylaying a merchant vessel. Pascent led them, his conscience free and light for a man preying on his own kind, for Pascent had never staggered through life under a heavy burden of scruples.

The merchant ship was captained by one Saius, who had come from Nantes around the rocky, perilous coast of Lesser Britain with a cargo of corn his backers hoped to sell at high profit in Britain itself, where harvests the previous autumn had been bad. Beamy and fully laden, the grain ship was accompanied by a Celtic longship hired as escort. Saius was not sure how far he trusted the Celts, but at least their presence should discourage most pirates.

Then two swift ships flashed from behind a point of land. Saius gave them a quick, assessing glance. One was a light scouter and raider of the Pictish sort, holding two dozen men, the other a longship of Saxon make, with overlapping oak strakes and a huge steering paddle on the right quarter. The mast carried no betraying sail.

Saius's escort, the pine planks set edge to edge in its hull, was swifter but on the whole less seaworthy. It showed the swiftness by turning at once to run. Its sail strained bright in the sun as it fled, for its captain had not lurked in ambush. Saius snarled a curse at its stern.

His heavy trader had no chance to flee. The Pictish raider reached him first, and its master actually was a Pict, wiry, red-haired, blue-eyed, and compact, naked but for sandals and a leather kilt. A bunch of four eagle's feathers sprouted from his ornate hairslide, and he'd painted blue spirals on his skin for the fight, an ancient custom the other tribes of Britain had long abandoned. His followers were North Britons, Dal Riata of Kintyre, four of his own tribe, and one stocky, bat-eared Coranian covered with mouselike fur.

Swarming over the merchant's decks, they were soon joined by the crew of the Saxon longship, boarding from the other side. Although short, the fight was hard; eight corpses had to be dragged to the side when it was over, to lie stiffening in a row on the reddened deck. Many men bound up their wounds with torn shirts or tunics. Saius yielded, seeing there was no other hope, but his humor was murderous.

Seeing the dark-eyed man with big cheekbones and heavy russet moustache did not sweeten his mood, although it took him aback. He made a gurgling noise.

"Saints and martyrs!" he choked. "Pascent, you devil!"

Pascent nodded affably, cleaning blood and brains from his beaked war hammer. "That's right, Saius. I've changed my trade. You'd have done the same in my place. Let you not boggle at me. What's your cargo? Corn, oil, or wine? It must be bulk from the way you ride. You'd better not be traveling in ballast only."

"It's corn, for Britain, damn you. Some oil, but no wine. *You* can spare a drink, can't you?"

"Surely. Maybe we'll drink together at the *Dolphin* again, if you keep your mouth clipped about this. Your backers can afford it. Meanwhile—hey, Hemming, fetch that wine jug under the stroke thwart! Two men here deserve it."

"A third deserves crucifixion, and he'll get it if I can contrive! What did you pay that double-dealer Cago?"

"Who's Cago?" Pascent asked innocently.

"I know you know. Come! That prince's henchman who was supposed to protect me from the likes of you, and was paid too much for the charge! He ran too easily at the sight of you. In league with you, wasn't he? Took my pay and yours, too. That's how you knew where to lie in wait."

"I don't understand you, Saius," Pascent said again, in the tone of a warning. "Be glad I do not, and leave it."

"Oh, no! His lord doesn't know about this, does he? Cago dealt with you slyly, on his own account. I'll see him hang for this."

Pascent sighed regretfully. "You shouldn't have said that, gossip. You always did talk too much. I see now that you'd blab about me, too, and I want to go back to merchanting in time. It's too bad."

Raising his beaked hammer, he brought it down like a thunderbolt. Saius dropped to the bloody deck like a butchered ox.

Pascent gave an order, and his pirates made short work of the witnesses.

Some hours later, having tallied the cargo and washed the decks clean, he sat in Saius's tiny cabin. Here, if anywhere, goods of tiny bulk and high value would be stored. Searching the cabin with the help of stolid, suspicious Germans, Pascent had found a box of coins, some silk skeins, a few middle-quality cowries and bits of coral. One of the Goths had opened a leather drawstring bag, sniffed the contents and demanded, "What is this muck?"

Pascent had sniffed it himself. Shackling reaction, he had said carelessly, "It's elephant dung. Some think it cures poison and protects against the yellow sickness. Maybe a noble somewhere will buy it."

Now he sat alone, tossing the little sack in his palm, smiling broadly. Born in the wickedest port of southern Gaul, used to trading for strange goods from the east, he knew what the sack contained. It wasn't elephant dung, but poppy gum, the legendary lotus which stupefied and unmanned Odysseus' crew. He held enough in his hand to daze a cohort. It should certainly bring a high, high price, and it occurred to Pascent that he might find a use for it himself.

Smiling still, he went on deck. This round-bellied *corbito* was too vulnerable to take to Sarnia with the guests they were expecting, welcome though its cargo would be to the pirates, with their bottomless bellies. He would go to Lesia instead, that larger neighboring island with its friendly chieftain, who would have it milled for Gudrun, even if he wouldn't fight three kingdoms for her. The wiser man he, too.

Before their empire had crumbled like sand in the west, the Romans had built a hard stone fort at the mouth of the Seine, and called it Grannona. Still garrisoned under the Frankish kings, it still guarded its harbor. The guarding was far less efficient in these times. A man named Quintian had the thankless responsibility, and the satisfaction of knowing that his barely adequate standing force would be without support worthy the name in any emergency.

Gudrun had a cheerful appreciation of his problems, and made life interesting for him when she could, since she often passed that way. Yet even she had never given him the shock the fleet from Thanet did when it appeared over the horizon, late on the second day since its departure.

His sentries saw only five ships at first, and those were cause for the entire garrison to stand to the walls. Signal banners flew. A rider was sent galloping inland with the news, and as more Saxon galleys rowed into sight until the count reached eleven, Quintian's dread for the countryside grew. Saxons had raided Gaul in great numbers before; there were settlements of them in the Charente; they had rowed up the main rivers in the past, and beseiged cities as great as Angers and Nantes. What was impossible about Ratuma?* Nothing!

"Sir," a pale-cheeked sentry said to him, "I've counted four more. Until now they rowed out of sight of the shore, it appears, with their sails down."

"Fifteen galleys," Quintian said. "A host of savages, and there is no more doubt that they are coming this way. Send two more riders with that news."

The riders departed, glad to be gone. The dust of their going had scarcely settled when the first Kentish keel gashed the sand. Quintian watched the savages leap into the water and splash ashore, whooping. To his Romanized sight they were the most squalid creatures breathing, in their motley wadmal and cowhides, their rawhide-gartered breeches, huge lousy beards, and simple round iron caps (those of them who wore even that much protection on their witless heads). None wore bull's horns on their helmets; that was a tale.

They were not even as great in stature as frightened legends made out. It didn't matter. They were yet a lethal crew of hundreds, able to devastate a wide swathe of country and burn a number of towns before they returned to the sea. The fort was all that prevented them.

"Who are you and whither do you go?" Quintian challenged.

"I am Ricsige, King of Kent and son of Oisc, who was the son of Hengist, who descended from Wotan," answered a man in a sea-stained but still magnificent tunic. He placed a hand on the pommel of his sword and jutted it forward. "My comrades . . ."

He introduced them, being long-winded and fulsome about it. They stood beside him while the ships were dragged ashore, one by one; a living mountain of blubber who surely could scarcely walk; a burly, thick-muscled redbeard who still ap-

*Rouen.

170

peared almost slight beside that amazing other; and a magnificent tawny-haired youth of about twenty who really did look like the stories fanciful scribes told of the Germans.

"We camp ashore tonight, and range for food in the morning," the youth said arrogantly, "and as many other days as we like. After we do that, we will go our way. There is nothing else here that we want."

"Even if I believed you, I might not let you have even that," Quintian told him. "I am charged by my master the Count of the Lower Seine to protect the land, its people, and their foodstocks. A muster is forming from the countryside even now, and you will have a host on your backs if you should try to plunder here."

The fat monster of a man answered. Quintian expected a breathy wheeze from him, but instead he heard a rich baritone.

"In the days of the legions you might give me pause with that tale. Not now. The most you will get is a levy of yokels in, say, three days. Your count will not relieve you with a real force in less than ten, supposing he's not feuding with his neighbor lords. Then he would fail to come at all. No, Commander, I say you're alone. Do not mind us. We have larger fish to grill and little time to spare, as Cynric says."

Quintian sighed in disbelief. Even if the savages told the truth at that particular moment, they could always change their minds, and probably would, once they stretched their legs and found diversions of burning and torture. He watched their camp fires burn and made his plans.

That night he led a surprise attack against their sprawling camp, counting on the savages' lack of discipline. He hoped to rout them and burn some of their ships. His plan failed when a tall old man with wolves at his heels raised the alarm, seeming to be everywhere at once. Quintian dismissed the wolves as fanciful embellishment when he heard about them, although some of his men had had their throats most convincingly torn out; but it was certain that he'd been forced to retreat to the fort pursued by numbers too great for him.

When the barbarian host scattered to forage, he tried again, sending bands of fifty here and there under his officers to annihilate the raiding parties. Sometimes they succeeded, sometimes they failed, and the levies he had summoned so promptly never came.

A gray old man was seen here and there by the invaders'

fires, talking of war and battle fame in words that inflamed like potent drink or the finest poetry, until his hearers were furious with the desire to level Sarnia's granite cliffs into the sea. The berserks frothed at the mouth and began a stamping, circling dance in which the entire host joined before morning, weaving among the camp fires.

Quintian watched from the fort's walkway in mingled wonder and disgust, while his signal beacons burned. When the barbarian's ships departed on the morning tide, he simultaneously thanked God and pitied the towns farther west.

The levies he had summoned did not appear for two more days. Then they proved to be not Gaulish peasants from the estates, but Frankish soldiery who had fed themselves on the march in the same way as the Saxons and Kentish Jutes. When their commander found that the savage ships were gone, he implied that Quintian was a fool who had dreamed the monstrous fleet.

"Then bide here until my dream returns!" Quintian snarled, out of patience after three sleepless days and nights of striving his utmost. "My entire garrison, each frightened hamlet on the coast, and all this twice-devastated champaign have had the same dream. Some folk will never awaken from it."

The avenging fleet was far away by then, rowing for two tides in succession in order to round the deadly peninsula beyond which lay Sarnia. For swiftness, it was no bad decision; for safety, an ill one. The second favorable tide occurred at night.

The Children of Lir were waiting.

XVI

Sunlit changing water above,
  And darkness fathoms below,
Shrouding the ooze where nothing has changed
  Since millions of years ago.
Starlight, tide, and a thousand rocks,
  Sculpted by no one's hand,
Breaking ships with hideous shocks
To make a feast for the demon flocks
  Who will never dwell on the land.
Warm is our blood while theirs is chill—
  We are closer kin to man—
But they and we belong to the sea
  As no earth children can.
                        —Felimid mac Fal,
                          The Children of Lir

Nacrantal lounged in the stern of his ship, one hand on the carved tiller bar, his face like a mask of angled bone, and a hungry look on his mouth. His nameless witch-leman stood a little before him in ornaments of green *findrina*, the magic metal. Behind them loomed deadly sea rocks with the appearance of a bizarre, buttressed castle.'

"They are staying well out to sea, avoiding these shores and the tide race of Ridune both," Nacrantal said. "So should I in their place! Vithils will have pilots with him who know of these rocks, for all the benefit he will receive from that. Ha ha ha! Niamh should be here to see this happen."

"Niamh is a-couch yet, weary and ill from driving this pact," the sea witch said. "She has done her part, and by Lir, I'll do

173

mine! The Cold Ones desire a greater blood sacrifice than the Kentishmen made, before they will league with us? That they shall have.''

Held safely to sea by the ebb tide, the Kentish ships passed Coriallo of evil repute. Midnight faded in their wakes, and their crews looked forward to the morning. The rasp of whetting spear heads and axe edges carried far across the water.

Ragged clouds blew, obscuring the stars, and somewhere waves beat against rocks. They sounded like the bellowing and sighing of some great starving beast. King Ricsige grew fearful in the leading ship, not liking the darkness after midnight or these treacherous waters. He wrestled with his fear and his pride for a long time, which seemed to him even longer, but at last he shouted through his cupped hands to the following ships, and those men passed his message to Edric.

Tireless as he was gross, the chieftain remained awake, handling his great rudder oar. He answered Ricsige's plea—which the king had framed as a suggestion—by bringing his three ships forward as Ricsige's eight dropped back, and so leading the fleet. Some shrewd jokes were exchanged, and two ships collided, to a clamor of oaths and aspersions. Then they rowed on in their new sequence.

Before long a white mist crawled over the sea. Edric saw it first as a pale glimmer ahead, then as growing skeins of wool spun out of the night. It came with the light breeze to engulf them.

"This is no right weather for fog," a sailor of thirty years' seasoning declared. "Nor did I ever know fog like this. Njord! It doesn't even feel damp."

"Quiet," Edric told him. "I listen to the sea."

The crying breakers sounded much nearer.

"Are we close inshore, lord? We should not be."

Edric displayed his concern with a phlegmatic grunt. "Umph. I say it is waves upon sea rocks, not the main shore, and they are off this bow."

"What was that?"

Something had risen, splashing, and dived again. The sound was repeated from behind the ship in another moment, and then the night was alive with swimming bodies. Men glimpsed scaly arms with glowing phosphorescent patches, and square-muzzled heads maned with external gills. Music, sweetly eerie, rose above the deadly noise of breakers.

"Someone reckons us children," Edric said. Then he thundered from the depth of his immense chest, for the ships following him to hear:

"Steady after me, men of Edricsburg! We're played with by spooks. Trust only this voice of mine and go forward as I bid."

That's a foolish speech, he chided himself then. *How are they to know it is my voice and not some mocking sea thing's?*

From his tun of a chest he raised a chantey his Saxons had often heard from him in the midst of storms, pirate attacks, or sweet blue weather. The noise carried far over the nighted sea, and warriors laughed to each other in relief.

"That's Edric, indeed! Nothing else has so fearful a voice!"

Hard must Edric strive to sing so lustily while he pushed the great rudder oar and watched monstrous shapes wallow around his ship. One seized that very oar with webbed hands, clasped and rode it. Edric raised the oar wholly clear of the water with a grunt of crucifying effort, then allowed it to fall back, knocking the sea demon clear. Two spearmen hastened to his side as he resumed his interrupted chantey.

> "*. . . and when we come home we will make the beds*
> > *creak,*
> *Ho! So sail we, and ho! ho! ho!*"

The mist rolled apart before him, forming a sea lane down which the ship's bow pointed, a long open corridor through obscurity. Edric halted his bawling in sheer amazement, which could pass as a gap between stanzas, and fortunately did, so that his men did not suppose there was anything amiss. Edric looked upward. The stars showed clearly again.

"This smells of a trap," he growled.

"Wreckers?"

"I think not. Blackhair slew the worst of them. It must be Blackhair herself instigating this."

The sea chantey roared from his mouth once more.

"Lord, look yonder!" his second spearman urged. "Do you see anything, or am I mad?"

"I see a shape like a woman's, and it walks on the sea," Edric answered, staring. "We may both be mad."

"But not all three," declared the first man, glaring at the vision. "A woman's shape it is—and what a shape, chieftain! See! The monsters vanish!"

"She comes near! By the ice of Hel! See how she points the way! Yes, that path is clear, but is it good or ill?"

Gyrth, the spearman at his left, said wryly: "It is to decide such things that you are chief, lord, and tonight I had rather it were you than I. Say, and we'll do as you bid. All I have to say is that I don't trust witch's work."

"Then let me think."

Edric pondered, listening to the crash of surf on rocks, which seemed to come from everywhere in the curious fog. He felt the sea through the responsive keel of his ship, smelled it, heard it, and knew he was deciding between wreckage and life. Experience, hunch, and suspicion were his bases, he leading, none before him, eight hundreds behind him, and all their lives perhaps depending on him.

"Away from here! Listen to me, you ships of Edricsburg, and give the word back! Turn seaward after me; I will light flares and sing! Never heed this channel through the fog or the fay who would lead you there; it goes to destruction. *Out to sea!*"

He plied the huge rudder oar hard, and raised his desperate voice in something his best friend might have called song. His ship obeyed him, though with cries of anguish from her timbers as the waves struck her abeam. His men lit sputtering flares of pine wood and set them up in the stern beside him. The yellow light splashed over his gross figure, standing steady as a boulder.

"Ho! So sail we, and . . . ho . . . ho . . . ho!"

The creatures from the deep swarmed about his ship again. They swiftly learned caution as spears found their bodies. The rowers panted as clutching webbed hands hampered their stroke.

"Lord! We left the clear path the fay showed us, and these nicors have come back!"

"Aye! We shouldn't have strayed!"

"We keep on as we go!" Edric ruled, his voice like iron. Indecision was worse than being wrong in this foul a situation. "They are not doing much. They cannot. They are angry because we did leave the path of our disaster. They would like us to go back to it . . . press on."

His two ships from the Elbe stayed close to him. Horns blew

aboard one, and shields were loudly beaten on the other. They desisted only long enough to call instructions astern to the Kentish ships, and King Ricsige plucked his beard in inability to decide.

"No!" he said at last. "The fay is friendly, and a power. We risk making a foe of her if we flout her. Then, indeed, we would never see morning! Follow the clear water."

Aur the wizard sniffed the breeze and the sea. The berserks hulked in the darkness below him, stinking. He said obsequiously, "Lord, that clear water may be too clear. None has ever said that fat man does not know the sea. We could do well to follow him. Even if he does go to rending doom, his fate will warn us and we will have time to avoid it."

What he had been impelled to say by trust in supernatural portents, Ricsige was driven by envy to confirm. He straightened his shoulders.

"I am king. Steersman! Follow the clear water."

"No!" Aur shouted in sudden certainty. "No. Mighty Odin speaks to me now. The clear water leads to death, the way through the fog to the open sea offers life! My head upon it. You servants of Odin, act as he inspires!"

The berserks rose growling, fondling their weapons, and surrounded the King of Kent. The thirty Kentishmen aboard outnumbered but could not outfight the monster seventeen, who laughed and slavered at them.

"We do your bidding, at this cost," Ottar said to Aur. "If Odin has not sent you knowledge, we will find time to hack the ribs away from your backbone ere we drown. That's the price of a fool's lie."

"Agreed," Aur said, past a sudden stiff blockage in his gullet.

"You will hang for this!" Ricsige told him.

Thrain leered. "Maybe if your idea proves wrong, you should hang, king. For the luck of the venture, as a gift to Odin."

Confusion spread among the other Kentish ships. The contradictory orders given had their effect compounded by inconsistent notions among the captains of what had taken place on the king's vessel. Most followed the White Horse, but two fled down the narrow lane between the writhing, swelling walls of fog, after the beckoning vision of a white sea witch treading the waves. No sea demons molested them as they rowed on that course.

Without warning they struck on shelves of rock beneath a gentle surface. Strakes cracked. Ribs broke out of the ships. Water surged through tilting the hulls sideways, dragging timbers free, widening the rents. The rocks, so unobtrusive a moment before, gored and battered the Kentish ships, splintered their oars and broke their backs. A dragon figurehead parted from its prow with a rending like the creature's death skirl. Foam seethed among the benches, washing men out of their pitiful shelter on a rush of Aegir's salt ale.

Their shrieks and the sound of smashing timbers carried far. Ricsige heard it where the berserks surrounded him, and hung his head abashed even as he stared at them in renewed fear. They were capable of doing what they had said. Kings had been sacrificed before.

"No," Aur said, to that very suggestion from Thrain. "His folk would turn against us. We require them to defeat Blackhair. Odin himself commanded that."

The sea demons that had remained below now rose to the feast spread for them, one whose delights they knew. Urbicus the wrecker lord had made such banquets for them many, many times. They dragged struggling men beneath the waves as they essayed to swim. They caught the battered, broken meats that washed from the rocks and devoured them as readily as flesh that struggled. If they did not altogether gorge full, their taste for warm blood was aroused and their demand met.

"They have had their greater sacrifice now," Nacrantal said. "Yes, fourfold greater than the one Ricsige offered, and all of warriors! The Cold Ones cannot withhold their aid from us now. We've met their terms in full."

The Children of Lir were blithe. They felt no remorse for what they had done to their victims. The astonishment and horror of shipwreck, the ugliness of being battered out of human shape on submerged rocks, was simply the way of their father the sea. Before long the same might happen to them—and until it did, they had given a sharp lesson to those who usurped the waves from them.

Edric did not accept that lesson. Nor did Vithils, who had followed his brother-in-law through the fog. When they met each other again in the morning, their meeting was a glad one; and all of their ships were intact.

Shaken and chastened, Ricsige ploughed the sea a humble distance behind the Saxons in his six remaining keels. The berserks were in good spirits. The loss of two ships with all who fared in them was no great matter to Ottar, Thrain, Leidolf, and their kin. Odin's favor had been shown to them yet again. They had survived, fighting was imminent, and they would then get revenge for the attempt to drown them as surely as axes broke through shields and the berserk fit was a glorious state.

Cynric, still lagging behind, had beached his three decrepit ships and waited for the morning. Since his rowers were well rested and had escaped the terrors of the night, he met with his allies off the island of Ridunia shortly after Vithils, Edric, and Ricsige themselves had gathered there.

The story of those terrors had not lost fat. He was assured over ale that the sea had opened and vented fire, the warriors had battled monsters fathoms longer than their ships, and the very stars had gone dark and fallen out of the sky. Ran herself had appeared, spreading nets to trap and destroy ships.

Vithils and Edric indulged in no such nonsense, nor did the Kentish captains, who were ashamed of their king but too loyal to say so; yet others did. Cynric heard it, and laughed in his beard.

"You came through all that with no damage? That you lost two ships, I know, but all those who survived are untouched. There is a wonder."

"No wonder," a Kentish warrior retorted, "just good ship-wright's work. Had it been your rotten ships put to such a test, they'd have shattered at a touch."

Cynric remembered Ulfcetel's advice about growing a thicker hide. He answered with humor.

"So? Fellow, it will soon be known how your Kentish ships hold together at Gudrun's touch. Come and boast to me then."

"We are going to make fish food of her."

"We are going," Cynric said more grandiloquently, "to pull Sarnia's granite cliffs down into the waves and bury the remnants from sight. I myself will burn or shatter the last of her ships as she made drenched cinders of ours — and if I do not, may I never see my father's face again! How Kent shares in the work, with all his fine ships, is to be seen."

Then he went to hold council with the other leaders and their henchmen. Ulfcetel went with him, his two captains, and half a dozen picked warriors for his honor's sake. Vithils was accompanied only by his half brother Cudebehrt and his reputation;

he had no need to display power or standing, and seldom cared to. Edric the Fat sat on an improvised chair among his own captains and ten spearmen of good lineage.

Ricsige, whose bruised self-love perhaps called for it, stood among his counselor Anlaf, the leader of his household troopers, Stur Worferth's son—who stood nearly seven feet tall—and his famed captains Chamo and Black Ealdred. Twenty hall warriors armed with bright swords also escorted him. All around them on the shore of Ridunia, their hundreds of men ate their last meal before the battle. For some it would be the last meal of their lives. Many of Ricsige's men had already eaten that; rock garnished with kelp.

"I claim the right to be first in the advance," he said. "I and mine. Some of you are greater warriors than I, some have equal griefs to avenge, but mine is the strongest force even now, and . . . I am the only king."

Although concerned for his own name, he was honestly enraged for the reasons he gave, and spoke with straightforward dignity. He could do that. What he could not do was sustain it.

Vithils nodded agreement. Cynric argued that he was weary of bringing up the rear and did not wish to hear more gibes about the state of his ships.

"If you will follow Ricsige," Edric said, "Vithils and I will follow you. There is nothing in that to hurt your honor, atheling."

Cynric agreed that there was not, and assured them he would not forget the offer. He sensed that somehow Edric had shown himself a bigger man by yielding place than he had by demanding it. However, he did not dwell on that, being eager to come to Gudrun's lair.

They sailed on the last short stage of their journey the next day. Ricsige's six proud vessels led as arranged, the White Horse of Kent bright in the sun. After them wallowed three of Westri's worst ships, filled with the best of that kingdom's fighting men, to the number of one hundred fifty. Behind Cynric, patient, stubborn, and tenacious, rowed the Elbe Saxons; and Sarnia drew ever closer.

XVII

They paid for the mead their lords gave them,
The yellow, bright, ensnaring mead;
They boasted aloud on the feasting benches,
And went by the whale's road to warlike death.
                                        —Felimid mac Fal

A lace-winged bird of air flew through the day, seeking Felimid. It found him in the shadow of granite cliffs fifty men high, where gray-green waves rushed up the shore of a bay holding five ships in its arms. It found him in his walrus-leather cuirass, helm, and boots made by the dwarves and strengthened with etched whalebone in places. He greatly preferred it to metal, since it was lighter and almost as strong. A targe with a triskele emblem rode on his arm, a sheaf of javelins on his shoulder, and the sword Kincaid hung sheathed at his hip. For once he did not carry his harp. She lay safely stowed in the boat he was about to enter, with a bigger, more practical shield beside her.

The bird-sprite flew down. "They come, they come! Put away your weapons, man of the harp, and give me poetry. Give me fine stories. Then I will tell you all I know!"

Felimid heaved the javelins into the waiting boat. "Alas, my friend, there is no time, and this is not a day for putting weapons aside! We know they come, and that they come now. The Children of Lir have told us. You're behind the fair, and I must leave."

"The sea people do not know all I know. Harp song and tales for one short hour, and I undertake to save you from Fate itself."

"Poetry and tales!" Felimid yelled angrily. "Poetry and tales! Harp song! Is that all you can chatter to me? Is it all of me that—'' He snapped his mouth shut. "There is a time and a place, and by all the gods you choose the wrong one. Trouble me again today and it is punishing satire you will get, not stories, my importunate child. Go!"

He sprang into the boat. The bird of air flew upward to spiral above the cliffs. Felimid spared it one glance before he turned his gaze to *Ormungandr*, riding beyond the breakers. The sight of Gudrun a-shine in her mail sent a fresh spasm of anger through him, richly hot. While foes came to destroy her, that bloodless child of wind wasted his time asking for songs!

He noted men looking at him oddly. One asked, "Are you touched in the head, Bragi?"

"Not I! Listening to spirits who tried to distract me from battle. They displeased me. It's fighting I need."

"I reckon you do. There's no cure for woolgathering like it. You stop thinking of other things or else you lose your tripes."

The boat bumped against *Ormungandr*'s side. Felimid heaved up the javelins and other gear. Taking Golden Singer last, he climbed nimbly aboard and met Gudrun with a swift embrace. It was scarcely a satisfying one, while they both wore their battle gear, but perhaps that was better.

"They reached us after all," Gudrun said. "Let us go and make them sorry for it, my man. Even Vithils will find there are more pleasant things than to face the swords Kissing Viper and Kincaid together. If they outnumber us, why, we shall just have to kill three each."

Felimid answered with a quip and scanned the other ships. *Whale's Sister* was there, with Hromund in command, and the Franks Waldin and Arnehad each captained a single-banked galley of essentially Roman pattern, altered somewhat by northern shipwrights. Zucharre the Basque waved from the other side, in a ship built by his own people and meant for the violent waters of Cantanabria. She rode the waves like a gannet.

"Welcome, lady," Zucharre called, grinning. "We will be hospitable, eh? Even though these northrons have come to supper uninvited, we will give them all we have in the pot."

"Yea, everything!" Gudrun answered. "A hot meal with many surprises, and they shall eat it to the last mouthful! Hromund, that mast step you doubted; did Tiumals repair it well?"

"It's all I could want, by the look. The man should be a shipwright himself. Now let's test it!"

Waldin, slouching and morose, straightened out of his dark mood to look like a captain. "We will test more than a Goth's carpentry," he said loudly. "We're about to test to breaking the hearts of Kent and Westri!"

Arnehad raised his axe and yelled.

Ormungandr led them out of the bay. High above the rower's heads, some helmed, some bare, rose the mast of northern fir. Wind whistled in the naked rigging, and the sky turned gray. A few small drops of rain speckled the sea.

Down from the north came the vengeance fleet, under sail. It spread across a mile of water. Felimid felt a strange, tight unease which had little to do with the coming fight; perhaps a fifth part. His heart told him that something other than armed warriors came with that fleet.

Gudrun raised her face to the spitting sky and uttered a defiance. "You will not stand between me and Vithils this time, wind lord! Row faster, my heroes, for they are sluggish even though the wind is with them! Can they be less than eager to taste the fare we have for them?"

Can you be fey? Felimid wondered.

"Kent leads! That weakling Ricsige! Where is Vithils?"

The White Horse on the leading sail rushed ever closer. A deep-voiced war chant rang from within the ship's sides. For a moment it ceased, and the king cried on a shrill note he doubtless hated to hear in his own voice, "I have come for my father's ship, wolf's head! Did you believe you could keep it?"

"You may get the bow of it through your tub's side," Gudrun answered, "But naught else! Shoot them!"

Setting the example, she strung her bow. From *Ormungandr* and *Whale's Sister* the Danish arrows hummed. Men fell, transfixed. More yelled or swore in the sudden pain of wounds. Then a hugely tall figure in a blue cloak rose in the bow, making himself a mark. In one hand he weighed a bright-headed spear.

"Have you a welcome for *me*, daughter?" he demanded.

Gudrun screamed wordlessly. Then she shot at him. Her bowstring twanged a curse. The greybeard's hand moved too swiftly for sight, and suddenly he held an arrow of Gudrun's red-and-gray fletching in his fingers. Deliberately he snapped it, and cast the pieces away.

Gudrun gripped her bow until her toughened palms bled. The bard went to her side. By the time he reached her, the figure in the blue cloak had gone.

"Earth-mother Danu!" Felimid said passionately. "He will not play with us, nor we with him! Let me come within sword's reach of that one and I will be showing him what Fate is! See, Gudrun, they have lost the stroke for all his attendance upon them. Let's ram that ship and sink it."

He boasted and raved, because he had seen Gudrun blanch and detested the one who had caused it with a mocking word. Gudrun shuddered once, then took command of herself and thought. Swiftly, in her usual fashion, because time for long musing or speeches there was none.

She said, "No. That ship, instead."

She had chosen Black Ealdred's, which sailed a little apart from the rest. If they murdered the king, they would have to slay all his men, who would not bear the shame of deserting a dead leader—or would at least fight all the harder until they saw their case was hopeless. But Ricsige was the weakest man there and might turn back if his courage was broken, taking his ships with him. Depriving him of a redoubtable captain like Ealdred was a good way to begin.

At her sharp command, the steersmen and rowers turned toward Ealdred and drove ever more swiftly through the sea. Gudrun's bowmen shot volley after volley into them, until the black captain's ship resembled a hedgehog and two dozen dead or wounded rolled in the bottom. Their efforts to evade the monster racing through the brine at them grew frantic—those who were yet able to make efforts.

Other Saxon ships turned to his aid, awkward as they presented their sides to the waves. They rolled like drunkards for the brief time it took them to come about. The nearest was still more than a bowshot away when *Ormungandr*'s braced and reinforced prow smashed through her victim's side to the noise of rending strakes and shattering, springing ribs. Yet the impact shocked *Ormungandr* from end to end and cost the enchanted vessel dearly.

The bracing within her bows gave way at last. Weakened from other reckless rammings, craftily joined beams shrieked and burst. Jagged splinters whizzed about like Gudrun's arrows. None had time to observe the damage closely; angry Kentish Jutes grappled and bound to *Ormungandr*, mad to hold her fast for killing. They were not grateful for their lesson in Danish archery!

The pirates worked like devils to push off from the damaged

ship. The Saxons clung as furiously, with poles, ropes, hooks, and their grasping hands. Ealdred's ship slewed around in the rolling waves until she wallowed side by side with *Ormungandr*. Grapnels flew and bit, to be chopped away as quickly as they lodged in timber.

Black Ealdred roared, "Sunder them!" and led the way. Murder boiled along the ships' sides. Saxons hurled themselves over *Ormungandr*'s shield-rail, to be impaled on pirate spears even as they crashed down into the ship, careless of life so long as they broke a hole in the pirates' defense. They killed even as they were killed.

Ealdred, lean and thin-lipped, raged like a wolf within *Ormungandr*'s sides. Some of his men rushed after him, widening his path to right and left. They did not survive long. One went down with a spear in his thigh. He tried to close the wound with his hands while blood burst in a fountain from the ripped artery. Finding it hopeless, he rose and fought, roaring with laughter until he was butchered by three pirates. One he took with him, finding cause in that for a final laugh.

Felimid fought at the rail, his sword darting through gaps in the press that might have frustrated a mouse. He cut, thrust, saw one of the locked, advancing shields slip sideways and down, then saw the line close and met a glare new to him, from bloodshot, sandy-lashed eyes beneath an iron cap. Warding a leaf-shaped spear head from his throat, he cut at the stranger's legs, and was knocked sprawling over two bodies before he knew if the stroke had been effective. He never knew whence the impact that toppled him had come, or even precisely where it had struck him.

His armor saved his bones. Giguderich perhaps saved his life, by jumping over him in the full weight of a scale byrnie to confront his attackers.

"Lazy, Bragi?" the Gothic pirate rasped. "You can't rest yet."

Between them they killed both Kentishmen and sealed the gap at the rail.

Felimid looked for Gudrun. His heart lodged at the back of his throat when he saw her in the Kentish ship, her red shield like a moon of destruction. Half a dozen pirates fought with her. The bard recognized mad, merry Rowan among them, but had no thought to identify them one by one. He began fighting his way into the Saxon ship, shouting her name.

She recognized his voice. "No, Bragi!" she shrilled, like the sea eagle he sometimes called her. "If I die you must sing of me—"

The words were like hot skewers in his heart. His throat raw and his legs weary, he slew one more man, then another, as he forced his way across the locked rails toward her. His long-jawed, snub-nosed face was white in the frame of the walrus-leather helm. Giguderich came beside him.

"Out of this!" Felimid cried to his lover. "Now! We will have another ship binding to *Ormungandr* on the far side at any moment."

He spent his remaining strength like a wastrel to keep the way open for her return to *Ormungandr*. She cut her way back, but three of those with her died as they went. The last fell at the very rail, to be trampled like rubbish by the striving Jutes as Gudrun passed out of their hands. Her sword dripped a dozen men's mingled blood.

Black Ealdred had been hacked to pieces. No one man could claim to have been his death, though many bore red wounds as his gift. Someone threw his unrecognizable head into his own ship like a cabbage as the two war dragons slowly drew apart.

Zucharre's tough ship now drew level with *Ormungandr*. Shields were battered aboard, Zucharre's own was broken, and some of his oars were shattered stubs. His spirits remained high.

"We fought them hard, then broke from the fight," he called through his cupped hands. "We could have taken them!"

"Until some o' their friends joined in!" Felimid called back. "Na, we've done enough. Have we not, Gudrun?"

"For now. We have made sure they will follow us. But they are slow!"

A Kentish ship loomed close enough to be hit with a tossed knucklebone as *Ormungandr* turned southward again. The pirates gifted it with a hail of arrows, and received javelins back. The volley seemed ragged and ineffectual. Then Felimid beheld the reason.

Kelp entwined the Kentish oars. A formless, crawling mat of it surrounded the ship. As fast as the beating oars broke its feeble grip, it clung again. The Jutes might as well have been rowing through honey.

"The kelpie," Felimid said in a drenching of ice-cold memory. "The water horse."

Ormungandr moved sluggishly, too, for that enchanted ship.

Water came in at the damaged bow for a while, but then the boards seemed to swell and close of themselves, as a live thing heals.

Gudrun passed near King Ricsige's ship to throw a taunt. A thicker tangle of kelp darkened the water around it. One man had descended the ship's side to chop the stuff away. Appalled, Felimid shouted a warning. The man replied with a contemptuous gesture. He slid lower, hacking with his heavy knife. The stuff enwrapped, then engulfed him, drawing him under. His comrades fished a corpse from the sea, pallid and trailing streamery brown leaves.

"The gift Urbicus dared send me," Gudrun whispered. "The blood weed! Those merfolk have driven a pact with the sea demons."

A man with scattered gray hair, in a wolfskin cloak, moved to the ship's side in a space quickly cleared for him. He carried a short iron sword of ugly shape. Gazing to the sky, he lifted his hands and spoke an invocation. Then he slashed his own arm.

The blood that ran into the sea looked nastily pale, and appeared to fume. Kelp clotted thickly around it, writhing. Then the entire mat weakened and dispersed as though poisoned.

"Was that the one who greeted you before, lady?" Giguderich asked. "He flattered himself if he called you daughter."

"No," she said curtly. "No, he is too small and he has—" She stopped. She had been about to say, "He has both eyes." To remind her men of the One-Eyed and his displeasure was not needful. "He has the look of a wizard, and those were berserks near him or I cannot tell one. Ricsige travels in low company."

Pigsknuckle Hromund had barely won clear of the skirmish he had entered. The Frankish captains came to his aid before he was overwhelmed, and their galleys showed their sterns to the fleet just as Cynric rowed up at his fastest. He raged in exasperation to see them escape.

"They won't flee far," Ulfcetel consoled him.

Rain fell heavily now, making the world dim. The five Sarnian ships beat southward, close together. *Ormungandr* came last, to be closest to the pursuit and delay it if that were called for.

"On! After them!" King Ricsige raved. "Their magic failed,

their attack failed. They have my father's ship, and they row slowly to stay behind their comrades. We will catch them now! I will have *Ormungandr*!''

The berserks cheered him, as they had threatened and mocked him two nights before. The king abandoned the ship Gudrun had rammed; Chamo and Anlaf were left to take the surviving warriors off before it sank. Then all five Kentish ships raced after the pirates, sails spread to the gusty wind. Cynric joined in the pursuit with his three ships, nursing all the speed he could from their waterlogged hulls.

''Well, brother,'' Edric bellowed to Vithils through the rain, ''shall we run after them likewise?''

''No!'' Vithils was definite. ''Someone must pick up the pieces later. Can we run them down before they make Sarnia, well and good. If not, let's talk some sense into young Cynric, for Ricsige seems beyond it. Dangle that cursed ship before him and he forgets all else.''

The solid Saxon warships plunged through the rain. Though no man could see more than a few ship's lengths now, they found Cynric by hailing him. The atheling was glad of them.

''Ricsige will be needing us,'' he said. ''They have five ships, and he has no more, now. He follows them closely.''

''Then he's a fool,'' Vithils answered. ''Look around you, Cynric. Should we chase them to Sarnia in this weather, half blind? And it grows worse! They know every rock on their own shores. I'll follow them as resolutely as any, but by the gods, if we cannot catch them on the open sea, let them go until the weather clears. Recall what happened to Ricsige but a couple of nights past.''

The sense in that was absolutely plain. Besides, it came from a renowned fighter and seaman whom Cynric could respect. Their ten ships tossed through the running waves, while men handled wet lines, chafed their backsides on wet seats, and kept the rust off their weapons as best they could.

In Ricsige's ship the berserks howled and chanted. Some of their madness entered the Kentish warriors, who roared each time they mounted a wave, clashing weapons on shields. Aur stared through the rain with wizard's eyes. His gray elf locks were drenched to his scalp now, and the shape of his head thus accentuated did not look wholly human. But he was human enough to have bound the wound in his arm. The bandage steamed slightly.

''Shall we have them?'' Ricsige asked. His eyes were those

of a feverish man. "Are they near?"

"Lord, they neither gain nor lose."

"Then where are those supposed friends of mine?"

Aur turned around slowly, to look back. He lifted his ugly sword and let it move in a questing arc, back and forth. Now and again it quivered in his hand.

"They follow, but close together and at Cynric's pace."

"Much use is that. We will take Blackhair ourselves, then!"

Weak when he should not be, rash when he should not be, Ricsige held to his course. White spray soaked him; gray rain washed the salt away. His war gear dripped unregarded.

In a while the rain eased. The Kentishman heard breakers hurling themselves to a furious death against cliffs to the east. Sunlight broke faintly through the clouds.

"There they are!" Teg yelled, he, the youngest, smallest, and worst of the berserks.

The clouds drew together again. Rain resumed, steady in its fall but lighter now. Through the gray curtains they saw *Ormungandr* spider walking on ten oars into a bay a furlong wide, a little but secure harbor. Before the serpent ship, brown smears on a gray vagueness, went the other Sarnian hulls.

"We have them!" Ricsige gloated—much too early, it seemed to Stur Worferth's son, listening to him. "Or if they flee, I will have *Ormungandr*, and the pirates later."

"Have a care, lord," Stur said quietly. He peered into the rain. "This is a time to go forward boldly, yet not all Blackhair's men are in those ships."

"Bah! The others cannot even find us in this wet," Ricsige told him.

They rushed into the bay on surging rollers, among fantastic sea rocks, each sculpted by Lir into a shape unique, and all deceptive. Gudrun's pirates toiled waist deep to drag their vessels ashore, yet before they could do it, the Kentishmen were upon them. They threw out anchors in desperate haste and came to hand grips with their enemies where water swirled about their calves.

"Get *Ormungandr* ashore, you nitwits!" Gudrun screamed. "Beach her, get back into her; hold her like a fortress at any cost! You will be more secure within her anyhow."

She cursed and beat fifty men into doing so while the Kentishmen pressed through the waves. Ottar's berserks came first, the madness of their kind seething in them. Throwing their clothes away, they raged ashore with their eyes white and slaver in their beards. Their strength tripled. Weapons did not bite on their noisome bodies. Only the most skilled or powerful blows wounded them at all. Even those gashes closed at once and scarcely bled. They left corpses wherever they went.

Felimid, still weary, found himself facing one of the maniacs. He moved away, playing his foe, evading his wild blows and striking in turn when he saw chances, yet doing little harm. Not even Kincaid's edge cut the berserk deeply, and he seemed tireless. A glancing blow from his axe nearly shattered Felimid's arm.

The bard tried another way. Turning as if to run, he lured the berserk into a blundering rush. Then, with all the agility he could yet summon, he spun on the wet sand and slipped past his adversary. A hard drawing cut to the back of the knee crippled the berserk.

Felimid circled him then, forcing him to turn on his bad leg, hopping and growling. When he saw his chance, Felimid threw his utmost skill and timing into a slash which opened the berserk's throat. He thrashed on the beach, arteries cut and windpipe opened. None of those vital parts lay far beneath the skin.

Leaving the dying man, Felimid sought Gudrun. She had gathered her pirates into some sort of order and withdrawn ashore. Ricsige's household troopers followed behind a shield wall which steadied and grew firmer as they came dripping onto the beach.

The two forces struggled back and forth while the berserks mangled Gudrun's flanks. Eighty Jutes fought to board *Ormungandr* while the pirates holding her fought as savagely to keep them out. The great advantage was theirs, for they stood above their beseigers on *Ormungandr*'s wales. No Jute dared burn or damage that ship. Vithils would have done it at need, in the face of Loki himself, but Vithils was not there.

Spears hard-driven from above pierced shoulders and bearded throats. Blood gushed around the ferrules; men dropped to the trampled sand. Axes broke skulls and faces. Panting, thwarted, the Jutes drew back and argued among themselves.

"Throw up a ramp of sand! We'll make it wide and charge them, six abreast!"

"Ha! While they throw javelins and their fellows chop us apart?"

"Drive Blackhair away! Then we'll deal with these scum."

They joined the main fray. Gudrun and Felimid were there, side by side in the center. Gudrun hewed over the rim of her shield; Felimid sent Kincaid pouncing around, below and over his own. He had taken wounds.

Still man after man fell to Kincaid's edge and point. The deadly surprise of having a sword thrust at them, when to their minds only the sword's edge was of use, claimed many a Kentish life. For what seemed the thousandth time a spear drove at Felimid's face. He turned the thrust aside with the convex surface of his shield. The point skidded over it, after an impact that jarred in Felimid's bones. Kincaid punched through leather into a shrinking belly. The bard twisted him and drew him back.

Now a war club smote at him in a brawny hand. This time he was too late with the large northern shield. Only his helmet saved his skull and the brain within. Triple-ply walrus leather, lined with padding, plated with whalebone over the crown and temples, it spared his life and gave him cause for a lifetime's gratitude to dwarvish workmanship. Still, he sank sideways into the sand, head filled with burning mist and distance, mouth filling with grit.

Out of his daze he sent Kincaid slanting upward to open the clubber's thigh. Gudrun Blackhair finished the man as he sagged on his weakened leg. Felimid struggled upright, and the fray continued.

Ricsige fought well among his household troopers, those seasoned warriors who gave little joy to any who came against them. He had not yet encountered Gudrun, and he was not to do so, because she ordered a retreat.

"Withdraw!" she cried. "Back, I tell you!"

This was so unlike her that the Kentishmen should have been warned. They were not. Heartened, they pursued the pirates up to the beach. As the latter reached the rocky ledges which effectively ended their retreat, Njal and his Danes charged from the western end of the bay where they had waited concealed, aided by the weather. Hardy and fresh, they came out of the drizzle to fall on the Kentishmen, tearing their flank apart. The line rolled up.

Now it was Kent's turn to withdraw, to know rout. But theirs was real. Three berserks lay dead. Most of the others were past their frenzy, and staggered or crawled from the fight in their resulting weakness. Thrain was the exception. He remained, snarling like a werewolf, red from head to foot, and killed two allies who tried to budge him from the slaughter. The rest left him there.

He slew five more pirates, also, and sorely hurt six, but with his madness passing, he weakened. A whetted axe in the hands of long-armed Sigar let out his entrails. Even then he fought on. Sigar went in behind the berserk's faltering axe, to chop away his shoulder and arm. Thrain fell at last, with a snarl and snap of teeth, his great body like something in a butcher's yard. Sigar decapitated him.

"By Tyr," he panted, "we'd best bury this one with his head under his knee, lest he walk."

The Kentishmen had gone in their ships by then.

They found as they rowed away that their troubles were far from over. As Vithils had said, they did not know Sarnia's coasts. An island three miles long, surrounded by islets, rocks, and a tricky sea, can offer many fatal surprises even in clear weather.

The Children of Lir could offer the same.

As Ricsige groped his way to the narrow passages between Sarnia and Brechou, two phantom ships moved in behind his wretched fleet. Unseen, they proceeded to harry it as dogs harry foolish sheep, nipping, barking, slashing.

One galley shattered on a rock after its rudder oar was lost, and scaly sea demons swarmed around the wreckage to feast well. A second was granted the sight of *Naglfar* bearing down, the ship made of dead men's nails and crewed by corpses, with Loki at the tiller. Then they found their ship's planks pried asunder from below, the sea pouring in, fanged monsters waiting for them—and that part was no illusion. With special and particular cruelty a third was allowed to win clear of Sarnia's southern coasts and its crew to breathe in relief. They ceased to be relieved when sentient kelp rose from the sea bottom to enwrap their oars, and bone-barbed faerie missiles began to sing from nowhere.

Two ships only escaped that rain-wet nightmare. Ricsige's was one, Chamo's the second; and Ricsige did nothing but stare into the grayness, mumble, and shudder. The experience had cost him his wits.

XVIII

The Norns weave fate which may not be altered;
Face it fearlessly, free of care,
For if you run you will find it before you.
Turn your back and it takes you there.
—Felimid mac Fal,
Gudrun's Saga

Felimid sat as comfortably as he might in the sting of his hurts, which were neither fatal nor crippling, and therefore not of much moment in this company. Only one was even deep. He had washed it with wine and sewn its edges together himself, Gudrun being occupied with many worse injuries among her men, and several determined little fiends were now probing it with hot needles.

He drank more of the light, heady mead he preferred to the thick variety. Although he should have been looking at the hall through a golden haze by now, the drink might as well have been transparent water. He played glorious songs on Golden Singer, and to him they sounded hollow.

The pirates celebrated triumph. Nothing was too good for their allies, the Children of Lir. They sat in places of honor at Gudrun's table, Niamh first among them, looking exhausted but holding herself straight. The bard could guess why she looked worn.

Nacrantal laughed and joked with the pirates, a bit supercilious still, but mighty good-humored. Turo the otter man played knucklebones with Rowan while a soft-eyed earthling girl drank his green wine beside him. Decius talked tactics with Gudrun, Waldin, and Pascent, who had returned from Lesia after reach-

193

ing an agreement with the chieftain Laban concerning the lifted grain.

Two of Laban's sons had returned with him, wanting a part in the battle so close to their own island. Felimid had met them before, young men like himself, reckless and changeable, but simpler of heart than he.

He stroked his harp, dreamy-eyed, using the instrument to lift himself out of himself. He played the irresistible laughter strain because the hall should be mirthful. He played it because it went with the pirates' own inclinations and mood. He might as easily have harped grief or slumber on all those present, but he had been sternly taught not to indulge such cranky whims of power. The pirates should laugh.

Their enemies had been reduced by a third in a single day!

Gudrun laughed and was merry with them. As their leader she could not show a gloomy face, and perhaps she did not even feel gloomy. Felimid knew her too well by now, though, to take her chaffer for just what it seemed.

Sliding Golden Singer into her bag, he slung the bag in its accustomed place on his back. One corner of it showed above his right shoulder as he moved with liquor-slowed grace to join the group of captains. If his drinking had not much affected his mind or heart, it did make itself known to his legs. He seated himself beside Waldin, across from Gudrun.

"Tonight we should divide the Champion's Portion among all of us present," he remarked. The irony passed unseen, or at any rate without comment. "As for tomorrow—what would you do, Gudrun, if you were Vithils?"

"I would bide for clear daylight, and meet with the king of Kent," she answered. "Vithils has shown that he's no such idiot as to blunder about my shores when he cannot see. Ricsige should have had as much wisdom!" She smiled mirthlessly. "But it is well that he did not."

This from Gudrun, who would a month before have been magnificent in her rage at the bare suggestion that sea demons be summoned to do the smallest share of her fighting, touched Felimid's blood with a little more cold than already resided there.

"Edric and Vithils will own the voices which decide wisdom in that fleet, after today. Even the Kentishmen will look to them as leaders."

"The Kentishmen who still breathe air!" Arnehad said, and guffawed.

"We're not troubling our heads with the others," Pascent assured him. "If I were Vithils, which God prevent, and had six hundred men, as he has, I'd land on the northern part of the island and make sure I controlled it. Then I'd take the southern part."

"As easily as that, so."

"It wouldn't be easy to force the Hatchet's Edge, but with those berserks to lead—"

"I believe that is how Vithils will think." Gudrun pondered the clay relief map of Sarnia which covered a part of the table. Felimid had sculpted it with his hands. "He will find no food on the northern side . . . yet I am not minded to let him have that, either. It is mine, every yard. I will fight him for it if he comes."

"Better to let him land, since he cannot be prevented. All our people, cattle, and ships are here in the south. There he will be, frustrated on the far side of the Hatchet's Edge with nothing to eat but wild rhubarb, and such a mighty host cannot hold together long when bellies start aching. Old quarrels will be remembered. They will melt away, and never come back with such a host again. They have had such losses already as no war leader ever forgets."

"Our food will not last long, either," Waldin said.

Naf, Laban's fifth son, put in a word. "Our father is having your grain milled this minute, lady. You will not hunger while he holds Lesia."

"That may not be long, if he angers Vithils," Waldin sneered. "It will take another sea fight to get the bread here."

"It will take a simple glamor, no more," Niamh told him. "I will answer for your food arriving. Let us talk of difficult things."

Gudrun rested her chin on her hand. She did not have to study the clay map. It was for those less familiar with Sarnia's shores; Felimid had made it partly for his own instruction, with Decius and others to correct his errors.

The northern and larger part of the island, cliff girt like the south, had several fair harbors. The southern part was almost wholly separate, and there Gudrun's hall stood. It could be reached in three ways, short of flying; by two paths fit for goats which led up the cliffs from two small coves, and across the high isthmus known as the Hatchet's Edge, one hundred paces long, two wide, and with cliffs falling away to the deadly sea on either side.

Gudrun's ships all rode in one of the small coves, *Ormun-gandr* included. Someone made the point that Vithils might attack there and destroy the ships, thus trapping them at his mercy.

"No," Decius said. "The northern part is all that's open to him. My trusty little onagers will see to him if he comes by daylight. If he tries it at night, I'll grieve for him."

The onagers he mentioned were small skein-powered catapults emplaced on the cliffs, able to hurl stones or fiery missiles seaward at different ranges. Part of his Roman heritage, they had sunk attacking ships before, and he trained and drove the crews who worked them until their accuracy was fearful. He'd earned the prideful affection with which he spoke.

"Your whanging toys won't stop Vithils, Spaniard."

It was Waldin, of course, trying to be more Roman than the Hispano-Roman bred for generations. Too casually, he drew his short cape over the barbaric tattoos on his bare arms.

"Vithils is a great and crafty fighter, but he's a savage withal," Decius said, smiling. "He won't respect the onagers enough until it's too late, even supposing he wins past your folk, my lady"—he inclined his head to Niamh—"and the demons."

Gudrun once again let that mention of demons pass. Waldin silently choked on the word savage, as Decius had intended he should.

"Now, about the order and array of battle."

They settled that in open council with Gudrun's drunken devils over the next couple of hours. Men shouted at each other, demanded precedent, cited examples of how heroes had done it, counter-cited other figures of legend, battles from tribal history, garbled accounts of Roman tactics, on and on until the strongest and clearest heads there prevailed—more because their opponents were unconscious than for any other reason.

Gudrun and Felimid were among the finalists, their sight blurred in the yellow torchlight. Not until then did Felimid ask the question that had hung in his mind all day, since the event.

"Why did you do it, Gudrun? Why leap into Ealdrad's ship like that, as though seeking death? And forever why turn me back from coming to get you out of that trouble, as though I hadn't the right? 'No, Bragi,' " he mimicked. " 'You must stay alive to sing of me' Well I know that is why you took me from Pascent's sinking ship in the beginning, yet I have become more than that to you since. Any man of your pirates would fight for you. Why shouldn't I?''

"You grow windy, my dearest man. I could have asked that in half the words." Gudrun smiled bitterly. "You saw the One-Eyed call to me today. He has come for the price of my disobeying him, and I am fey. I knew it when I saw him. I am fey, but you may not be."

"And nor may you! Cairbre and Ogma! He showed himself in Ricsige's ship, and what has happened to Ricsige since, we all do know! If that is what happens to those Odin favors, you whom he flatters with his ill will are likely to die of old age."

Gudrun laughed, truly amused. "That is a good saying, Bragi, though you should say his name so lightly. Use his titles; he has enough of them. Wanderer, Battle-Glad, the Abaser, Greybeard, Victory-Father, Death-Worker, Stirrer-of-Strife, Wakeful, Grim, and a hundred more. All safer than Odin."

"Safer," Felimid said, smiling. "That must be why men come to you; to be safe. I am not likely to walk out of this business alive if you do not, my heart, so I had better believe your doom is not here on Sarnia. And there is a large mouthful of negatives for you. My instructors in the bardic college would say my years in wandering have rusted my word skill."

"And a fearful thing that would be. My ears tell me you are apprehensive for nothing, Bragi. Let us go to bed."

She and Felimid left the hall with arms about each other's waists. They were kissing when they reached her chamber. They loved once with urgency, then slowly for hours, until the pallet was damp with sweat and they had said things to each other that neither had said at all before. When at last they lay together, sated, Gudrun shed tears on Felimid's neck and said, her voice muffled:

"I would have remained in your land with you, Bragi, not sought the Otherworlds."

He felt moved, but did not believe it, though he was sure she did in that moment. It didn't matter. She said "would have," and that meant she was still sure she was fey; marked by Fate to die. He held her, and hated a certain one-eyed god as he had not hated anything before.

The bird of air did not come back. Felimid wondered a little, in passing, in the early morning, what news it might have given him. *Sing to me! Give me stories in exchange for my news!* He knew now why he had dismissed the sprite so curtly when it made that request. He'd been reminded of Gudrun's words on more than one occasion. Maybe he was only that, a trader in music and words, with no more to offer. Treasures of cloud, towers of air . . .

His wound hurt. That, he told himself, was the source of this melancholy, nothing deeper. With Vithils bent on retribution, somewhere nearby, it was a fine thing to be glooming about.

Vithils was indeed somewhere nearby. On the trembling shores of Angia, a larger island neighbor to the pirate lair, the Kentish remnant met with him, Edric, and Cynric. Ricsige maundered and wailed until his henchmen were ashamed for him.

"So Gudrun Blackhair allies with demons, does she?"

"No doubt of it," Stur Worferth's son said.

"The Serpent writhes," Ricsige said usefully. "Maggots and ordure of the sea bottom stir, and stir, and foul the broth with their bodies. Aegir's ale is tainted. Ran casts her nets and all is caught within them. The rotten meshes close. . . ."

"Get away," Vithils said brutally. "The men lose heart because of you."

"Blackhair's demons will not save her," Aur the wizard declared. "Odin favors us!"

Vithils stared at him so forbiddingly that he backed away somewhat.

"That is what Ricsige said before we put to sea. Now look at him! Odin seems ever to be on the side of the greatest slaughter, wizard. Maybe that's why he aided me to come this far, but I never have trusted him. For my people's honor I have to go forward. I'll go forward alone if it comes to that. . . ."

"Not alone," Stur assured him.

"Yet I must give heart to the men somehow. They have lost it with these events."

"Consult an augury," the wizard advised. "Some of Blackhair's men were taken in battle, and Stur is about to behead them anyhow. Let me sacrifice them to the Victory-Giver instead, and read the omens in their deaths!"

"The blood on our keels did precious little to help Ricsige," Edric rumbled. "Behead them cleanly, I say."

"I'd rather," Vithils admitted, "but the other way should hearten the men—if the omens are good."

He said no more, only regarded the wizard bleakly and fingered his axe. Clear in his manner and stance was his meaning; that the omens had better be good. Oars from the warships were lashed together to form a gallows of ash wood; the captives, dedicated to Odin, shortly dangled from it. Before they died they were thrust through with spears. Aur crouched below like a gray wolf, watching each jerk, each angle of a dripping spear shaft, the patterns in the falling blood.

"If we fight on the water, the cost will be our destruction," he announced at last, above the sea's hollow roar. "If we land and fight them on Sarnia itself, we will gain the victory."

"A good prophecy," Vithils muttered under his breath, "for it's what I intended." In a full-throated voice he addressed the host to be heard. "Cynric, atheling of Westri, are you with us? Men of Kent, are you with me, and will you follow me under your own leaders, Stur and Chamo—outstanding leaders both? Berserks of Odin, are you with me? *Men of Edricsburg, are you with me?*"

Their assent nearly brought down the cliffs. The Kentishmen cried loudest—for vengeance, for grief, for shame, and in Odin's inspiration of bloodlust. Their king sat apart from them and mumbled.

Later he took a rope and crept to the unguarded gibbet, hanging himself from it beside the four victims already there, a fifth and royal sacrifice. So he was regarded by his Kentish eaters when they found him, and so he was remembered thereafter—until time swallowed even his name, which did not take long.

Nothing could have made the Jutes more wholly committed to their venture. The worst shame they could bring on themselves would have been to break faith with their dead lord. Cynric would not turn back for his name's sake, and he accepted Vithils as the expedition's leader as he would have accepted few other men above himself.

The wind shrieked, and clouds blew ragged. A few raindrops pelted past the creaking gallows, the beached warships, the hundreds of men in their leather and iron. Whitecaps crashed landward. Yet sunbeams lanced through the torn clouds, too, striking gray water to a gold-green lucency in places.

The fleet made for Sarnia in the first clear weather.

XIX

A gray god smiles in the shrieking tempest,
Frost kings march out of Niflheim,
Heroes whiten and kingdoms sunder—
Worlds break apart at the tread of time.

What gods imprisoned, now Fate releases—
Hear the breaking of Fenrir's chain!
His father's fetters, too, lie in pieces,
And Loki is steering to Vigrid Plain.
—Felimid mac Fal,
Ragnarok

"They come."

Gudrun spoke calmly as she looked across the sea. The dozen ships remaining of her enemies' power still made a mighty fleet. Kingdoms had been founded or overthrown with much smaller forces. The White Horse, Vithils's green-and-black sail, the vivid orange and white of Cynric's three, bore them landward before the breeze to their chosen landing place, the best and safest harbor on Sarnia's eastern side. Gudrun awaited them on the skyline above it with three hundred men.

"A pity we're so nearly out of arrows," she went on. Her own quiver was full, but no other bowman in her host could say that. They had half a dozen shafts each.

"We have other surprises for them," Felimid said, the pain of his wound forgotten. There was no time to pamper it. "So has Niamh, as she said."

"That filthy blood kelp!" Gudrun spat. "I'm as bad as Urbicus for having a thing to do with it. Not that it has been effective . . . why did it not slither aboard their ships and attack men on the seats? Why did it hamper no more than two or three ships?"

"I suppose the sea demons do not have so much of it," Felimid guessed. "It must be nourished with hot blood. They would have to feed it, on men, cattle, and maybe the rare whale, and they are not brave. At the dark bottom of the sea they could scarcely be raising whole fields of it."

"If that is all—"

"No, Niamh spoke otherwise, and I believe her. There will be more, and it may prove more than we want to see. The worst is that we cannot gripe!" Felimid smote the flat of his hand upon a rock. "We do want it."

"There are no sea demons in sight. You spoke the truth, man o' mine; cowards are they all. They deserve life in the black dark! I have lived mine in the daylight, at least."

Felimid put a smile on the pang it cost him to hear her talk as though her life was done. "You will not let any persuade you against death, will you? I'll drink you under the table at the end of the day, girl."

"There is Niamh."

Between the shore and the approaching fleet stood a rock shaped like a crouching dragon. Niamh stood on its triangular head in all her haughty poise. She lifted her arms.

"Father Lir, hear me, your daughter of royal power! Hear me call on your strength! Master of the green sea, of all waters the world around, send me a mighty wave! Let your servants thrust the waters landward, let them dash the waters in a high wall against the shores of yonder bay, let the ships I see be shattered, ground upon the shore, broken and strewn with all their mariners! Let their figured prows crash! Shake your green mane, Father Lir! Roar and ravage the fleet that comes here! Children of the sunlit waters, creatures of the black depths—"

"Cease."

The voice was deep, hard to resist as a moving glacier, and as cold. Niamh's own voice locked in her throat as she slowly turned her head.

The stranger with the rune-carved spear stood upon the rock. His gray beard blew. The single eye held Niamh as though she were impaled. His spear glittered no more terribly.

"This is not your affair," he said. "We will do without your meddling henceforward. Take your people; go from Sarnia and Brechou. Do not return."

"Lord . . ." she whispered, and lost the courage to speak

further. She braced herself erect and tried again, with success. "Lord, I have promised my help to Blackhair, and I am royal."

The Wanderer spoke implacably. "Think of your own people first. Raise the wave you intend, and tonight the men who drowned in Ricsige's folly will come from the sea to leave nothing alive in the caves of Brechou. They will come with dead eyes, kelp stranding their beards. The edges of their weapons are keen yet. The remnant of your folk will die to the last babe.

"Summon your wave now, sea woman; dash my fleet ashore. Why do you look back and forth?"

"Lir is my god! Those dead who drowned belong to the sea. You cannot claim them."

"Enough. When I hung on the ash, myself sacrificed to myself, I became a king of death. Even less than the sea am I held within boundaries, and these dead are mine. You know I can raise them. I can be neither polite nor patient if you gibber."

Niamh shuddered.

"Choose."

Niamh bent her head. "I yield to you, lord. But Gudrun Blackhair will not."

"For that I chose her. Now watch the fleet land."

Niamh obeyed, her mind a wilderness for once.

Edric's ship came on. The sea demons she had allied with at such cost were nowhere in view. Niamh thought in bitterness that they were too coldly wise for that. Risking naught themselves, they would have scavenged the results of her wrecking. Now they had doubtless fled back to the depths.

Yet was she better? *One sea is every sea.*

They were strange thoughts for a daughter of Lir to have.

One by one the brown-hulled ships grounded and men waded ashore in their war gear. Gudrun watched them, grinding her teeth at Niamh's failure to do anything, yet knowing why. She had seen the blue-mantled figure confront her, and Niamh bow in capitulation.

"By every power, I will not go tamely!" she said. "We still have our strength. It will serve us."

She assessed the host below with a warrior's eye.

"Slay Vithils now," Felimid advised. "We will be better off if they lack him for a leader."

"I will when I have a clear shot," Gudrun answered. "The bow is my weapon; do not jog my arm."

Both spoke coolly. They had few uncertainties left, and they had planned how to meet what was coming. The Children of Lir had failed them. There was no time to bewail that truth. As Gudrun declared, they had their own strength.

She searched for the great figure with the rusty beard. Yes, there he was, in gray Gothic helmet and scale byrnie, conspicuous among the surrounding war men.

Get away from him, you dogs, let me see him plainly for a moment!

They did not. He held his shield in a wary fashion, too. He knew where he was. Then he advanced into the broken rocks rising beyond the beach, and a clear shot was impossible. The mixed host advanced behind him. A quarter of it stayed behind to guard the beached vessels.

Gudrun's men toppled boulders on the climbing foe. They bounded and rebounded down the broken, receding cliffs, some missing entirely, some smearing men like beetles in their leather sarks. They did not stop.

Now they were gaining the top, and falling to the last arrows the pirates had left. Saxons returned the fire with their own short bows, better supplied with arrows. Berserks pranced in the front of the advance, naked and blackened with charcoal in animal fat, more hideous than ever. And Vithils moved inexorably forward among his comrades.

"Blackhair!" he thundered. "Let's finish that fight we once began! I have work to do this summer, and a wife to go home to!"

"She will have to find another man!"

Gudrun's desperate crew charged. They wore trousers and kilts, tunics and furs, leather armor, iron armor, lamellar, scale, and none. Dirt and tarnish mingled with looted finery. They carried weapons of every design and make, from the short-handled Frankish axe to the wide-bladed stabbing spear. Their swords ranged from simple lengths of beaten tanged iron, through the professional single-edged *spatha*, to magnificent heirlooms like Kissing Viper and Kincaid. They spoke twenty different tongues, and their common shout was "Blackhair!"

Their numbers drove the few Saxons to have gained the skyline back down among the rocks. They did not stay there. Doggedly they fought their way back through the broken granite. By fours and fives they advanced, at times hiding among granite boulders while their comrades came behind them, then moving forward again. Sometimes an arrow would find a man who exposed himself too long, too plainly.

The little groups of climbing Saxons met similar fours and fives of pirates coming down to stop them, and red skirmishes would leave corpses among the rugged stone. Gudrun was not being heroically magnanimous on this day, and her men had never been so inclined. No thought entered her mind of generously allowing the foe to come up in force, arrange his lines, and join battle on terms that denied her the high ground's advantage. Nor would Vithils have respected her for it.

"Let them pay for every yard!" Gudrun said.

"We will," the attackers replied with their weapons. "We will pay for it, and then take it."

The day grew two hours older. By a sort of common consent the two sides rested, with some forty of Vithils's Saxons established among the rocks just below the skyline. Cudebehrt led them. Scattered among the ledges and boulders below, three hundred fighters waited to move. Gudrun's bowmen had spent their last arrows.

Felimid's helmet was off, the smooth brown hair pressed close to his head. Bread, cheese, and an apple lay sliced on the surface of his shield. At the moment he was not eating. With Golden Singer in his hands he sent a humiliating satire down through the rocks to the Saxons' ears. His harp notes hummed like wasps and stung in the same way. The words lifted skin to rub in salt. Worse, they made men feel foolish to be where they were, doing what they were about to do. They undermined the will to fight.

"I'll break that singer's harp to pieces and use the shards to kindle a slow fire beneath him," Cudebehrt said. "Put rags of cloth in your ears if you have not the will to ignore him. Then follow my sword. Roar loudly to drown his song for those coming after!"

Knives in hard-palmed hands slashed little strips of wadmal; fingers stuffed them in hairy ears. Then Cudebehrt raised sword and shield, shouted, and charged with his forty behind him. The remainder of the host seethed out of the rocks like ants from a broken nest. Cynric of Westri in his fineness of royal armor came well to the fore, gold winking on his arms.

"Westri is here! We come for you, Blackhair!"

Cudebehrt's forty closed with the pirates. At their head, conspicuous in her silvered mail, Gudrun showed even to Cudebehrt's short-sighted eyes. He called her name as he raced toward her. She laughed a welcome, then asked:

"Where is Vithils? Did he have to send you?"

"Vithils will speak for himself!"

"So? You take this one, Bragi."

"The leavings you do not want? Ochone, you're greedy, my black darling."

Cudebehrt saw green eyes and a smooth face incongruously framed in a hard leather war hat with whalebone cheek pieces. Felimid had donned the helm again, and his harp was being carried to the hall by an old Celt who understood the importance of such things. Still, Cudebehrt guessed at once that here was the bard he had promised a somewhat fancy death. He slashed at Felimid's legs.

Knees bent, the bard moved aside so swiftly that his legs were not in the path of Cudebehrt's cut. He replied with a sharp blow at the Saxon's helm. Cudebehrt raised his shield and his own sword darted forward again. Felimid tilted his shield sideways to ward his left hip, and Cudebehrt's edge shrieked across the surface. It came within an inch of breaking on the boss.

Felimid rammed that iron cone into Cudebehrt's middle. The two shields locked together, edge under edge, and the pair strained together while men struggled and stamped about them. Cudebehrt slowly levered the bard's shield aside and struck through the gap like deadly lightning. Felimid fell, gagging. The stroke had not opened his cuirass, made with such art by the red dwarves, but the sick pain of the impact dropped him to his knees. Cudebehrt struck downward with his shield's edge at the bard's skull. Barely did Felimid lift his own shield in time. They met with a boom. Then Felimid slashed the Saxon's legs, shearing all the way through one shinbone, and it was Cudebehrt's time to go down. Felimid drove Kincaid's point into his throat.

Rising to his feet, he saw Vithils. The massive body and thick limbs combined with the great red beard made that identification certain. Then the figure was gone, wading into the fight's thickest part.

The stark naked berserks with their blackened skin rushed through the fray like figures from Helheim. They raged irresistibly, the terror of their convulsed faces freezing those they met as they smote with their axes in terrible joy.

Felimid moved lightly yet, whenever the press of the fight allowed it, and in one-to-one fighting he was always the victor. Kincaid darted, flashed, and licked forth, those who opposed its master as likely to feel the point as the edge, while they themselves knew only the use of the edge and could be hideously surprised by a simple thrust. And Felimid's swordplay was rarely simple. Any leisured watcher—there were none—might have called it a juggling display. Yet the results were as fatal as any crude slasher's.

He fought and slew. Always there were more coming. Always the confusion of the battle kept him from gaining any idea of who was winning. He shouted "Blackhair!" until his voice gave out, and fought in silence thereafter.

He and Gudrun lost each other, found each other again, and guarded each other's sides. Between them they killed another of the berserks, and when the monstrous black-and-red figure finally sank down in his last convulsions, they were each a standing, panting ache. And the fight went on.

Then Gudrun cried, "Come, guest!" Felimid had the hot premonition that she spoke to Vithils, even before he saw the heavy-limbed figure in the Gothic helm striding toward them. His axe was notched and dripping, his byrnie spattered, his shield hacked almost to pieces, and still he looked indestructible. If the strain of wearing and wielding iron so long told on him, it remained his secret.

"I will take no help against this one, Bragi," Gudrun said swiftly. "I mean it."

"Cairbre and Ogma!" he retorted. "I would take the help of a bear and a wild ox against him, if I could get it! Do not be a fool, my own."

"Come between us and you will hang from hooks," she spat, and swept Kissing Viper in a circle that claimed lone conflict.

Felimid would have ignored her mandate, if two Saxons had not engaged his attention just then with stabbing spears. She did not turn to aid him.

The bard stood his ground and saw only glimpses of the fight between Gudrun and Vithils. Her bright helmet flashed; the axe of Vithils rose. Behind his ragged shield was an arm thick as most men's thighs, and Gudrun concentrated on it, working to reduce the shield even more while placing more strain on that massive arm. She knew it was his weakness, since she had nearly cut it off the previous summer.

Zucharre the Basque came to Felimid's aid out of nowhere, by placing a knife neatly in one of the spearmen's kidneys. His dark, narrow face smiled, and he still moved with his tireless bouncing energy. Felimid said, "One . . . I owe you

. . . mountain walker," and cut through the shaft of the second man's spear before killing him.

Because of that exquisite timing on the Basque's part, Felimid saw how Gudrun's fight with Vithils ended. The giant's arm had mere shards of his linden protection hanging from it now, and at Gudrun's next calculated stroke that hand fell helpless to his side. He raised his axe, but slowly, with a tired arm, for the weapon weighed all of half a stone. Gudrun aimed her sword at his sweat-dark beard.

The arm gripping the shield boss came up and around in a scything punch with that iron cone on the end of it. Gudrun was hurled sideways by that terrific buffet, her jaw smashed. Vithils struck three devastating blows with his axe, and Felimid's whole body reacted to each as he ran forward. The first split Gudrun's own shield in two as she struggled, half conscious, to ward herself; the second drove broken ribs of half her side into her lungs, the fearful impact doing the work without having to split her mail or the hard leather beneath it; and the last turned her thigh to splintered bone in a tube of torn meat.

Felimid's tortured howl was involuntary. He flung himself at the great Saxon, making his helmet ring and Vithils stagger. Then his sworder's training caused him to drop into a rational, bent-legged stance for his attack.

"Sa-ha," Vithils said, tiger softly. "The slayer of Cudebehrt. I'll see you again, no beard, fear not."

He retreated then, dropping the remnant of his shield, for Felimid had only obtained a new one minutes before and the advantage was too great. Vithils was as careful as ruthless, and if he said he would see the bard again, that promise would be kept.

Felimid let him go. Gudrun lived yet, though horribly maimed. One glance at her shattered thigh as it jetted great fountains of blood was enough to know she had predicted her own death truly. She clawed the earth in her pain. Turning an agonized glance toward Felimid, a look in which there was hardly even recognition, she thrust herself into a half-sitting position with the strength of both arms. Her head stretched far back and her mouth stretched wide. Her pride turned a scream of mortal agony into a high, shaking shout of *"Mor-ri-guuuuuu!"*

With the name of the Celtic war goddess in her mouth, she fainted. Zucharre, Hemming, and Rowan made a litter of spears to take her from the moans of fighting, while Felimid vainly tried to stop the blood spilling out of her. When at last he gave up and looked at her face, he saw scarlet froth on her mouth. All hope left him then.

He never remembered much else of what happened. He knew he went beside Gudrun's bier in the long, hard-fought retreat across the plateau to the Hatchet's Edge, where fifty pirates had been posted to guard it for any losers who might require it, and a rear guard to cover their crossing. He battled beside Zucharre and Hemming to hold back the Saxons while his comrades crossed the blade-thin isthmus, and so did Rowan, fighting as well as any of them until a spear in the body ended his life of seventeen years. The three who survived him were the last to cross the narrow path to safety. Only Felimid glanced back at what had been Rowan; his look was envious.

Then he looked at the sky, caught by a glimpse of movement there. Great flocks of ravens were flying out of the north on a freezing wind. Among them, between the ragged clouds, rode the war god's dreadful servants, the *waelcyrior*, the Corpse-Choosers, with taut, enraptured faces and arms bloody to the elbows, shrieking their joy at the sights below them.

"Yes, send your scavengers, evil-worker," Felimid cried. "They will not have her. By your own word she is no more yours. She died calling upon the Morrigu."

"Easy, Bragi," Hemming advised. Clearly he was concerned for the bard's sanity; all he beheld in the sky was birds. Felimid was used to that reaction and paid it no heed. His lover was dead. *Dead.*

The truth of it struck home. He felt pain again, pain of entire belief, as though an arm had been torn out of him, out and away from his living body with a rending of bone, flesh, and nerves, making him forever less than whole. He groaned aloud.

"Bragi." It was Decius. Tears ran unregarded from the Spaniard's one living eye. His voice was steady. "Come into the hall. There are things that must be done. Wash yourself and *her*, wasting no time. Then come down. It's for us now to hold these wild wolves together to the end."

"Yes." The bard lifted his head. He was glad there was so much to do and more fighting to come; glad of it for once. The activity would fill his mind and maybe preserve it. He entered the hall.

By then all the fighting men in it knew that the Children of Lir had deserted them.

XX

Be not overwary, but wary enough,
First, of the foaming ale,
Second, of a woman wed to another,
Third, of the tricks of thieves.
— The Words of the High One

There was a wicked, desperate air in the hall that was thicker than the smoke. Felimid smelled it. Gudrun had been the living talisman who held these varied outlaws together as a coherent force. Their leader, their center, their luck, had departed, and so had their supernatural allies, gone like fading smoke. They were ready to split into factions and separate, fleeing at random; or worse, to turn on each other, with Vithils just beyond the Hatchet's Edge. That had to be prevented.

Felimid stood before them. Gudrun's litter of spears had been exchanged for a true bier covered with furs. She had been wrapped in a long silken cloak, one fold of it covering her ruined jaw. Her black hair flowed loose. The wild flowers of Sarnia surrounded her, primroses, bluebells, and ferns.

"We are leaderless now, or some of us may think we are," Felimid said. "True it is that we'll find no leader like the lady again. But we have captains here to match any among our bloody foes, and I know that one or two see themselves as the new lord of Sarnia. That's foolish until we have settled with Vithils the Axe and his friends. Now all of you know me. I was the lady's spokesman while she lived, and I speak with her voice now that she is slain. The Hatchet's Edge is well guarded, like the cove where our ships are. We can last longer than they can. Tonight we hold the lady's grave-ale feast, and tomorrow we hold back the tide until it ebbs."

209

"Who are you to say what we'll do?" demanded a belligerent Goth. "You were the lady's pet, no more, you bench ornament! When we want a song, we'll call upon you. What we need now is a new leader, and I say let it be Decius."

"Helmuth, isn't it?" Felimid asked, knowing well that it was. "You went on *Ormungandr*'s northern voyage and came back. Not all of us did. I showed then that I can do more than sing, and I showed it this day. The lady's pet? Maybe. But she chose me for her spokesman, and she made a good choice. Do you disparage it? And I'm as ready to have Decius lead us as you are, so that he leads us against the Saxons." His voice husked suddenly, and his eyes burned. "They owe us payment for this day's work."

"Yea, and we'll take it!"

Other vengeful shouts arose. Felimid shook his head sadly.

"Is that the best you can do, now? I have heard you roar louder when the meat was late. Were you ever Blackhair's men? This is what her foes have done to her! *Vengeance for Blackhair!*"

"Vengeance for Blackhair!"

This time it was a satisfactory thunder.

"Then let's be drinking to that, and to her name. Later we can see her to her gods, and better gods than the one she used to worship! I loved her, and I say we should send her as she would have wished to go, as Danish chieftains go, in her burning ship with loot and trophies around her! Those Kentish bunglers do not deserve to have *Ormungandr* again. In one summer that ship became the lady's, and hers only! Who says no?"

"I do!" growled Pigsknuckle Hromund. "I do! Burn *Ormungandr*? You crazed poet, she's the fastest ship on any sea, and we may be needing her to outdistance Vithils and Cynric! Or hadn't you thought of that?"

"True for you," Felimid replied at once. "I hadn't. I will not be fleeing before them. I stay, and they leave. But there is this about your idea, Pigsknuckle! *Ormungandr* will hold eighty men. What happens to the others? How do we decide who has which ship? We'd be killing each other in moments if it came to that. No. No talk of fleeing. Now let us make this a true wake, such as we hold in Erin for the dead."

"It's not settled yet, or so lightly! What if only eighty can go? That's not to say none should go! *Whale's Sister* is good enough for me—I'm not honing to take *Ormungandr*—but we

may not have ships enough as it is for all of us! What do the
rest of you Sarnians say?''

Dispute followed. Decius supported the bard. Arnehad was
against him, as was Waldin, though he said wryly that he hated
to agree with Arnehad. The pirate crews were divided.

"I'm for it," Pascent said, surprisingly. "She was a rare
chieftain, and should be given a rare funeral, with nothing
shoddy in't. I'll take my chances in my own ship. If it comes
to that, as I don't reckon it will. Not a louse-bitten man of
them will cross the Hatchet's Edge if we resist them.''

It was agreed, and Waldin was angry. He asked Pascent
furiously, later as they drank in a corner:

"Why? We can use *Ormungandr*!''

"Can we?" Pascent asked sardonically. "Take her into any
honest port and we'd hang. Nor am I minded to leave her intact
for foes to follow us. Bragi's lovesickness works for us, so I
gave him support, and so should you.''

"Ha! It's late for us to go from here!''

"That's foolish, and you're no fool, child. Our ships are in
the cove where we can reach them. None bars our way out of
here—yet.''

Torches illuminated his big-featured, raffish face. He wiped
foam from the moustaches bracketing his mouth and peered at
Waldin. The Frankish captain writhed his lips and looked blue
fire in response.

"The woman is dead and the merfolk have run. It's time to
go.''

"Not without a goodly share of the treasure.''

"I like the way you think," Pascent said. "No fear, my lad.
You see this?'' He produced a stoppered flask of Rhineland
glass.

"What is it?'' Waldin asked obligingly, though with a yawn.

"A syrup I brewed from poppy gum. I've been in the east.
I know how. Hear me, Waldin,'' the Gaul said, low-voiced.
"I'll mix this in one small keg of ale, and divide that keg
among a few barrels. The cohort that emptied 'em would snore
until morning. Our own men won't get any, because I've arranged that they will be guarding our ships tonight. We'll just
walk out with as much loot as pleases us, and Vithils can clean
up what we have left.''

"By Attila's red tomb!'' the Frank exclaimed. He shook his
head. The long flowing hair of his rank, or the rank he claimed,

shone honey-colored in the torchlight. "You are a devil, Pascent. Nonetheless . . ." He gnawed an end of his moustache.

"None the less, what?"

"Hell is for traitors and oath-breakers."

"It yawns for pirates, too," Pascent retorted, "and for all heathen. I'll take the sin on my soul, if there is one. I never had any choice about joining Blackhair, save to die, so I should get absolution easily enough. You had better not back out on me now, Waldin."

"Am I so mad as to stay here now? Oh, no, you had better not try to go without me, my friend, or it is you who will stay. With my axe in your skull."

"Then we've agreed," Pascent said. "It's a fine thing, is it not, to have a partnership of trust?"

Waldin took his hand, smiling like a wildcat thinking of robins.

Across the isthmus Vithils laid plans of his own with his allies. Cynric, splendid as Balder, stood with his thumbs jauntily thrust in his girdle, flashing with gold. Ulfcetel sat at his feet, squinting over the camp fire. Stur and Chamo, leaders of the Kentish remnant, squatted on their left. Aur the wizard occupied the last quadrant of the circle.

"There are three ways to reach them," Vithils said. He indicated the ways on a crude map, embroidered by the Queen of Kent in colored wool. "Over the Hatchet's Edge. Up the cliffs by a path well suited to goats, from this cove where their ships lie. Up the cliffs by another path on this side, from this little bay. Which looks best?"

"We have been through this," Chamo complained. "It's not like you to repeat needlessly, Vithils. The Hatchet's Edge is best. It's the shorter way, and they cannot roll rocks on us from above, either."

"Yet it would be a great thing to seize their ships," Cynric said thoughtfully. "I would not have to scale the cliffs to do that."

"Are you saying you would try it?"

"With three *good* ships and all my own men, I would. I'd succeed, what is more. The Children of Lir have gone, deserting the pirates. We have Aur's word for that."

"Yes." Vithils did not say that Aur's word was hardly the vow of Tiw, but the dryness of his short assent conveyed that meaning. "It would be fine to have them wholly trapped, and to know they cannot trap us. Nor would it be bad to have *Ormungandr* in our hands. Yet they will guard her with every trick and power they have. You might go into worse danger than fighting your way over the Hatchet's Edge.''

''There is room for just so many on the Hatchet's Edge.'' Cynric laughed. ''I am for trying my luck on blue water.''

Yes, you're young and full of juice and have done nothing truly notable on this venture yet. It pinches, atheling, doesn't it, for all your good humor? Yet it's the hard truth that you can lead. No dreaming Ricsige you.

''You will deserve all the honor you can win if you do this,'' Vithils conceded. ''You ask for three ships, good ships. Which three will you have?''

''Neither of ours,'' Stur Worferth's son said flatly. ''No offense, atheling. They are all we have to take back to Kent.''

''Then I'll lend three, or persuade Edric to,'' Vithils said. ''See!'' He stabbed his finger at the needlework map. ''We have one hundred men with our own ships, *here*. Cynric will take one hundred fifty. If we cannot carry the Hatchet's Edge with two hundred fifty men, berserks among them, belike it cannot be done at all. We can spare one hundred for an attempt on this little bay with its other cliff path. They have hidden no ships there so far as I know. Maybe it will be less secure, though they are sure to have guards at the top, at least. All we require is a foothold there.''

''That's all,'' Ulfcetel said.

''I will try that if one of your pilots will steer the first ship,'' Stur offered.

''Not so careful of Kent's last vessels now, are you?'' Cynric gibed.

''No need for that,'' Vithils said. ''We had better speak to them all, and Edric must hear the plan before it is settled.''

They settled it at last, and clasped hands in agreement to their three-pronged onslaught. By then the hours until dawn were few. Indeed, it was cockcrow.

The war host ate a solid meal from its dwindling supplies. Cynric led his men aboard the designated ships to await the tide, and Stur did likewise. They must row down Sarnia's eastern shore and round its southernmost point to reach their goals. Cynric admitted that he would be less ready for the gamble if the Children of Lir were still involved.

''If Aur should be wrong and they appear again, to my last

sorrow," he told Vithils, "I ask a favor. Slay that he-witch."

"I shall."

The time came. Vithils, his wounds throbbing like his heart, stood before Cudebehrt's pyre of driftwood and broken houses. The pirate's bane raised cold, tearless eyes to the sky.

"Wait you, kinsman. I will not light your flames until I have made your offerings or gone with you. At least I have given you Blackhair, but there is your own slayer, too. I have promised to see him again."

XXI

I grieve for thy loss,
Red-buttressed fort in the encircling sea.
I grieve for thy slaughter,
Swordwoman of unsurpassed valor, of warlike beauty;
Greater than my own ruin is my cause of lament.
> —Felimid mac Fal,
> *Dirge*   .

Rude hands were on Felimid's shoulders, shaking him so that his head flew back and forth. Then one of the hands steadied him in a sitting position while the other slapped his face.

He'd have responded before that, had he been less weary, but the slap provoked him to move even while half conscious. He seized the unknown's arm, guided by the hand on his shoulder. The unknown was shortly flat on his face in the rushes that covered the floor, his hand twisted up between his shoulder blades and Felimid's knee in the small of his back.

"If you are an enemy," the bard said, "I may forgive you. If you call yourself a friend, it had better be nothing less than utter calamity that moves you to such actions. Who are you?"

The hall was very dim in the hour before dawn, with all the torches out. He could not see.

"Brac," the man beneath him gasped. "Remember me? You spared my life when you fished me from the river that day."

Felimid did not remember. His mind in that moment was as bleary as his eyes. Nor did he find it easy to be considerate when he had just been roughly awakened from badly needed sleep.

"That's a mistake I can always correct, so," he snapped. "Is this your gratitude? Wait! The man who floated down on

215

a brewing-vat cover? Is that you?''

"Yes! Lord, your men are all asleep—the ones guarding the Hatchet's Edge, too.''

That was far worse than the slap. Felimid released the baker.

"Asleep? All? Let's have some light on this.''

He arose, rubbing crusted eyes, and saw Gudrun's bier sur- rounded by the dying flowers. He'd forgotten. Now the knowl- edge that she was dead pierced him through again. It had not been some bitter dream which would vanish in the morning; it was the truth, and he would never escape it. Neither by time or magic could it be undone.

He had not even a moment to grieve over her now.

Brac was kindling torches. Felimid helped him. The few lights partly illuminated the hall, a gloomy cave filled with drugged, inert men. Felimid went from one to the next, shaking, kicking, slapping, aware within minutes that this was no ordi- nary slumber. Some were deeper in it than others, and after a maddening eternity of trying, he had thirty on their feet, som- nolent and stupid.

Decius was not among them. Njal and Arnehad were.

"Wake the rest, if you must do it with hot coals,'' Felimid said. "I'm told it is the same at the Hatchet's Edge. I'll go and see.''

Njal stifled a yawn. "Busk yourself first . . . in your war gear.'' Thinking had become a huge vague effort for him. The news that the way across the Hatchet's Edge might lie open did not have any effect. "Wha' happened last night?''

"Treachery. Maybe we were all given a sleeping potion, or enchantment is in it. If Vithils crosses that narrow path, we will none of us be long concerned. I must go there *now*. Send a man to the cove for news of the ships. We may have to take to them after all.''

Felimid buckled and strapped his gray corslet on as he gave his orders, never pausing to wonder why he should, or why the captains obeyed. He had always been content to let Gudrun lead, because she wanted to and he did not—but now there was no Gudrun, and his was the clearest, swiftest head present. Not that that said much.

He rode like the wind under a lightening sky. The Hatchet's Edge was less than a mile distant. Flinging himself from the back of his horse, he found only a few pirates awake, desper- ately trying to rouse their mates. One was urinating in another's face, cursing him vilely, urging him to stand like a man, while he sat on the ground, chuckling and indifferent.

"Enough," Felimid told the furious pisser. "It's the same at the hall. What caused it? Are you after knowing?"

Foolish question. How should they? Yet he received answers.

"We've been enspelled."

"Not enspelled," another man contradicted groggily. "It was the ale. Pascent sent it here, a barrel for us to share."

"Pascent?" All Felimid's doubts of the man rushed back. Could he have drugged the ale? And where was he? Felimid couldn't recall. Curse him, rot him, shrivel him, ghouls desecrate his grave . . . but it might not be so, and there wasn't time to curse him effectively.

"Awaken them," he said harshly. "Start to skin them if nothing else will serve. Drive brooch pins under their nails, but have them upright, whatever. We are lucky Vithils is not here now."

He ran to the crude barricade of stones they had thrown across the Hatchet's Edge the previous night. A dozen lurching men went with him, game to fight even in their poppy stupor. The sky lightened further; the Saxon encampment on the far side of the isthmus became visible.

One hundred yards away! Gods! If they had known the barricade was not even manned, or if he had come a little later, the Saxons would have walked across unchallenged!

They were approaching now. Pirate after pirate staggered to the rough barricade, clutching weapons, woolly headed but foul of humor and wholly willing to strike blows.

First to attack were the berserks.

Felimid whirled his sling until the thongs creaked. Releasing, he sent a murderously heavy lead missile straight to one blackened figure's brow. The head should have burst apart like an egg let fall. Instead, it snapped back perhaps two hands' widths. The beserk stumbled, groped at his brow as though bewildered, took his fingers away and blinked at the redness upon them. The lead ball was sunk in his forehead, nesting among cratered bone, and his eyes had rolled up until only the bloodred sclera showed. Unconscious or dead—surely dead!— he did not acknowledge it. Stumbling onward with three shocking crimson eyes, he clawed his way over the stone rampart. Braining one pirate who stood before him and smote, he laid hands on another and plucked him apart like a chicken while the man shrieked and drove a knife into his side seventeen times. Not once did it penetrate far. Only then did the berserk slowly sink to his knees and die.

The pirates began to fall back before these men become monsters. Felimid sprang from the barricade into their path. Swinging Kincaid with perfect skill and timing, he hewed into one berserk's rib cage. It was like hacking an oak barrel packed with clay. Flesh, bone, and gristle locked over the blade like a clamp. The wound hardly bled.

As Felimid wrenched at his sword, the creature smote with a club like a troll's. Felimid let go his weapon, dropping and dodging like a flame twisting in the wind. The club barely missed. He darted back as the berserk's own mighty stroke spun him around, then sprang high in his corslet and landed on the filthy back. He pressed his legs around the blackened torso, plucked at Kincaid with one hand, and raised his targe with the other. Fiercely he smashed it down at the back of the creature's neck.

His sword came free. The berserk threw himself backward atop the bard and stumbled to his feet. He lifted his club. Felimid had rolled over, winded, and begun to rise. This time he would be too slow to dodge the club.

Gudrun, we'll meet sooner than I expected. . . .

Spears winged at the berserk, four or five lodging in his body, and pirates rushed from the barricade to bring Felimid safely behind it again. Hemming was first among them. The bard's action had had the effect he wanted.

Coughing pink foam, dragging the spears, the berserk lumbered after them. It had all taken moments. The sane fighters, coming on the berserks' heels, followed them to the barricade and pressed to surmount it. They met a wall of spears atop the wall of stone. The berserks smashed through, making corpses wherever they smote, but the shield wall closed again, trapping them among the pirates. Murder seethed then on both sides of the barricade.

"Smash their knees or the back of their necks!" Felimid shouted. "Open their throats if you have the skill. Elsewhere it is like hewing a tree."

The berserks roared their glee as men rushed them. Each one slaughtered nine or ten before falling. Whenever two had the wit to stand back to back, the tariff was higher. Yet they died, one by one.

Meanwhile the Saxons, led by Vithils, had broken through the pirates' line and forced the barricade. More crossed the Hatchet's Edge each moment, to scramble over the piled stones.

"Where are you, you harper they call Bragi, who killed Cudebehrt? See if you can do the same for me!"

Felimid knew that bass voice. "Here I am, Vithils! You slew my lover, and I am wishing to do the same for you, indeed. Even if that didn't lie between us . . . you are just not welcome on this side of the Hatchet's Edge, dear man."

He went forward boldly, knowing that if he faltered, the others might turn and run, infected by his pusillanimity. Bold words were easy; to walk smiling toward Vithils the Axe was less so. . . . *Na, Felimid, none of that!*

He had to die. Gudrun had counted on his weakened shield arm and died for it; Felimid must not make that error, or any different one, either. Maybe Vithils's shield arm had recovered better than he had let anyone know. Maybe *he* had spread the rumor that he was partly crippled to take enemies off guard; he was cunning enough. Felimid saw again in his mind's eye that terrible punch with the shield boss, and Gudrun's dead shattered face, and fury burned all trepidation out of him.

A shifting, slashing ghost, he cut at Vithils's byrnied side. Metal scales gave way. The Saxon smote with his half-stone axe. Felimid sprang out of its devastating path and leaped back in again, reckless of his strength. He cut in the same place. Kincaid's razor edge sheared through a few more scales. Vithils chopped at the bard's hip. Felimid interposed his shield, and even though it was not a full stroke he warded, the impact staggered him. He twisted, and sent a backhand slash viciously at the Saxon's face, swift as a wildcat's claw. Vithils's shield, a fresh, barely marked one, came up to cover his throat and chin. Kincaid skidded around the rim and snagged his ear, drawing blood.

In that moment's surprise, Felimid drove his own shield downward at Vithils's knee, hoping to smash it. The Saxon merely straightened his other leg and shifted to one side. His axe whirled up and around in a looping figure-of-eight which would have beheaded Felimid, taken off at least one of his legs, and divided him twice at the waist, had he lingered in its way; but he leapt like a grasshopper. Once more he hewed into the Saxon's byrnie in the same place.

The pattern was established. Coming swiftly back in, he

broke it, warding one of those short but fearfully powerful chops and then aiming a thrust at Vithils's throat. Vithils shifted aside; the long thrust went past his ear, harmlessly. Using the sword's point was not going to surprise him as it did lesser men. So much for that.

Felimid wasn't dismayed. He simply tried something else. Nothing if not inventive, he tempted the burly man by appearing to stumble. Vithils laughed contemptuously and ignored the bait.

"You are a juggler, not a fighter," he jeered.

Kincaid and the heavy axe met with a shriek of metal. Sparks flew. Rock steady while Felimid shifted and darted around him, Vithils nearly lost fingers when the bard cut home on his axe haft. A chip of the fire-hardened wood flew away after the binding wire parted. Vithils shoved the blade aside and struck overhand at the top of Felimid's shield. Hooking the head of the axe behind it, he yanked Felimid forward, off balance. As the bard fell, he turned his fist over and rammed his sword through Vithils's foot, pinning it to the earth.

The Saxon howled in astonishment and fury. His axe rose for one of the mighty strokes nothing could avoid or resist. Felimid raised his shield like a hat, thinking, *my knife* . . . but he knew he would not even have time to release Kincaid's hilt. Only a crippled foot to pay for Gudrun's life and his own! He couldn't face her.

The huge axe twisted in Vithils's hand as it fell. The stroke did not arrive cleanly; Felimid's shield endured it, although his arm was numbed. Astonished, he looked up.

The short haft of a Frankish throwing axe stuck out of Vithils's beard. The edge must reach as far back as his spine. His jaw was cleft in two. He swayed. As Felimid scrambled to his feet, the Saxon legend fell, still holding his great weapon firmly. Felimid did not believe it.

"What were you trying to do?" Arnehad bugled at him. "Follow the lady?"

Men were running from the direction of Gudrun's hall. They ran like drunkards, or drugged men, which they were, but they were arriving, and the cry of Vithils's death was spreading like a stain of ink in milk. The berserks were dead or useless.

"Push them back . . . across the Edge," Felimid gasped.

"No! It's no use, you fool! We'd be caught atween two hosts. Cynric is in Ran's Basin; he's taken our ships, he holds them against us! Pascent and Waldin ran before he came, may the lucky bastards writhe in fire. The sea people are gone, most of us are stupefied asleep. I tell you, it's lost! All we can do is get out. Some of us."

"Ay, you croak like a raven, you know. Where is Decius? Maybe I can get some man's language from him."

"Why?" Arnehad snuffled. "Do you want him to hold your hand? Man's language, by the Nails! I may cut your heart out and save some Kentishmen the trouble."

"Where is he?"

"Dragging limp men out of the hall when last I saw him, and three parts unconscious himself. I reckon he does not know what he's about."

"Well, he's needed here. Best you tell him so, whether he's drugged or not. Cynric has taken the ships?"

"He holds the cove where they are, and he'll be breathing up your arse in moments!"

"How? He cannot get up the path. Twenty good men at the top could bottle him below, and here we can yet do the same. . . . Bring Decius. *Then help me drive these Saxons back*!"

"You do that, you lovelorn hero," Arnehad said. "I am leaving while I can, with some fighters who also have sense!"

Gudrun would have struck him for that, or cut him down in his insolence. Felimid laughed at him, and then asked derisively, "How? By swimming, or will you fly?"

But by then he was asking it of the Frank's back.

For a moment his wits raced along ten disordered paths at once, and he was near panic. Then he controlled it. What if Cynric did hold the cove, and did appear across the lea? It wouldn't be important if they lost the Hatchet's Edge. The fray wouldn't wait, and he could not be in more places than one. Settling his shield in a more comfortable way on his arm, he returned to the fight.

For a savage half hour the outcome was uncertain. They forced the Saxons back over the barricade, only to have them come again and cross it anew; but the pirates fought until their adversaries had all gone back once more, or died on the barricade's southern side. Felimid cleaned his sword, feeling as though he had passed through the entrails of a bear. But there was no rest yet.

All around him men lay broken or hacked on the bloody earth. Some lay very still while flies buzzed over them. Others writhed and screamed—for water, for their mothers, for death. Others only lay and moaned. Broken or fallen weapons lay scattered about, blood drying in dark ridges upon them, the reek of it fetid and cloying as its freshness faded. To Felimid's bardic sight there were worse things present, also; bright red flitting shadow-forms like scarlet crows, the spirit host his people called the *badb*, battening on the rage, anguish, and agony which is the psychic crop of battle, from high-hearted beginning to soured aftermath. The bard clenched his teeth until an urge to spew had passed. Then he braced himself to hearten the men he had fought with.

"Now that was excellently well done," he said, standing jauntily erect, "and only Gudrun Blackhair's men could have done it." Using her name hurt his belly, but he had to hold them together, and he knew the source of their greatest pride. "Vithils is slain, and we hold the Hatchet's Edge, in spite of treachery."

"It's Vithils who holds the Hatchet's Edge, Bragi!" someone called out. "Fairly between his eyes he holds it."

"Aye!" laughed someone else. "Edric will go home the sadder for his meddling here."

"They may come again, and if they do we must hold this crossing as we have done. And we will! Who are their leaders now?"

"Eglinth the Chapman, that stinking wizard whose name I do not know, and Stigand Seavain. They are none of much account beside Vithils."

It was Hemming, lame and gore-spattered, cleaning his weapon with a torn piece of some unlucky warrior's striped cloak. Blood from a slash on his cheek caked one side of his beard.

"Maybe they will send word to Edric before they do anything more. Who's this coming yonder?"

It proved to be Giguderich, the effects of the poppy gum evident upon his face. Six men accompanied him.

"Decius sent me," he told the bard without preamble. He spoke dully, without urgency, although the situation must have been as urgent as he had known in his violent life. "He says he is going to fire the hall for Gudrun Blackhair's pyre, sending her plunder and all the good things within where no Saxon or Kentishman can get it. We cannot let them have everything, he says. Do not think it is the enemy's work."

"Burn the hall? It's too soon for that," Felimid protested.

"We've held them here and will hold them as long as we must. Gudrun's pyre was supposed to be *Ormungandr* . . . wait. Cynric has *Ormungandr* now?"

"No, he has it not. Maybe you have heard. Pascent and Waldin deserted us, slipping out of the Basin in a swift ship just before Cynric came in — and they burned *Ormungandr* first. They ruined the catapults on the cliff ledges, too. Cut the torsion skeins."

"No wonder Cynric was able to enter and have things all as he desired them!" Felimid's shoulders lost their jaunty set. "If the gods are very good to me, I'll see that pair again some day." It didn't seem likely. "But it's too soon to fire the hall. We can hold out for a long while yet, and we have cost them dearly, even with the curse of the men of Ulster upon us.* Go back quickly, and tell Decius to wait."

"Wait for what?" Giguderich asked glumly. "Cynric is at the top of the cliffs with his men, not confined to the bottom."

"Ah," Felimid said slowly. "Now that is bad news. How was it ever allowed to happen? Idle curiosity it may be; still, if I am going to be cut into as many pieces as there are stars in the sky, I would like to know which of my friends I have to thank for it."

"It happened because Pascent slew all the onager crews and left the Basin unguarded, or nearly so, and because Cynric moved quickly while the hall lay asleep. The pup has six or seven score men with him, and he musters them even now. If he comes to the hall, he will take it. That's why Decius is making sure there is nothing to take. Then he will join you."

The leaden, indifferent voice set Felimid's teeth on edge. Doubtless it was an effect of the drug, but Giguderich had always possessed a somewhat cadaverous appearance, and now talking to him was like holding converse with a dead man.

"Join me?" he asked, thinking of the helplessly drugged men Decius would leave behind if he did that. Still, he could scarcely carry them with him unless they were very few, and Felimid had wounded of his own to care for. He set about doing that, under the tender spring sky where the insubstantial *badb* flapped and croaked.

It was not long before smoke and fire rose from the long

---

*The men of Ulster were cursed for nine generations, with the helpless weakness of a woman in childbirth, whenever their enemies approached and their need was the greatest.

roof of Gudrun's hall. He imagined the smashed benches and rushes from the floor, piled under the table that upheld Gudrun Blackhair's bier to make her pyre; and atop the table, all around her, the trophies of her voyages and raids. The weapons and armor would be the most ordinary part of it, fine though these were. The war banner from Svantovit's temple should be draped over Gudrun herself for a shroud, with the pelts of monster red ape and white bear on either side of her. Gold and garnet, silver, amethyst, and pearl, swords and spears and many fine shields could be scattered lavishly on the floor around her, like the furs — sable, ermine, fox, beaver, seal, and bear, all charring and smoking as the flames took hold. Since *Ormungandr* had been destroyed, it was the best cremation Gudrun could be given, and Decius was right; it would not do to let the foe have everything. Least of all the body which was the most valuable thing being consumed.

Only the ravens will bury us, my darling. But none of us will care.

Decius led his shambling crew across the Sarnian plateau, with the rolling smoke of the hall behind him. He saluted Felimid as he approached, in the Roman fashion.

"You've done well here, Bragi. Vithils is dead, I am told."

"True for you, Decius. Our half-nosed friend Arnehad did it with his tribe's axe, in time to save me from dying in two pieces; but then he decided to follow Pascent. I fancy he has left it late, though."

"Cynric will have holed the rest of our ships," Decius agreed. His voice sounded deeply weary, and his tough shoulders sagged within his war harness. Both events and the poppy-drugged ale Pascent had given him had cost him much energy, but determination kept him moving. "His own will be out of reach. Wait, though . . ."

He swayed.

"What?" Felimid asked as the Spaniard steadied himself.

"There might be a way. We guarded the Hatchet's Edge, the cove, and the Red Bay in the southwest, if you remember — because there is a way up the cliffs from there, too. Vithils sent two ships there to destroy our men, but they lost."

"Who lost, now?" Felimid knew that Decius was drugged, but suspected that his own mind was working no better. He felt tired.

"Our enemies lost, man! I thought you drank none of that

damned, drugged ale! Our enemies lost, and our men won. Those two Kentish ships are in their hands now.''

''A hundred men could get away, then, if the rest covered their retreat.'' Felimid drew a long, considering breath which was pure pretense, as he had decided at once what he would do. ''I am staying. I'd like you to go your way, Decius, if you can. You are one of the few I'd rely on to deal with Pascent for me.''

''It's the one real reason I have for wishing to go,'' Decius admitted, his false eye flashing redly. ''With the lady dead, I do not care to follow any other leader, and I cannot return home, unlike you. Give some thought to that, youngster . . . for you are young. Maybe you ought to see to Pascent, and I should remain, for you have your magic to give you a better chance of escape.''

''My magic is nothing to Odin's. Na, na, Decius. If I were to go, I should have gone long ago, and I chose not to. I'll not be reversing that choice the same day Gudrun has died, and saving my own skin to leave her ghost alone on Sarnia. I stay.''

Decius sighed. ''I'm sorry to hear it. I think you will regret it in Hell, but it's your right to choose your own way of dying.'' He clapped the bard on the shoulder. ''Cynric may change both our plans for us anyhow. See, he comes now.''

''I do see him. His byrnie is too bright to miss, and he has too many friends to ignore. Let us make a round shield burg and welcome him, so. There is great news before us, my son; wetting of swords, destroying of life, shields with broken bosses, after the fall of night. Our horses are tired; we are riding the horses of the Sidhe; although we are alive, we are dead.''

''Do not be so sorrowfully morbid, you damned Celt! Help me manage these men and get the cart into position, instead. That is useful.''

He backed up the creaking wain and saw the worst wounded men carried close to its sides, while the others arranged themselves in concentric circles around them. The outer circle of warriors locked shields defensively together.

''What is in the cart that would interest me?'' Felimid asked.

''Water and the last ale—and even the water will interest you by nightfall, Bragi. Weapons, of course. Your harp, too; I wrapped it in fleeces. We may be glad of a song before we are done.''

"I'm glad of my harp now. She is one of the treasures of
Erin, and I did wrong to leave her when I went to fight, and
to have her clean out of my mind so long! My thanks indeed,
Decius. It is no good of a guardian I was to her then."

Cynric marched through the blue morning at the head of his
followers. Young, splendid, and very able he looked, with the
delight of his victory upon him and a deed worth talking about
achieved at last on this venture. He strutted a little. Felimid
did not begrudge him that.

"Welcome, Cynric," he said. "I might ha' known you would
find your way to us, though a traitor and his crew did help
you. I fear all we can offer you is hard knocks; our hall caught
fire."

"Greetings, Bragi," Cynric said pleasantly. "Or do you
prefer to be killed under your own name? I know your hall
caught fire, for we passed that way and none of the men who
lay ensorcelled asleep there will ever have the trouble of awak-
ing. You might have taken a sleep thorn yourself."

Felimid shook his head. "I have too much to see yet. There
are still some of the lady's men living."

The Saxons were moving south across the narrow blade of
the Hatchet's Edge for the last onslaught. Felimid held two
spears, one in his skilled left hand, the other clasped against
the back of his shield. Kincaid hung sheathed at his right side,
cleaned and honed as he seldom needed honing. Sweat ran in
little streams within the bard's war harness; he itched, felt
grimy and smelled gamey, and ginger stubble had sprouted on
his jaw in the past couple of days. It was not really much
consolation that the pirates who locked shields with him on
either side smelled worse than he did.

*If I must die, why could I not die well washed and shaved,
in clean garments?*

The men of Westri raised a long, rolling shout and charged.
The pirates yelled taunts as they braced themselves for the
shock, and the Saxons scrambled over the blood-slimed stones
of the barricade on the Hatchet's Edge to be in at the death.

Felimid's eyes picked out a yellow-bearded corsair rushing
for him. Briefly they glared into each other's faces and knew
each other, although they had never met. The man from Westri
swung a scourge of chains at Felimid's head, a weapon so
unusual that it seemed to the bard he should have heard of this
man—but he hadn't.

226

No matter. He let the chains wrap themselves around his spear, and when the warrior yanked, he simply went with the heave, thrusting in the same direction so that his spear head entered the stranger's throat. As the man fell, Felimid pulled back his spear, and the brutal weapon came with it. Swiftly the bard stuck it in his belt.

The fight was a matter of attrition, and Gudrun's pirates proved hard to abrade. An axe-man broke one of Felimid's spears and thought he had him, but discovered his mistake when the sharp splintered end of the shaft was thrust through his thigh from underneath the bard's shield, and he crawled away swearing.

Some time later the man on Felimid's left dropped with his legs mowed from under him, and Felimid speared the Kentishman who had done it before closing the gap with another pirate who stepped forward with an unmarked shield from the wagon. There were very few of those left on the island by now.

Cynric's long sword offered arguments that were never successfully rebutted, though he was wounded twice. Stigand used a longer-handled, lighter axe than Vithils's to good effect, and Ulfectel belied his age wherever his blade struck. Aur the wizard fought also, the interlinked iron circles on his shield conspicuous, his strange, misshapen sword with its poisoned edges reaping a harvest of men. No berserks were in sight, and none of the pirates missed them.

Their circle shrank inward, toward the wagon, and finally it was plain that the next attack or the one following would break them into little, doomed groups. When their foes dropped back for the dozenth time, panting, mauled, and still determined, Decius seized the moment to speak with him.

"It's time we made our run for it, Bragi, or we'll never go anywhere again. Wet your throat. Before they charge anew we'll slay all our desperately wounded and go."

Felimid drank. Knives made short work of those who were plainly crippled or dying, and those who could walk got grimly to their feet. If they couldn't go far, they would delay the devils behind them while those who could move effectively did.

The distance was a mere six furlongs and more than a hundred leagues. Fallen men marked the way with their bodies and their blood, until a mere eighty pirates reached the cliffside path leading down to Red Bay. Thirty stayed at the top to hold off pursuit, while the rest, led by Decius, scrambled down one at a time to the waiting ships held by their comrades. Those comrades might have left long before, had the tide been with them, but only now was it favorable—as Decius had known when he chose his time to move. It would still be a near shave.

Felimid sighed and faced his enemies. He had long since cut the straps of his cuirass and let the dwarf-made armor fall on the grass of the Sarnian plateau. The afternoon breeze lifted sweat-drenched cloth from his body and prowled over his skin with cooling fingers. He still wore helm, carried sword and shield, and retained his harp in her accustomed place on his back. She defined who and what he was, not the war gear he could assume and discard when it suited him. He did not expect to be anything much longer, but while he lived, he would carry Golden Singer.

The struggle went on. Sweaty, panting, he resisted among the thirty pirates. The light sword in his hand grew heavier with each stroke. Hemming, nearby, came face to face with Aur and felt the deadly kiss of his weapon. As the venom from the ugly sword spread through his veins, he seized the wizard in his arms and drove a dagger into his side some forty times. The other Jutes trod over them while they struggled in their murderous embrace on the ground.

Two pirates were forced over the edge of the cliffs. They fell to the sea with fading screams, and the rest knew it was time to withdraw down the path. Few were likely to reach the bottom alive.

It happened that Felimid was among the first to go. Two dozen men in single file were between him and the foe. If they all fell, he would have his turn to fight again, but in the meantime he had only to descend the path as slowly as possible. Wiping his sword on the padded tunic he had worn under his cuirass, he sheathed it, and shed the tunic, too. Now he was down to trousers and shirt.

Two thirds of the way down the path, it widened into a ledge where they could stand and move. Lopsided stone cairns high as a man had been erected there for some reason.

"It's a good enough place for a last stand," the bard said. To himself he said, *Cairbre and Ogma, but these glorious last stands make better telling than living. I always did think it, and now I can guarantee to know.*

"Ho, Decius!" he shouted to the men on the beach. "Are you yare to depart? Our company here is the smallest thing insistent."

"Hold them off a little longer if you can. We have space for a few more. Let those at the rear come down here!"

At that moment rocks fell down the path in a bounding, rattling, rebounding chaos, threatening to brain whatever stood in their way. One pirate's hip was shattered, another's arm broke with a sharp, clearly heard snap, and Felimid was struck on the head by a chunk the size of two fists. But for the dwarf-made leather casque, he would have been killed at once.

He fell on his face. The casque rolled off and went leaping down the path to the beach. Now Felimid had nothing left of his gains with Gudrun except the walrus-leather boots, and was quite unaware of that. He did not move, then or for some hours.

When he opened his eyes he did not know where he was, or care. His vision was blurred, and everything he saw had a double. Someone was slowly driving a wedge into his head above his right ear, with regular blows timed to his heartbeat.

He recognized other sensations in time. He had wet gritty sand beneath him, and waves were lapping gently nearby. The jovial talk and boasting of weapon men emerged bit by bit from what had seemed empty, torturing noise. He stirred.

"Huh! He's awake, lord," someone called.

Hard hands dragged him upright. His head flew away from his neck on unsteady wings, then swooped nauseatingly back to him. Brassy light attacked him through his flinching eyeballs. Cynric's twinned image floated before him, tall and strong, with a steady gray-green stare. Pride forced the bard to brace his legs and stand.

"We reckoned you dead with the rest at first," Cynric said to him. He grinned. "You might have deceived us if you had not moaned."

It meant little to the bard. Laboriously he nailed the words like pointers in his pounding head. They had thought him dead. With the rest. Who were "the rest"? Gudrun. Ataulf. No, Ataulf had died in the jaws of a monster, months past. Decius?

"Did Decius win away?"

One of the men holding his arms cuffed him.

"Not until I tell you," Cynric ordered. He grinned once more. Felimid saw little that was funny. "Yes, he's clear, with you to thank. You did well. Now you face the little matter of paying for it. You should perhaps have stayed dead."

"If I may choose," Felimid croaked, "you could allow myself to drink me to death."

The atheling chuckled. He'd become expansive, his mood

a curious mixture of the cruel, the cheerful, and the generous. He and Felimid were acquainted; he did not particularly want to kill the bard. Sated with mere slaughter, he yet did not care to appear weak, or to give an enemy the better of him. A playful alternative came to his mind.

"You had luck," he said. "A man should respect luck, or his own may turn. I'll see whether the gods allow you to keep yours. I don't know this bay, but I would guess the high tide reaches to . . . there." He tossed a bit of driftwood to the spot he meant. "What say you, Ulfcetel?"

"I reckon it's so, to a fathom above or below," the old sailing master said.

"Dig a hole," Cynric said, "and we'll see."

Understanding, his men guffawed. Felimid was slow to comprehend, so Cynric explained.

"You shall go in the hole they dig, to your neck. If you are breathing still when the tide goes out, I'll have you dug up and you may go free, with just what you had when I first saw you—your harp and sword. If you drown . . ." He shrugged. "Your luck was not of the best, after all. And what do you think of this chance I give you?"

"I think," Felimid said with care, through the milling in his head, "that I will do as much for you some day." Because his double vision plagued him, he added a bit foolishly, "both of you."

"Tell me that again when the tide has gone out."

"Edric will not like it, lord," a sycophant muttered. "This man slew Cudebehrt, and may have slain Vithils, too."

"Cudebehrt I would believe; Vithils I doubt. But I know he killed Tosti Fenrir's-get, and for that alone he deserves a bare chance. Leave Edric to me."

Before the Jutes thrust Felimid into the seeping hole, they robbed him of boots, belt, collar, and everything else save his breeches and shirt. They threw the wet sand in around him and stamped it down until it was mounded below his chin. They also took care to bury him facing seaward, so that he should have a fine view of the marching waves. Felimid reckoned they were not very imaginative. It would have been more cruel to bury him facing the cliffs, so that he could not see the waves coming at him.

"Time your breathing, scut," one of them advised with a laugh, "and learn to hold it."

Felimid gazed at the quiet greenish blur so close to him. Bit by bit his concussed mind appreciated the situation. Decius was safely away, and the tide was apparently turning. It had been about to ebb when Cynric's men had hurled rocks down the path. The light on the waves shone a brassy yellow; the afternoon must be far spent. Then he must have been unconscious for hours.

The little waves grew higher by degrees. Watching with interest, the Jutes laid wagers while the issue remained doubtful. Felimid let his mind slide into apathy. There was nothing he could do. King Oisc of Kent had once hung him by the ankles from a beam above a pit of hungry wolves, and he had escaped that. But then he had been allowed a couple of hours unobserved, and been able to move within limits. Now, the packed moist sand held him as in a giant's fist.

The first bubbles of foam collared his neck with wetness.

Felimid felt no real concern. It maddened him that his vision would not clear, or focus to a single image, and that his mind remained woolly, stumbling where it used to dance. The imminence of death did not really touch him. His spirit had drifted away.

The next few waves did not rise as high. The following one surged around his neck and dragged at it like a soft, fluent hangman's rope as it slipped seaward once more. Felimid remained untouched even when the next wave slapped him wetly in the mouth. Irked perhaps by his lack of response, a Jute squatted before him and asked whether the Lord Aegir's ale was to his liking, or if he did not begin to wish he had remained on land.

The gibe aroused Felimid to talk back.

"Crow now, my cock," he said. "It may be yourself next time, and you can judge . . . the taste of Aegir's ale, as served by Ran, with no need to ask another. Now it's in my mind that this . . . predicament . . . of mine deserves to be remembered in a stave or two, so leave me in peace to compose them. My head's aching, so. I do not want your breath distracting me as well."

He made twenty staves before the water was almost continuously over his head, witty, insulting, speculative, wry. He had not lied about the state of his head. They were far from his best. Still, it amused and delighted the Jutes that he made poetry at all, in such a trying position.

Then he began to drown, and to truly realize that he was drowning. He breathed with care, timed his inhalations well, held them long and then longer yet. Still he was choking beneath a foaming, sand-gritty surge, and the tide had not reached its highest point. The Jutes began to settle their bets.

"His luck was not with him after all," Ulfcetel said.

"No." Cynric smoothed his beard with a trace of regret. He had wagered on Felimid. "No, the tide is still rising. He can't hold out."

Felimid's ears rang. A mounting pressure in his lungs screamed for release. Then through the ringing and seething, a voice spoke in his ears, close as his own heart.

"Live, Bragi . . . live and sing of me."

Wet hair swirled about his face, too long for his own. Fingertips touched his skin. Cool lips molded themselves to his, breathing air into his throat where he had had access to nothing but smothering brine. The lips left his. He exhaled a storm of bubbles, unable to help himself, and before he must suck in the green sea, that ghostly, life-giving mouth returned to his.

He knew it as he knew his own. Amazed, awed, he kissed it hungrily time after time, for it was all he would ever have again of Gudrun Blackhair now that they were parted.

Yet the air she brought him did not come from above the waves, or from any land on the ridge of the earth. As he drew it through his throat, he saw visions of a Sarnia whose cliffs were gray, not red, a wholly barren island in black seas, where wrecked ships and corpses were continually washed ashore for monsters to eat. He saw phantom armies locked in unending, joyless battle, and clusters of stone tombs in a landscape without water. The springs and rivers flowed with blood, instead, and a fortress of bones roofed with broken shields stood where the ashes of Gudrun's hall had been. There were gibbets in the place of trees. It was Odin's realm, and Hel's.

"Live, Bragi. Live. Never think death will join us anew."

Other visions, other knowledge came to him in the gold-green, sand-flecked dimness while he breathed that strange air. He never knew how long it was until the tide went out, only that he glimpsed a white shape crowned with black vanishing seaward on the ebb. He knew he would not see it anymore. Tears flowed from his eyes into the great green body of Lir.

Some vestige of ordinary guile urged him to feign unconsciousness while his head emerged from the water. He let it turn and joggle on his neck as limply as cord in the waves. Finally, as his hair streamed brine into the exposed, tide-rippled sand, he counterfeited spasms of loud coughing.

He performed for no audience. The Jutes had gone.

Acting on Cynric's orders, two returned at last to dig him out, living or dead. They voiced noisy amazement when they found him alive. One swore in disgust, for he had won a bet when Felimid apparently drowned, and would have to give back the stake now. His companion had wagered on the bard to live, and was bigger. Felimid thought that was probably as well.

"We are not carrying you up that path, though," the larger Jute told him positively. "If you cannot climb it now, get your strength back and come to our camp for your harp when you're able. Here's food to help you and my cloak to warm you. I'd expected to use both myself! Your luck is even better than the atheling said."

"Luck," Felimid said, wondering, *why me?* He added abstractedly, "Yes, I've had my share and more."

He wrung out his own garments, spread them on the rocks, and spent the night on the beach. No voice came to him in the wind, saying, *"Live, Bragi; live and sing of me."* He did not have to hear it. Once it had spoken to him from beyond the gap of death, and that was enough. But he did hear the clashing of weapons and the sound of ghostly ships passing from Sarnia in the dark. He did listen to the wild sea with ears he had not owned a year before.

The morning dawned blue. Felimid saw great flocks of ravens like clouds in the sky, moving against the wind as they departed into the north. More sinister shapes flew that way, too, the war god's shrieking corpse-choosers, silent now, with dead men slung before them across their gaunt horses, riding home to their mother Hel. The bard's mobile lips thinned over his teeth.

"It isn't over, Ill-Wreaker," he said quietly. "Not yet."

He went for his sword and harp.

Epilogue

Three fewnesses that are better then plenty:
  a fewness of fine words;
a fewness of cows in grass;
  a fewness of friends around good ale.
                                    —Irish Triad

The soft, rolling sea strain faded like the noise of surf. For a little while there was silence. Then Laban, chieftain of the island of Lesia, poured from a jug for the bard who had been harping. His other guest, the black-haired Spaniard with a patch on one eye, signed that he was content with what he had in his goblet.

"I left with a fisherman," the bard said. "These two months I have spent in Lesser Britain, roving about and gathering what news I could. Of Pascent I have heard nothing."

"Nor will you," the Spaniard answered with grim certainty. "I caught him. He and Waldin have been feeding fish since May, and because of it I'll never eat fish again, though I sin on every Friday."

"Ahhhh. That is one thing I could never quite rest until I knew. I'm glad of it, Decius."

"No gladder than I. Many a ghost should be more contented now that those two have joined them. But since then the sea has turned to lead for me, and the world is flat." He sighed. "I'd as soon settle here as anywhere else, but it's too close to Sarnia."

"The world's wide," Laban said. "You are welcome here always if you should change your mind. There isn't a one of my daughters who hasn't an eye for a good man, and sea captains like you are not found every day.''

"Why . . . you honor me, Laban.'' Decius grew thoughtful for a moment. The prospect of a family and a bride made him realize that he was lonely. It came too soon, though, too soon after the destruction and vengeance of the summer. He wanted time and a taste of civilization again before he gave an answer.

Felimid came to his rescue. "And honor it is. This is a fair isle with true folk. I'd live here myself, did I not have a home and kindred to go to that I haven't seen for five years. You did say you would give me passage to the west of Britain before the summer ends, Decius.''

"I'll keep my word. You needn't be anxious.'' The Spaniard turned his head to look at Felimid, and the side of his mouth Laban could not see curled in a faint smile. "You will see the shores of Erin again.''

Laban sighed deeply. "Aye, his own hearth calls to every man. I have a notion, lads; let's all three get mightily drunk tonight, for from tomorrow we tread different paths. Blackhair and Sarnia linked us together. But all's changed now.''

"*Blackhair and Sarnia*,'' Felimid echoed over the brimming cups. Laban spoke truly. All had changed now. The great pirate stronghold might become a lair of wreckers again. Laban or some other chieftain might make it his own, to pasture cattle and work its mines. Some seafaring band of monks could even establish a community there. Maybe that would be better. None of it had anything to do with Felimid mac Fal any more. From tomorrow, as Laban said, they trod different paths. It was as though, beyond the clay-plastered walls, beyond the rolling waves, he saw the thatch of his clan's home rising above a timber palisade, the gates open in welcome and the broad blue Shannon flowing past into the Western Sea.

Coming Soon!

BARD V
FELIMID'S HOMECOMING
by
Keith Taylor

When Felimid mac Fel returns to the land of his fathers, to the glorious shores of Erin, all is not as he left it. The Company of Bards is sullied by members who take advantage of their talents and spread disenchantment among the people – ruining their livelihoods with Satires of Cursing and other such abuses…

**For more information
visit:** www.SpeakingVolumes.us

On Sale Now!

**For more information
visit:** www.SpeakingVolumes.us

On Sale Now!

On Sale Now!

For more information
visit: